THE DIARY
OF A CATHOLIC BISHOP

THE DIARY OF A CATHOLIC BISHOP

BY EDWARD CARBEN

CROWN PUBLISHERS, INC.

NEW YORK

© 1974 by Edward Carben
Library of Congress Catalog Card Number: 73-91155
All rights reserved.
No part of this book may be reproduced or utilized in any form or by any means, electronic or mechanical, including photocopying, recording, or by an information storage and retrieval system, without permission in writing from the Publisher. Inquiries should be addressed to Crown Publishers, Inc., 419 Park Avenue South, New York, N.Y. 10016
Printed in the United States of America
Published simultaneously in Canada by General Publishing Company Limited

Book design by Carol Callaway

For Evelyn

ANY RESEMBLANCE OF CHARACTERS IN THIS NOVEL TO PERSONS LIVING OR DEAD IS PURELY COINCIDENTAL.

INTRODUCTION

It seems strange to be writing an introduction to a book which the author did not want published. Indeed, Bishop Peter Faber, the author, specifically requested that the notebooks from which I constructed this book be burned. As his secretary, perhaps I should have complied with his wish—as I did with all his others—but after perusing the manuscripts, this is one request that I could not bring myself to fulfill. I do not know whether you will agree with the morality of my decision or not, but after reading this book, I think you will understand what prompted me to act as I have.

Shortly after Bishop Faber died, Mrs. Owens, his housekeeper, discovered his notebooks in an old trunk which he kept under his bed. The bishop had pasted a note to the lid of the trunk, which read: *IN THE EVENT OF MY DEATH, PLEASE BURN THIS TRUNK. DO NOT, UNDER ANY CIRCUMSTANCES, OPEN IT.* Mrs. Owens, a woman who possesses an insatiable curiosity, disregarded the bishop's instructions, searched for a key, and when she found it, promptly opened the trunk. When she saw that the trunk contained nothing but notebooks, she was tempted to burn it as the bishop had requested. Not wanting to destroy anything of value, however, she asked me to have a look at the notebooks first.

There were more than two hundred large notebooks in the trunk, and in these notebooks, Bishop Faber had kept a record of his life from September 8, 1937, the day after he entered the seminary at the age of fourteen, until he died in his sleep at the age of forty-eight on Christmas Eve, December 24, 1971. There are some large gaps in this mammoth diary, created when the bishop was just too busy to make any entries; but for the most part, he was very faithful in recording the major events and thoughts of his life. As you will see from reading the diary itself, Bishop Faber wrote mainly for two reasons: to dispel loneliness; and by referring to earlier entries, to have some measure of how much he had grown in holiness.

Although I did not work for Bishop Faber very long—he served as bishop for only a little more than four months before he died—I consider myself fortunate in having gotten to know him at all. He was so humble and unpretentious that he seemed ordinary; and before coming under his influence, I had never been interested in forming friendships with ordinary people, whether they were clergymen or laymen. I was impressed by the position a person held, by what I then considered culture and polish, and by sheer ostentation and egotism. In other words, I was beguiled by phonies.

If Bishop Faber had not become my bishop, he most certainly would never have attracted my attention. He had been Bishop Connolly's secretary for many years before he succeeded him, and although I had visited Bishop Connolly's office several times during that period, I had completely ignored him. True, he was the bishop's secretary—an important post in the diocese—but he wasn't even a monsignor. I had already reached that pinnacle of what I then considered success, and I wasn't going to waste my time talking at any length with a man I considered little more than a clerk.

A few days after Bishop Faber's consecration as bishop, I went to see him about a transfer. I had been chief chaplain at Saint John's Hospital for five years, and the position was starting to grate on my nerves and wear me out. I was rarely able to get away from the sick and dying for any length of time, and I was in a state of profound depression.

Bishop Faber listened to my problem in the attentive, quiet way he had, and then he said: "You've come at a good time, Monsignor. I need a secretary, and the job is yours if you want it. I promise that the work will not be especially difficult, and you can take a few days off anytime you want. What do you say?"

When I told him that I had no experience as a secretary, he commented: "If I could do it, you certainly can. I'll teach you."

Although I was still reluctant, he finally persuaded me. After I had an opportunity to reflect on the matter, I realized how kind he had been. Most men would have chosen one of their friends for such a post, or at least someone they liked to have around them.

Introduction

I'm sure that Bishop Faber didn't especially like me—at first, anyway. We were so very different in temperament and outlook. Nevertheless, he saw a fellow human being with a problem, and that's all that mattered to him. This was characteristic of the man.

When Bishop Faber said that he would teach me to become a secretary, he meant it. He never broke a promise. I should add, though, that my lesson lasted about half an hour. Then I was on my own. That was something else which was characteristic of him. Once he gave a man a job and told him what was expected, he never interfered with him. I was surprised to learn how well this system worked. Because he made people feel independent and responsible, he always had willing workers who gave their best.

Bishop Faber's predecessor, Bishop Connolly, was often referred to by subordinates as the boss. I never heard anyone speak of Bishop Faber in like manner. I think that was because he considered everyone his equal, something which was perfectly obvious from his manner. There were times when I thought he went too far in this regard, and I frequently told him so. After all, as bishop, he possessed almost unlimited powers within the diocese. In a sense, he was king, and he was answerable only to the pope and to the common law of the Church. He had the power to interpret, teach, judge, censor, confirm, ordain, and appoint. But instead of acting like a king, he behaved more like a janitor, and a very humble one, at that.

Especially when I noticed that he was quite obviously ill, I wanted to fend off some of the bores for him, but he wouldn't let me. He not only eventually got around to seeing everyone who wanted to see him, but he would spend hours of his precious time patiently discussing trivia with numskulls that most people would have refused to see in the first place. It pained me to hear fools and idiots openly disagreeing with and even ridiculing a man who was so much their intellectual and spiritual superior. I had never before encountered a person of his stature who not only tolerated, but welcomed conversation with people so inferior to himself.

Although Bishop Faber was an excellent administrator, fools and personal charities took up so much of his time that the two auxiliary bishops, the chancellor, and myself had to assume the task of taking care of the many minute business details which are involved in running a diocese. We liked that kind of work, though, and since we felt that we were co-workers rather than subordinates, we were willing to do everything required of us and then some. Meanwhile, Bishop Faber, who really didn't care for business—he hated to have to go to the chancery—had more time to minister to men's souls, and that was the work he enjoyed most.

While Bishop Faber was brilliant in most of what he did—a genius, in fact—he was certainly not a politician. He never sought the office of bishop, and he was more surprised than anyone when he found himself sitting on a bishop's throne. When he became bishop at the age of forty-eight, he was a very young man by church standards. True, some bishops had been younger when appointed, but he had not had their advantages. He had not studied at Rome, had no really important political advocates, and was usually considered too liberal by those who knew him well. For some reason, his predecessor, Bishop Connolly—who was certainly no liberal—had taken a liking to him and was responsible for his rise in the Church.

Although Bishop Faber impressed me in life more than any other man I have known, I think he has become even more impressive in death. For one thing, it was only after his death that I learned he had been slowly dying of cancer and knew it. Yet, I had never heard him become impatient, brusque, or sharp with anyone. He was a tall, muscular man—handsome in a rugged sort of way—and he smiled a lot.

Even when he was hospitalized and I visited him, he inevitably appeared cheerful and never indicated that he was seriously ill. After he got out of the hospital, he continued to give me the impression that he had undergone a minor operation; when in reality, it had been a gastroenterostomy. I noticed that he looked ill and had continued to lose weight, but he assured me that he was quite well. Although death was then only two months away, you will see from his diary that he expected to live for several months. I am sure that he thought he would have time to burn his notebooks before he died.

Introduction

I consider Bishop Faber a saint. I realize that there are many who will disagree with me, but that is their privilege. I personally doubt that the Church will ever canonize him, though. After reading his diary, I think you will understand why. Nevertheless, I see Bishop Faber as an embodiment of the transition between the old and the new in the Church, and I think he represents the best of both worlds. I believe that he was a saint of our times, and considering the times, I think that is a great deal to say for any man.

In editing his diary, I have not changed any of the bishop's words intentionally. At times, his handwriting was very difficult to read, but I did my utmost to discern and record his words as he wrote them. For purposes of clarity and continuity, I have taken the liberty of dividing the diary into sections. Moreover, since the bishop's notebooks would fill numerous volumes, I have had to eliminate thousands of entries in order to get the diary into one book. I have tried not to leave out anything of real importance, although that has not been easy.

And now, it is time for Bishop Faber to tell his own story.

Monsignor Francis J. O'Malley

The Feast of St. Joseph

PART ONE

September 8, 1937

Today I am starting a diary. The idea is not mine, but was given to me by Monsignor Grosclaude, who is rector of the seminary. I saw him shortly after I got here yesterday, and he asked me if I thought I would get homesick. When I told him that I didn't know, he said that a lot of boys get homesick when they are away from home for the first time. He said that the best thing to do, if that happens, is to have a good cry, and not be ashamed of it. He told me that even he cried when he first came to the seminary. He said that if I do my crying when the lights are out in the dormitory and I am all alone in bed, no one will ever know about it.

I think his idea about the diary is even better than the one about crying. He said that I could talk to the diary just like I talk to a person, and if I did that, I'd always have a good friend close to me and never be lonely. Besides, he said that I could tell the diary things I might not want to tell anybody else, and that way I could get everything off my chest, and still not have people getting mad at me. He told me that when I get older, I should have a look at what I have already written, and see if I have become a better person. He said that I might discover some day that I have become a saint. Although I don't think that will ever happen, I think it is a good idea to be able to look back and see if I have gotten any better.

If all the priests here are like Monsignor Grosclaude, I don't think that I'll be doing much crying. He's one of the nicest priests I've ever met. The big sign on his door reads: *VERY REVEREND JEROME GROSCLAUDE, RECTOR.* When I first saw it, it scared me a little bit. But as soon as Monsignor Grosclaude shook hands with me, I knew that I didn't have anything to worry about. He said to come to his office anytime I have a problem. He told me that he likes my smile and hopes to see it often. Anyway, I haven't cried yet, and I don't intend to.

September 9, 1937

When I saw Monsignor Grosclaude in the hall today, he asked me how the diary was coming. I told him that I had written something yesterday, but couldn't think of anything to write today. I told him that even what I wrote yesterday had happened the day before, and he said it's all right to do that if you are keeping a diary. So now I am going to say more about September 7, my first day at the seminary.

Women are not allowed in our dormitory, so I had to kiss my mother good-bye and leave her in the seminary parlor, while my father helped me with my luggage. The dormitory is divided into metal cubicles, which are covered in front by curtains. When Father Clancy, who is vice-rector of the seminary and prefect of high school students, learned that my name is Peter Faber, he assigned me the first cubicle in a row of cubicles near the door. Father Clancy has a room right across the hall from me.

No sooner had my father left than I did something pretty stupid. Father Clancy had told me to report to the rector's office at once, but one of the boys was touching the wall with his hand, and he asked me to put my hand on the wall for a second, and without thinking, I did it. He then withdrew his own hand, and told me that I was now holding up the wall and would have to keep my hand there until I found another boy to take my place. A lot of the boys were laughing, and they laughed even more when I told them that Father Clancy had asked me to see the rector right away. Then another boy came into the dormitory, and he smiled when he saw the fix I was in. I told him that I had to see the rector and asked if he would take my place. He said that he would. His name is Karl Wright, and I think it was awfully nice of him to do that for me, especially since he is in second year.

Karl Wright did something else for me that day. We played ball after supper, and I wasn't pitching very well. I think that was because there were so many priests and boys standing around watching. Some of the boys yelled that somebody else should pitch. Karl shouted back at them: "Give him a chance!" After that, I started to pitch very well. When the game was over, Karl patted me on the back and told me what a good job I had done. I really like him.

September 10, 1937

Being in the seminary is like being in the army. We have to line up and march to just about everything. Even in the refectory, we have to sit in a certain place. Although the table of the faculty is located across the room, near the wall, it has been placed at an angle which is vertical to our tables, so that the priests always have a good look at what we are doing. Father Clancy keeps a bell on the table, and if a boy does something he isn't supposed to do, Father Clancy rings it and corrects him. He also rings the bell for prayers before and after meals. These prayers are said in Latin. Most of the time, we eat in silence, while one of the boys reads from a spiritual book. We have to take turns doing that, and if a boy doesn't read the way he should, Father Clancy rings the bell and tells him what's wrong.

We are not permitted to smoke as long as we are in high school, but after we get to college, we will be allowed. Father Clancy opens our mail and reads it before we get it, and when we send letters out, we have to leave the envelopes unsealed, so he can read them. We are not permitted to receive or read secular newspapers. Even when we take books from the library, a record is kept for each student, so that the faculty knows what books a boy has been reading. We are never allowed to talk in the library, dormitory, study hall, chapel, lavatory, and showers. In fact, we are not supposed to talk outside the time provided for recreation. The Father Prefects are everywhere. They even watch us while we take our showers.

All of our days begin at six o'clock in the morning, with the loud clanging of a bell. I hate to be awakened that way, but once I get my eyes opened, it's not so bad. After we get washed and dressed, we have to make our beds. Then we line up for chapel. When we get there, Father Clancy says morning prayers. Then we meditate—something which they are still teaching us to do. After we get done with that, Monsignor Grosclaude offers High Mass.

Breakfast comes next, followed by a fifteen-minute recreation period.

Latin is always our first class, then algebra and a study period. After that, we go to chapel again, where Father Clancy reads to us from Sacred Scripture for half an hour. Dinner is next, followed by fifteen minutes of recreation. Then we have classes in English and ancient history. After a long recreation period, we study until five thirty, at which time we gather in chapel for recitation of the rosary. Supper is at six, followed by a half-hour recreation period and benediction in chapel. Then we study until nine thirty, when we go to chapel for night prayers. Lights are turned out in the dormitory at ten o'clock.

September 11, 1937

Every time I see Monsignor Grosclaude, he mentions the diary. I told him today that I am running out of things to write, and he suggested that I write about my early life, until I get more interested in what is going on here. I was going to give up on the diary altogether, but now I'll try to see how much I can remember. He told me to start with the day I was born, but since he smiled when he said it, I don't think he was serious. Anyway, I can't remember anything about that. The first thing I remember happened when I was a little kid, but I'm not even sure how old I was.

We had an old Victrola at home, and I remember listening to a song called "The Builder." After a while, I seemed to hear the words and melody even when the Victrola wasn't playing. Sometimes I'd even join the imaginary voice in singing the song. One day, I asked my mother where the song was coming from, and she told me that it was coming from my mind. I was thinking the song. *Mind* and *thinking.* These were funny words. When you heard things and no one was saying them, it was your mind, and your mind was thinking. I asked my mother: "Why does your mind think if you don't tell it to think?" She told me that my mind would not think unless I told it what to think. I persisted: "How can I tell it what to think if it thinks when I don't tell it to?" Then she said that I would understand when I got older.

September 12, 1937

That's what my mother and father always said when I didn't understand something. But now that I'm older, there are still a lot of things I don't understand.

I remember kneeling at my mother's knee and saying my prayers. "Holy Mary, Mother of God!" Holy Mary was God's mother, and I loved her because she was like my own mother. Our Father was like my father, and I grew to love Him for the same reason. "Give us this day our daily bread," I prayed. Our Father gave us our bread, and it was the bread my mother baked in the oven. There were times when my father got angry and spanked me, and sometimes I didn't understand why. But God made it thunder and lightning, and I couldn't understand that either.

When I played indoors during the winter months, I sometimes put on my father's long overcoat. I always felt happy and secure when I wore that coat. I thought that since priests and nuns wore long clothes, they must have felt the same way. My parents taught me that priests and nuns were the most important people in the world, and priests were even more important than nuns. When my parents took me to church, everything was always quiet and scary, and they told me it was because God was on the altar. Not only that, everyone wanted to watch the priest and listen to him, since he took the place of Jesus.

September 12, 1937

When I got big enough to go to school, my parents said that since Catholics practiced the only true religion, they were sending me to a Catholic school. Moreover, they said that nuns did everything for the love of God and received no salary, and that made them better teachers than the public schools had. My friend, Jimmy Hicks, was a Protestant, and one day I told him what my parents had said. When he said it wasn't true, I got into a fight with him and punched him in the nose. Although I won the fight, I know now that it was only because my arms were longer than his.

My first teacher was Sister William. Before she did anything else, she made sure that all the kids knew how to make the sign of the cross. "In the name of the Father, and of the Son, and of the Holy Ghost. Amen." She said the same words over and over again, and each time, with her right hand, touched her forehead, chest, left shoulder, and right shoulder.

There was a big chart in front of the room, and Sister pointed to it every day with a pointer. There were pictures on the chart, with words in large letters under the pictures. One picture showed an angel with his arms around a boy and girl. The words read: *GOD GAVE ME AN ANGEL. MY ANGEL LOVES ME. MY ANGEL HELPS ME TO BE GOOD. I LOVE MY ANGEL. DEAR GUARDIAN ANGEL, HELP ME TO BE GOOD!*

Sister said that guardian angels often saved people's lives by making them miss buses or trains which were later in accidents. I remember wanting to ask her why the people who had been killed had not been saved by their guardian angels, but I didn't dare. My best friend, Chris Sullivan, had once asked a question like that, and she had slapped his face and told him he was as bold as brass. When she was explaining how God had made everything in the world, Chris had asked: "Sister, who made God?"

Sister liked to tell stories about the Christian martyrs. She said that when the pagans were torturing Christians by roasting them over a fire, the Christians sometimes joked with their tormentors by saying they were done enough on one side and should be turned over. Sister said that when some of the martyrs were thrown to hungry lions, even the lions recognized their holiness and refused to eat them. She told of other martyrs who walked around carrying their heads in their hands after the pagans had cut them off.

Almost every day, Sister told us about some miracle that God had performed for His saints. She said that Jesus Himself often spoke to them from a crucifix on the wall. At other times, He appeared to them and looked just as He had when He was on earth. To indicate that saints were really saints, God never allowed their bodies to decay after death.

Sister said that God performs even greater miracles for Mary, His mother, and that Mary is especially devoted to people who wear her scapular. Sister liked to tell a story about two boys who went swimming. One wore a scapular, while the other did not. When a big wave came along, the one with the scapular was saved.

The other boy drowned. She also liked to tell about a boy who came home from school one day and found his house on fire. The firemen couldn't put the fire out, so the boy took off his scapular and threw it into the flames. The fire went out right away. Sister said that according to a promise made by the Blessed Mother, the soul of a person who dies wearing a scapular will never go to hell. If the soul goes to purgatory, it will have to stay there only until the first Saturday after death.

Sometimes Sister told real scary stories, like the one about the boy she used to teach who was bad in school. Every time he did something wrong, Satan put another link in an invisible chain that was tied around his leg. One day, when the chain got very long, Satan pulled the boy right out of the room and dragged him screaming into hell. I remember wondering why Sister had not helped the boy by throwing holy water at Satan. There was a holy water font in every room at school, and Sister had said that when holy water hit the Devil, it hurt him very much and a loud sizzling noise could be heard. I remember thinking that if only I had been there, I would have thought of the holy water in time.

September 13, 1937

Monsignor Grosclaude came down to the athletic field today, and we got to talking about my diary again. He suggested that I say something about my pastor, Monsignor O'Shea. "But be honest about it, son!" he cautioned. He winked and smiled when he said that, so I have an idea that he knows Monsignor O'Shea pretty well himself.

During my first year at Sacred Heart School, Monsignor O'Shea gave us catechism instructions every Tuesday morning. When he strode into the room, everyone stood at attention and greeted him in unison. Sister William made us practice for hours until we could keep together when we said: "Good morning, Monsignor O'Shea." We had to remain standing until Monsignor told us that we could sit down. Then we would put our feet flat on the floor and clasp our hands on our desks. Except for lunch and recess, we always had to sit that way.

Monsignor taught us that there were big sins and little sins. He explained that big sins were mortal sins, and he said that people committed such sins when they broke the third, fifth, and sixth commandments. He would write a big three, a big five, and a big six on the blackboard to emphasize his point. He said that big sins were terrible sins, because Jesus was nailed to the cross and died on account of them. Moreover, God sent people to hell for these sins, where they remained for all eternity. Sister told us that Satan burned them in a huge fire and ran his pitchfork into them.

Most of the kids were afraid of Monsignor. Sometimes he asked Sister for the names of pupils who had missed Mass the previous Sunday, and if they could not prove that they had been sick by producing a written excuse from their parents, Monsignor would scold them until they cried. If it was a boy who had missed Mass, Monsignor often boxed his ears. Even when a pupil went to Mass, he had to attend the nine o'clock children's Mass, or Monsignor would throw a fit. He sometimes got madder when boys and girls attended the wrong Mass than when they didn't go to Mass at all.

One morning, Monsignor told my friend, Chris Sullivan, to come to the front of the room. He asked Chris why his father had not been to Mass for two Sundays. When Chris said that his father had been sick, Monsignor asked: "Why didn't your mother bring his envelope with her?" Chris answered that his father did not have any money. Monsignor got mad and said: "When your father does come to church, he never puts more than a quarter in his envelope. What can you buy for a quarter? Where else could you and your family go to church and school for a quarter a week? It costs more than that to go to the movies!"

"But we never go to movies, Monsignor," Chris protested.

"Don't talk back to me, boy!" Monsignor growled. "Your father is a drunkard, and he spends his money in speakeasies. He was drunk, and that's the real reason he wasn't in church." When Monsignor opened the door to leave, he shouted: "It's a sin to squander money on drink and not support the Church!" Then he banged the door shut.

On the way home from school that day, Chris told me that his father had called Monsignor a big, fat-faced pig, who never worked

September 13, 1937

hard and spent most of the day eating and sleeping. Chris said that Monsignor and Sister liked rich people. That was the reason the poorer kids were always being punished at school, while when someone like Richard O'Brien, whose father was a judge, misbehaved, Sister laughed and joked about it. That was the reason Sister had given Richard O'Brien a nice rosary for his birthday and had the class sing "Happy Birthday" to him, while she never said anything to poorer kids on their birthdays. I told Chris that we should both ask God to make us rich. Sister had said that if somebody prayed for something hard enough, Jesus would give it to him. In fact, Jesus had promised that a person could even move a mountain by praying. Chris said that it wouldn't work. He had already tried it.

A few days later, Chris's father died. The whole school attended the funeral. In his sermon, Monsignor O'Shea said that Mr. Sullivan was in heaven, since he had been lucky enough to receive the last rites of the Church before he died. He praised Mr. Sullivan for his large family of nine children and promised that God would take care of them. He quoted the Bible: "Look at the birds of the air: they do not sow, or reap, or gather into barns; and yet your heavenly Father feeds them. Are not you of much more value than they?"

After the funeral, my father asked my mother what Mrs. Sullivan was going to do. My mother told him that she intended to take a job working for rich people, so that she could keep the children together. When my father said that it was unfortunate Mr. Sullivan had left so many children behind, my mother told him it was the will of God. I asked my mother why God wanted Mr. Sullivan to die. She said that it was just something God wanted, and there was nothing anyone could do about it. I asked her why Mrs. Sullivan had called the doctor if there was nothing anybody could do. My mother said that the doctor helped when God was not ready for the person yet. I told her that I could not understand why the doctor was called at all if it was entirely up to God whether someone got better or not. Once again, she said that I would understand all of these things when I got older. Do you know something? I don't understand them yet.

September 14, 1937
When he gave us catechism instructions, Monsignor O'Shea often quoted the words of Jesus: "I am the living bread that has come down from heaven. If anyone eat this bread he shall live forever. For my flesh is food indeed, and my blood is drink indeed. He who eats my flesh, and drinks my blood, abides in me and I in him." After quoting these words, he would always tell us that only priests had the power to change bread and wine into the body and blood of Christ. Even the Mother of God did not have such power. Only priests were permitted to hold Jesus in their very hands, while it was a sin of sacrilege for anyone else to so much as touch the Host. The body of a priest was so sacred that to strike him was a sin of sacrilege, and could result in spending eternity in the fires of hell. Although I was impressed with what Monsignor O'Shea said, if he had been the only priest assigned to Sacred Heart Church, I don't think that I would be here at the seminary. I never felt that I wanted to be like Monsignor.

It was different with Father Kelly. He was one of Monsignor's curates, and all the boys at Sacred Heart liked him. While Monsignor stopped our games when we made a lot of noise during recess, Father Kelly often played ball with us. I first thought of becoming a priest in the second grade when I heard Father Kelly quote the words of Christ to the rich young man: "If thou wilt be perfect, go, sell what thou hast, and give to the poor, and thou shalt have treasure in heaven; and come, follow me." After hearing those words, I began to attend Father Kelly's Mass every morning, even though I had to get up before five o'clock and walk two miles.

When I was in the third grade, my mother sent me to the rectory to obtain blessed candles, and that was when I really got to know Father Kelly for the first time. He told me that he saw me at Mass every morning and asked why I got up so early. The words seemed to stick in my throat, but I managed to say: "I think I want to become a priest, Father." It was then that he talked me into becoming an altar boy. He taught me my first Latin prayer, and I learned it so fast that he said I was a genius. Then he gave me a book which had the picture of a priest and altar boy on

September 14, 1937

the cover. It was called: *How to Serve Mass.* I was so excited that I would have forgotten my candles if Father Kelly hadn't reminded me.

I memorized all of the Latin prayers in the book that very day. Father Kelly had told Sister Constantine, who had charge of altar boys, about me; and when she looked me up at school the next day, I told her that I already knew all the prayers. She didn't believe me, but when I proved it to her, she was speechless. She took me over to church for practice a few times, and by the end of the week, she said that I was ready to serve Father Kelly's Mass.

When Father Kelly saw me, he couldn't believe his eyes. "I always told you that you were a genius," he said, "and now you've proven it. They should have called that book I gave you: *How to Serve Mass in One Week.*" When the Mass was over, Father Kelly told me that I was already the best altar boy Sacred Heart ever had.

I served Father Kelly's Mass for two weeks, and then Sister Constantine appointed me to serve Monsignor O'Shea's Mass. Since I wanted to do everything right, I got to church very early on the first day I was supposed to serve for him, long before he arrived. Everybody knew that he always offered a High Mass, so I went into the sanctuary and lit six candles. There was a joke in the parish that if Monsignor had a sore throat and was unable to sing, he'd whistle the Mass rather than allow one of his curates to sing it.

When Monsignor finally entered the priests' sacristy, I said good morning to him.

"Good morning, boy," he responded in a gruff voice. He removed the cape he was wearing over his cassock and stood there holding it. "Wake up, boy!" he grumbled. "Take this and hang it in the cupboard."

While I was putting the cape in the cupboard, Monsignor walked to the door of the sacristy and looked out into the sanctuary. "Why did you light those candles?" he demanded.

"I thought—"

"You are not supposed to think," Monsignor interrupted me. "Put them out this instant!"

The candles were tall, and I had to stretch and stand on tiptoe to reach them, but I finally put them out. When I got back to the sacristy, Monsignor ordered: "Now light them."

I felt like an idiot because the people in church had just seen me extinguish the candles, but I went out and tried to light them again. I found it more difficult this time to get the taper inside the gold cap which surrounded the wick of the candle. I finally got one lit and was lighting the second one when the church bell began to ring.

When the bell stopped ringing, all the lights in the sanctuary went on, and I felt more embarrassed then ever because the people could see me more clearly. I got the third candle lit, genuflected before the tabernacle, and tried to light the candles on the other side. I glanced toward the sacristy, and I could see Monsignor standing in the doorway, waiting to enter the sanctuary. It was only because I had a lot of luck that I was able to finish lighting the remaining candles.

"Dummy!" Monsignor yelled when I got back to the sacristy.

Before I could catch my breath, he gave me a shove, and we were in the sanctuary. When we reached the altar steps, I turned at the corner of a long rug, in order to permit Monsignor to pass in front of me. In doing this, I kicked the end of the rug, and it curled up a little bit. I intended to straighten it when I knelt to say the prayers at the foot of the altar, but Monsignor stopped before the rug and refused to walk on it. "Fix that rug!" he commanded. I got down and fixed it.

By the time Monsignor began to say the prayers at the foot of the altar, I was so excited that I forgot the responses to some of them. Suddenly Monsignor stopped. "Say those prayers!" he shouted in a voice that everybody could hear. I did my best, but he stopped again. "Louder!" he commanded. "Don't you know your prayers? You dummy!"

At the Offertory, I tried to hand Monsignor the wine cruet, but he just stood there and glared at me. Finally he said: "Take that thing out of there." When I hesitated because I didn't know what he meant, he yelled: "Did you hear me, boy? Take that thing out of there this instant!"

September 14, 1937

"What thing?" I whispered.

"That stopper, you dummy!"

I removed the stopper and handed him the cruet.

"Dummy!" he grumbled as he roughly handed it back to me.

When we finally entered the sacristy at the end of Mass, he grabbed my arm and squeezed it. It really hurt. "Who taught you to serve Mass, boy?" he asked.

"Father Kelly and Sister Constantine," I replied.

"They never taught you to serve like that," Monsignor grumbled as he released his grip on my arm. "You'd better practice before you come back tomorrow!"

I tried not to cry, but by the time I reached the altar boys' sacristy, I was bawling like a baby. I decided right then and there that I would never serve another Mass as long as I lived. When I saw Sister Constantine at school that morning, I told her I was quitting. She said she would tell Father Kelly.

After school, Father Kelly was waiting for me. He asked me what had happened, but I refused to tell him. I just said that I was quitting.

"I am disappointed in you," he said. "I thought I could depend on you to serve my Mass sometimes."

When he said that, I started to bawl again.

"It's Monsignor, isn't it?"

I finally told him that it was.

"I thought you wanted to become a priest."

"I do."

"Well you can't become a priest if you're going to act this way," he said. "A priest has to be strong like a soldier, and a soldier never gives up, especially over something that just hurts his feelings."

I cried even more when he said that. "It's just that he's a priest," I told him.

"And I'm a priest, too," Father Kelly reminded me. "Will you give it another try? Just for me?"

I finally said yes, and Father Kelly smiled and offered me his big handkerchief. Then he put his arm around me and hugged me close.

When I think about it now, it all seems pretty funny. But it wasn't very funny then.

September 15, 1937
When I saw Monsignor Grosclaude today, he gave me some more advice about my diary. He asked me if I had ever heard of Emerson and Thoreau, and when I told him that I hadn't, he wrote down their names for me. He said that both of them had written diaries, and he suggested that I go to the library and have a look at the way they went about it. Monsignor Grosclaude told me that it is all right to put anything at all into my diary if I find it interesting or if it appeals to me. He said that I can write about current events, or even about things I have read in history and literature, or when I get older, in philosophy and theology. According to Monsignor, Emerson and Thoreau put all of their observations and ideas into their diaries, and then used these observations and ideas for writing and lectures.

Until I get a chance to read Emerson and Thoreau, or find some other interesting things to write about, Monsignor suggested that I write about my sins. He said that Saint Augustine and many other saints had done that, and there was no reason why I shouldn't do the same. This made me think of what happened to me when I was in the seventh grade at Sacred Heart School.

On a warm Sunday afternoon in May, I went on a hike with some of my classmates. When we came to a creek, we decided to go swimming. We had not brought our trunks with us, so we ended up swimming in the raw. Although the water was cold, we were having a good time dunking each other. Then one of the boys started to joke about the beards some of us were sprouting. I had never noticed before that certain boys had beards, while others did not. In fact, I had never even noticed that I was beginning to grow one. Then a few of the guys started to talk and laugh about girls and babies.

For some reason, when I got home that day, I couldn't get what had happened out of my mind. In fact, I couldn't sleep that night, and my thoughts kept going back to the creek where we had been swimming. A very strange feeling had come over me, and

September 15, 1937

when it was still with me the next day at school, I decided that I should ask somebody about it. At first, I didn't know who to ask, because I didn't think there was anybody who would understand. Then I thought of Father Kelly.

That afternoon, when classes were over for the day, I went to the rectory and rang the bell. When the door opened, Monsignor O'Shea was standing there. For a few seconds I didn't know what to do, but then I thought of my rosary and quickly got it out of my pocket. "Will you bless my rosary, Monsignor?" I asked him.

"Let me have it," he replied impatiently. He made the sign of the cross over it and gave it back to me.

"Thank you, Monsignor."

"You should have left your rosary in school to be blessed," he snapped. "You should learn to be a little bit considerate of other people." He slammed the door shut.

I was glad he hadn't noticed that the rosary I asked him to bless was my First Communion rosary which he had already blessed five years before. If I had told him I wanted to see Father Kelly, he would have asked the reason, and I knew I never could have explained anything like that to him.

On my way home, I still felt very uneasy and strange, so I decided to stop at the public library for a while. I went into the children's section and began to browse. Before, I had always been able to find an interesting book to read, but on that particular day, I couldn't find anything. Then, for the first time, I wandered into the adult section. I looked through a few of the books on each shelf until I came to a shelf of books on medicine. I picked up one of the books and began to page through it. Then I turned to the back of the book and glanced at the index. Suddenly I saw the word *Sex*, and for some reason, I experienced a strange thrill. Then I noticed three words with page numbers beside them: *Autoeroticism, Heterosexuality, Homosexuality.*

I sat down at one of the tables and began to read. There were words which I did not understand, and I looked them up in a large dictionary that was on the table. Whenever the librarian passed by, I'd get embarrassed and quickly turn to another page so she wouldn't know what I was reading. But as soon as she left, I'd start to read again. When I had finished with the one book, I got up and picked out some more. One of them had pictures and diagrams of different parts of the body. I looked up the words *Vulva, Clitoris, Vagina,* and *Uterus.* Some books had the pictures and diagrams of genital organs torn out. A few had been marked up with words and drawings—words and drawings like I had seen in the lavatory at school.

At first, I thought that what I had read at the library was going to help me, but it didn't. In fact, everything seemed to get worse. I still thought of discussing my problem with Father Kelly, but then I decided that it was even too late for that. I had sinned. Or had I sinned? The medical books said that what had happened to me was perfectly normal and happened to almost all boys of my age. Still, I had been taught something entirely different in my religion classes at school.

Worst of all, I realized that if I really had been committing mortal sins, I was compounding them with the sin of sacrilege; for I continued to receive Holy Communion every day. I had intended to stop, but each time Father Kelly stood before me with the sacred Host, I had received. I feared that if I did not receive, he might suspect what had happened. Each day the struggle went on, and each day I worried anew over whether I had committed another sin of sacrilege and new sins of impurity. I kept trying to decide whether the doctors or my teachers were right.

This went on for an entire month, and each day I envisioned myself slipping deeper into the fires of hell. When I continued to have trouble sleeping and eating, my father took me to a doctor. The doctor said that he could find nothing wrong, other than that I was growing up. And all the time I wondered if the doctor knew, and if my father and mother knew. There were times when I thought that even the people who saw me on the street suspected me. I felt unclean, and I thought that I must look that way.

Finally, I couldn't take it any longer. I decided to go to confession. Since I was ashamed to confess to Father Kelly, I decided to go to a church on the other side of town, which was operated by the Dominican Fathers. I thought that no one would know me there.

September 15, 1937

I was really scared when I entered the confessional. "Praised be Jesus Christ, bless me, Father, for I have sinned. My last confession was one month ago." I had carefully memorized my list of sins, but suddenly I couldn't remember them. "I have committed sins of impurity, Father," was all that I managed to say.

"What kind of sins of impurity did you commit?" the priest asked. "With yourself?"

"Yes, Father."

"How many times did you commit such sins?"

"Every day, Father."

"Did you have bad thoughts?"

"Yes, Father."

"How often?"

"Every day."

"Do you know how many times a day?"

"Very often, Father. I have also read bad books."

"How old are you?"

"Twelve, Father."

"Are there any other mortal sins?"

"I received Holy Communion sacrilegiously."

"How many times?"

"Every day since my last confession, Father."

"Now why on earth did you do a thing like that?" the priest asked angrily.

"I was afraid, Father."

"If anyone ever crucified Christ, you certainly did! It is bad enough to commit sins like that, without receiving Communion on top of them yet. Do you realize the sinfulness of what you have done?"

"Yes, Father."

"Do you realize that if you had died before you came here to confession, you would have gone straight into the fires of hell for all eternity?"

"Yes, Father."

"It is easy to live a pure life if you know how to go about it," the priest said. "When you are tempted to commit an impure action, or when you have an impure thought, you should not dally around. You should immediately distract your attention to something else. Saint Philip Neri once said that with this type of sin, it is the person who runs away—the coward—who always wins. You should pray, too, to the Mother of God when you are tempted. You should also join the Angelic Warfare Confraternity. Do you know what that is?"

"No, Father."

"If you stop at the rectory after you leave here, one of the Dominican Fathers will explain it to you and enroll you. He will give you a white cord, which you should wear around your waist, under your clothing, at all times. If anything like this ever happens again, get to confession right away, even if you have to get a priest out of bed. For your penance say fifteen Our Fathers and fifteen Hail Marys. Make an Act of Contrition."

As I said the Act of Contrition, I closed my eyes and envisioned a bleeding Christ hanging on the cross. Tears welled up under my eyelids as I pictured myself helping to drive the nails into Christ's hands and feet. But when I had finished this Act of Contrition and walked out of the confessional, I felt as though I had left a great burden behind me. I felt clean again.

September 16, 1937

Now that I have been here at Saint Mary's Seminary for a week, I think I am going to have a whole lot more to write about. Although it was hard to get started, I'm beginning to think it's fun to keep a diary. I am glad Monsignor Grosclaude recommended it.

In a way, I'm surprised that I'm still here. I've thought of giving up and going home many times, but Karl Wright always talks me out of it. I don't much care for the idea of keeping quiet most of the day, and having to be everywhere and do everything whenever a bell rings. I told Karl how I felt, and he quoted the following words of Saint Augustine: *"Fecisti nos, Domine, ad Te, et inquietum est cor nostrum donec requiescat in Te."* Then he helped me translate them: "You made us, O Lord, for Thyself, and our heart is restless, until it rests in Thee." I think Karl is very bright to know that.

September 17, 1937

Karl keeps telling me what Father Kelly always said: that I should become a priest to save my own soul and the souls of others. If that is what I am going to be able to do as a priest, then I guess everything I have to put up with here is worth it. Karl doesn't seem to mind the seminary at all. He claims you get used to it after a while. I said he is sharp, and I really mean it. Although he is only one year ahead of me, he can write poems in Latin. Today he said that I am his best friend, and I told him I feel the same way about him.

September 17, 1937

Until today, I never really understood what people meant when they talked about mystics. Karl explained how the relationship between the mystics and Jesus is much like that between a bride and bridegroom. In other words, mystics love the body of Jesus in a very special way.

During summer vacation, Karl hitchhiked all over the country and visited several mystics. He met a woman who has the wounds of Jesus in her hands, feet, and side. Her wounds bleed every Friday, and on the first Friday of each month, Jesus appears to her. She gave Karl a small bottle of water which Jesus Himself blessed for her.

Karl met a philosophy professor who has been visited by the Blessed Virgin. The Blessed Virgin told him that a war between Antichrist and the pope would soon break out, and although many people would be killed, the armies of the pope would win. She gave the professor some orange scapulars, and promised him that anyone who wears one will not be killed in the fighting. The professor gave Karl one of the scapulars.

Karl took the orange scapular from around his own neck and placed it around mine. He also gave me the small bottle of water which Jesus blessed. He said he was doing it because he likes me so much. He told me how the Bible says that Jonathan loved David as his own soul, and how David's love for Jonathan surpassed even the love he had for women. The Bible also says that Jesus loved Saint John, his disciple, in a very special way. Karl said he feels the same way about me.

November 3, 1937

Today Karl told me something very interesting. He said that I could always trust Monsignor Grosclaude, but to watch out for Father Clancy, the vice-rector. He said that Father Clancy wants to be rector himself, and will do anything to cause trouble for Monsignor Grosclaude. I guess Father Clancy was vice-rector for ten years before Monsignor Grosclaude became rector, and he thinks he should have been given the job.

Karl said that Father Clancy is especially angry because Monsignor Grosclaude is not an Irish rector. He told me that most of the Irish priests on the faculty feel the same way. Like Father Clancy, they are always trying to cause trouble for the rector, hoping that Bishop Connolly will remove him. According to Karl, Father Clancy and most of the other priests think Monsignor Grosclaude is too holy, and that's another thing they don't like about him. When I said I couldn't understand why priests would resent another priest just because he's not Irish and because he's holy, Karl remarked that it's politics. I guess that's what it must be, because I still can't understand it.

December 9, 1937

The seminary is full of surprises. When I was an altar boy at Sacred Heart, I used to meet a lot of seminarians, and from the way they behaved, I always thought all seminarians were very holy. Now I know that I was wrong. Some of the guys here are really pious, but others are downright hypocrites.

When Monsignor Grosclaude and certain other priests are around, the hypocrites pretend that they are living saints. In fact, some of them look like they are going to sprout wings and take off. But at other times, I see them cheating on their examination papers. Some of them, when they haven't done their homework, write on small sheets of paper what they should have memorized the day before, and insert them in their missals. Then, while they wear angelic expressions and pretend to pray during Mass, they study for their examinations and recitations.

Father Clancy and some of the other priests actually encourage such dishonesty. Sometimes they even join the hypocrites in breaking rules. For some reason, they seem to like these phonies, and even when they do reprimand them, they do it in such a nice and humorous way that they give the impression they really approve.

But priests like Father Clancy don't treat everybody the same. If a boy who is careful about observing rules happens to break one unintentionally, Father Clancy and the priests like him go out of their way to make things rough for him. Even if a boy like that does something just a little bit wrong, they embarrass him before everybody and send him to the rector. This is something else about the seminary which doesn't make any sense to me.

December 14, 1937

I really had a shock today. I found out that we have girls at the seminary. Well, in a way, we do. One of the older seminarians told me that some of the guys are called "she." I guess it has a lot to do with the way a guy walks and talks. Some of the priests are called "she," too. Monsignor Grosclaude and Father Clancy are called "he," but Fathers Tierney, Foley, and Couts are called "she." Father Tierney teaches Latin, and I just found out today that some of the boys nicknamed him "Kitty." That's because he always jumps up on the windowsill when he comes into the classroom and teaches from there. Father Foley is known as "Mamie," and Father Couts has been named "Bubbles."

It's all very strange, but I'm beginning to understand better some of the things that have been going on. A few days ago, Monsignor Grosclaude gave a talk on the dangers of particular friendships. He said that we should associate with all the boys in the same way, rather than with one favorite boy. Now I know why Monsignor gave that talk. Two boys from the senior class have been expelled for being particular friends. I guess they held hands when they thought nobody was looking. One of the boys, Paul Dunn, was known as a "he," because he was interested in sports. The other boy, John O'Neill, was a "she." Paul Dunn was caught in John O'Neill's cubicle at night, and they were in a clinch. The next day, Monsignor Grosclaude expelled them.

When I saw Karl Wright during recreation this afternoon, I

told him what I had heard, and he said it was true. I said I didn't want the guys to consider us particular friends, and he said they didn't. He said that we are good friends, but not particular friends. I told him I sure hope so.

January 10, 1938

During recreation period today, Karl and I almost got into serious trouble by breaking a rule. Karl wanted to show me a poem written by Saint John of the Cross, a great mystic. He had left his book of poems in study hall, and although we were not supposed to go there during recreation, we went to get the book. Karl had just picked it up when Father Clancy seemed to appear out of nowhere.

"Why are you two not outside for recreation?" he demanded.

"We wanted to look at a poem, Father," Karl answered.

"Oh a poem, was it now!" Father Clancy exclaimed in a disbelieving tone of voice. "And may I see that poem?"

Karl handed him the book.

"So it is Saint John of the Cross, is it? Do you have permission from your spiritual director to read this, Wright?"

"No, Father."

"And you, Faber, do you have permission from your spiritual director?"

"No, Father."

"Saint John of the Cross is not to be dabbled in by boys who don't know what they're doing," Father Clancy admonished us. "You should never read Saint John of the Cross unless your spiritual director explicitly tells you to. I have a doctor's degree in philosophy, and I have never read him—not even once, mind you. And do you know why? It's not because I'm lazy—as you might think. It's because I was never told to read him. Instead of reading Saint John of the Cross, you two should be outside where you are supposed to be. Did you know that you are breaking a rule by being in here?"

"Yes, Father."

"Well then why are you here? I won't report you to the Very Reverend Rector this time, but if it happens again, I shall. Now go outside and play ball or something—as you are supposed to do—and wipe all that foolishness about Saint John of the Cross from your minds."

January 11, 1938

After night prayers last night, Father Clancy asked me to wait for him in his office. I thought he was going to reprimand me again for being in study hall during recreation period, but he surprised me by saying: "I attended a party yesterday, and they gave me this big cake. I was wondering if you would be good enough to help me eat it."

I said that I would, and he cut a large slice of cake and handed it to me.

"It's good cake, isn't it?"

"Yes, Father."

"You know, son, you lads don't know how lucky you are. When I was a boy at the seminary in Ireland, our professors never would have thought of inviting one of us in for a piece of cake. If they invited us in, it was for a sound thrashing. Let me tell you, my boy, they were strict with us. More than once they boxed our ears. But they made men of us. Everyone had to memorize something every day. I can still recite poems I learned when I was just a boy like you. Would you like to hear one of them?"

"Yes, Father."

Father Clancy recited the poem, and then he began to ask me questions about it. "Do you know who wrote that poem?"

I told him that I didn't.

"You should be ashamed to say that you don't know," he said. "It was written by John Keats. The title of it is: 'On First Looking into Chapman's Homer.' Do you know who John Keats was?"

"Yes, Father. He was a poet."

"And do you know who Homer was?"

"Yes, Father. He was a Greek poet."

"And do you know what he wrote?"

"The *Iliad* and the *Odyssey*, Father."

"And who was Chapman?"

"I don't know, Father."

"You should know that, too, my boy. I am not going to tell you who he was. You go to the library tomorrow and look it up, and then you will know next time. Do you know who Cortez was?"

"Yes, Father. He was the Spaniard who conquered Mexico."

"And do you know who Apollo was?"

"He was the Grecian god of poetry, music, and manly beauty, Father."

"For a boy your age, you know quite a bit. Quite a bit! But you should have known Chapman, too. Long before I was in the class you are in now, I knew Chapman. My professors would have pulled the ears off any boy who did not know Chapman.... You know, son, when I think back on my school days in Ireland, I feel homesick and lonely. I left there right after I was ordained. I had to leave my mother and all my friends behind. Have you ever felt lonely, son?"

"Yes, Father."

"Then you know how I feel. Do you think we can be friends, my boy?"

"Yes, Father."

Father Clancy came over to where I was sitting, knelt down, and kissed me on the cheek. "Now you are one of my boys," he said. "There are so many things I want to teach you."

I felt funny when he kissed me. My father always told me that men who kiss each other are sissies.

"You can stay with me tonight," he said.

"I can't, Father."

"Nonsense! my boy." He went to the doorway of the adjoining room and turned on the light. "Do you see how big my room is? I know you'll like it. Why don't you stay?"

"I can't, Father."

"What do you mean, you can't? You can stay with me for just a little while if you don't want to stay all night, and then you can go back to your own bed in the dormitory."

"I can't, Father," I told him again.

Then I got up and ran out of the room. I felt my way in the darkness to my cubicle, undressed as quickly as I could, and got into bed. I felt sorry for Father Clancy. He looked very unhappy, but I couldn't help it. I just couldn't do what he wanted.

January 12, 1938

I was almost expelled from the seminary today, and it was all because of Father Clancy. It's still hard for me to believe that anyone could have done what he did, especially a priest.

Monsignor Grosclaude sent for me this morning, and he was very upset. "Why was Karl Wright in your cubicle last night?" he asked.

I almost fell off the chair. "He wasn't in my cubicle, Monsignor," I told him.

"You might as well tell me the truth. Father Clancy said that he caught you."

"That isn't true, Monsignor."

"Are you calling Father Clancy a liar?"

"It isn't true."

"Let us just suppose—and remember, I said just suppose—that Father Clancy made up the story. Can you give me any reason why Father Clancy would do that?"

I was tempted to tell him everything, but I didn't want to cause trouble for Father Clancy. I finally said: "I don't want to answer that question, Monsignor."

"If there is a reason, you had better tell me now. Otherwise, I'll be forced to believe Father Clancy, and you know the consequences. What did I tell you would happen to a boy who went to another boy's cubicle, and to the boy who did not immediately report him?"

"You said they would be expelled, Monsignor."

"That's right. So what do you have to say for yourself?"

"Nothing, Monsignor."

"Is Karl Wright a good friend of yours?"

"Yes, Monsignor."

"And that's all?"

"Yes, Monsignor."

Monsignor Grosclaude was silent for a time and sat looking intently at me. "In a case such as this," he said slowly, "it is not always necessary to expel both boys. The expulsion of one is sometimes sufficient. If I have to expel one of you, which one do you think it should be?"

"I think you should expel me, Monsignor."

"And why do you think that?"

"Karl Wright will make a good priest, Monsignor."

"And what about you? Don't you think you will be a good priest?"

"He will be better."

Monsignor Grosclaude shook his head slowly. "I don't think so," he said. "No, son, I don't think so. But I am not going to expel either one of you. I have already talked to Karl, and now that I have talked to you, I believe that both of you will make good priests. Karl talks a great deal about mystics and that sort of thing, doesn't he?"

"Yes, Monsignor."

"And what he says is very fascinating, isn't it?"

"Yes, Monsignor."

"You and Karl Wright are fine boys," Monsignor Grosclaude said, "and I am glad that you are such good friends. You will notice I said that I am glad you are good friends—not particular friends. There is a big difference between the two. Particular friends associate with each other to the exclusion of everybody else. Good friends associate with each other because they have common interests and compatible personalities, but their friendship never degenerates into maudlin sentimentality and possessiveness. Do you understand?"

"Yes, Monsignor."

"If you are wise, you will see Karl only when you have really important common interests to discuss, and I would do my utmost not to be seen by Father Clancy during any lengthy conversation with him. Moreover, I wouldn't mention this incident to any of the other boys or priests. I would be friendly with Father Clancy and pretend that nothing has happened—even though you might believe that he did not tell the truth. Is that clear?"

"Yes, Monsignor."

"Do you think you can do it?"

"Yes, Monsignor."

Monsignor Grosclaude smiled. "If you ever get to thinking about any of these things, and you make any discoveries, let them be our secret. Will you?"

I had to smile, too, when he said that. I promised him I would.

PART TWO

November 17, 1944

I went to see the rector again today about joining the army, and although I was really determined to do it this time, no matter what he said, he once again talked me out of it. When I told him that there are guys younger than I am who are dying in my place, just because I happen to have a seminary deferment, he said that those who follow Christ die daily for others, and there is no reason to feel that I'm not doing my part. Even this argument would not have convinced me, if Monsignor Grosclaude had not added another one. He said that he expects the war to be over within a year, and if I went now, by the time basic training was completed, I would be stuck in the army with no war to fight. This argument makes a lot of sense to me, so I guess I am going to stay here, and in the words of Monsignor, continue my basic training for becoming a soldier of Christ.

Monsignor Grosclaude is an expert in talking people out of going to the army. Many seminarians have wanted to join up, but so far, only three have actually gone. Karl Wright wanted to go, and I'm especially glad that Monsignor managed to dissuade him. I'm afraid Karl is still the inveterate romantic he always was. He's against all the weapons used in modern warfare. In fact, he's against all killing. His idea was to use only his bare fists. I almost had to laugh when he told me, but I managed to restrain myself. He's a very sensitive fellow, and brilliant— about *some* things. In the end, he probably would have thrown an orange scapular at the Axis, confident of ending the war with one blow. I think both he and the army are much better off that he's still here.

Although Karl's attitude seems rather unrealistic to me, I think it is healthier than that of many seminarians and priests who have grown to hate the Axis. I shudder when I hear a seminarian or priest refer to a Japanese as a "gook," a "Jap," or a "slant." I still believe that it's possible to fight for a cause without hating the people you have to fight against. They are all children of God, and in everything that really matters, they are not one bit different than we are.

Father Tierney, who was a chaplain in the First World War,

has taken his uniform out of mothballs, and every chance he gets, he puts it on and goes to different churches and meetings of civic organizations, where he preaches patriotism and inflames people against the Germans and Japanese. I don't think that's something a priest should be doing, especially a seminary professor. He's even written a song called: "When It's Taps for the Japs." This song has been circulated nationally.

I think it's our duty to pray for *all* the people who are caught up in this disaster. The politicians—not the fighting men—are responsible. All of the major powers played a part in creating the conflict, and not one of them can be considered guiltless. That includes our own country. Wars are seldom fought for the immediate, emotional reasons given by governments to their people; but for longstanding economic and political ones. It is in these spheres that the leaders of nations are responsible. They are the real war criminals.

But now that the war is here, I believe we have to follow our consciences. Certainly Hitler is a menace to the civilized world, and I do not believe that any decent person, who knows him for what he is, can permit him to win. But while we fight him, I do not believe that we should feel anything but compassion for those unfortunate people who are being misled by him.

Even the pope bears a heavy responsibility for this war. Instead of behaving as the Vicar of Jesus Christ should, he has been playing politics with the lives of people, just as the leaders of nations have been doing. The pope has certainly delivered enough sermons lamenting the war, but these sermons are entirely meaningless, since he never points out the real causes of the war or accuses the individuals responsible. He has never condemned Hitler or Mussolini, and he has never forbidden Catholics to fight in their armies—armies which, for the most part, are made up of Catholics.

Instead, we have seen the sorry and contradictory spectacle of Catholic prelates and chaplains championing the leaders and soldiers of their particular nation, when they should have been speaking out on those moral principles which involve the good of mankind in general. If only the Church had done this, it would now be stronger and more respected than it has been since the

Middle Ages. Instead, the pope concluded a concordat with Hitler, which gives him a prestige and power he would not have had otherwise.

I especially cannot understand why Pius XII has not done more to help the Jews. After all, if anyone is our brother in Christ, they certainly are. Not only is the pope to blame in this regard, but the Christian nations—including our own—which would not accept them, when it became perfectly obvious that their lives were threatened in Europe. The Christian attitude toward Jews has always been difficult for me to understand. Even in our own country, they are often excluded from neighborhoods and country clubs, yet the same Christians who exclude them go to church every Sunday, where they worship a Jew and venerate His mother. But what can one expect when the pope didn't even speak out to save the lives of those courageous Polish and German priests who dared to criticize Hitler? It is all so depressing.

February 2, 1945

Someone once said that no matter how much things change, they remain that much more the same. I am beginning to think that is a very accurate description of the human situation. When I first came to the seminary, I thought that getting out of the high school department and into college would make a big difference. It didn't. Then I thought that when I completed my first two years of college, had my own room, put on a cassock and Roman collar, and got into philosophy, I would be much happier. I'm not. In fact, now that I am completing my fourth year of college and taking my final credits in philosophy, I feel more ignorant and confused than I did when I first entered the seminary. I keep thinking of those words of Saint Augustine, which Karl Wright quoted to me shortly after I arrived here at Saint Mary's: *"Fecisti nos, Domine, ad Te, et inquietum est cor nostrum donec requiescat in Te."* How true! How *very* true!

Even Father Clancy hasn't changed. Now that he's my philosophy professor, I can't get over what a really ignorant man he is. A chimpanzee could pass his courses, if he had the ability to memorize definitions in Latin. Almost every day, he repeats the same idiotic statement: "Mind you now, memorize your definitions capital for capital, comma for comma, and period for period!" On those rare occasions when someone dares to ask him a question, he uses another refrain: "How many times must I tell you! You do not know enough yet to ask questions in the classroom. Haven't I told you that often enough already? Just be humble and obedient and memorize your definitions, as you're told to do."

Father Clancy has asked us to write a paper on the proofs of Saint Thomas for the existence of God, and when he sees mine, I know that he'll have a fit. But I can't help it. It's what I really think. Today I recalled again when I was in the first grade at Sacred Heart School, and my friend, Chris Sullivan, asked Sister William: "Who made God?" Ironically, that is the question I still have to ask after studying the elaborate and reportedly invincible proofs of Saint Thomas. Poor Chris was a philosopher, but nobody realized it. Out of the mouths of babes! Once again, it goes to prove that things don't change as much as people usually think they do. After almost sixteen years of schooling, the questions—although they are now coated with a complicated technical jargon—are exactly the same; and the answers are as elusive as ever.

In his first three proofs for the existence of God, Saint Thomas stated that everything in the world is either moved, caused, or dependent upon something else. But he said that it is illogical to suppose that this process goes on indefinitely. He concluded, therefore, that there must be a first mover or cause, and he called this *God*. I ask in my paper how we know that what Saint Thomas called *God* is not also moved, caused, or dependent upon something else. Who has ever traced everything which is moved, caused, or dependent, to a point where he could prove that such and such a thing were a mover and yet unmoved, a cause and yet uncaused? But even if such a point of absolute causality and independence were capable of being observed, I ask how anyone could possibly say that it would be the same thing as Christians understand by the word *God*.

I believe that Saint Thomas's fourth and fifth arguments are even more flimsy than his first three, and I indicate that in my paper. His fourth argument is nothing but semantics, and if it were followed to its logical conclusion, the Devil would become God. Not only are there beings in the world which are more and less good, true, and noble, as Saint Thomas points out, but there are other beings which are more and less evil, false, and ignoble. If one were to be consistent in pursuing Saint Thomas's line of reasoning, he would have to say that such beings derive the qualities of evil, falsity, and ignobleness from some being which possessed those qualities in a maximum or unlimited degree. Such a being could be called *God* just as logically as the being which possessed maximum or unlimited perfection.

In his fifth proof for the existence of God, Saint Thomas stated that since the universe is governed in an orderly fashion, a perfect designer exists, and he called this designer *God*. Even if Saint Thomas had been able to prove that the world is governed in a perfectly orderly way, I ask in my paper how he could have proven that it is God, in the Christian sense, who governs the world in such fashion. Moreover, the basic question still remains: What perfect designer created the perfect designer who supposedly created the perfectly designed universe? But Saint Thomas never proved that the world is governed in a perfectly orderly fashion. How could he have proven with reason alone, for example, that a perfect designer created a world in which animals—including man—had to kill each other in order to obtain food? What about floods, earthquakes, sickness, wars, and death? Religion attempts to explain such phenomena, but the fifth proof of Saint Thomas, from the standpoint of reasoning alone, does not explain them; nor does it prove the existence of God.

I conclude my paper by saying that we know God exists only through faith. I quote part of the Epistle of Saint Paul to the Hebrews, where he points out in the eleventh chapter that "faith is the substance of things to be hoped for, the evidence of things that are not seen." Saint Paul said: "By faith we understand that the world was fashioned by the word of God; and thus things visible were made out of things invisible." This is the only "proof" I have discovered so far that makes any sense to me.

February 9, 1945

Although I knew that Father Clancy would be anything but happy with my paper on Saint Thomas's proofs for the existence of God, I never expected his reaction to be as vehement as it was. He walked into our theodicy class today just as he always does, with an armful of books—which he never uses—and a pencil wedged between his teeth. After he had ceremoniously removed the pencil and said a prayer, we sat down as usual. Then it started.

"I should make you get up and sit down again," he complained. "I have told you time and again that you should sit down quietly. Now you know that! Don't make me tell you every . . ."

He suddenly stopped talking and glared at me. Then he asked: "What are you laughing at, Mr. Faber?"

"I wasn't laughing," I told him.

"You weren't what, Mr. Faber?"

"I wasn't laughing."

He banged his desk with his fist. "I am a priest, Mr. Faber, and I demand the respect which is due me. You should have manners enough to address me as 'Father.' Even though you are stupid, I believe you should have learned that much."

"I wasn't laughing, Father."

"That is somewhat better, Mr. Faber. You know, Mr. Faber, there is something wrong with people who laugh at other people and don't know they're doing it. Maybe you should be locked up! We'll have to see. . . . But no wonder Mr. Faber laughs at me. He even laughs at Saint Thomas Aquinas—the greatest philosopher of all time—mind you. You do laugh at Saint Thomas Aquinas, don't you, Mr. Faber?"

"No, Father."

"I read your paper, Mr. Faber. In it you said that the philosophical proofs given by Saint Thomas for the existence of God are invalid. You said that, did you not, Mr. Faber?"

"Yes, Father."

"Stand up, Mr. Faber, when I talk to you!"

I stood up, but I had already decided that I wasn't going to let him do what he had in mind. He wasn't going to ridicule me before my classmates and get away with it.

February 9, 1945

Father Clancy banged his fist on the desk to emphasize his words. "I have told this class again and again, Mr. Faber, that there can be no disagreement between philosophy and theology. How could you be so foolish as to indicate in your paper that there can be?"

"I was not being foolish," I told him. "There are philosophers who disagree with certain theologies, including our own; and there are theologians who disagree with particular philosophies, including the scholastic philosophy which is taught here at the seminary."

"You cannot call people who disagree with Catholic theology, philosophers," he said. "Catholic philosophy is the only philosophy, because it is the true philosophy."

"I'll answer that with a typical scholastic argument," I countered. "By calling Catholic philosophy the true philosophy, you are admitting the existence of false philosophies. Consequently, there are other philosophies besides Catholic philosophy."

"Since you know so much about philosophy, Mr. Faber, perhaps you could give us the names of one or two of the people whom you call philosophers and who disagree with theologians."

"Hobbes, Spinoza, Kant, Nietzsche, James—"

"You don't have to go on, Mr. Faber," Father Clancy interrupted me. "I think it is apparent to everyone how wrong you are. How can you call atheists, pantheists, voluntarists, and pragmatists, philosophers? The very word *philosophy* comes from the Greek words which mean 'love of wisdom.' How can you say that the men whom you named loved wisdom?"

"I think that some of them loved wisdom as much as Saint Thomas," I replied.

Father Clancy shouted and pounded the desk: "It is sacrilegious to say such a thing! The Canon Law of the Catholic Church states clearly that the method, doctrine, and principles of Saint Thomas are to be held sacred. *Sacred,* mind you, is the very word used in Canon Law."

"Saint Thomas would have been the last person to want his work considered sacred," I calmly told him. "He himself opposed certain teachings of Saint Augustine, and he was condemned for heresy by the archbishops of Paris and Canterbury."

"That is all beside the point, Mr. Faber. Can't you see that? How dare you compare the men you mentioned with Saint Thomas, the Angelic Doctor? I wrote my thesis for the doctoral degree on the relationship between chastity and truth. If a person does not live a pure life, his intellect cannot possibly discover the truth."

"I don't see how that can be true, Father," I said. "We believe that the Catholic religion is true, yet there have been unchaste individuals who have accepted Catholicism, while there have been chaste individuals who have rejected it. Besides, the Angelic Doctor himself was opposed to the dogma of the Immaculate Conception, which all Catholics must now accept as one of the truths of Catholic faith. If a man has to be chaste to be a good philosopher, then we would have to disqualify some of the greatest philosophers who ever lived; from Plato to modern times."

When Father Clancy saw that he was losing the argument, he attempted to use the ploy of becoming conciliatory. "But that's all beside the point," he maintained. "Surely you can see that! Don't you think that the vice-rector of a seminary, who is head of a philosophy department and who holds the doctoral degree, knows more about philosophy than you do? Don't you think you should accept what he tells you?"

"I believe it was Saint Thomas," I said, "who claimed that the argument from authority is the weakest of all arguments. *'Locus ab auctoritate quae fundatur super ratione humana est infirmissimus.'* "

"Don't try to impress me with your Latin!" Father Clancy shouted. "Sit down this instant, you stupid ass! You have clearly demonstrated before this entire class what a conceited and arrogant simpleton you really are. But now I have all the evidence I need to do something about you. I am going to report you to the faculty—that's what I'm going to do. Perhaps you can try to explain to the Very Reverend Rector what you said here this morning."

I'm sure Father Clancy will carry out his threat, and if he does, I do not think the faculty will permit me to receive tonsure this spring. Although that will be a big disappointment, I'm not sorry I acted as I did. It was something that somebody should have had the courage to do a long time ago. In the end, maybe it will do some good. I hope so.

February 12, 1945

Monsignor Grosclaude asked to see me today about my recent altercation with Father Clancy, and although he was quite perturbed at first, he was quick to accept my version of what had happened. I denied Father Clancy's claim that I had been ridiculing him. "I had to defend myself," I told the rector. "Father Clancy was treating me like a child, and I—"

"And you don't like to be treated as a child, do you?" Monsignor Grosclaude interrupted me, a tinge of sarcasm in his voice. "You're so big now! All of twenty-one, I think. Imagine that!"

"I'm sorry, Monsignor."

"You have become something of a hero to some of the other seminarians," Monsignor Grosclaude said, "but there are often serious liabilities to being a hero; and sometimes one of those liabilities is that you must suffer the consequences. Christian patience and forbearance are not only important spiritual virtues, but they are important virtues for everyday living as well. By not practicing them, you have made an enemy of Father Clancy."

"I'm not so sure that Father Clancy was not my enemy already," I pointed out. "I think his enmity goes back a number of years."

Monsignor Grosclaude nodded reflectively. "Yes, son," he said slowly, "you could very well be right. But there is something else that troubles me a little bit. In proving the existence of God, you stressed the primacy of faith over reason. Why did you do that?"

"I did not find the proofs from reason satisfactory, and I decided that faith was the only answer."

"What about your own faith, son?"

I was startled by the question. Monsignor Grosclaude had

been looking intently at me, and in doing so, he seemed to have penetrated my very soul. "I have had some doubts about matters connected with our religion," I admitted.

"Sometimes I think every lad of your age has something in him of the agnostic," Monsignor Grosclaude remarked. "It is all part of growing up, and usually nothing very serious."

"What bothers me more than anything else," I said, "is the authoritarianism found here in the seminary."

Monsignor Grosclaude smiled. "My, that's a big word!"

"I'm serious, Monsignor. It often seems that the seminary is little more than a place for indoctrinating students in certain beliefs, and training them to be docile instruments of those in authority."

"That is one of our aims here," Monsignor Grosclaude said. "We attempt to train men so that they will be obedient to their bishops."

"In other words, bishops are always right."

"I do not know if that is the best way to express it, but it is the general idea."

"I can respect authority when it's right, Monsignor, but I cannot respect it when it's wrong."

"That is because you are still very young," Monsignor Grosclaude commented, "because you think a great deal, and because you have not yet developed the spiritual qualities necessary for such respect. Most students accept the training we give them as a matter of course. But there are exceptions, and I think perhaps you are one of them. In such instances, a different approach is indicated. Unfortunately, under our present system, that is not always possible."

"I often feel that I am getting an inferior education here," I said. "It seems that the real scholarship is being done in secular universities."

Monsignor Grosclaude smiled. "If we are as bad as all that, why don't you attend a secular university this summer?"

I couldn't quite believe what I was hearing. "Are you serious, Monsignor?"

"Entirely serious! I think it would do you a great deal of

good. Is there any subject in which you have a particular interest?"

"History, Monsignor."

"Well, then history it will be. Choose a good secular university—one that has the program you want—and I'll take care of all your expenses."

"I couldn't let you do that, Monsignor."

"Oh, but you can, and you will! I have no use for the money. Besides, I happen to think you're a good investment."

"You're so honest, Monsignor!"

Monsignor Grosclaude laughed. "Honesty, like being a hero, has its consequences. Did you know that this is my last year as rector?"

I was stunned. "No, Monsignor."

"I have been appointed spiritual director. Father Clancy will become rector."

"If that is the case, I am not going to return to the seminary next year," I told him. "With Father Clancy as rector, there is no chance of my ever being ordained. I knew that I would not receive tonsure this year, but now I can see that the situation is altogether hopeless."

"Perhaps not as hopeless as you think," Monsignor Grosclaude commented matter-of-factly. "Father Clancy wanted to use me as his instrument for getting rid of you, but when he becomes rector, I believe that he will do everything possible to win your favor. He is more afraid of you than you are of him, and if you think about it, you'll understand why. And you will receive tonsure. I still have some say in such matters. Moreover, if you return next year, you will not be without a friend. The spiritual director of a seminary has something to say about policy."

"But how could they do this to you, Monsignor? How could they demote you in this way, and how can you take it so well?"

The rector smiled. "You must learn to see the hand of God in these things. If you can accept the primacy of the spiritual over the material, then you might even say that I have been promoted. As spiritual director, my sole concern will be the spiritual welfare of the students. Besides, I think Bishop Connolly knows what he's doing. They complained about me so much that he had no choice. But this does not mean that he agrees with them. I am not entirely without influence. But the most important thing is that we have to look at these things the way God sees them. After all, we are all in His hands."

"You are a great man, Monsignor," I said.

He laughed. "And you are a great lad! But once again, let all of this be our secret."

"You can count on me, Monsignor," I told him.

"I know that, son. God bless you!"

PART THREE

June 28, 1945

This morning I arrived in Jefferson City by train. Even before I started to search for a room, I left my luggage at the station and had a look at Jefferson University. I have to say that it is all very impressive. The buildings are mammoth, and the library is the largest I have ever seen. One of the librarians told me that they have over a million volumes. We only have about fifteen thousand at the seminary. During the regular school year, ten thousand students attend the university. When I heard there would be more than that during the summer, I decided that I had better get busy and find a room before they were all gone.

Fortunately, I got a room on the first try. They gave me a list at the university, and I sort of closed my eyes and picked out a name and address. The place is not far from the university, and a Mrs. Duffy is the proprietress. She wanted eight dollars for the room, but I got her down to five. She was very reluctant to lower the price—the demand is such that she didn't have to—but then she asked me which church I attend. When I told her that I am a Catholic seminarian, she said that I could have the room for five.

I have an idea that she is something of a religious nut. She sat down and told me everything about herself. *Everything* is the right word. I kept wondering if she would ever shut up. She told me over and over again how she attends Mass every day, and never misses Benediction in the evenings. Then she started on her deceased husband. She said that he had broken the laws of God and man by committing suicide. I thought she seemed pretty callous about the whole thing. She said: "He played a dirty trick on me. I would have gotten more money in insurance if he had died a natural death." After about two hours of this, during which she served tea, I had a notion to tell her that her husband was lucky to have gotten away from her, no matter how he did it. But I restrained myself.

The room itself is going to be fine. It has a sink and a large bed that comes out of the wall. It is near the front door on the first floor, and that means I won't have to be running into Mrs. Duffy all the time. She has a large apartment in back of the house, and there is a young guy who has a room right in her quarters. I have my suspicions about that, but it's their business, not mine. There are several other roomers in the house, and Mrs. Duffy claims they are all very quiet. I hope she's right. I know that I'm going to have a lot of work to do.

I telephoned Dr. Mannheim, chairman of the history department, and he asked me to see him at his home tomorrow morning. He sounds like a nice guy. He speaks with an accent, but his English is easily understandable and unusually precise. "Yes, Mr. Faber," he said. "I remember your letters very well. It makes me happy to know that you are finally going to be with us at the university—even though it be for so short a time. But do not misunderstand me! Much can be accomplished in a short time. It is quality—not quantity—with which we are concerned."

I am anxious to meet him.

June 29, 1945

Now that I have met Dr. Mannheim, I don't know whether I like him or not. I get the impression that he is anticlerical and very hostile to the Church. That is only a first impression, though. I do have to say that on the surface, at least, he was very gracious and even extremely kind. He offered me a seat in his cluttered study and proceeded to fill a pipe. I mentioned that when I came up on the porch I had heard a violin and thought I might be interrupting him.

"I do not play the violin, Mr. Faber," he informed me. "It was my daughter you heard."

"She plays very well," I said.

Dr. Mannheim didn't seem very impressed with my comment. "She plays well," he smiled, "but one day she will play better. I hope to see much improvement. You see, I come from a family of musicians. I once studied music, but I was not very good, and when I am not good at something, I do not pursue it. Consequently, I no longer play at all. But my daughter shows possibilities. What will come of those possibilities remains to be seen. If you would like, I shall introduce you to my daughter after we have transacted our business."

"Fine!" I told him.

"From your letters and application, I understand that you attend a seminary," he said. "What kind of place is that?"

"It is a school for training priests."

"Yes, I know all that, but what did they teach you there? I have never heard of your school."

"You will have to judge the product yourself, Dr. Mannheim. I am sure that you will soon learn whether they taught me anything or not."

"What about this priest who recommended you? I believe his name is Grosclaude, or something like that. I never heard of him."

"He was rector of the seminary."

"Yes, yes, I understand that, but I want to know more about him. In his recommendation, he said that one of your best qualities is your honesty. Now what I would like to know is whether or not you think Monsignor Grosclaude himself is honest. Do you see why that is important? If Monsignor Grosclaude says that you are honest, but if he is dishonest himself, then his recommendation of you cannot mean very much. Is that not right?"

"Not entirely," I said. "I think it presents another question. If Monsignor Grosclaude says that I am honest, but if he is dishonest in saying it, of what value could my opinion of Monsignor Grosclaude's honesty possibly be?"

Dr. Mannheim lit his pipe and smiled. "You are a clever young man, a remarkably clever young man! Your answer was properly scholastic, and the professors at the seminary would be proud of you. But tell me, Mr. Faber, do you believe that you can be honest in your study of history?"

"I have always tried to be."

"Perhaps you have, but we do not study history here as you studied it at the seminary. You studied what you thought was history in such a way that it increased your belief in your religion. Here, we study history scientifically. You must be willing to examine the facts, and examine them closely. We are not dogmatists here, Mr. Faber. We want you to investigate, we want you to question, and we want you to prove things to your own satisfaction. Do you think that you will be able to do what we expect of you?"

"I am willing to try."

"I noticed that you intend to take the course in medieval history. That is the course I teach, Mr. Faber. I keep wondering whether or not your seminary background will interfere with your studies. The people of the Middle Ages were not—how shall I say it?—very saintly."

"People have never been conspicuously saintly in *any* age," I told him.

"That is true, Mr. Faber, but you must remember that the Catholic Church controlled society during the Middle Ages, and you must also remember that the Catholic Church usually tries to make people of that time much better than they actually were. The Church often attempts to give the impression that if the whole world were Catholic, people would be much better than they are now. But the truth is that they would be much worse, and I think the history of the Middle Ages proves that what I say is true. Clergymen themselves during those times were anything but saintly."

"There have always been bad priests, Dr. Mannheim."

"There were more than you probably realize, Mr. Faber, and they were not just a little bit bad. Monasteries and nunneries were often little more than houses of prostitution. But do not take my word for this. Go to the library and read for yourself what medieval councils of the Church had to say. Read what Archbishop Rigaud of Rouen, an archbishop of the thirteenth century, said in the *Register* about his visitation of convents, monasteries, and churches."

"I'll do that, Dr. Mannheim."

"You will find, Mr. Faber, that when I discuss the corruption of the Middle Ages, I always quote what Catholics themselves have had to say. Otherwise, Catholics will call me prejudiced and say that I am quoting sources which are inimical to their church. That is a favorite Catholic trick to avoid the truth. Did you ever learn it?"

"No, I didn't," I stated emphatically.

Dr. Mannheim smiled when he noticed that I was becoming angry. "That will be enough for now," he said. "I hope I have given you something to think about."

"A great deal!" I told him.

"Good! I'll introduce you to my daughter."

Dr. Mannheim is a very ugly man, but his daughter, Maria, is a beauty. She has long, dark hair, and for the few moments I saw her, she had a radiant smile. But I think her eyes are the most striking feature about her. They seemed to look at me from bottomless depths.

After she had gone, Dr. Mannheim asked: "What do you think of my daughter?"

"Very beautiful!" I said.

Dr. Mannheim smiled. "On that, I think we can agree."

July 2, 1945

There are times when I think that Dr. Mannheim is going to have a heart attack during his lectures. He sweats, shouts, flails his arms all over the place, and at times, even jumps up and down. Today he lectured on the corruption of popes, cardinals, and bishops. By the time he finished, his shirt was wet, sweat covered his face, and he was breathing heavily. I expected him to collapse at any moment.

He began his lecture by saying that popes and cardinals had been guilty of everything from adultery, fornication, incest, and sodomy, to murder. He quoted Saint Bridget—once again, using his *Catholic* sources—to the effect that Pope Innocent VI was a greater traitor than Judas; his cardinals being consumed by the very fire that devoured Sodom. Then he read a passage from Saint Catherine of Siena which lamented that the popes were expending the treasures of Christ on harlots.

Dr. Mannheim seemed to especially relish telling about a party which was held at the palace of Pope Alexander VI on the eve of All Saints' Day. He said that the party was given by the pope's son, the Duke of Valentinois, who had been a cardinal until the pope permitted him to marry. He emphasized that the pope himself was present, as well as the pope's daughter, Lucrezia. He added that the pope's son had only recently murdered his sister's husband. Finally, he quoted from the diary of Burchard, the pope's master of ceremonies.

I wrote down the quotation. It goes like this: "That night fifty of the more decent prostitutes, who are called courtesans, dined with the Duke of Valentinois in the Apostolic Palace, and after dinner they danced with the attendants, first in their clothes and then nude. Lighted candles were then placed on the ground and chestnuts between the candles, and the naked women, crawling between the candles on their hands and knees, had to pick up the chestnuts, the pope and Lucrezia looking on. At the end, gifts were given to those who had intercourse with the prostitutes the largest number of times. This was done openly in the hall, and the gifts handed to the winners."

Despite all this immorality, Dr. Mannheim claims that the *real* sin of medieval church officials was not immorality, but greed. He pointed out that popes like Boniface IX, Alexander VI, and Leo X, continuously created new church offices and sold them to the highest bidder. Thus, drunkards, murderers, debauchees, and brutal warriors—who sometimes could not even read and write— became bishops. Dr. Mannheim said that positions were sometimes created after the fashion of Pope Alexander VI, who poisoned Cardinal Giovanni Michele, seized his possessions, and then sold his office to someone else.

Dr. Mannheim then told another of his favorite stories. It seems that Pope Leo X fabricated a plot against his own life in order to blackmail five of his wealthy cardinals. As the price for sparing their lives, he demanded huge sums of money. He had them tortured into falsely confessing that they had hired a physician to poison him; and he had one of the cardinals, who was especially difficult, secretly murdered. To make the false accusation appear authentic, he had a doctor and a steward of one of the cardinals publicly put to death. Their flesh was torn from their bones with red-hot pincers during the journey to the place of execution, where they were finally hanged, drawn, and quartered.

After Dr. Mannheim's lecture, I went to the library and looked into the sources he had used. I have to admit that he was entirely honest in his facts. I still detect a very definite prejudice, however, in the special exuberance with which he imparts them. Nevertheless, the best historians—Catholic and non-Catholic alike—support what he said. All of this has been quite a revelation to me.

July 5, 1945

I heard on a newscast this morning that the United States has recaptured the Philippines. Perhaps Japan will be defeated very soon now, and the war will end. I hope so! I can't wait for the suffering and killing to stop. I keep praying for all those who are still experiencing the horrors of this war, whether they be Americans or Japanese. Although I have never met a single Japanese, I still think of each Japanese as my brother. I guess I am not easily influenced by all the propaganda to the contrary.

I don't know whether it was because of this morning's news reports or not, but today Dr. Mannheim delivered a lecture condemning the Catholic Church for bringing war rather than peace to the world. He said that the popes of old had declared it necessary for all the people of the world—under pain of eternal damnation—to be subject to them even in temporal matters. He cited Pope Boniface VIII's *Unam Sanctam* as an example of these declarations.

According to Dr. Mannheim, when emperors and kings refused to pay the exorbitant taxes demanded by the pope or refused to hand over their lands to him, the pope would excommunicate them and order other rulers to join him in a war against them. Dr. Mannheim pointed out that because of this, Europe was involved in senseless wars for centuries at a time. He said that the popes not only granted plenary indulgences to Christians who went to the Holy Land to slaughter Moslems, but to Christians who fought on the papal side in unjust wars against other Christians.

Dr. Mannheim maintained that the popes gained their power over secular rulers by means of fraud and trickery. He said that in the eighth century, when Pope Stephen II wanted the military aid of Pepin, he composed a letter to the Franks, which he pretended

Saint Peter himself had written and sent down to earth from heaven. In the ninth century, when the popes demanded territories and civil authority to which they had no right, they forged a Donation of Constantine and the False Decretals. Each fake decree of the False Decretals was assigned to a pope or council as far back as the second century; and Dr. Mannheim claims that these fake decrees not only helped the Church establish its power over secular governments, but also helped the popes gain power over other bishops in the Church.

Dr. Mannheim said that it was common for Church historians to manufacture events which never took place. As another example, he mentioned Bishop Agnellus, the ninth-century bishop of Ravenna, who wrote that when he was preparing the biographies of his predecessors and could discover nothing about one or the other of them, he simply prayed and composed the biography himself. Dr. Mannheim pointed out that innumerable saints—including some who never even lived—were given exotic biographies in this way.

Right after Dr. Mannheim's lecture, I went to the library and looked into what he had said. Once again, I found that he was absolutely right. These lectures are certainly giving me quite a bit to think about.

July 14, 1945

As I was leaving church this morning, I met Dr. Mannheim's daughter, Maria. We started to talk, and I asked her if she wanted to walk over to the university library with me. She gave me a big smile and said yes. Then she asked me if I attend church even on weekdays.

"Every day," I told her.

"Why do you do that?" she asked.

"Maybe from habit," I smiled.

"Do you really believe in God?"

"Most of the time."

She laughed when I said that. "Aren't you sure?"

"Most of the time. How about you?"

"I have never been able to take religion seriously," Maria said.

"My father does, but that's because he is always searching for final answers. I don't believe one way or the other. If there is a God, we have no way of knowing anything about Him. I think if all the wonderful things some people say about God are true, then He is intelligent enough to understand me; and to realize that I—and a lot of other people—can't find out anything about Him. So I don't think I have to worry."

"I detect the reasoning of a woman in what you just said," I smiled.

Maria didn't seem to like my comment. "And what is wrong with that?" she demanded.

"Nothing, nothing at all," I told her. "You have every right to talk like a woman."

"Why do *you* take religion so seriously?" she asked.

"It is the only way I can take it," I replied. "I am caught on the horns of a dilemma. If God exists and I make a mistake about it, that mistake will last as long as eternity. On the other hand, if God does not exist and there is no eternity, then I shall have messed up for nothing the only life I'll ever have."

"But no final answer is possible," Maria insisted. "There are so many different religions, and with their contradictory teachings, all of them cannot possess the truth. Hindu, Buddhist, Moslem, Jew, Christian. Who is to say? They convince themselves that their part of the earth is the entire world. Christians look around and see only Christians; often not realizing that non-Christians outnumber them by a ratio of over two to one. The members of each religion think that the Bibles of the other religions contain myths. They never seem to consider the awesome possibility that all religions—including their own—might be mythical and untrue."

"That is an awesome possibility, indeed," I admitted.

"It is just as I said," Maria continued to insist. "There are no absolute answers."

"There must be answers," I said, "and I have to find them."

"The knight in shining armor goeth forth!" Maria commented rather mockingly. But then she looked at me and said: "I hope with all my heart that you will find your answers. I really do!"

"Thanks," I remarked.

"Although I know that you won't believe me now," she said, "I really meant what I just told you. But you're too serious! You talk like an old man with a long, grey beard. Let's go on a picnic Tuesday."

"I really don't have the time," I smiled, "but since it's the professor's daughter . . . Actually, I'd love to come!"

July 16, 1945

Today Dr. Mannheim delivered the most scathing attack on the papacy I have ever heard—or ever expect to hear. He began his lecture by shouting: "The popes lived in luxurious palaces; they held lavish and immoral banquets; they surrounded themselves with male and female prostitutes; they used fraud and forgery; they committed murder. Will any of you still tell me that they are the Vicars of Christ on earth? If Christ ratified in heaven what the popes decreed on earth, then Christ is a criminal. If Christ did not ratify their nefarious deeds, then the popes do not have the power to bind and loose in heaven; something which they claim for themselves. Either Christ is a criminal, or the popes are liars. I maintain that they are liars!"

After these opening comments, Dr. Mannheim went on to say that the popes gained their power over other bishops chiefly through using military force. He said that force was even the decisive factor in determining what orthodoxy and heresy were to be. According to Dr. Mannheim, what was heresy one day became the true faith the next; depending on which side had the stronger army.

Dr. Mannheim emphasized that there is nothing to indicate that Saint Peter ever visited Rome. He said that even if he did, there is no proof that he thought of himself as head of the entire Christian Church; or that the other apostles considered him to be such. Dr. Mannheim then brought up the Gospel of Matthew, where Jesus tells Peter: "Thou art Peter, and upon this rock I will build my Church." He said that this statement never appeared in the original versions of the New Testament, but was forged and inserted later by church officials to prove the pope's claim that he was head of the Church. He pointed out that even in the Gospel of

July 16, 1945

Matthew itself, Jesus tells the apostles the exact opposite: "None among you shall be placed higher than the others."

Next, Dr. Mannheim attacked the theory that the Church possesses a complete list of popes—from Saint Peter down to the present pope. He said the Church claims that a Pope Clement, who was supposed to have been the fourth pope, recorded in his *Homilies* that Peter was the first pope. Dr. Mannheim maintained that the *Homilies* attributed to Clement were never written by him; but once again, were forgeries. He said it is quite possible that Pope Clement never lived.

Dr. Mannheim went further. He emphasized that from an historical standpoint, nothing at all is known about any of the first few popes on the Church's list—even those described as saints and martyrs. He said there is every reason to doubt that they ever existed. As for the other popes on the list, he pointed out that historians have been confused by the names and the numbering. He said that often more than one pope was elected, and in such cases, the placing of a particular name on the list was done arbitrarily. Moreover, according to Dr. Mannheim, the popes did not always immediately succeed one another. Sometimes there was a period of years between them.

After he had made this point, Dr. Mannheim lectured on the Great Schism. He said it proves conclusively that the Church's entire theory of continuous papal succession is fraudulent. He stressed that while the Church claims there was only one valid pope during this period, history teaches something quite different. He said that Saint Antonius, who lived during the time, wrote that it was never possible to decide who the true pope was, without doubts remaining in the minds of most men. He pointed out that the very same cardinals elected both lines of popes and participated in the election of the third line. Even when the schism ended, the compromise pope was elected by cardinals who had been appointed by three different lines of popes; and he himself had supported a pope whom Catholics do not recognize as having been a valid pope.

Dr. Mannheim seemed very satisfied with himself. He calmed down somewhat, picked up a pipe, filled it, and lit it. I could tell that he was about to begin one of his favorite stories. He said that near the end of the ninth century, Pope Stephen VII brought one of his predecessors, the dead Pope Formosus, to posthumous trial. According to Dr. Mannheim, Pope Stephen had the body disinterred from the grave, vested in pontifical robes, and set up before a council of bishops. First, the pope and bishops condemned the former pope. Then, carefully following the prescribed ritual, they declared that he had never been pope, and stripped the body of all ecclesiastical insignia. Finally, a mob threw the desecrated remains into the Tiber River.

Before he went on with his story, Dr. Mannheim smiled broadly and puffed on his pipe a few times. Then he pointed out that Pope Stephen had declared all of his predecessor's ordinations null and void. "Even the Holy Spirit must have gotten confused at this point," he winked. He went on to explain how Pope Stephen himself had been consecrated bishop by Pope Formosus, and was thus making his own consecration invalid.

Dr. Mannheim said that when Pope Theodore II came to the throne, he must have confused the Holy Spirit still further; for he announced that all of Pope Formosus's ordinations were really valid. In addition, he reinstated all the clerics deposed by Pope Stephen. The next pope, Pope John IX, annulled completely all the acts of Pope Stephen. Dr. Mannheim hastened to point out that since the Catholic Church recognizes all of these men as legitimate popes, the Holy Spirit must still be trying to figure out what to do about the mess. After all, He has been told to depose a pope and yet not to depose him; to annul ordinations and decrees and yet not to annul them.

Dr. Mannheim gave each of us a mimeographed paper which lists numerous popes who supposedly came to the papal throne in devious ways. He said: "Even if the popes had become popes by strictly spiritual means, I still could never believe that they are infallible in faith and morals—or in anything else. But considering the manner in which some of them attained the papal throne, I do not know how any sane person can consider them infallible; or believe that the Holy Spirit is involved in their ascent to the papacy."

Then he started to rage again about popes who had gained the papal throne by castrating, blinding, poisoning, strangling, battering, or burying alive their papal predecessors. He singled out popes on his mimeographed list who had attained the papacy by conquering rivals in war. He mentioned others who had been appointed by a predecessor or by civil rulers; and he emphasized that in both instances, armies were sometimes used to back up the decisions.

Another point he kept stressing was the fact that a man would be pope for a while; be driven from the throne by a rival; and then, in time, drive out the rival; and sometimes be driven out again himself. Thus, a variety of men would alternate between being pope and not being pope. Dr. Mannheim emphasized that while the cardinals did not begin to elect the pope until the eleventh century, even they, in their efforts to become pope, fought among themselves and resorted to bribery, murder, and war.

I can only say that I am thoroughly confused by Dr. Mannheim's latest revelations. I am going to have to study all of this very carefully. I have already looked up the first three names on Dr. Mannheim's list—Heraclius, Eusebius, and Liberius—and once again, what Dr. Mannheim had to say is substantially true. It will be a long time before I get to all the names on the list, but I am going to keep digging. I hope that I'll eventually find something to prove that Dr. Mannheim is wrong.

July 17, 1945

Maria had prepared a delicious meal, and I complimented her on it a number of times. After dining at the restaurants in Jefferson City, it was quite a treat. When we had finished eating, I suggested that we play some tennis, but Maria said she wanted to show me a grotto. I asked her where the grotto was located, and she said it was a considerable distance away, along the rocky bank of a creek. I told her that since it was already late, I didn't think it was such a good idea. But in the end, she talked me into it.

"It is strange that you want me to see a grotto," I told her as we walked toward the creek. "I thought you had no interest in religion."

"I like simple things—even religious things," Maria said, "but they must be plain, direct, clear, and without pretence."

"Is that why you play the violin?"

"I love music because it is beautiful, and there are no questions involved—no difficult problems. Like the song of the nightingale, it just is."

" 'Beauty is truth, truth beauty,—that is all ye know on earth, and all ye need to know.' "

"Who said that?"

"Keats."

"Is he your favorite poet?"

"One of them."

"When I first saw you, I knew that you had the soul of an artist."

"I also love what is plain, clear, and direct, but I am not a musician, not a painter, not even a poet. I can only try to bring clarity, order, and precision to my thought; and there are times when I think I might not even succeed at that."

"That, too, is an art, and because you were born to be an artist, you will succeed."

We walked along in silence. The bank of the creek was very steep, and it was covered by large rocks. Maria stumbled, and I took her by the hand. We walked for a long time, until I noticed that she was getting tired. I asked her if she wanted to rest.

"I can make it," she panted. "It's not much further."

A short time later, we could see the grotto through the trees. When we reached the crude wooden kneeler which rested at the foot of the grotto, I released Maria's hand and knelt down. I looked up at the statue of the Virgin on its pedestal. The statue looked worn and weather-beaten. Suddenly, I felt Maria's hand resting on mine.

"Why did you let go?" she asked.

"I thought you didn't need me any more."

"But I do need you."

I stood up.

"Don't you want to kiss me?" she asked.

July 17, 1945

"Here?" I smiled, glancing toward the statue of the Virgin on its pedestal.

"Why not?"

Before I knew it, my arms were around her. Then I brought her slowly, carefully to the ground. I kissed her again and again as she lay there on her back, and I on my stomach. Then I lay on my side, and with my right hand, I held her close against me. I ran my left hand up and down her back. Then I relaxed my right hand, and I slowly placed her on her back again. Now I ran my hand over her breasts, and then over her thighs.

Suddenly Maria stood up. "Let's go swimming!" she exclaimed.

I smiled. "I didn't bring a bathing suit."

"Neither did I."

"Well, you can see that's out."

"Didn't you ever swim without a bathing suit before?"

"Not with girls."

Maria laughed. "Don't be so old-fashioned!"

Then she began to undress. I watched her as she removed her slip and brassiere. She stood there looking at me for a moment, and then she removed her panties. I continued to watch her, and as I did so, I could feel my heart pounding. I removed my shirt and trousers—everything, except my shorts.

Maria smiled when I did not remove them. "You'll be awfully wet going back if you don't take them off," she said.

Night was approaching, and most of the day's heat had subsided; but I could feel myself perspiring all over. Maria just stood there and looked at me, almost mockingly. Even in my shorts, there was no concealing how I felt. I slipped them off, and Maria turned and ran toward the water. I ran after her, and before she could reach the water, I caught her, and pulled her down on one of the huge rocks which jutted out from the bank into the creek. The dying sun cast its shadows upon the rock, and I watched as the shadows recorded my every movement. Again and again I stopped to kiss her breasts. Then, suddenly, I held her tight. Except for the chirping of crickets, there was silence.

After a long while, I stood up. I looked toward the grotto. In the semidarkness, I could barely discern the statue of the Virgin, high above me on its rocky pedestal. As I gazed up at the statue, I experienced—for only an instant—a feeling of remorse and revulsion at myself. I picked up my shirt and lay down again beside Maria. She told me that she was beginning to feel cold. I kissed her, and then I draped my shirt around her.

August 2, 1945

When I attended Mass this morning, once again I asked God to strengthen my faith in Him and in the Church. I have been unable to find any errors in Dr. Mannheim's account of the Church's history, and this has begun to worry me a great deal. I sometimes have the feeling that I really am losing my faith. I keep thinking that perhaps my crisis in faith is due to the fact that God is punishing me for doubting Him, and for endlessly questioning His ways.

Then, too, there is Maria. It is difficult for me to believe that I have been sinning with her; but according to the teachings of the Church, I know that I have. This morning at Mass, I once again resolved to break off the relationship. But this evening, when she came to my room, I immediately took her in my arms. Only in the mornings, when I attend Mass, do I feel a sense of sin. In the evenings, when I hold her close, I think of paradise rather than of hell. On a number of occasions, during the Holy Sacrifice of the Mass itself, I have been unable to stop myself from envisioning her beautiful breasts and thighs; and even then I have wanted her.

Perhaps the only answer is to accept God and the Church with the blind faith of a little child. Or is it already too late for that? Maybe I have already probed and sinned too deeply. Before, when the priest held up the sacred Host at the elevation of the Mass, I had always been able to exclaim: "My Lord and my God!" Now when I utter this act of faith in the presence of Christ in the Holy Eucharist, the same words always come back to me: "Is it *really* true?"

Because of my soul's state, I still feel unable to receive Holy Communion. I am beginning to think that I should give up my studies for the priesthood. Even after spending eight years in the seminary, it is something which I must now seriously consider.

August 9, 1945

I cannot recall a time when I have been so depressed. When I heard that the United States dropped the atom bomb on Hiroshima three days ago, I thought the world had gone completely mad. Now Nagasaki! These two events not only leave me numb, but physically sick. While I am relieved that the Japanese will almost certainly surrender now, I keep asking myself if we were morally justified in letting loose in the world this monster of destruction—a monster which can annihilate entire cities and all living things therein with a single blow. Surely there must have been other ways to achieve our objectives. I just hope and pray that the monster we have created will never be unleashed on us.

While I am distressed to think that we are responsible for introducing a weapon of this nature into modern warfare—which was already barbarously cruel and a threat to mankind's very existence—I am particularly appalled by the civilian casualties incurred in these two bombings. It is one thing to bomb supply depots of the enemy, but I believe it is quite another to obliterate hundreds of thousands of men, women, and children. There had to be another way!

Many people at the university keep saying that if the Germans or Japanese had invented the bomb first, they would have used it on us. While this is probably quite true, I do not believe that it is a justifiable excuse. After all, we pride ourselves on being a Christian nation. People flock to our churches on Sundays, and they pray to a God Who is supposed to be the father of *all* mankind; a God Who sent His Son to make all men brothers and to redeem them. Although we are determined to win this war, I believe that we should take *everyone* into consideration. If we followed the injunctions of Christ, we would be *especially* concerned about the welfare of our enemy.

This evening I was going to tell Maria that I have decided to return to the seminary. I know now that Jefferson City is not the place to determine whether I should continue my studies for the priesthood or not. After a few months in the comparatively quiet atmosphere of the seminary, I'll make my decision. The decision may very well be to leave, but at least I'll be sure that it is a rational one.

In the end, I did not inform Maria because I was too depressed. I needed another human creature to put my arms around; someone to let me know that all love in the world had not died with the bomb.

August 10, 1945

My final examination in medieval history is scheduled for tomorrow, and after that, I'll be leaving the university. I finally decided not to tell Maria that I was leaving, but to write her a letter. I thought this would be kinder than a complicated farewell. At least, it is what I told myself I thought. Maybe I was just afraid to face her. Anyway, it turned out that I had no choice. Maria came over this evening, and she kept knocking at the door until I had to let her in. I'm sure she would have persuaded Mrs. Duffy to unlock the door for her if I hadn't answered.

When I finally opened the door, Maria was in tears.

"Don't you want me?" she asked.

"You know I do," I told her.

"Then what's the matter?"

"Don't you know?"

"You've decided to go away."

"Yes."

"But you can't," she cried. "Don't you love me even a little bit?"

"I love you very much."

She sat down on the bed. "I don't understand."

I sat down beside her and put my arm around her. "I wanted to write you a letter after I had gone," I said. "I thought it would be easier for both of us that way."

"But why are you leaving? My father told you that you can work as his assistant until you get your doctorate. He likes you very much, and says that you show greater promise than any student he has had in years. He is offering you a career. Why won't you accept it?"

"I have decided to return to the seminary."

"But why?" Maria demanded. "Why do you want to go back there?"

"At this point, I only know that I have to go back. I'm not sure why."

"That's nonsense!" Maria exclaimed. "Why would you go back to a place when you have no reason?"

"It's just something I feel I should do," I tried to explain. "I haven't found the answer here, so I must go back."

"What makes you so sure that you will find it there?"

"I'm not at all sure, but I'm going to try."

"You are not going to leave," Maria declared. "You can't leave! I'm pregnant."

"You're what?"

"I'm *pregnant.*" This time there was even more determination in her voice.

"By whom?" I asked in astonishment.

"By you, of course. Who else?"

"You can't be."

"But I am," she insisted. "You weren't as careful as you thought you were."

"I'm sure you're not," I maintained.

"You're the only one I've ever done it with. I was a virgin."

"You weren't a virgin," I protested.

"I bled."

"Now, Maria, stop being ridiculous! You didn't bleed, and you know it."

She began to cry. "That's why you don't want me! You want a virgin, and you think I wasn't one."

"Maria, that's absurd!" I told her. "Can't you understand that? Virginity is a stupid technicality; and it means nothing to me one way or the other. I love you, and that's all that matters."

"You don't love me," she sobbed, "or you wouldn't be leaving."

"But I do love you," I insisted, "and that's one of the reasons I'm going. I'm so confused right now that if I stayed, I'd only make both of us miserable."

"You don't love me!"

"Now, Maria, look at me. Look at me! If you're really pregnant, I'll marry you—no matter what. But I want you to tell me the truth."

She wouldn't look up. She hesitated, and then she began to sob even more. I attempted to console her, but she pushed my arm away and ran crying from the room.

PART FOUR

October 4, 1945

Now that I have been back at the seminary for a few weeks, I'm not so sure that I haven't made a mistake in returning. I miss Maria very much, and I keep wondering if what I've done is fair to her. After all, she was very much a part of my life, and I don't know if it was right to make a decision on my own that involved her as well as myself. Still, when I told her that I would make both of us miserable if I remained in Jefferson City, I was being entirely honest. Even now, I am completely confused as to what I should think or do. If I went back to Jefferson City, I'd probably leave within a short time—for the very same reasons I left in the first place. I'm not even certain Maria would want me back now; but even if she did, I know that she would end up being hurt again.

So here I am, back at Saint Mary's! I certainly can't say that I'm happy as a first-year theologian. Although all of my professors hold elaborate degrees in theology and canon law, their courses, for the most part, are dull, boring, and uninspiring. Dr. Mannheim may have jumped around like a whirling dervish, but at least he was always *very* interesting.

In dogmatic theology, we do almost nothing but memorize our Latin textbook. Lectures are given in some courses, but they are the same lectures that have been given here for many years. In fact, in years gone by, several enterprising seminarians pooled their notes and made master sets for every course. These notes were then mimeographed and sold to each successive class by the class ahead of it. I have a set. Although attendance at lectures is compulsory, the lectures never differ in any important respect from the mimeographed notes.

Our course in church history is especially disappointing. Compared with the course Dr. Mannheim gave, this one borders on the ridiculous. Father Glenn, our professor, is in his eighties. His voice is so fragile that it is difficult to hear him; and what he says is often incorrect. In this course, the mimeographed notes are a real asset, since they are much more accurate than the lectures themselves. Sometimes during a single lecture, Father Glenn gives four or five different dates for the same event. We use one textbook in the course, and it is old and outdated. It has been translated from the French, and the translation itself is poor and contains many inaccuracies.

Even though his course is boring, I feel very sorry for Father Glenn, who happens to be a kind old man. Most of the seminarians talk, laugh, and write letters during his lectures, and I don't think that's right. Worse still, some of them actually ridicule Father Glenn himself. They do not ridicule him for what he says in his lectures—few of them know enough, or care enough, to do that—but they mock him for the infirmities which come with advanced age. Mercifully, he is too deaf to hear the remarks and hilarious laughter; and nearsightedness keeps his eyes on his notes most of the time rather than on the class. When he does notice the seminarians laughing, he laughs along with them, thinking they are enjoying some remark he has made. I guess God has His own way of looking out for the sensibilities of older people.

October 12, 1945

As a group, my classmates continue to disappoint me. While there are notable exceptions—like my good friend, Karl Wright—I can't help but wonder what most of them use for brains. Today, during Monsignor Grosclaude's talk on the spiritual life, they were busy harassing him. Only a few months ago, these very same seminarians, awed by his high office, had shown him the greatest deference. But now that he has seemingly lost his power, and urged on, I suspect, by Father Clancy, the new rector, they show him only contempt.

It is incredible that something like this could occur in chapel, before the Blessed Sacrament. Several seminarians kept kicking kneelers and stamping their feet on the floor during Monsignor's entire sermon. Although Monsignor has a loud voice, they were successful in preventing some of the things he had to say from being heard. I was amazed by the manner in which Monsignor accepted all of this abuse. At one point, he did tell them that he hoped they would grow up a little bit and become gentlemen, but even this was done without rancour. He seems to possess infinite patience.

Even when Monsignor Grosclaude was rector, there were

priests who referred to him as "that pietistic fool." Now the students have taken up this refrain. In his capacity as spiritual director, Monsignor has begun to preach openly those principles which he previously expressed only tacitly—by the example of his own life. Many thought it bad enough that he himself had lived such a life, but they consider his preaching of it intolerable. He keeps warning the seminarians against those very pleasures which they have come to expect as prerogatives of the priestly class: new cars, expensive clothing, luxurious food, elaborate entertainment, and the adulation of society.

October 19, 1945
In today's talk on the spiritual life, Monsignor Grosclaude attacked the pride and arrogance of the clergy. He quoted from Mark 12, where Jesus said: "Beware of the Scribes, who like to walk about in long robes, and to be greeted in the market place, and to have the front seats in the synagogues and the first places at suppers; who devour the houses of the widows, making pretence of long prayers. These shall receive a heavier sentence." He also quoted from Matthew 23, where Jesus said of the Scribes and Pharisees: "In fact, all their works they do in order to be seen by men; for they widen their phylacteries, and enlarge their tassels, and love the first places at suppers and the front seats in the synagogues, and greetings in the market place, and to be called by men 'Rabbi.' But do not you be called 'Rabbi'; for one is your Master, and all you are brothers. And call no one on earth your father; for one is your Father, who is in heaven. Neither be called masters; for one only is your Master, the Christ. He who is greatest among you shall be your servant."

Monsignor Grosclaude lamented the failure of priests to practice the virtue of poverty, which he described as "the most elementary lesson of the gospel." He said that the love of poverty is not only a necessity for priests, but for every Christian who sincerely wishes to live according to the teachings of Christ. He emphasized that it is impossible for anyone to serve God, and at the same time to comply with the accustomed norms of human society; which stress the seeking of power, wealth, and sensual gratification. He quoted the words of Jesus from Luke 16: "No servant can serve two masters; for either he will hate the one and love the other, or else he will stand by the one and despise the other. You cannot serve God and mammon." He also quoted Matthew 19, where Jesus said: " . . . it is easier for a camel to pass through the eye of a needle, than for a rich man to enter the kingdom of heaven"; and Luke 6: "Blessed are you poor, for yours is the kingdom of God."

Once again, Monsignor Grosclaude chided priests for preaching against materialism, while giving, by their own example, the impression that people could enjoy the pleasures of the world, and heaven besides. He said that it is the example of the clergy which makes Christians materialistic—rather than Christlike—in their attitudes: such as in their love of luxury and comfort, their devotion to success, their social snobbishness, their racial consciousness, their nationalistic prejudice, and their contempt for the poor.

October 28, 1945

Monsignor Grosclaude has been called many things, but today was the first time I have heard him called a radical and a heretic. The sermon which he gave at Mass this morning has electrified the entire seminary. I had my notebook with me, and I copied part of it down verbatim. It went like this: "Today is the Feast of Christ the King, and for a number of reasons, I think it is a very significant feast. Christ is depicted as sitting on a gilded throne, a crown on His head, and a scepter in His hand. I suppose that we just couldn't stand Him as He was. His stark simplicity and utter poverty were too much for us, so we placed Him on a throne and made a wealthy monarch of Him. I think He would look much better as He was—perhaps something like some of the derelicts of our large cities. But we took all the dirt and grime and rags off Him; we dressed Him up as a king—all because we cannot stand the truth."

I think that Monsignor Grosclaude could have gotten away with saying some of these things if he had spoken in theoretical fashion, couching his message in the customary theological jargon

January 17, 1946

and verbiage. But it is characteristic of the man that he presents his ideas in much the same way that Jesus Himself taught. His language is plain and clear; his examples concrete and practical. Instead of remaining in that rarefied atmosphere of theory and the definition of complex terms, he applies the clear and simple teachings of Jesus to everyday life.

After he had talked at length on the significance of the Feast of Christ the King, Monsignor Grosclaude attacked the gluttonous clergy for dining like kings. He cautioned us to eat a sufficient amount of food because we need healthy bodies to serve God, but he advised against eating merely for pleasure. He also criticized the use of intoxicants and smoking. He said that while these habits gave pleasure to the senses, they did not bring an individual closer to God; but usually had the opposite effect.

Then he recommended something which really caused an uproar. He said that if all students and priests at the seminary gave up smoking cigarettes, a quarter of a million dollars could be saved each year. He suggested that this money be given to the poor. Although I am sure that most seminarians and priests will never accept Monsignor Grosclaude's suggestion, I am equally certain that they will never forgive him for having made it.

January 17, 1946

Once again, I am seriously thinking of leaving the seminary. I am bored by the courses, appalled at the attitudes of my classmates, harassed by doubts about the faith, and very uncertain of my own spiritual state. My experiences of the past summer have a way of coming back to haunt me. Even though I went to confession before returning to the seminary, I keep wondering if I possessed the necessary contrition for forgiveness.

Sometimes it is still difficult for me to believe that I sinned. Indeed, there are times when I think that if I did commit a sin, it was the sin of leaving Maria. There are many nights when I cannot help but recall the pleasures of her beautiful body and the spontaneity of her spirit.

I keep trying to convince myself that I made the right choice in leaving Jefferson City, but I'm still not sure. Not sure at all!

January 26, 1946

Today, in sheer desperation, I sought the advice of Monsignor Grosclaude. He listened intently as I revealed my numerous woes, occasionally interrupting me to comment briefly. He said he realizes the courses are boring. Even so, he feels that attainment of the priesthood is more than worth the agony. In regard to the seminarians who are ridiculing Father Glenn, he said: "Never make the mistake of expecting seminarians and priests to behave as saints. Every profession has its good and bad, its kind and unkind; and the priesthood is no different. Anyone who believes that he can escape the evils of the world by entering a seminary or monastery only deludes himself. We all bring the world, the flesh, and the Devil right along with us. Our real reason for coming here should be the hope that through mutual dedication, we might gain individual strength to overcome evil."

When I alluded to his own trials and tribulations, Monsignor Grosclaude told me: "I have never believed in running away from evil. I do not believe that one really can. Evil always waits in another guise in another direction. If it is to be conquered, it must be confronted; and the conquest—if it is really going to be a conquest—must ultimately be spiritual. To win spiritual victories, we must often appear in the eyes of the world to have lost. But real victories are spiritual victories, and spiritual victories are measured not by what happens outside of us, but by what happens to us on the inside; not by what happens in time, but by what happens in eternity. Always be a big man. Never let the little men—the evil men—force you to run away. If you do, you will allow them to control not only your own destiny, but the destiny of the world."

I finally told Monsignor Grosclaude that I am still having problems with faith, and he repeated what he had said once before. He feels that this problem is temporary and will disappear in time. He pointed out that it is not an uncommon difficulty. Then he said: "Now tell me about the girl."

January 26, 1946

Once again, I was stunned by the keenness of his perception. "It happened this summer, Monsignor," I said.

"Yes, I know. Tell me about her."

"She is very beautiful."

"And you succumbed?"

"Yes."

"And now what?"

"I don't know. I frequently think about her. I often wonder, too, if I did the right thing by returning here. I feel a certain responsibility toward her. But it's more than that, I think. I really do love her."

Monsignor Grosclaude reflected for a short while, and then he said: "Each of us is responsible for everyone in the entire world, because we belong to the mystical body of Christ. We are our brother's keeper, and we are responsible for what he is and for what he does. When our brother suffers hunger, illness, and despair, we should also suffer; and when our brother suffers from sin, we should carry the burden of his sin on our shoulders. But in this instance, I believe that leaving the seminary would impose an even greater burden on the girl's shoulders and on your own. I believe that you are meant to become a priest. You do have a vocation from God. It may be a somewhat different vocation, but it is there nonetheless."

"But do you really believe, Monsignor, that I am justified in remaining at the seminary?" I asked him. "Do you think that I could ever become worthy again, after what happened during the summer?"

"You do not have to become worthy," he answered. "You are already worthy. It is unusually easy for you to love, and that means it is also easy for you to sin. When you first walked into my office over eight years ago, I looked at you and told myself: Especially watch over that youngster; he has a good soul. I have not changed my mind. I still believe that you have a good soul. But even when God has given a young man a good soul, that soul must be purified; and sometimes sin helps to do that. Sin places us on the level of other men, and it teaches us to understand and sympathize with their weaknesses—no matter what those weaknesses happen to be. Sin also helps us to remain humble. It proves to us that we are not strong enough to stand alone, and that we need the constant help and guidance of Almighty God."

"It is your opinion that I should remain then?"

"I would be very disturbed if you left. I feel that you would be running away from your God and from yourself. Promise me, son, that you will give the matter much more thought before deciding to leave."

"I promise."

Monsignor Grosclaude smiled. "I hope you don't mind that I still call you 'son.' I know you're pretty big now, and I recall you're rather sensitive about the matter."

"I very much want you to call me that, Monsignor."

He smiled again. "God bless you, son," he said. "I also like the arrangement."

March 7, 1946

When mail was distributed this afternoon, I received another letter from Maria Mannheim. I was somewhat surprised, since I answered her last letter only a week or so ago. Although Maria hinted in earlier letters that I was right in believing she had lied when she claimed to be pregnant, only in this one have I finally gotten her to unequivocally admit that fact. She also says that she has reconciled herself to the reality that I will not be coming back to Jefferson City. Moreover, she now agrees that it was probably best for me to return to the seminary. She says that she still does not fully understand my reasoning, although she is beginning to comprehend it better. She added, however, that if I change my mind, her father is still willing to make me his assistant. She concluded the letter by saying she still loves me enough to marry me.

This letter has already made a great difference in my thinking. Now that Maria is reconciled, I feel much better about everything. Tonight I recalled Jesus' conversation with the rich young man, and I reread the entire passage in the Gospel of St. Matthew. Part of it goes like this: "Jesus said to him, 'If thou wilt be perfect, go, sell what thou hast, and give to the poor, and thou shalt have treasure in heaven; and come, follow me.' But when the young man heard the saying, he went away sad, for he had great possessions."

In view of what has happened, these words have taken on a new significance for me. For the first time in my life, *I* have great possessions. I really have something to offer Christ. Maria's father still wants me to become his assistant, and Maria is willing to accept me as a husband. But tonight I have decided to choose Christ instead.

Just before writing this, I turned to the Gospel of St. John, where Jesus says to Thomas: "Because thou hast seen me, thou hast believed. Blessed are they who have not seen, and yet have believed." In so far as belief is concerned, I hope to do better than Thomas did.

Yes, dear Lord, I am going to remain in the seminary. Please help me!

PART FIVE

February 1, 1949

Karl Wright came to visit me today. It is still difficult to believe that he is already a priest. I asked him how he likes being an assistant at Saint Paul's, and he said it isn't too bad. I know from experience that when Karl isn't enthusiastic about something, that means he doesn't like it. He eventually told me that he thinks he'd rather be teaching. He is seriously thinking of leaving the diocesan priesthood to become a Benedictine monk. One thing that hasn't changed about Karl is his romanticism and unworldly outlook. I'm sure that Monsignor Grosclaude is proud of him. Unlike most of his classmates, his first purchase after graduating from the seminary last spring was not a new car. He arrived here by bus.

In so many ways, Karl possesses the same, simple, blind faith of our early seminary years together, when he was such an ardent devotee of the mystics. I often wish that I had his faith. I told him today about some of the problems I am having with Sacred Scripture, and he had to laugh.

"My God, Pete, what's wrong with you?" he asked. "You are always creating unnecessary problems for yourself. Why can't you be the kind of student everyone else is? You study everything so thoroughly that by the time you finish, it has no meaning. I'd like to hit you over the head and take all of your books away from you. In fact, if I had been the bishop, I would have ordained you before you ever had a chance to study philosophy and theology. When you graduated from high school, you *already* knew enough to last you through a dozen lifetimes."

I'm afraid that maybe he has a point. Karl's bent is mystical, and mine is analytical. Of the two, I think he's better off. Faith is always much easier for the mystic than for the thinker. I asked Karl if he believes the Biblical account of how Jonah, after three days and three nights, was released unharmed from the belly of the whale. I asked him if he really believes that Noah's ark, which the Bible indicates was not as large as many modern ships, was able to hold not only Noah and his family, but hundreds of thousands of birds, hundreds of thousands of animals, over a million insects, and enough food to keep that vast menagerie alive not only for forty days, but until the flood had subsided and new foods could be planted and harvested. Finally, I asked him if he believes that Adam, Noah, and other Biblical figures lived for over nine hundred years, and that Noah fathered children at the age of five hundred.

"I see no reason for disbelief," Karl answered. "I am willing to believe whatever the Church tells me to."

That's the way Karl is. I'm sure that if the Church told him to believe that Jonah swallowed the whale, and that it was released unharmed from *his* belly after three days and nights, he'd believe it.

I asked Karl to consider two facts. First of all, scholars have never seen a single page of an original manuscript of the Bible, and in so far as present knowledge is concerned, it is impossible to prove for certain who wrote it. It is obvious, for example, that Moses did not write the sections attributed to him, since his own death and burial are recorded in those very sections. Secondly, when the Old and New Testaments were put together, many manuscripts existed which people claimed were the word of God; and it was merely the majority vote of religious leaders that finally determined which of the numerous manuscripts were to be considered the *real* word of God and go into the Bible.

"I still don't see the problem," Karl insisted. "In the sixteenth century, the Council of Trent settled all of those matters once and for all. It decreed formally which books were to belong to the Bible; and it became an article of faith for all Christians to believe in their divine inspiration. That's enough for me."

I had a notion to tell him that I wish it were enough for me, but I didn't.

February 9, 1949

It seems that the more I study the Old Testament, the more difficult it becomes to reconcile what I read there. Until this school year, when I began to study the Old Testament formally, I had never read much of it. When I read the Bible in the past, it was usually the New Testament.

I am still puzzled by the fact that in passages like Exodus 34, Exodus 32, Exodus 11, and Exodus 14, God is portrayed as

February 9, 1949

showing emotions which even civilized human beings are able to control. He is prone to jealousy, anger, vanity, and pettiness. I keep wondering how God—or even any stable human being—could be concerned with the gruesome, savage, and nonsensical ceremonial laws found in the Old Testament. In Exodus 29, for example, God tells Moses—along with other highly repugnant and ridiculous things—that in consecrating priests, a ram is to be killed and its blood put on the tip of the ordinand's right ear, on the thumb of his right hand, and on the great toe of his right foot. The remaining blood is to be thrown against the altar round about.

Even more disturbing is the fact that in Leviticus 25, God tells Moses that slavery is permissible. In Exodus 21, God says that a slave can be beaten to the point of death by a master, because in the words of the Bible, "the slave is his money." Deuteronomy 22 says that if a bride cannot prove her virginity by producing a bloody garment, she is to be stoned to death. Women were to be treated in this way not because they had transgressed virtue, but because prospective husbands had to pay the fathers of brides a sum of money and expected unused merchandise.

I am also bothered by Exodus 15, Deuteronomy 20, and Numbers 31, where God is depicted as a pitiless lover of war. God orders the Israelites to attack innocent peoples; to seize lands which do not belong to them; to make slaves of people who surrender when faced with an unjust attack; to completely annihilate the men of those nations which defend themselves; to murder all the people of certain nations; to murder innocent children and women; and to save virgins for brutal warriors to violate.

Some Biblical scholars have attempted to explain troublesome passages of the Old Testament in terms of myths, allegories, partial inspiration, and so forth. This makes very little sense to me. If I can say that one part of the Bible is mythical and untrue, why can't I say the same thing about another part? I am convinced that the authors of the Bible—whoever they were—wanted readers to consider their accounts literally true; and that is the way the Church did consider them for centuries. If God did not tell the Israelites to commit all of the atrocities which are depicted in

Exodus 15, Deuteronomy 20, and Numbers 31, as the Bible says He did, why should I believe that God is the author of the Ten Commandments, as recorded in Exodus 20? That's the dilemma!

March 18, 1949

Now that I have been on the lookout for them, I have begun to discover more and more flaws in the New Testament as well as in the Old. For one thing, I have found that the purported prophecies concerning Jesus in the Old Testament—the supposed link between the Old Testament and the New—do not exist. When the writers of the New Testament were unable to make such a connection, they apparently resorted to fabrication.

Matthew 2 states, for example, that in order to escape Herod, the parents of Jesus fled with Him into Egypt and remained there until Herod died. Matthew says this was done "that what was spoken by the Lord through the prophet might be fulfilled, 'Out of Egypt I called my son.'" It is evident, however, that the words "Out of Egypt I called my son" apply to the Lord's delivery of Israel from Egypt, and could not possibly have anything at all to do with Jesus. The entire passage from Hosea 11, where the author of Matthew got his so-called prophecy, makes this abundantly clear: "When Israel was a child, I loved him, and out of Egypt I called my son. The more I called them, the more they went from me; they kept sacrificing to the Baals, and burning incense to idols."

I have found many other inconsistencies. Matthew 1 and Luke 3 contradict each other not only as to the number of Jesus' ancestors, but even as to their identity. Luke assigns Jesus almost twice as many ancestors between David and Joseph as Matthew does. But even more perplexing is the fact that Matthew and Luke give Jesus entirely different ancestors. These two accounts do not even list the same father for Joseph himself. Matthew 1 states that Joseph is the son of Jacob, while Luke 3 says he is the son of Heli.

There are even contradictions connected with Jesus' death and resurrection. Mark 15 says that Jesus was crucified at the "third hour," while John 19 reports that Pilate handed Jesus over to be crucified at the "sixth hour." According to Matthew 27, Jesus' last words were: "My God, my God, why hast thou forsaken me?" But Luke 23 has Jesus say: "Father, into thy hands I commend my spirit"; and John 19 gives these words as: "It is consummated!" Matthew 28, Mark 16, Luke 24, John 20, and John 21 not only differ as to the number and identity of the women who were said to have come to the tomb on the morning of Jesus' resurrection, but they give entirely different descriptions of what those women saw, the number of angels at the tomb, and what the angels were doing. They also give contradictory reports in regard to what Jesus Himself, the women, and the disciples did following the resurrection.

All of this is creating another crisis in faith for me; perhaps the most serious I have yet experienced. The New Testament has been the anchor of my faith for so many years that now I don't know what to do. But there must be an answer. At least, that is what I keep telling myself. Each day I ask God to help me find it soon.

April 14, 1949

The weather was very good today, so I decided to take a long walk around the grounds of the seminary. For the first time this year, I got down to the lake. I think we have more ducks this year than last. In just one spot, I counted thirty. The benches haven't been painted yet, but I found one that was still in pretty good condition and sat down on it.

I had my Bible with me, and after I had looked out over the water for a while, I began to page through it at random. "Blessed are you poor," I read. "Blessed are the meek. . . . Blessed are they who hunger and thirst for justice. . . . Blessed are the merciful. . . . Blessed are the peacemakers. . . . Blessed are they who suffer persecution for justice' sake. . . ."

Who could deny the truth of these words which the Bible said Jesus had spoken? Who could doubt that they were, indeed, the words of God? What did all of the contradictions matter, provided that these words were true? It almost seemed as though a miracle had occurred. I knew that I had my answer.

To love and serve the poor, the ill, the old, the lonely, the oppressed, the outcast, the sinner—this was what I really wanted to do. I now realized that it was faith—faith alone—which built character, homes, nations, and civilizations. I kept asking myself if I *wanted* to live in a world without Christ—not the Christ of the books I had read; not the Christ of the history I had studied; but the Christ *I* had known. The answer was an emphatic *no*.

I am now certain that God has finally responded to my prayers by giving me the faith I need to serve Him. I only hope that I can repay Him by serving Him well. To that end, I once again implore His help with the following prayer:

> *Lord, make me an instrument of your peace.*
> *Where there is hatred, let me sow love;*
> *where there is injury, pardon; where*
> *there is doubt, faith; where there is*
> *despair, hope; where there is darkness,*
> *light; and where there is sadness, joy.*
>
> *O, Divine Master, grant that I may*
> *not so much seek to be consoled as to*
> *console; to be understood as to understand;*
> *to be loved as to love; for it is in*
> *giving that we receive; it is in pardoning*
> *that we are pardoned; and it is in dying*
> *that we are born to eternal life.*

May 24, 1949

When mail was distributed this afternoon, I received a letter from my father. The letter is such that I want to record the following part of it: "Soon you will be a priest of God. You have no idea how your mother and I have waited for that day. When you were just a few days old and the priest baptized you, he told us he would pray that you, too, one day would become a priest. Now that priest's prayers have been answered, and our prayers, also; for although we dared not hope that God would ever be so good to us, we prayed all through these many years. And now God has answered us. The happiest day in our lives will be when your mother and I receive Our Lord in Holy Communion from the hands of our son. God, through you, has now given us everything."

May 27, 1949

A printed invitation was enclosed with the letter. It reads:

> *Almighty God, through the imposition*
> *of the hands of the*
> *Most Reverend William J. Connolly, S.T.D., D.D.,*
> *will ordain our son,*
> *the Reverend Peter Faber,*
> *to the Priesthood of Jesus Christ*
> *in the Cathedral of Holy Name,*
> *at nine-forty-five o'clock in the morning*
> *on the fourth day of June.*
> *You are invited to be a witness.*

> *To thank the Heavenly Father*
> *for His goodness and power,*
> *he will solemnly offer to Him the*
> *sacrifice of His Son*
> *which is given to us*
> *under the sign of bread and wine.*
> *We invite you to join with him*
> *in the offering of this Holy Mass*
> *and to receive the fruit of this sacrifice*
> *by eating the Bread of Life in Holy Communion*
> *in Sacred Heart Church,*
> *at ten o'clock in the morning*
> *on the fifth day of June.*
>   *Mr. and Mrs. John Faber*

May 27, 1949

Monsignor Grosclaude sent for me this evening. When I got to his office, he was all smiles. "Congratulations!" he said. "I think we can safely say now that you've made it. Ordination is right around the corner."

"Thank you, Monsignor," I responded. "I owe much of it to you. I don't think that I'll ever be able to repay you."

"Repay me by helping other young men to become priests," he said. "When they become discouraged, tell them to be patient. You should have learned a great deal from your own case. It only took time. In the end, Our Lord gave you the necessary strength and faith."

"Yes, I think I now have the necessary strength and faith."

"I'm sure that you do.... I have been trying to think of something I could give you as a little memento. It seems that this crucifix is all I have. It is very old. It was given to me on the occasion of my own ordination to the priesthood."

As Monsignor Grosclaude was handing me the crucifix, it dropped to the floor. When I reached down to pick it up, I found that it had broken and that the corpus was completely detached from its cross.

"Because of the material from which this is made," Monsignor Grosclaude commented, "I do not think that you will be able to put it back together again."

"I'll cherish it and keep it as it is," I promised. "I cannot thank you enough, Monsignor."

I knelt down. "Please bless me, Monsignor."

As Monsignor Grosclaude blessed me, I felt closer to God and the Church than I had ever felt before. Following the blessing, I took Monsignor Grosclaude's hand and kissed it.

"Your life offers great possibilities for service," he said. "Go now, my son. Work out your salvation with diligence!"

June 5, 1949

Today I said my first Mass. I had made arrangements for a very simple ceremony, but Monsignor O'Shea, my pastor, went to great pains to make it an elaborate affair. When I walked down the aisle of Sacred Heart Church, I wore golden vestments. Monsignor permitted these vestments to be used only on the most important occasions. I was preceded in procession by singing choirboys, who were dressed in red, green, and white cassocks. The choirboys were followed by little girls in white dresses and veils, who carried baskets of flowers and strewed the floor with petals. Next came the cross-bearer, the altar boys, and the priests who were officers of the Mass.

In his sermon, Monsignor O'Shea was lavish in his praise of both my family and myself. Although he went out of his way to be kind, there was much which I did not like about his emphasis. He kept repeating that I was now "another Christ." Among other things, he said: "Just as Mary and Joseph cared for and nurtured the child Jesus, Mr. and Mrs. Faber have cared for and nurtured this other Christ, Father Peter Faber." I wanted to stand up and shout: "Please look at me! I am still Peter Faber, and I am no different than anyone in this church." If it had not been for embarrassing everybody, I think I would have done it.

I remembered an article which appeared in the May issue of *The Voice of Christ*, the student publication of Saint Mary's Seminary. It was called *"Ecce Electi!"* I can still quote one of the paragraphs which I found particularly obnoxious. It went like this: "Now, ere many weeks have passed, we shall have joined our colleagues in taking up with gladness the awesome tasks of being *alter Christus* to a world reeling in darkness, indifference, and ungodliness. Please God, it shall be our part to serve Thee in some small way, that the souls Thou hast fashioned for Thyself may rest at last in Thee." I was appalled by the pride and arrogance of that passage, and I still am. The words of Monsignor O'Shea brought it to mind again.

At the dinner which followed the Mass, my friend, Father Karl Wright, acted as toastmaster. When the meal was over, he introduced Monsignor O'Shea, who once again expressed his great personal pleasure at the fact that a member of his parish had been ordained to the priesthood. He pointed out that he had baptized me as an infant and had watched me grow up. He added that it was significant I had been an altar boy while I attended Sacred Heart School. He said that almost all priests were once altar boys, who had gotten their love for the priesthood from serving Christ at the altar.

After Monsignor O'Shea's brief comments, Father Wright introduced my father, who on behalf of himself and my mother, thanked the people of the parish for their thoughtfulness in connection with the ordination and first Mass. He repeated what he had already said many times before. This was the happiest day of their lives.

"Now," Father Wright said, "let us have a few words from this other Christ, from Father Faber himself."

I was so grateful to everyone that I was really at a loss for words. I simply said: "I want to thank all of you for your many kindnesses throughout the years. If I can ever be of service to any of you, do not fail to call on me."

Father Wright rose to his feet again. "To all of those," he said, "who on the day of a priest's first Mass, devoutly kiss the palms of his hands, the Church grants an indulgence of one hundred days. Will all of you who wish to gain that indulgence, please line up to the right. Father Faber will give you his blessing, and he will present his hands for you to kiss."

As the people pressed forward to kiss my hands, I began to feel ill. The feeling had been building up all morning. I think that every time the words *other Christ* were applied to me, I had felt a little sicker. I was sorry I had eaten dinner. When the first person knelt to kiss my hands, I darted from the room. I entered a washroom and stood over one of the urinals. I vomited until it seemed there could be nothing left. I stood there by the urinal and inhaled its pungent odor. Then I vomited again and again.

Father Wright entered the washroom to see if he could be of help. "It must have been the wine," he commented. "You aren't used to it yet."

"I don't think it was the wine," I said. "I'm certain it wasn't the wine."

PART SIX

June 21, 1949

A registered letter arrived from the chancery this morning, informing me of my first two assignments in the priesthood. I am to become an assistant to Father Linehan at Saint Anne's Church; as well as the Catholic chaplain of Juvenile Home. My parents aren't very enthusiastic about the assignments. I'm afraid they expected something much better for their son. My classmates also received assignments today, and a number of them telephoned to find out how I had done. They likewise expressed reservations and dismay.

Because I graduated at the top of my class, my parents and classmates thought I would receive one of the choice appointments. They tell me that I have gotten the worst. I don't feel that way about it, though. As far as I'm concerned, my assignments are the best of the lot. I didn't spend twelve years in the seminary so that I could work in some swanky neighborhood, where most of the people are wealthy phonies. I want to work with the same kind of people as Jesus did. Both of my appointments will fulfill that desire.

Although these appointments do not become effective until July 1, I decided to visit Saint Anne's this afternoon. I had never been there before, and I must say that I encountered several surprises. Before reaching the entrance to the church, I had to pass through a large garden—called "the monastery garden"—which was enclosed by a wall. The garden was cluttered with life-size statues of the most popular Catholic saints. One entire corner of it was taken up by a huge replica of the grotto at Lourdes. There was a faucet at the base of the grotto, with a plaque above it which read: *LOURDES WATER*. I especially noticed the collection boxes. Each statue had one attached to its pedestal. Moreover, six such boxes had been placed at strategic spots near the grotto.

When I entered the church itself, the first thing that attracted my attention was a marble staircase. Thinking that the staircase led to the main part of the church, I ascended the numerous steps, only to find myself inside a small chapel. There was a giant statue of Saint Anne in the chapel, as well as a large collection of crutches and braces, which hung from the ceiling. These items had been left there by people who believed they had been cured through the intercession of Saint Anne. When I got downstairs again, I noticed a door behind the stairway. This led to the vestibule of the church proper.

In the vestibule, I noticed a rack which had booklets and envelopes in it. There was the inevitable iron box attached to the rack for depositing money. I picked up one of the envelopes and looked at it. In large letters across the top were the words: *REMEMBER YOUR BELOVED DEAD.* Beneath these words were a pair of folded hands engulfed by flames. Under the folded hands were the words: "Why not make an offering in memory of a loved one whom God has called to Himself? The merit from your charity might easily speed this poor soul on its way to heaven." At the bottom of the envelope were the words: "*OFFERING*—Low Mass . . . $1; High Mass . . . $5; High Mass with Organ . . . $10; Series of Gregorian Masses . . . $45."

I left the vestibule and entered the church itself. Considering the poverty of the neighborhood, I found it quite elaborate. Once again, there were statues everywhere. Some of them rested on altars, while others stood on pedestals. The largest and most brilliantly clothed statue was the one of Saint Anne. It rested on an ornately decorated pedestal, directly above the main altar. Numerous vigil lights burned before all of these shrines.

After looking at the church, I went over to the rectory, where I introduced myself to Father Linehan, a pleasant-looking fat man of middle age.

"Welcome to Saint Anne's, Father," he said as we shook hands. "Have you seen the church yet?"

"Yes, I have," I told him. "I almost got lost in it. I went up a stairway and discovered the chapel before I found the main part of the church."

Father Linehan laughed. "Many people do that, Father," he said. "You went up the *Scala Santa*, a replica of the original Holy Stairs which Our Lord Himself ascended during His passion."

I wanted to ask him some questions about that, but I decided to leave them for later. "How do you like working at Saint Anne's, Father?" I asked him.

June 21, 1949

"I *don't* like it," he replied. "I just wish that I were starting out, like you are now. But I'll never have that chance again. Here I am in this broken-down parish, with these stupid nobodies for parishioners."

"Do you think that you'll always be pastor here?"

"I'm not sure, but I know that I'll never be top dog. My chances for that are all gone. It's the young fellows like you who will get the breaks. The Linehans are out and the Fabers are in. But don't spoil it! Don't spoil it! Do what Bishop Connolly wants you to do, and you'll go places. I've seen your records, and I've been around long enough to know why the bishop sent you to a place like this. He knows you're good, but he wants to test your humility. If you do well here and at Juvenile Home, there's no stopping you. You'll be top dog. You might even become a bishop."

"I doubt that very much," I smiled.

"You just don't understand how these things work," Father Linehan said. "I wish that I could have started out with your grades. I was never a good student, and I sometimes think I'm here because of all those D's I got in Greek and Latin. We had a theology professor at the seminary, a Father Cronin, who used to point his finger in the direction of a small mining town that was over the hill. He'd say: 'You better study hard and get good grades, boys, or that's where you'll be ending up. And what are those coal miners ever going to give you?' I know now that he was right."

I wanted to comment, but I didn't. Although I can already see that Father Linehan and I have diametrically opposed philosophies, I hope that I'll be able to work with him effectively. I have my doubts, but I'll keep my fingers crossed. He has certainly gone out of his way to be kind. He assigned me a very large bedroom, with a connecting study and private bath. With all the poverty which exists in the parish, I have to say that he manages to keep the physical plant in good shape.

June 22, 1949

I visited Juvenile Home today, but in so far as accomplishing anything was concerned, I could just as well have remained at home. I did meet the superintendent, Mr. Pearson, and I'm afraid that I didn't come away with a very good impression. If I were going to describe him in a phrase, I'd say that he's a rather supercilious, pompous, officious bureaucrat. I wanted to inspect the facilities of the home, but he refused his consent. "You are not our chaplain until July 1," he told me. "At that time, come to see me, and I'll be happy to explain our program to you. Until then, I really don't have anything to say to you."

If it had not been for Mr. Pearson's secretary, the day would have been entirely wasted. She was kind enough to tell me a little bit about the institution. Boys who have either lost their parents, or who have been abandoned by them, live there until the courts find them foster homes. Most of the boys, however, are committed to the home for being delinquent in one way or another. These boys sometimes remain at the home for as long as four or five years. Although a number of euphemisms are used in connection with the place, it is primarily a local reform school for boys between the ages of eight and sixteen.

Fortunately, the boys are not locked up in cells, but sleep in dormitories. Even so, there are bars on the windows, and from all the guards I saw around, I don't think it would be very easy to escape. I'm anxious to meet the boys themselves and hear what they have to say.

June 28, 1949

Karl Wright telephoned today and asked me to accompany him to Saint Michael's Abbey, to meet Abbot Cecil, his future abbot. Karl has definitely decided to become a Benedictine monk. He enters the novitiate on July 1, the same day that I begin work at Saint Anne's and Juvenile Home. As soon as his novitiate is over, Abbot Cecil is going to send him to the University of Louvain in Belgium to work on his doctorate in philosophy.

Abbot Cecil seems to be a rather worldly man for an abbot. He spent most of the time we were there showing us around his abbatial suite. He was elected abbot only a few months ago, and it appears that he has done little since then but remodel and redecorate his personal quarters. His office looks like a large ballroom. There are chandeliers on the ceiling, thick red carpeting on the floor, and even the abbot's throne-like chair has a crimson pillow on its seat. The walls of the entire suite are adorned with expensive paintings.

As for the abbot himself, he has big jowls, a double chin, and sensuous lips. He is tall and quite rotund. His voice is unusually high-pitched for that of a man. He kept trying to get me to join the order. "What about you, Father Faber?" he asked a number of times during our conversation. "We need men like you."

Each time, I respectfully declined.

July 3, 1949

Apparently Father Linehan doesn't think that I'm capable of delivering a sermon yet. At my Mass today, he did the preaching himself. Since this is my first Sunday here at Saint Anne's, I let him get away with it. If he tries to do the same thing next Sunday, I am going to have a word with him. After all, if I wasn't ordained to preach the gospel, then why *was* I ordained?

I think that Father Linehan's sermon itself left a great deal to be desired. He is starting a new novena to Saint Anne next Tuesday, and he made that the theme of his preaching. What he said went pretty much like this: "If you seek special favors, increase proportionately your almsgiving to Saint Anne's Church. When you ascend the Holy Stairs on your knees, say short ejaculatory prayers on each step; such as: 'Good Saint Anne, pray for us!' and 'Jesus, Mary, Anne, pray for us!' When you reach the top of the Holy Stairs, visit Saint Anne's Chapel and say special prayers at the foot of her miraculous statue. While there, look at the crutches and braces hanging from the ceiling, and realize that if you earnestly seek Saint Anne's help—and if it be for the good of your soul—she will cure you of your physical illness."

As the sermon went on, I got the distinct impression that I was listening to a charlatan. "Burn candles and vigil lights before the shrine of Good Saint Anne," he urged, "and come to the rectory for oil that has been blessed in her honor. Many people are cured when they apply this blessed oil to the afflicted parts of their body. A copy of the magazine, *Good Saint Anne*, can be purchased in the vestibule. Even the mere application of the pages of this magazine to the sick has been effective in obtaining miraculous cures. Other cures have been obtained through merely purchasing the magazine or subscribing to it."

Father Linehan concluded his sermon by saying: "When you come up front to kiss the sacred relic of Good Saint Anne at the end of next Tuesday's services, kiss it with special fervor, remembering that it is part of the body of Jesus' own grandmother. After the fragments of the true cross, the relics of Good Saint Anne remain the most precious relics on earth. We do not have relics of the Blessed Mother, because she was taken bodily into heaven. But right here in your parish church, we have a part of that body which gave birth to the Mother of God. . . . May God bless you, and through the powerful intercession of Good Saint Anne, grant you those things which you need for your spiritual and physical welfare."

I'm afraid that one of these days, I'm going to have to tell Father Linehan how I feel about some of these matters. I certainly don't want him giving *that* kind of sermon at my Masses. People might get the idea I agree with him.

July 5, 1949

Things sort of came to a head today, and I think it may be a good thing. I can see now that Father Linehan intended to dominate every aspect of my priestly life. He'll probably still try to do that, but I think he became aware tonight that it's not going to be easy. At least he finally knows that I completely disagree with his philosophy and methods.

He asked me to assist him with the service this evening, and before it began, he instructed me as follows: "After the first hymn, Father, you will lead the rosary. Next, I want you to read the announcements I wrote out for you. Then I'll give a short sermon. After the sermon, you will have charge of the novena prayers and benediction. At the conclusion of the service, I'll carry the relic of Saint Anthony along the communion rail for the congregation to kiss, and you'll carry the relic of Saint Anne."

Everything went smoothly until the time came for making announcements. On the paper which Father Linehan had given me, he had written the words: "Emphasize money!" After a bit of hesitation, I finally said: "Your pastor also has asked me to remind you to be generous in your offerings during this novena."

Following the service, Father Linehan invited me into his private suite and offered me a chair in his lavish and expertly decorated parlor. I knew that something was bothering him, but I wasn't quite sure what it was. He came right to the point: "When you made the announcements, Father, I thought you would emphasize money. But you didn't."

"When I saw the words 'emphasize money' on the paper, I didn't know exactly what you wanted me to say," I told him.

"That's exactly what I expected you to do, Father," he stated in a tone which indicated that he was clearly irked. "I expected you to emphasize money. You are new here, and I think if you had gone about it properly, we could have taken in a good haul tonight. You should have appealed to their sympathy. You could have pictured yourself as a newly ordained, struggling priest."

"I had no idea that's what you wanted me to do."

Father Linehan looked disappointed, but his appearance mellowed somewhat. "It's really my fault, Father," he said. "I should have told you. You'll learn some of these things as you go along. Will you have a drink with me?"

"If it's not inconvenient," I told him.

"It's not inconvenient at all. That mahogany cupboard in the corner turns into a bar. It even has a refrigerator built in at the bottom. You would never know what it was by looking at it, would you?"

"No, you wouldn't."

"What will you have, Father? Some wine?"

"That will be fine."

"Maybe you would rather have a good whiskey. You just name it. I have bourbon, rye, Scotch, Irish, Canadian. What will it be?"

"Anything will be fine, Father."

Father Linehan laughed. "You don't know your drinks very well, do you?"

"No, I guess not."

"That's another thing you'll have to learn, Father. You'll have to learn your drinks, and you'll have to learn to be discriminating about what you drink. After all, you're a priest now, and you want to be a gentleman-priest. Why don't you try some good Irish whiskey?"

"All right," I said. "How long have you been at Saint Anne's, Father?"

"Almost seven years now," Father Linehan replied ruefully. "At first, I despised the place. But now I've gotten used to it a little bit. When I get depressed, I always pray to Saint Anne, and she usually helps me. I guess that is one of the many miracles she performs for us."

"Are miracles really performed here?"

"Haven't you seen the crutches and braces in Saint Anne's Chapel? Scarcely a day goes by without some great miracle here."

"I have seen the crutches and braces, but I seriously question their significance."

"What do you mean, Father?"

"I don't believe that Lourdes Water, Saint Anne's Oil, burning candles, going up stairs on the knees, and making novenas, can, in themselves, cure anyone's illness. If people think they feel better after doing such things, I believe that the basis of their illness is emotional rather than physical."

"But doctors themselves have verified the cures at Lourdes," Father Linehan protested.

"Doctors have also verified the cures of faith healers," I pointed out. "The question is not whether a person is cured or not. The question is: Why is he or she cured? If the reason for a person's cure is emotional—if it can be explained by the psychiatrist—then it is certainly not miraculous."

"But the people cured at Lourdes and Sainte Anne de Beaupré were hopeless cases," Father Linehan argued.

"In their ordinary practices, doctors often see cases which

look hopeless get better," I told him.

"What sort of proof do you require to believe that miracles take place at our Catholic shrines, Father?"

"Not long ago, I read an article in our diocesan newspaper by a Father Walsh," I said. "Father Walsh ridiculed the cures claimed by Christian Scientists and other Protestant faith healers. He said that all such cures resulted from the power of suggestion. He stated that only Catholic cures are legitimate, because God would never show his approval of Protestantism—a false religion—by performing miracles for Protestants."

"Father Walsh is absolutely right," Father Linehan interrupted.

"But Father Walsh made a very strange statement," I continued. "He said that he would believe the claims of Protestant faith healers only if people who had no arms and legs were made to grow new arms and legs. In saying this, he unwittingly defeated his own contention that the supposed cures at Lourdes and other Catholic shrines are miracles. People who visit Catholic shrines do not grow new arms and legs either. But this proof which Father Walsh demanded, I also demand. Whenever you can show me a person without an arm or leg, who has been made to instantly grow a new one at Lourdes or through the intercession of Saint Anne, or whenever you can show me a person with no eyes at all, who has been instantly given new eyes; then—and only then—will I say that a miracle has been performed."

"Do you believe that the Blessed Virgin Mary appeared to Saint Bernadette at Lourdes?" Father Linehan asked.

"No, I don't," I answered.

"Do you believe that she appeared to the children at Fatima?"

"No, I don't, Father. These intermittent and belated revelations of so-called secrets in connection with Fatima are childish. There is something very shady about the whole business. I don't think that any intelligent person, who really looked into the claims of Fatima carefully, could believe in them."

"Are you saying that the Church is intentionally perpetrating a fraud, Father?"

"I don't know what the motives of Church officials are," I

replied, "but whatever their motives, I think the entire affair is unfortunate. I imagine that you have ecclesiastical permission to display for veneration the relic which I carried tonight. But I am certain that what I carried was no more a relic of Saint Anne than my shoe is."

Father Linehan paled. "It's the drink talking, Father. That relic of Saint Anne was authenticated by a cardinal of the Church."

"No one even knows for certain who Christ's grandparents really were," I pointed out. "There is merely a tradition in the Church which says their names were Anne and Joachim. Saint Anne and Saint Joachim are nowhere mentioned in the Bible; nor is there any historical evidence to indicate that they ever lived. Where did the body of Saint Anne come from then? I should say *bodies*. In France alone, during the Middle Ages, at least two different towns claimed to possess the entire body of Saint Anne."

"What do you think the people were venerating tonight then?" Father Linehan asked sarcastically.

"I don't know," I replied. "It could have been a piece of bone from an animal or human being, but I am certain that it was not a piece of Saint Anne's bone."

"In other words," Father Linehan commented, "you are saying that the relics which our people venerate are spurious."

"Anyone who knows anything at all about history realizes that many of them are," I said. "During the Middle Ages, bogus relics were everywhere. Some of the more popular ones found in the churches were: the Virgin's milk, hairs from Noah's beard, dung from Job's heap, a piece of the bush in which God spoke to Moses, hay from the stall in Bethlehem, fragments of the loaves and fishes which were multiplied by Christ, and the tail from the donkey on which Christ rode into Jerusalem. There were others which even bordered on blasphemy; such as Christ's teeth, sweat, tears, urine, feces, blood, and umbilical cord. A great many churches were said to possess the head of John the Baptist and the foreskin from Christ's circumcision. Likewise, if all the pieces of wood which were supposed to have been part of the true cross had been gathered together, there would have been enough wood for thousands of crosses."

"It appears that you really think the Church has been deceiving people," Father Linehan noted.

"People are being deceived. I don't think there can be any question about that."

"You are treading on very dangerous ground, Father," Father Linehan warned.

"The Church does not demand that we accept private revelations, such as those at Lourdes and Fatima," I pointed out. "Neither does the Church insist that we accept any single relic as authentic; nor does it order us to venerate relics."

"That is all very true," Father Linehan granted, "but if I were you, I would hesitate to be critical of practices which the universal Church, taken as a whole, obviously encourages. When I first met you, Father, I saw great possibilities for you in the Church. Now I'm not so sure. You sound radical to me. For all I know, you might even be a Communist."

"My God!" I exclaimed. "You can't be serious."

"But I am serious," Father Linehan said. "It is quite possible these days. One cannot be too cautious."

"That's absurd," I smiled. "It's like my calling you a Nazi."

Father Linehan did not smile. "It's not the same thing at all," he maintained. He rose to his feet. "How about another drink, Father?"

"No, thank you," I replied.

"Surely you'll have one more."

"I'm sorry, Father, but I have some work to do."

October 28, 1949

Today I received another letter from Karl Wright. I guess that I should get used to calling him by the new name he acquired as a monk—Father Martin. But after all these years, that's not going to be easy. Karl seems quite content as a novice. Since he has always been a man of prayer, and since the novitiate is primarily a time of meditation and gaining spiritual insight, there is every reason why he should be happy. His letter was the only good news I received today, and it did a lot to perk up my drooping spirits.

I'm still very much appalled by the conditions at Juvenile Home. Once again, I tried to persuade Mr. Pearson to do something about the incompetent people he's hired to work there, but it does no good. Each time I present a complaint, he tells me that my predecessor, Father Parme, got along very well at the home. He continues to accuse me of being a rabble-rouser.

Almost every day I tell him that a potentially explosive situation exists at the institution, but he doesn't believe me. When I make concrete suggestions which I am sure would help, he invariably says: "That's none of your affair, Father. You are supposed to minister to their spiritual needs; and that's all." How can I get this fool to understand that "spiritual needs" involve much more than conducting religious services?

I informed him this morning that I am no longer going to eat lunch at the institution, since he will not permit me to sit with the inmates. He said that he doesn't care. He refuses to understand that the boys are not going to trust me if I have to sit at the special table where he and the other big brass eat. I told him that I wanted to circulate among the boys, eating at a different table each day. I suggested that he and the other officials do the same thing. He told me that I was out of my mind. He said that if I understood anything at all about the discipline required in correctional institutions, I'd never make such a suggestion.

That's what he thinks!

November 11, 1949

The situation at Juvenile Home seems to worsen each day. Today I talked with a thirteen-year-old boy who was unable to eat any solid food for more than a week. A guard had punched him in the face, knocking out several teeth and dislocating his jaw. According to the boy—and I believe him—the guard attacked him without provocation. The boy had just finished scrubbing the kitchen floor when the guard told him to do it over because he

November 11, 1949

had not gotten it clean. The boy could not see any dirt on the floor, so he asked the guard to show him where it was. It was then that the guard hit him.

I see evidence all the time that many of the guards are sadists. A number are perverts. They have forced some of the boys into homosexual activities with them, and the boys are powerless to do anything about it. If the guards find out that a boy has reported any one of them for any reason, they invariably beat that boy half to death. I have reported several cases of homosexual abuse to Mr. Pearson, but he always denies that the incidents ever occurred, saying that the boys make such claims to get attention. Then he adds—as always—that such matters have nothing to do with my duties as chaplain at the institution.

I readily admit that most of the boys at Juvenile Home are not angels, but I haven't seen one yet who has not come from an impossible home-situation. They come from backgrounds that the average person would not deem possible. They have been beaten, starved, rejected, betrayed, abandoned, and in some instances, even sexually molested by their own parents. Then a judge sends them to Juvenile Home, where they experience more of the same.

Most of the rules at Juvenile Home are stupid and petty. They contribute absolutely nothing to the rehabilitation of the inmates. For example, letters are censored, showers may be taken only once each week, and chewing gum is prohibited. The boys are even restricted as to the amount of toilet paper they are permitted to use. Moreover, visits are limited to one a month, and then only a parent or guardian is allowed to visit an inmate—the very same parent or guardian who is usually responsible for the boy's plight in the first place.

On the other hand, where rules should exist, there are none. Racial, ethnic, and all kinds of similar personal animosities are not only tolerated by the officials, but even encouraged. The outside recreation yard, for example, has been divided into sections by the inmates. Most boys are invited to join one or the other of these sections by the inmates who control it. If a boy happens to walk into a section where he does not belong, he is apt to be beaten or even killed. The whites and blacks have separate sections, and these major divisions are subdivided again on the basis of other hatreds and prejudices.

If a boy should refuse to join one of the groups, or if for some reason, he receives no invitation, he is constantly harassed by members of all the groups. He has to belong for his own protection. After a boy has been invited to join a particular group, he has to go through some sort of initiation. Two of the groups require that he masturbate the leaders of the group. In some instances, he has to engage in fellatio or submit to anal intercourse. These acts sometimes take place in the dormitories.

I have repeatedly appealed to Mr. Pearson to break up such divisions within the institution—the latest appeal was made today—but he steadfastly refuses. He maintains that the divisions are *good* for the institution, since they keep the boys from uniting and posing a disciplinary problem for the guards. "Besides," he said, "we don't want whites and blacks together for *obvious reasons*." When I asked him what those "obvious reasons" were, he refused to discuss the matter further. I came away with the impression that he is a bigot.

February 8, 1950

For a long time now, the boys at Juvenile Home have been telling me about Menlo Park, where many of them first got into trouble. The park is owned by the city, and it is a well-known haunt of homosexuals. The boys go there to sell their bodies to older men. Sometimes they beat and rob these men, and that is what usually brings them to the attention of juvenile court. Although some boys go to the park for the hell of it, many of them could not survive if they did not prostitute themselves. It is the only means they have for obtaining food and shelter.

This evening I went to Menlo Park to see for myself what was going on there. I buttoned my topcoat about the neck in order to conceal my Roman collar, and then I sat down on one of the park benches. A number of incidents occurred that I hadn't anticipated. I got quite a shock.

As it grew dark, the park quickly filled with boys and men. They paraded around the many paths of the park, all of which led to a central plaza. The boys wore tight-fitting dungarees, and despite the cold, they had their jackets open, apparently to reveal the T-shirts which clung tightly to their chests. The men eyed the boys suggestively as they passed them on the paths, and occasionally, one of the men would walk off with one of the boys.

Out of this gathering, I noticed a group of boys who appeared to be playing some kind of game. They'd stalk certain individuals from among the men, and every so often, they'd meet in small groups to exchange information and to decide on their next move. In time, they seemed to have decided to concentrate all of their attention on a tall, rotund man, who paced continuously around the plaza. Soon, three of the boys were talking to the man. After a short conversation, he accompanied them down the stairs to the right of the plaza, which led to the men's latrine. Immediately, a large group of boys gathered around the top of the stairs.

After about fifteen minutes, I saw the man running up the stairs. The boys who stood at the top of the stairs tried to keep him from getting out into the plaza, but he finally managed to struggle through. As the man ran across the plaza, the boys pursued him, punching him with their fists and shouting obscenities at him.

When I saw that no one else was going to come to the man's aid, I followed him and the boys out of the park. By the time I reached the street, I noticed that he was trying to extricate himself from the boys and climb into a Cadillac. After a fierce battle, the man did manage to get into the car, but he was unable to close the door because one of the boys still had him by the throat. I seized the boy by the hair and dragged him from the car. The man then closed the door and locked it.

While I grappled with three of the boys, three or four others were busy slashing the tires of the car with knives. Still others had surrounded the car and were rocking it. Then I heard the roar of the car's motor, and it pulled away—but not before a brick was sent crashing through the rear window.

Fortunately for me, the police arrived almost immediately after that, and the boys scattered. If the police had not gotten there when they did, I could have been killed. I didn't know any of the boys who were involved in the attack, and I had no chance to explain who I was.

I did get a pretty bad cut on the head from a stone, but one of the policemen dressed it, and it doesn't even hurt now. What does bother me is the revelation which took place tonight. I recognized the man who drove away in the Cadillac. I met him when I visited Saint Michael's Abbey with Karl Wright. It was Abbot Cecil.

February 17, 1950

It seems that Father Linehan and I will never agree on anything. Although I should have known better, I finally asked his permission to use part of our rectory for some of the homeless people we have in this area. We certainly have the space, but Father Linehan didn't see it that way. He hit the roof. "Over my dead body!" he exclaimed. "If you want to be murdered in your bed, that's your business, Father. But you'll have to wait until you're old enough to be pastor of your own parish. I'll not allow it here!"

I went to great pains to explain the situation as I saw it. I pointed out that most of these people not only have no place to stay, but they never get anything substantial to eat. It is true that many of them are winos, drug addicts, and former prostitutes—as Father Linehan keeps emphasizing. But if we as priests are not going to do anything for such people, really what is our function?

The more I try to help these misfits, the more I feel that they bear very little—if any—responsibility for their plight. Father Linehan disagrees with me. "They brought it on themselves, Father. If they hadn't violated the laws of God, they would not be where they are now." I told him that it does not really matter how they got in their present condition. I said all we should care about is that they are children of God who need our help. But Father Linehan remained unconvinced.

March 23, 1950

When I saw that it was useless to talk further about using the rectory as a refuge for the poor, I suggested renting a building for this purpose at my own expense. Since I don't have a car, I thought that maybe I could manage to scrape up enough money. Father Linehan made it very clear that he was opposed to the plan. He said that if I attempted to carry it out, he would report me to the bishop. He told me that I would be taking on a task which had not been assigned to me, and since this would take time away from my other work, I would be derelict in my duties. I pointed out that I was willing to use my free time for the project, but he reiterated his position and said that he would definitely report me to the bishop if I went ahead.

At first, I thought the situation was hopeless. But as I was kneeling before the Blessed Sacrament in church tonight, I had a brainstorm. I decided that I would ask some of the parishioners to open their homes to the poor. If these parishioners could provide one good meal a day for the homeless, and if they could provide shelter for just some of them—especially for the utterly exhausted and ill—a great deal could be accomplished. If the project were organized and run by individual parishioners, no one could prevent it—not even the bishop—and no one could accuse me of neglecting my duties. Before I left the church, I thanked Christ in the Blessed Sacrament for giving me that idea.

March 23, 1950

In so many ways, the parishioners here at Saint Anne's are remarkable. The fact that most of them are poor themselves seems to make them more sensitive to the plight of others. They were even more eager to help the homeless than I had anticipated. I asked Mrs. Russo to become director of the project, and she has done a phenomenal job. Under her direction, our parishioners now provide meals in their own homes for two hundred homeless men and women. They have made bedrooms available for one hundred.

For the first time in a long while, these poor unfortunates, who have spent days, months, and even years walking the streets, now have families to care for them and to love them. Many of them have become entirely different people. They voluntarily help with both the household chores and the children. Contrary to what Father Linehan keeps telling me is going to happen, their benefactors have not yet been murdered in their beds.

A few days ago, we began our new program for shut-ins. I asked Mrs. Vicari to take charge of that program, and from all appearances, it is going to be as successful as our project for the homeless. The women of the parish are preparing meals for people in the neighborhood—both Catholic and non-Catholic—who are too old or too sick to cook for themselves. These meals are kept warm and delivered each day by station wagon. If the recipients can afford to pay the small fee which is charged, they do so. Otherwise, the service is provided free.

Although Father Linehan would like to put a stop to these projects, there is nothing he can do. They are operated by parishioners, and although I give advice when it is requested, he is unable to say that I am formally directing them. Nevertheless, he still holds me responsible and often criticizes me. He maintains that I have gotten myself entangled in situations where a priest has no business. Moreover, he claims that parishioners involved in these undertakings are squandering money on them which should be contributed to Saint Anne's Church.

I couldn't disagree with him more. I think that we now have some *real* Christians in the parish, doing what *real* Christians should always be doing. These projects make me rejoice that I have become a priest. In fact, if I accomplish nothing else during my priesthood, just helping the homeless and ill has made all of my struggles and years in the seminary worthwhile.

April 18, 1950

Father Linehan hasn't given up yet on trying to convince me that I should do things his way. I suppose he considers it his duty to enlighten his assistant and to see that he gets started on the right path. This evening, he invited me into his private suite again, and as usual, served drinks. But our conversation ended up the way it always does—in a stalemate. Although I would like to please him by accepting his viewpoint, I feel that it would be intellectually and morally dishonest to do so.

Following our discussion, I went into the church to pray, as I do every night. The church was dark, and I sat down in the last pew. I felt slightly unsteady from the liquor I had drunk, and what happened next made me think for a while that I might be imagining things.

A little, stooped old woman entered the church and knelt before the altar of Saint Anthony, with its numerous, flickering vigil lights. She prayed for a long time, and then she got up and removed one of the lilies from a vase which rested on the altar. I watched in rapt astonishment as she placed the lily in her mouth and ate it. After she had eaten the lily, she knelt before the altar again for a few minutes. Then she rose and walked slowly toward the back of the church. I stood up as she passed my pew. She was startled at first, but then she recognized me.

"Oh, it's you, Father," she said.

"It's so dark in here," I remarked. "Aren't you afraid?"

"What is there to be afraid of, Father?" she asked. "Why would anyone bother an old woman? Saint Anthony will take care of me."

Although the woman's English was good, I noticed that she had a slight Italian accent. I walked through the vestibule with her. "I don't want you to be out this late alone," I said. "I'll walk home with you."

"But that is too much trouble for you, Father."

"It is no trouble at all."

"I live close," the woman said. "I will give you a cup of coffee."

We walked through dark alleys until we came to a frame apartment house. I followed the old woman as she slowly made her way up two pairs of rickety outside stairs. The steps creaked so badly under our feet that I thought they might give way. When we reached the third floor, I was startled by the meow of a cat and a bucket that upset when the cat jumped out of it.

"He keeps the rats away," the old woman said.

She opened the door to her apartment and switched on an electric bulb, which rested in a socket on the side of the wall. I followed her into the apartment.

"Would you like some coffee, Father?"

"Very much so," I replied.

I sat down on a chair that was painted a faded, sickly green. The entire room was very poorly furnished. It contained a cupboard, an old coal stove, a table and chairs, and a rusted iron bed in a corner. A crucifix hung on the wall, and on a stand beside the bed, there were pictures of the Virgin and Saint Anthony.

"I don't have any milk for your coffee, Father," the old woman apologized. "It's hard to keep milk here. I don't have a refrigerator."

"I never drink milk in my coffee," I said, sipping the coffee. "This is very good coffee!"

The old woman smiled. "It is nice of you to say so, Father, but I know you have had better." She sat down on a chair beside the table. "You don't have to worry about me, Father. I understand. A man has to drink sometimes. I had a man. I know how it is."

Her powers of observation surprised me. "How did you know that I had anything to drink?" I asked her.

"You can't fool me, Father," she replied. "You can't fool me about anything. I am too old to fool. You are a good priest, Father. Everybody says that."

"Do good priests drink?"

"You don't drink very much, Father. Some priests drink all the time."

"Are you retired now?"

"I work every day, Father. I work from ten in the morning until six at night."

"What kind of work do you do?"

"I scrub floors and clean."

I glanced at her shriveled hands. They were rough and red, and the bluish veins stood out as though they were about to burst. "How old are you?"

"Seventy-eight."

"Why do you still work?"

"I couldn't live if I didn't work, Father. My husband didn't leave me anything when he died. I had two boys to raise, and I always had to work."

"Where are your boys?"

"I never see them, Father. They have money now, and they are ashamed to come to my place."

"You have a nice place here."

"No, Father! It is not nice. But it is all I can afford. There are four rooms up here, but I can use only this one. If you go into the other ones, you fall through the floor."

"What do your sons do?"

"My oldest boy has a big store and sells flowers. My youngest boy is a lawyer. He is a smart boy. He worked hard to go to school, and I worked hard, too, and helped him. But after my boy went to school, he married a girl who is Protestant, and now he is Protestant." The old woman began to cry. "I still can't believe it, Father. He was even an altar boy. Now both of my boys have changed their names, and I never see them."

"How long has your husband been dead?"

"For over thirty years, Father."

"Was he a good man?"

"He was like all men, Father. He was good to me, and he was bad to me. He drank too much, and sometimes he hit me. But sometimes he was good to me. When he got sick, he started to act like there was something wrong with his head. He didn't act right. Then he didn't talk right, and I could hardly understand him. He got so sick that he had to be in bed, Father. After a while, he couldn't take care of himself at all. He was just like a little baby. I even had to make diapers for him. He was a big man, Father, and I had to lift him and change the bed for him. He was like that for three years before he died. People told me he got that way from bad women, but I never believed them. He couldn't have gotten that way from bad women, could he, Father?"

I looked into the sad, questioning eyes of the old woman. "People say many things," I answered, "and very often they have no idea what they are saying."

"I knew it wasn't true, Father," she sobbed. "He suffered so much. I prayed and prayed that he would get better, but God wanted to take him. I prayed to the Mother of God, I prayed to the Sacred Heart, I prayed to Saint Anne, and I prayed to Saint Anthony. But they would not listen to me. God doesn't love me, Father."

"What makes you think God doesn't love you?"

"I just know He doesn't."

"I am sure that God loves you very much."

"I go to Mass and Communion every day, Father. I go to church at night, but I know that God doesn't love me. I keep praying for my husband. I pray that he is in heaven. I have Masses said for him all the time. On Saturday, I had a Mass with three priests said for him. I like a Mass with three priests best. I like High Masses, Father, but I don't like Low Masses, because there's no organ and singing. I don't know if I gave Father Linehan enough for the Mass with three priests. Someone told me I should have given seventy-five dollars, but I only gave forty."

"That was too much," I told her. "You should never give more than twenty-five or thirty dollars for a Solemn High Mass. But even that is too much. You should have had a Low Mass said for your husband."

"But I want the best for him, Father," she protested. "I want to be sure that he is in heaven, because after I die, there will be no one to have Masses said for him. Wait! I will show you what else I do for my husband. I send money away for Masses, too."

The old woman went to the cupboard, got out several letters, and handed them to me. "All of these places say Masses for me," she said. "They send me nice things, too. I will show you." She went to the cupboard again and brought back a cheap rosary, a small medal, and a little wooden cross. "They sent me all of these," she commented happily. "They sent me the rosary for special Masses that cost forty dollars. Once a year I try to have these special Masses said for my husband. I can't afford it more than once a year."

After glancing at the form letters which various religious orders and seminaries had sent out in their quest for donations, I handed them back to her. "You just can't afford to send money to all of those places," I said.

"But I want to do the best for my husband, Father," she insisted.

"I feel sure that your husband is in heaven. You do not need to have any more Masses said."

"But Father Linehan said that I can never be sure. He told me that I should always pray and have Masses said."

"But your husband's case is different," I tried to convince her. "You go to Mass every day. You pray for him. You have had many Masses said for him already."

"If only I could be sure, Father!"

She went to the cupboard, took five one-dollar bills out of a jar, and handed them to me. "Here," she said. "I want you to say a Mass for my husband, Father."

I returned the money to her. "I'll say a Mass for your husband," I promised, "but there will be no offering."

She looked at me in astonishment. "You mean it is free?" she queried.

"Yes, it's free," I replied. "If you want any more Masses said for your husband, be sure to tell me. They will be free."

The woman began to cry again. "You are a good priest, Father. I wish I had a boy like you."

I got up from the chair, bent down, and kissed the old woman on the cheek. "I am your boy, and you are my mother," I said. "It is late and I must be leaving. But I will be back tomorrow after my Mass. If you don't mind, I would like to stop here every morning and have coffee with you."

"What time is your Mass, Father?"

"It is at seven o'clock."

"Then I can go to it!" she exclaimed enthusiastically. "I can go to it, and I can walk home with you! We can have breakfast before I go to work. I will make you good things for breakfast, Father."

I took out a small piece of paper, wrote the telephone number of the rectory on it, and handed it to her. "You can reach me at this number," I said. "If you need me for anything, just call, or have someone else call." I bent down again and kissed her on the forehead. "Now I must go. God bless you."

"God bless *you*, Father!" the old woman called after me as I descended the rickety stairs. "God bless *you!*"

When I neared the bottom of the stairs, the cat, which had been curled up on one of the steps, jumped out in front of me and ran down the alley.

April 19, 1950

After my seven o'clock Mass this morning, I looked for the old woman I met last night. When I did not find her in the church, Saint Anne's Chapel, or the monastery garden, I walked toward her home. With the sun shining, the neighborhood in which she lived seemed much less dreary than it did last night. On the other hand, the filth in front of her apartment house was more apparent. As I walked up the stairs, I noticed that they also were littered with papers and scraps of garbage; except for those which led directly to the old woman's apartment. They had been scrubbed until they were spotlessly clean.

When I knocked at the door, there was no answer. I knocked again, this time harder. There was still no answer. I finally tried the door and found it open. I entered the apartment and pulled up the blinds. As the morning sunlight streamed into the room, I went over to the bed and tried to awaken the old woman. I saw that she was dead.

For the first time, I became aware that I did not even know her name. I remembered the letters she had shown me, but I had not payed attention to the name on the envelopes. I began to search for the letters. In the cupboard, I found the jar which the old woman used as a bank. It had five dollars and seventy-five cents in it. An entire shelf of the cupboard was cluttered with crosses, statues, rosaries, and medals—all of them similar to the religious trinkets which the old woman showed me last night. Apparently they also had been sent to her in return for the money she contributed for Masses. After I picked them up to see if the letters were under them, I went through all of the dishes and clothes. I still could find nothing which revealed the woman's identity.

After I had thoroughly searched the room, I went into one of the adjoining rooms. It was empty except for a trunk in the far right corner. Although the floor beneath my feet was so fragile that I thought it might give way, I managed to reach the trunk by stepping slowly and carefully.

The trunk was old and worn, and its hinges squeaked as I opened the lid. I immediately realized that this was the old woman's hiding place for her most prized and personal possessions. The trunk contained several flowers which had been dipped in wax. She had apparently preserved them in remembrance of weddings and funerals. There was a ribbon from a funeral wreath, with the word "Father" printed on it in faded silver letters. I deduced that this memento must have been from the funeral of her husband. There was a wedding portrait in the trunk, and I could see that the old woman had once been very beautiful. It was also evident that her husband had been unusually handsome.

I noticed a marriage certificate, which bore the words: *WHAT THEREFORE GOD HAS JOINED TOGETHER, LET NO MAN PUT ASUNDER.* From this certificate, I learned that the old woman's maiden name had been Antoinette Sarto. Her husband's name had been Joseph A. Montini. From the children's baptismal certificates, I learned that Mrs. Montini's sons had been named Peter and Joseph. There was a newspaper clipping in the trunk which stated that a Joseph A. Jones had been admitted to the practice of law. I reasoned that the clipping referred to Mrs. Montini's son.

After going through the trunk, I returned to Saint Anne's and found the name of Attorney Joseph A. Jones in the telephone directory. I could see from the address that he lived in a very fashionable neighborhood. I dialed his number, and a woman answered. I asked the woman if Mr. Jones's name had once been Montini. When she said yes, I told her that I wished to talk to him about his mother.

"Joseph, darling," I heard the woman call, "it's for you, dear."

"Who is it?" I heard Mr. Jones ask in a gruff voice.

"It's a man calling about your mother," I heard the woman say.

"Who is this?" Mr. Jones asked brusquely.

"This is Father Faber from Saint Anne's Church. I have some bad news for you. I found your mother dead in her room this morning."

"It couldn't have been my mother," Mr. Jones said matter-of-factly. "My mother died many years ago."

"Wasn't your name once Joseph A. Montini, Jr.?"

"No it wasn't."

"Your wife told me that it was."

"She was mistaken. I am not even a Catholic. I am a Protestant."

"Your mother mentioned that you had become a Protestant."

"She was not my mother. I have never been a Catholic. I am very sorry. Now if you will excuse me, I am very busy."

Mr. Jones hung up on me. I then tried to find either the name of Peter Montini or Peter Jones listed under the heading of "florists" in the classified section of the telephone directory. When I could find neither name, I pondered the possibility of telephoning all of the many florists in the city. But then I considered my experience with Attorney Jones and decided to give up.

As soon as Father Linehan returned to the rectory from saying Mass, I told him that Mrs. Montini had died.

"Did you notify her family?" he asked.

"I tried to," I replied, "but the only son I could reach denied being related to her."

"I suspected as much," he said. "Did you go through her things?"

"Yes, Father."

"How much money did she have?"

"Five dollars and seventy-five cents."

"That means the Saint Vincent de Paul Society will have to bury her. You can turn the five dollars and seventy-five cents over to them. Since she was a member of this parish, we'll provide a Low Mass gratis."

"Can't we give her a High Mass, Father?"

"We can't bury a pauper like a princess, Father. The Saint Vincent de Paul Society will pay the undertaker, and I think we are doing our part if we provide a Low Mass and take care of the services at the grave."

"Mrs. Montini contributed more than she was able to Saint Anne's," I said. "I think she deserves a High Mass. She told me that just last week she gave you forty dollars to have a Solemn High Mass said for her deceased husband."

"That has absolutely nothing at all to do with the present situation," Father Linehan snapped.

"May I officiate at her funeral then?" I asked. "I could sing a High Mass, and that way there would be no offering to be paid."

"You could, but you're not going to. I am the pastor here. I marry them, and I bury them."

I took out my wallet and handed Father Linehan two ten-dollar bills. "This is for Mrs. Montini's High Mass," I said.

"Have you lost your mind?" Father Linehan asked in astonishment. "You are going to have to get over this foolish sentimentality of yours. It isn't your place to have funeral Masses said for every pauper in the city."

"Mrs. Montini liked High Masses," I said, "and I think she should have one. I can't see burying her like a dog."

"Have it your way then," Father Linehan sighed. "We weren't going to bury her like a dog. But if you want to do this, I can't stop you. I didn't realize you were so fond of the woman. If you want to offer her funeral Mass, you have my permission. In that way, I can split the twenty-dollar stipend with you, and you won't lose so much money."

"I do want to offer her funeral Mass," I told him, "but not because I want to save money."

"I understand perfectly," Father Linehan said, now somewhat embarrassed. "Here is your stipend for officiating at the funeral." He handed me one of the bills, and then he placed the other in his own pocket.

This evening, when I visited Gallagher's Funeral Home, I discovered that Mr. Gallagher wasn't interested in burying a "pauper like a princess" either. I passed six large and elaborately furnished parlors—all of them vacant—before I reached the cubicle where Mrs. Montini was laid out. Her coffin, which was unlined, resembled an ordinary wooden box. In order to view the body, I had to look over the side of the coffin, since the body was not supported by pillows. Mr. Gallagher had dressed her in the same dress she was wearing when I met her last night. He had placed the same bandanna on her head, to cover the hair he had not taken time to fix. A cheap rosary, sent to Mrs. Montini by one of the many religious organizations to which she had contributed, was wrapped around her hands. There were two baskets of flowers. I had sent both of them. On the ribbons attached to the baskets was the word *Mother.*

April 20, 1950

It was raining very hard when I awoke today. I kept hoping that it would stop in time for Mrs. Montini's funeral, and fortunately it did. But there were other problems. The funeral was scheduled to begin at ten o'clock. By fifteen minutes after ten, the sexton had not yet tolled the bell—the signal for me to walk to the vestibule and bless the coffin as it was brought into church. When I investigated the delay, I was shocked and angered to discover that the coffin was already in place before the communion rail.

Once I realized what had happened, I immediately entered the sanctuary, wearing a black cope and accompanied by the altar boys. Even though the coffin was already in place, I stood before it, sprinkled it with holy water, and recited all of the prayers which the Church prescribes for receiving the body. I then returned to the sacristy and vested for Mass.

When I reentered the sanctuary and began the funeral Mass, I noticed that there was no singing. I interrupted my prayers and turned around. The lights in the choir loft were out. The organist had not arrived, and I found out later that Father Linehan had not bothered to notify him. I was forced to offer the Low Mass which Father Linehan had wanted from the beginning. After I had said Mass, I entered the sacristy and exchanged my Mass vestments for the black cope. Then, together with the alter boys, I proceeded in procession to Mrs. Montini's bier. Since there was no organist, I sang the responses to my own prayers.

There were no pallbearers, and when I had finished the ceremony of absolution, Mr. Gallagher and another man removed the coffin from the church and placed it in a hearse. Mr. Gallagher drove the hearse, while the other man drove the only car in the funeral procession. I rode in the front seat of this car, and three of Mrs. Montini's friends rode in back. Although several old women had attended the funeral, there was space in the car for only three of them.

Following burial rites at the cemetery, Mr. Gallagher walked up to me as I was about to get into the car for the ride back to the city. "I really don't know you very well yet, Father Faber," he smiled as he removed his hat. "It would give us a chance to git better acquainted if you rode back with me—if ya ain't afraid to ride in a hearse, of course."

"I'm not afraid," I said.

"Good!" he exclaimed. "I do wanna git to know ya better, Father."

I climbed into the hearse with Gallagher.

"I suppose you wonder, Father, why I'm helpin' out today," Gallagher said as he headed the hearse in the direction of the city. "I usually don't do this sorta thing, but I'm doin' it as an act of charity. It sorta reminds me of the days when I hada drive one of these things to make a livin'. I hada work my way to the top, Father. Things ain't like they useta be, though. I have people who work fer me now, and I can take the wife and kids travelin' every year. Have you ever been to Italy, Father?"

"No, I haven't."

"It's nice, Father—real nice! Maybe you'll git to go some day. It's a lot different there than it is here. You take the woman we planted this mornin', fer instance. Where she come from, people like her know their place. But here, the low class expects to be treated as good as the high class. Some of her friends who come to my funeral home complained to me about how she was laid out. The nerve of those ungrateful wops, Father! They jist don't know their place over here. And it ain't right. We give her a better funeral than she ever deserved. Those kinda people never save no money, and then they expect handouts. If it wasn't fer the Church, the state would've got holda her, and she would've ended up bein' hacked to bits in some medical school. But do they thank us fer it? No! They think they din't git enough, and they want more. The Saint Vincent de Paul Society paid fer only a small parta this funeral. The rest comes outa my own pocket. But I'm glad to do my part fer the Church, Father. It ain't that. But these ungrates git under my skin."

"Perhaps you really came along this morning to cut down on expenses," I commented. "It's cheaper for you this way, isn't it? If you hadn't come yourself, you would have had to pay a man to do this."

"That ain't it at all, Father," Gallagher protested. "I don't mind payin' a man. I did this jist because I wanna do some charity. Everybody knows I'm no penny pincher. I'll tell ya what I'm gonna do, Father. I did git a little money outa this funeral, and I'm gonna give ya ten dollars outa what I got."

"I don't want it."

"I understand, Father. It's agin' the rules. But let's jist say that I'm givin' ya the money as a personal gift."

"I wasn't thinking of the rules. I just don't want it."

Gallagher looked at me in bewilderment. "You're not gonna always wanna pass up little presents like these, Father," he lectured me. "There's a lota things you young fellas have to learn yet when ya first git outa the seminary. I can tell you're still pretty green. I don't wanna tell ya what to do, or anything like that, Father, but you'll learn some day that you took too much time fer this here funeral. You could've left out a lota those prayers you said. Father Linehan only says all those prayers fer people who are somebody. You took more time to say your Low Mass than Father Linehan takes at a Solemn High Mass fer people who really amount to somethin'. Father Linehan can teach you quite a few tricks if you let 'im. Stick close to him, and you'll be all right."

"It seems that we have somewhat different conceptions as to what constitutes a *somebody*," I told him. "I believe that every

April 20, 1950

really good human being—no matter how unknown or how poor that person happens to be—is a *somebody* who deserves our utmost respect in life, and a funeral as decent as we can make it in death. Certainly Mrs. Montini was a somebody who really did amount to something—to use your manner of speaking—and she deserved all the respect both in life and in death that we could have given her."

"I don't think you're right, Father. That woman was even crazy. Father Linehan will tell ya that himself. She useta eat the flowers right offa Saint Anthony's altar. A lota people seen 'er do it."

"There are a lot of people in the world who think that you're crazy, too, Mr. Gallagher. Did you ever think of that? When you receive Holy Communion, for example, you believe that you receive the body and blood of Jesus Christ. It is very difficult for a great many people to comprehend that, and I'm sure that some of the less intelligent among them would say that you're crazy. What Mrs. Montini did was similar in some ways to what you do whenever you receive Communion. The flowers on the altar had been offered to Saint Anthony, and Mrs. Montini felt that by eating those flowers, which Saint Anthony now owned, she herself could get closer to him. Perhaps Mrs. Montini just had more faith than you do."

Gallagher's face reddened in anger. "You can't say that dead wop was a better Catholic than I am, and git away with it, Father," he raged. "I'll have you know that I'm one of the outstanding Catholics in this whole diocese. You jist haven't been around long enough to know who Peter M. Gallagher is. I'm a real power in this diocese. The bishop often takes me with him whenever he travels. We've flown all over the country together. And you're tellin' me that a stupid wop had more faith than I have! Why she couldn't even speak good English."

"Her English happened to be much better than your own is," I pointed out. "She had a slight accent, but her English itself was almost flawless. The same cannot be said for your own use of the English language, and you have spoken it all your life. Mrs. Montini began to learn it for the first time when she came to this country from Italy. I wonder how well you could learn to speak Italian if you moved to Italy. But in any language under the sun, Mr. Gallagher, you—as a human being and a man—are a sorry son of a bitch."

Gallagher's face turned sickly pale, and then it changed to flaming red. "I won't take that from no one—not even a priest," he commented belligerently. "No one calls me a son of a bitch and gits away with it."

"We can settle it right here and now," I offered. "Just stop the hearse!"

Gallagher's hands actually began to shake, and he turned pale again. "I can't hit you while you're wearin' that collar," he said, "and you know I can't. I'd commit a sacrilege."

"Don't let this collar stop you," I told him. "If any human being deserves respect, it is not because of what he wears on the outside, but because of what he is on the inside. What Mrs. Montini had was on the inside, and it was the sort of thing people like you can't touch; either with their fists or their malicious tongues. I did not know her long, but I knew her long enough to understand that she was worth any number of your kind."

Gallagher became conciliatory. "Look, Father," he said, "you're lettin' your feelings run away with you. You jist don't understand business. A businessman hasta accept things the way they are. You jist don't understand, Father."

"I understand enough to know that you don't have an honest mind," I told him. "Religion is something you use for your own selfish motives, just as you use everything and everyone. It makes you look respectable while you push the little fellow around. Your religion is one of forms and ceremonies, and fitting snugly into a niche in society. It is religion of the heart which you don't have, Mr. Gallagher, and religion of the heart is the only religion that really matters. It is religion of the heart which enables us to see God in everyone, and especially in saintly people like Mrs. Montini. And now stop the hearse. I'm getting out."

Gallagher looked stunned. "You can't do that, Father," he pleaded. "There's been a misunderstandin', and I think I should explain."

June 1, 1950

"I'm not going to sit here and help you repair your damaged ego. You need time to think over what I said. Now let me out!"

"I can't jist let you out on a highway like this," Gallagher protested. "What'll people think if they hear about it?"

"Let me out!" I demanded.

"Please be sensible, Father."

I grabbed the steering wheel and gave it a sharp turn to the right. Gallagher slammed on the brakes.

"Are you tryin' to kill us or somethin'!" he exclaimed. "You can't do this, Father! What'll I say if people hear about it? The car with the women in it is still behind us."

"You can always tell them that I'm crazy—like Mrs. Montini was!" I said as I jumped out of the hearse and banged shut the door. "I thank God for one thing," I yelled back at him. "I'm glad that only the dead are entrusted to your ministrations!"

June 1, 1950

What a night this has been! A little after eight o'clock, I received a telephone call from Mr. Douglas, the assistant superintendent of Juvenile Home. He asked me to come over to the home as soon as possible. He said that Mr. Pearson, the superintendent, and several guards had been taken prisoner by the boys, who were threatening to cut their throats. He added that the interior of the home was already a shambles. The boys had destroyed most of the furniture and equipment.

It was almost nine o'clock by the time I arrived at the home. The mayor and other city officials were already there. They told me that since the boys held me in high regard, they hoped that I would be able to do something to quiet things down. I learned that the ringleader of the insurrection, a sixteen-year-old boy by the name of Jimmy Jackson, had issued a list of demands. These included a new superintendent, replacing most of the guards, better food, more humane treatment, uncensored correspondence, more frequent and less restrictive visiting privileges, and of all things, an end to the racial and other divisions in the yard.

Although Jimmy Jackson and I had talked on occasion, he was not a Catholic and I did not know him well. I had suspected that he was a pretty bright fellow, but his demand in regard to the yard convinced me. Moreover, he was clever enough to insist that the mayor appear on radio and TV and state specifically which demands were being granted. Because of Jimmy Jackson's intelligence, I began to see some hope that the insurrection could be ended without bloodshed.

I told the mayor and other officials that I thought all of the demands were justified and should be met. They did not agree with me. The mayor said that if the demands were granted, other demands would follow, and it would be impossible for anyone to run the institution effectively. He maintained that since Jimmy Jackson was white, the Negro inmates would cooperate with him only up to a point. He insisted that when the showdown came, the boys would not dare to kill Mr. Pearson and the guards. He said that if I could not persuade the boys to surrender, a contingent of state and local police would storm the institution.

From my own experience in working with the boys at Juvenile Home, I knew that the officials were wrong in all of their assumptions, and I told them so. I felt certain that if they did not grant the demands, the hostages would be killed. I pointed out that boys were less likely to be concerned about possible consequences than adult prisoners might be. Although what I said about killing the hostages made them reconsider, the officials came to the conclusion that I was wrong and they were right.

They wanted me to address the boys over a loudspeaker, from outside the institution, and ask them to surrender. I refused to do this. I told them that I wanted to go inside and talk to the boys personally. At first, they were opposed to the idea. They said that the boys would make me a prisoner, too, and this would jeopardize efforts to get them to surrender. When they saw that I would not cooperate unless they let me go inside, they finally granted my request, albeit reluctantly.

The inmates had posted guards at all the doors of the building, but I had no difficulty in getting through to see Jimmy Jackson. When I told him that the local and state police intended to storm the building, he made it quite clear that the throats of the hostages would be cut. I tried to persuade him to consider the consequences, but he said: "If they are going to treat us the way they have been treating us, every guy here is willing to take his chances on the consequences."

I asked to see Mr. Pearson, and Jimmy readily complied. Pearson hadn't been harmed, but they had tied him to a chair. One of the boys stood next to him, holding a knife not very far from his throat. Pearson's face was ashen, and some of the old arrogance had disappeared; but not all. I told him that I thought the dispute might be settled if he gave me permission to inform the city officials that he agreed to the demands of the boys.

"I refuse to do that, Father," he said. "As I have told you many times before, I do not think that any changes in procedure are required."

Jimmy Jackson looked at me and smiled. "He wants to die, Father," he commented, "and I think he's going to get his wish."

When I saw that I could do no more inside the institution, I decided to go outside and talk to the officials again. Jimmy Jackson walked to the door with me, and once again I tried to convince him that what the boys intended to do wasn't the answer to anything. "Most of you will spend your entire lives in prison for murder," I emphasized.

He repeated what he had said before. The boys didn't care. "We all know that you're a good man, Father," he told me. "If we didn't like you, you'd never get out that door. I know you're against this place, too, and want to help us. But if we give up now, they'll treat us even worse than they did before."

As we were talking, several inmates walked up with cans of gasoline. "Look what we've got, Jimmy!" one of them exclaimed.

"Throw it on the walls," Jimmy told them, "but be sure there are windows nearby so you can get out. Then stand by and be ready to light it when I tell you."

Jimmy looked at me. "You can tell them when you go out there that if they refuse to meet our demands, we'll not only kill the superintendent and guards, but we'll burn the place down."

Suddenly I had an idea. "Why don't we do it this way, Jimmy?" I said. "Have the boys collect materials that can be used to make torches—wood, paper, and the like. Then keep half the boys inside the building, ready to light your fires and do whatever else you feel you have to do, while the other half marches around the building carrying the torches. If the marchers are attacked, you'll immediately set fire to the building. I'll write a letter to the mayor telling him what you intend to do, and you can have one of the boys deliver it."

Jimmy looked at me and grinned. "Why don't you deliver the message yourself?" he asked.

"Because I'm going to lead the march," I replied.

Jimmy hesitated, but I could see that he was impressed. "What will all of this accomplish?" he asked.

"A number of things," I answered. "When they actually see the torches burning, I think they'll be able to visualize what comes next—a burning building. This alone may persuade them to grant your demands. They'll certainly be under greater pressure to grant them, especially with the radio and TV crews recording the whole thing. Then, too, the fact that a Catholic priest is leading you—your chaplain, at that—will convince a great many people that your demands are really justified. I doubt that they'll be willing to risk not granting them under such circumstances."

Jimmy laughed. "Father, you're a real sharpie," he said. "We'll do it."

I wrote my letter to the mayor while the boys made their torches. After the letter had been delivered, we waited for about forty-five minutes. Then we lit the torches and filed out of the building. I led the procession, while Jimmy stayed behind to direct activities within the building. I asked the boys if they could think of a good song to sing as we marched, and one of them suggested "Onward Christian Soldiers." That's what we sang.

We had circled the building only a few times before the mayor approached me and said that he and the other officials were willing to grant all of the demands. The mayor then stood before the TV cameras and announced the decision. Jimmy Jackson and I, together with several of the other boys, appeared with him. Some of us, including myself, were still carrying our torches. Immediately after the mayor's announcement, Jimmy and the other inmates surrendered the hostages and themselves.

June 5, 1950

This is really a joyous night for me. Not only did I save people's lives, but I helped bring about some long overdue reforms at Juvenile Home. I thank the Good Lord for guiding me.

June 2, 1950

Poor Father Linehan! When I saw him this morning, he looked as though he were going to have an apoplectic stroke. He saw the torchlight procession on TV last night, and I'm afraid it was too much for him. He said that he had decided to ask the bishop to transfer me. "I'll be quite candid, Father," he told me. "I don't want an assistant like you. You're radical. As I said before, you might even be—God forbid!—a Communist revolutionary."

I tried to make Father Linehan understand that he was talking nonsense, but it did no good. The newspaper headlines didn't help matters. One of them read: *SAINT ANNE'S CURATE THREATENS TO BURN DOWN JUVENILE HOME.* Another stated: *FATHER PETER FABER LEADS ARSONISTS.* Although one of the newspapers did mention that I had saved at least several lives and the home itself from destruction, that bit of news was buried in an obscure spot on an inside page.

This afternoon I received a call from the mayor. He thanked me—rather grudgingly I thought—for my help. Then he went on to say that he was asking Bishop Connolly to replace me at the home. He said he had felt for a long time that I lacked the necessary insight to function effectively there.

Function *effectively!* My God! I had just saved a superintendent and guards from having their throats cut, and I had saved the home itself from destruction. I keep thinking of something Monsignor Grosclaude told me several years ago. He said that there are serious liabilities to being a hero, and one of those liabilities is that the hero must suffer the consequences. I guess that's what I'm doing now. People are so grateful for what I've done that they are going to try to have me fired.

June 5, 1950

Today the inevitable happened. Monsignor Hogan, the chancellor of the diocese, telephoned and asked to see me. I thought I knew what he would say, and I was right. He made it very clear that Bishop Connolly is dissatisfied with me.

"I do not know what we are going to do with you, Father," he said. "You have been a priest for only one year, and you have managed to alienate everybody."

"Not *everybody*, Monsignor," I corrected him. "Before you pass judgment, I think you should talk to our parishioners at Saint Anne's and the boys at Juvenile Home."

"That is beside the point, Father. The *important* thing is that you have alienated your superiors."

"I don't think it is," I told him. "A few people have been disturbed, but hundreds of others—perhaps thousands—understand and appreciate what I've been doing."

I could see that Monsignor Hogan was becoming uncomfortable. "The *important* people don't appreciate it," he said, "and it is with them that I am concerned."

"I thought that *all* of God's children were important," I commented.

"Yes, yes, of course," Monsignor Hogan spluttered. "I know that you are a conscientious priest, Father. Nobody questions that. Your intentions are good, but you give your superiors the impression that you are quite immature. Threatening to burn down Juvenile Home is just one example."

"I think I should explain the reasons—"

"You don't have to, Father," he cut me off. "I know what they are. But once again, I do not think they are pertinent. For a priest, you behaved in a most disgraceful manner. You should consider the *dignity* of your office. You even had the inmates sing "Onward Christian Soldiers" as they marched around the building. That's a *Protestant* hymn."

I was tempted to smile when he criticized me for having the boys sing a Protestant hymn, but I restrained myself. "I'm not concerned about dignity," I said. "I *am* concerned about helping God's children. I'm sure that any number of *superiors* considered many of Christ's actions disgraceful and undignified."

Once again, Monsignor Hogan displayed embarrassment. "I'm sure they did, Father! I'm sure they did! But this is quite different. You've been called a rebel, an agitator, *even* a Communist. We just can't have that, Father. No matter how good your intentions, we can't have it!"

I felt like telling him that Christ had been called a number of things, too, but I could see that it was no use.

He went on: "People are happy the way they are, Father. By trying to change the conditions in which they live, you'll just make them unhappy. In time, you'll learn that."

"I have never noticed that the homeless, the hungry, the sick, and the pariahs of society are especially happy," I commented. "What I've seen at Saint Anne's and Juvenile Home tells me quite the opposite."

"The trouble with you is that you've misinterpreted what you've seen," Monsignor Hogan said. "Father Linehan has been a priest for thirty years—a very dedicated priest—and he doesn't see things the way you do. Father Parme served at Juvenile Home for three years prior to your arrival there. He found the place very well run and thought that the boys were happy. The Protestant chaplain never saw anything wrong. You seem to have some special problem, Father."

Once again, I decided that it was useless to comment. I just waited for my sentence, and it wasn't long before Monsignor Hogan got around to it.

He said: "The bishop has asked me to relieve you of your duties, Father. You are to remain in residence at Saint Anne's until you hear from us. You will be permitted to say Mass, but you are not to serve the people of Saint Anne's in any other way. The bishop is appointing a new assistant to Father Linehan. He is also assigning a new chaplain to Juvenile Home. We want to offer you a chance to think things over. We hope that this *vacation* of sorts will give you an opportunity to ask God's guidance in prayer."

July 19, 1950

It looks as though the "vacation" is going to be a long one. But I'm not too concerned. I spend most of the time praying and catching up with my reading. In fact, I can quite honestly say that

I am content. I'm not ashamed of anything I've done. On the contrary, so far I'm quite proud of my work as a priest. I can live with my conscience. I just hope that the officials of the diocese can do the same.

I do regret that I cannot continue the work I've started. I have an idea that the parishioners here at Saint Anne's will go on with that work, but I'm not overly optimistic about the prospects for Juvenile Home. I'm sure that the new superintendent will make some changes for the better, but with the city administration looking over his shoulder, and without a really knowledgeable chaplain to goad him, I'm sure that the reforms will not be what they should and could be. But one has to be patient in this life. I believe that God permits all of us to do only so much, and we have to be satisfied with that. God has His own way of working things out in the world.

True, I could disobey the diocesan officials. But what would that accomplish? It might do something for my vanity, and it might even benefit people temporarily. In the end, however, my effectiveness as a priest would be destroyed, and I would be unable to help many times that number of people in the future. Although I believe that the diocesan officials are wrong in my particular case, the diocese as a whole, with its thousands of priests and religious, helps more people than I could ever help as an individual. Thus, the team is infinitely more important than I am.

Aside from all that, I made a solemn promise to God that I would obey my bishop. That was one of the requisites for ordination, and I intend to keep that promise. If a man cannot be counted on to keep his promises, I don't think he can be of much help to anyone.

PART SEVEN

August 10, 1950

What a surprise! I received a registered letter this morning from Monsignor Hogan, announcing that Bishop Connolly has appointed me a lecturer in history at Holy Spirit College. The appointment is to become effective on September 7, when the academic year begins at Holy Spirit. I am to live at the college, and Monsignor Hogan emphasizes that all of my time is to be devoted to my duties there.

Frankly, I don't know yet what to think of the appointment. My first impression is that the bishop wants to keep me out of trouble by turning me into an intellectual. Although I have always been a good student, I've never wanted to teach. I would much prefer to do work like I had been doing here at Saint Anne's and at Juvenile Home. But since I have no choice in the matter, I'll have to make the best of the assignment. I have already ordered some new books. I'll do everything I can to become a competent professor. That, too, is God's work.

Two of my former classmates, Fathers Jim McHugh and Bill Fagan, were here today, and when I told them about the appointment, they couldn't get over it. Holy Spirit College is a plush school for women, operated by the Sisters of Mercy, and it is apparently considered a choice appointment. In fact, Jim and Bill claim that the new assignment means I'll have the best post of anyone who graduated in our class. According to Bill, my appointment proves that the best way for a priest to get ahead in the diocese is to displease his pastor, the city officials, and the bishop. Although I passed the comment off as a joke, I think that Bill was rather serious. He'd like to be teaching instead of serving in a parish, and I suspect he's envious.

August 23, 1950

This afternoon I had my first conversation with Sister Prudentia, the president of Holy Spirit College. Although I had an appointment with her, she kept me waiting for an entire hour. I think this was done deliberately, in an attempt to impress me with her importance. When her secretary finally ushered me into the office,

Sister Prudentia rose from her long, mahogany desk and rather condescendingly offered me a chair. She is a large woman, probably in her forties. She has a reddish and bloated face, with lips that are quite thin. Her speech is extremely affected.

"It is such a pleasure to meet you, Father," she said with feigned graciousness. "I regret that I had to keep you waiting."

I tried to be polite. "I was enjoying your air conditioning," I told her. "It's very hot outside."

"*Everything* is enjoyable at Holy Spirit College, Father," she stressed.

"I was surprised to be assigned here."

"We are happy to have a priest who has already done some graduate work in history," Sister Prudentia said. "Most of the young priests His Excellency sends us have had no specialized training in the subjects they are to teach. His Excellency feels that if a young man is trained in theology, he is competent to teach almost any subject. A few years ago, His Excellency assigned a young priest to our department of English. He did not have any training in literature beyond a survey course which he had taken six years previously in the seminary. The students would ask him questions about certain authors, and he had never even heard of them. It was most embarrassing for us at times. However, I must say this in his favor, Father. He was an excellent literary critic. He could determine immediately whether a work in literature were immoral or not—even when he had not read it—merely by having it summarized for him. Perhaps you know him. His name is Father O'Donoghue. He is now doing parish work."

"I don't know him, Sister."

"I do think that Father O'Donoghue is better suited to parochial work. We have standards to meet, Father, if we are to maintain our recognition by the secular authorities. It is always more impressive to print in our catalogues that our instructors have done graduate study in the subjects they teach. But I must point out, Father, that we are curious as to why you elected to do your graduate work at a secular university."

"The history department at Jefferson has a good reputation, Sister."

August 23, 1950

"Did His Excellency send you there?"

"No."

"Did you deliberately act against His Excellency's wishes?"

"My seminary rector suggested it."

"He had no right, Father! He was acting in violation of canon law. But I am happy to know that you did not take it upon yourself to make such a decision. If you had, you would not be welcome here. In philosophy and theology, we closely adhere to the teachings of Saint Thomas Aquinas. Father Sheehy, our chaplain and professor of theology, is an expert in such matters. You will share an office with him."

"I met Father Sheehy when he delivered a sermon at Saint Anne's."

"He is a fine man, Father. How did you like Saint Anne's?"

"I enjoyed my work there."

Sister Prudentia grimaced as though she were in pain. "But it's located in such a horrible section, Father! Someone has to do that kind of work, but it is hardly the work for a bright young man like you. Our girls come from only the best homes. You will find everyone at Holy Spirit thoroughly cultured. This fact will be especially appreciated by a cultured person like yourself, who has had to work with—how shall I say it?—*uncouth riffraff*. My father, Magnus Carlin, owned most of the dwellings around Saint Anne's. My brother now manages these properties. He tells me that this blighted area is spreading to other sections. Some of the best people in the city used to belong to Sacred Heart Parish, but now many of them are moving away. I feel sorry for Monsignor O'Shea, the vicar-general. He is pastor of Sacred Heart, you know."

"Yes, I know," I said. "Sacred Heart is my home parish."

"Then you must know all about the problem, Father."

I was angry. "My family lives on the *border* of Sacred Heart Parish," I pointed out. "I happen to come from the other side of the tracks, Sister."

Sister Prudentia blushed. "I had no idea, Father," she said. "I am sorry. But there is no reason to be ashamed. Many of our bishops—even popes—have risen from the sordid conditions of their childhoods to become illustrious disseminators of culture."

"I am not ashamed, Sister," I told her. "I am proud. The poor have a culture of their own, and I see nothing inferior about it."

"Certainly, Father! Certainly!" Sister Prudentia rose hastily to her feet. I could see that she was furious. "You will have to excuse me, Father," she announced curtly. "I have several other appointments this afternoon."

That ended our meeting.

August 25, 1950

I know that I'm not going to be able to sleep tonight. This evening, for the first time since he got out of the novitiate, I visited my friend, Karl Wright. Karl—I still can't get used to calling him Father Martin—wasn't very happy to see me; and I can understand why. I also know now why he hasn't written to me for the past two months. I found him in a deplorable state. It was evident that he had been drinking heavily. He was very pale, and while I was talking to him, he had to leave the room in order to vomit. I still can't get over the shock. During all the years of my friendship with Karl, I had never known him to accept even one drink.

Although he was obviously not interested in discussing the matter, I asked him when he was leaving for Europe to begin his doctorate in philosophy at the University of Louvain. He said that Abbot Cecil had decided not to send him. When I asked him why, he refused to give me an answer. I got the distinct feeling that Abbot Cecil had a great deal to do with his present condition, and I questioned him about that, but once again, he was evasive. It was then that I decided to tell him about the incident in Menlo Park. At first he said nothing, but soon he started to cry. After he had calmed down somewhat, he finally told me the truth.

The very first night that Karl was out of the novitiate, Abbot Cecil entered his room while he was asleep. He woke Karl under the pretext of wanting to discuss Karl's impending studies abroad. Karl said that he still doesn't know how it happened, but it wasn't long before Abbot Cecil was performing fellatio on him. The next night, Abbot Cecil came back and tried the same thing. This time

August 25, 1950

Karl hit him in the face, knocking out two of his teeth. Abbot Cecil then went into a rage and informed Karl that he was no longer sending him to Louvain.

I told Karl that he should get out of the abbey right away. I added that he had an obligation to report Abbot Cecil to Rome. But Karl wouldn't listen. He said that he felt cheap and dirty. He went on to say that he didn't deserve to leave Saint Michael's Abbey alive. I suggested that he make a good confession, but he said that he had already done that. He was of the opinion that God could never forgive him for what had happened. I tried to convince him otherwise, but he started to cry again. It was then that I became convinced he was having a nervous breakdown.

Before leaving, I told him that I would return soon again, but he shook my hand and said: "Pete, you're the only really good friend I've ever had. I want you to know that. But I never want to see you again. I'm unworthy even to look at you. Just let me stay here and die in peace." Once again, I tried to reason with him, but it was no use.

On my way back here, I stopped at Saint Mary's Seminary to discuss Karl's problem with Monsignor Grosclaude. I told him that I was going to report the matter to the apostolic delegate, but he advised against it. He said that in all likelihood the Roman authorities wouldn't believe me, especially if Karl maintained his silence. He added that even if Karl reported the matter himself, it was doubtful that they would believe him. They might think he had a grudge against Abbot Cecil and was lying in order to get even with him. Monsignor Grosclaude reminded me that such things did happen. He said that the apostolic delegate was apt to think the same thing if I reported Abbot Cecil. Then there was Karl's mental state to consider. Monsignor Grosclaude pointed out that it would be very easy for Abbot Cecil to say that Karl had made the accusations because of mental illness.

After returning here to Saint Anne's and thinking about the situation more carefully, I came to the conclusion that Monsignor Grosclaude was right. He promised that he would visit Karl. Meanwhile, all I can do is hope and pray for the best. I don't think I have ever been sickened so much by anything as by this.

September 4, 1950

After saying Mass this morning, I once again visited Saint Michael's Abbey, but Karl still refuses to see me. Now that Monsignor Grosclaude has been unable to get anywhere with him, I don't know what I am going to do. Perhaps the only answer is to confront Abbot Cecil personally. Monsignor Grosclaude continues to advise against that, though. He seems to think that Abbot Cecil has the influence to cause serious trouble for me. He may be right, but if the situation doesn't improve soon, I'll have to take that risk.

I have finally gotten most of my belongings into my suite here at Holy Spirit College. I didn't have much to move in the way of clothing, but there were hundreds of books. I never realized that I owned so many. The suite is pretty nice. I have a large bedroom, a sitting room, a comfortable study, and a private bath.

This afternoon I met Sister Margaret Mary, the chairman of the history department. I don't know what to make of her yet. She is not a beautiful woman, and I get the impression she tries to compensate for that by being overly gracious. She is unusually tall and thin, and her large teeth are very noticeable when she smiles. Her lips are full and sensuous, and there is something almost childish about her voice and actions.

"I have been waiting for you, Father," she drawled when I entered her office. "Sister Prudentia should have introduced us. You shouldn't have had to telephone me."

"She's probably busy," I smiled.

"She likes to have people think that," Sister Margaret Mary commented, "but she's not as busy as she pretends to be."

"Well anyway I'm here."

"I know you are!" she beamed. "I recognized you the moment you walked into the office. Even if I had seen you outside, I would have known you from the picture that came with your records. You have a face that's easy to recognize."

I smiled. "Gruesome, isn't it?"

"I didn't mean it that way at all!" she exclaimed. Then she added playfully: "And you know I didn't. It's just that your face shows you're unusual and different—if you know what I mean."

"Unusual and different in a gruesome sort of way."

"Now you're teasing me, Father. You know what I mean."

"Can you tell me something about the department, Sister?"

"There are only two of us in the history department—you and I. We *are* the department. You will teach ancient and medieval. I will teach modern. I get first choice because I'm older than you. How old do you think I am, Father?"

"I don't know."

"I bet I'm older than you think I am. I'm thirty already."

"Thirty isn't old."

"But I'm a little over thirty."

"That still isn't very old."

"You're just being good to me."

"I'm telling you the truth, Sister."

"I still think you're being good to me."

"Have you worked out our schedules yet?"

"You will have five classes. I hope that won't be too much for you."

"I'm here to work," I said.

"Did Sister Prudentia tell you that you're going to share an office with Father Sheehy?"

"Yes, she mentioned that."

"You'll like him. He's a nice little man."

"I met him once."

"He's our confessor, Father. I think he's a much better teacher than a confessor."

"What's the matter?" I smiled. "Are his penances too long?"

"You're teasing me again," Sister Margaret Mary drawled. "You know very well what I mean. Father Sheehy doesn't have deep spiritual insight."

"What do you mean by *deep spiritual insight?*" I asked.

"You just like to tease me," she replied. "You know what I mean."

"What makes you think so?"

"I know that you've read Saint John of the Cross, Saint Teresa of Avila, Saint Francis de Sales, and all the rest."

I smiled. "How can you be sure?"

"I knew as soon as I saw your picture. Have you read them, Father?"

"Yes."

"I knew you had, and that's the big difference between you and Father Sheehy."

"I guess Father Sheehy and I should change places."

"You're teasing me again, Father. Why can't you be serious? I do wish that you were our chaplain instead of Father Sheehy."

"I believe you did have a priest here who knew quite a bit about Saint John of the Cross. He wrote a book on the subject. Did you know Father Calvin?"

Sister Margaret Mary paled. "I hope you're not friends!" she exclaimed.

"I never met him," I said. "I did hear a lot about him at the seminary, though."

She breathed a sigh of relief. "You had me worried, Father. I thought you might be one of his followers. He's an extremist. He believes that all pleasure is evil. When he was here, he caused a split in our community. The nuns who followed his teachings became eccentrics. Once I asked him why God had made so many good things if He didn't want us to enjoy them, and he said that God had made them so we could give them up."

"Perhaps he had a point."

"Surely you don't agree with him!"

"Did you ever hear Father Calvin say that all pleasure is evil? Were those his exact words?"

"I never heard him say it in so many words, Father, but he implied it."

"Perhaps you misunderstood him," I suggested. "Certainly John of the Cross, Teresa of Avila, and Francis de Sales preached detachment from the things of the world. So does the Bible."

"I just didn't care for him, Father," she said. "He was a very independent person. When he spoke, he could be very sarcastic."

"It was probably a matter of clashing personalities," I smiled.

"He's a very proud man, Father. He seemed to think that he

was always right. He acted as though we had to believe what he said."

"Isn't that what Christ did?"

"Father!" she exclaimed. "That's sacrilegious! Christ was God."

"And *man,*" I added.

Sister Margaret Mary appeared to be irritated. "I can't understand why you would defend Father Calvin this way," she said.

"I have never met the man," I emphasized. "If I ever do meet him, I might feel altogether differently about him. I don't know."

That seemed to satisfy her. "If you meet him, you won't like him—just as I don't," she said. "Can I get you a glass of milk, Father?"

"Maybe next time. I still have a lot of unpacking to do."

"And here I am keeping you back. I'm sorry."

"You have been very helpful, Sister."

Before I left, she grabbed my hand and kissed it tenderly. I noticed that there were tears in her eyes.

October 12, 1950

For some reason, my students insist on believing that the Church consistently champions democracy. I suppose this is because they consider our own government a democracy, and would not like to think that the Church favors something else. Then, too, cardinals elect the pope, and the students apparently think that the word "elect" is synonymous with democracy. I don't like to disabuse them of this theory, but in the interests of truth, I have no choice.

In my lecture today, I presented a number of pertinent facts. I pointed out, for example, that in the twelfth century, Bishop John of Salisbury declared in his *Policraticus* that the Church should exercise absolute power over the state. I added that when Dante, on the other hand, stated in *De Monarchia* that the popes were not supreme in political matters, he was exiled and his book placed on the Index. I also gave the students an example from the fourteenth century. I told them that if the emperor had not saved Marsilius of Padua, he would have been burned as a heretic for saying in his book, *Defensor Pacis,* that the source of all civil authority was the will of the people rather than the pope.

I explained that this attitude has not changed appreciably in modern times. I pointed out that Pope Leo XIII, in his *Christian Constitution of States,* criticized the idea that governments should be based on the will of the people. I also mentioned that Pope Pius IX, in his *Syllabus of Errors,* denounced the principle of separation of Church and state. I went on to say that the same pope opposed the idea that every man is free to embrace the particular religion which he considers true. I emphasized that our present pope, Pius XII, believes that Catholics have the right to demand religious freedom for themselves, because they possess the truth; while non-Catholics have no such right, since they are in error.

One of the students asked me what I thought of these principles, and I said quite frankly that I am against them. I went on to say that such teachings were responsible for the horrible tortures, mutilations, and murders of Christian heretics and Jews during the Middle Ages. I added that I believe the Inquisition itself committed heinous crimes against humanity.

A nun in the class tried to dispute this. She said that Father Sheehy had told them that it is sometimes necessary to burn people's thought in order to save their souls. I tried to explain to her why burning people at the stake serves neither the interests of thought nor those of the soul. I doubt that I convinced her.

Another nun asked me if I thought the Church would ever accept Communism. Although the question didn't seem especially relevant, I answered it anyway. I said that it is quite possible that the Catholic Church might one day work out an accommodation with Communism. I pointed out that the economic theories of the Catholic Middle Ages have much more in common with Communism than they do with capitalism. I emphasized that it was the Catholic philosophers and theologians of medieval times who provided the basis for Communism's labor theory of value.

I could see that the nun was anything but happy with my answer. In fact, many of the students seemed quite perturbed at what I said today. I'm sure that Father Sheehy will hear about it, but that can't be helped. I still hold the truth sacred. I just hope that Father Sheehy does, too.

October 23, 1950

This morning I once again telephoned Saint Michael's Abbey, and I finally learned something about Karl. Considering the number of times I have called, I think it is pretty evident that the switchboard operator had been told not to give out any information. When I called today, a young scholastic happened to be taking the place of the regular operator for a short while, and he was much more helpful. He told me that Karl had fallen asleep while smoking in bed, the mattress had caught fire, and Karl had been seriously burnt. He said that this happened over a month ago and that Karl has been in Saint John's Hospital since that time.

Even though I knew that things had not been going well for Karl, this additional information gave me quite a jolt. I was surprised to learn that his injuries had occurred while smoking. Before entering the monastery, he had never smoked, just as he had never been a drinker. I asked the scholastic whether Karl had been drinking before the fire started, and he said that he did not know. I think he must have been.

I telephoned Saint John's Hospital, but they would tell me nothing. They even refused to confirm that Karl is a patient there. I went over to the hospital, but I had to leave without seeing Karl and without learning anything new. I even talked with Sister Clarence, the administrator—all to no avail. She was polite enough, but she made it clear that no information would be forthcoming.

When I saw that there was no other way, I went out to Saint Michael's and asked to see Abbot Cecil. His secretary talked to him briefly on the telephone and then told me that he was too busy to see me. When I tried to make an appointment for another time, the secretary said that he would be unable to talk to me at any time in the future. I decided that there was only one thing to do. I walked right into the abbot's private office and confronted him.

Abbot Cecil appeared stunned when he first saw me, but his appearance quickly changed to one of fury. "I hope I am not going to have to summon the police, Father Faber," he told me. "I don't know whether you realize it or not, but you're trespassing."

"Call them if you want," I countered. "We can tell them about you and Menlo Park."

Abbot Cecil hesitated. I could tell that he had recognized me that night, but until now he had not known for sure that I had recognized him. He finally said: "I don't know what you're talking about."

"I'm sure you do," I told him. "And you owe me something. I saved your life that night."

"I still don't understand what you're talking about."

"I also know that Father Martin is in Saint John's Hospital, and I know the real reason for his illness."

"I won't listen to this," Abbot Cecil snapped as he picked up some papers and started to make notations on them.

"I guess I'll have to spell it out for you," I said. "I'm talking about your *homosexual* activities."

Abbot Cecil slammed down the papers. "How *dare* you!" he shrieked.

"You are responsible for Father Martin's condition," I said, "and at this point, you are the only one who can help him. He needs psychiatric treatment, and I insist that you see to it that he gets it."

"*You* insist!" Abbot Cecil scoffed in his effeminate manner. "I will have you understand once and for all, Father Faber, that I am the sole ruler of this abbey. Father Martin is a rebellious monk, and if he insists on drinking himself to death, then that is his funeral—not mine. His problem is not one of illness, but one of sin. It is not my duty to encourage my monks in the commission of sin. As I have told Father Martin himself, I believe in giving a man enough rope. If he wants to hang himself, that is his business—not mine."

"Father Martin is mentally ill," I said, "and—"

"I'll not listen to this," Abbot Cecil shouted. He picked up the phone. "Father Jude, please get the police over here," he said. "Father Faber refuses to leave."

I could see that it was useless. I knew that if the police did arrive, I'd be the one in trouble. Before leaving, I told Abbot

Cecil: "If anything further happens to Father Martin, I am holding you personally responsible. You will have to settle with me, and I'm telling you beforehand that you won't have time to summon the police."

I think I would have hit him then and there if I hadn't felt that it would have made things even worse for Karl.

November 6, 1950

What started out to be a very promising day ended in tragedy. Father Jim McHugh telephoned this morning and said that Karl had been released from Saint John's Hospital last week. Jim's sister, who is in charge of nursing at the hospital, finally obtained the information for us. Even she had a great deal of difficulty in finding out. Father Martin had been admitted to the hospital under another name, and it was only by doing quite a bit of detective work that she was able to unravel the mystery.

As soon as I knew that Karl was back at the abbey, I tried to telephone him, but I was informed he was away. When I asked when he would return, I was told he would not be back for several months. I asked to speak with Abbot Cecil, but I was told he was also away. I asked when he would be back, and once again I was told that it would be several months.

I could see that they were still giving me the run-around, so after thinking about it all day, late tonight I decided to make an unannounced visit to the abbey's cloister. I knew where Karl's room was located, since I had visited him there in August. If Karl was no better, I had decided to get him out of the abbey, even if I had to use force. I realized that Abbot Cecil might carry out his threat to have me arrested, but I decided that I would have to risk that.

I experienced no difficulty in getting into the abbey's cloister. A side door was unlocked. When I reached the floor where the rooms of the monks were located, I crept quietly down the hall, all the while trying to escape notice. I was just going to open the door to Karl's room when I heard excited voices coming from inside. The few words which I understood made me stand closer to the door. There was no mistaking the voice of Abbot Cecil, and although I could not immediately place it, I thought that I had heard the other voice before.

"But are you sure you understand?" Abbot Cecil was asking. "This must be kept absolutely quiet."

"I understand, Abbot Cecil," the man said.

"These things happen in the very best of places," Abbot Cecil apologized, "and unfortunately, nothing can be done about them. We sent Father Martin to the best specialists, but something had snapped inside his mind, and there was nothing they could do for him. Until this happened, we thought he was getting better. He was perfectly all right yesterday. I do not know where he got the wine he drank today. He must have broken the lock on the wine cellar again. You know—the cellar where we keep the wine which is used at the Holy Sacrifice of the Mass. And just look at what he did to his room! Yesterday we had it all cleaned for him. Today he must have gone on a rampage and torn everything apart."

"It's too bad," the man commented, "but bein' an undertaker fer so many years now, I'm useta things like this."

"I knew you would understand, Mr. Gallagher. That is why I called you immediately."

"I do understand, Abbot Cecil," Mr. Gallagher emphasized.

"If something like this got out, it would do untold harm to the Church," Abbot Cecil stressed. "I have already called our own physician, and he will write out the death certificate in the morning. He will say that Father Martin died of a heart attack. That is also the story which we will give to the newspapers. That is the story you are to give in the event you are asked. You are certain that you understand now, Mr. Gallagher?"

"I understand, Abbot Cecil."

"The funeral will be similar to all of our other funerals—in keeping with our vow of holy poverty. But in this case, Mr. Gallagher, please try to do something about his face. I shall give you a photograph of him from which to work, and I do hope that you will do your very best to make him look as natural as you possibly can. We shall be glad to pay extra for that service."

"I'll do my best, Abbot Cecil," Gallagher promised.

"I know you will," Abbot Cecil said. "You have always been a fine Catholic gentleman, and I know that the Church is your first interest. You can rest assured—"

Before Abbot Cecil could finish his sentence, I abruptly opened the door. On the floor, I saw the body of Father Martin. A rope was still fastened about his neck. Another piece of rope was tied around three clothing hooks on the wall. I looked at Abbot Cecil who had turned ashen and was trembling.

"Leave this abbey, Father Faber!" he ordered in a weak, tremulous voice. "Leave immediately!"

As I walked toward him, Abbot Cecil backed away until he was leaning against a dresser and could go back no further. "Don't let him touch me, Mr. Gallagher," he pleaded. "He's going to kill me. Protect me, Mr. Gallagher! Please protect me!"

Gallagher remained motionless, gazing dumfounded at what was taking place.

I grabbed Abbot Cecil by the throat and started to squeeze. His eyes had almost bulged out of their sockets by the time Gallagher tried to pull me away from him. I swung around and gave Gallagher a punch in the face that sent him reeling.

Then I addressed Abbot Cecil, who had fallen to the floor. "Are you satisfied now?" I asked. "You gave him enough rope. You murdered him just as surely as if you had tied the rope to his throat with your own hands. Are you satisfied now? Are you . . ."

I didn't say anything else. I saw that Abbot Cecil had fainted. Besides, I could feel the hot tears welling up in my eyes. I turned quickly and left the room.

November 9, 1950

This morning the monks chanted the Office of the Dead for Karl. Then Abbot Cecil, who could have won an Oscar for his performance, officiated at the Solemn Pontifical Mass. He was attired in black vestments, and he wore a mitre on his head. At the conclusion of the Mass, he presided at the absolutions over Karl's corpse. He then ascended the pulpit.

"It is no longer customary," he said, "to deliver eulogies at funerals. However, I feel compelled to break custom this morning in order to say a few words concerning the deceased. In all sincerity, I can tell you—his parents, his brothers, his sisters, and his friends—that it has never been my privilege, either as a monk of this community for many years, or as abbot, to have known a monk who better fulfilled the ideals of our order. As his abbot, I can assure each and every one of you that he was very close to God. He was a humble, prayerful, and obedient young man.

"Some of you, because of your great love for Father Martin, may be asking yourselves this morning why God chose to take such a splendid monk away from us in the very prime of his young manhood. I share these sentiments with you, because after all, I was his father in religion. I, too, loved him as a father loves his son. But if all of us loved him in a special way, we must remember that God loved him in a very special way also. That is why God, in His great wisdom and mercy, decided to take him immediately to Himself. Now, in this the hour of our agony, we must pray to our Heavenly Father in the words of Jesus: 'Not my will but thine be done.'

"Father Martin's sudden death came as a shock to members of his family, to his fellow monks, and to his friends. In one split fraction of a second, his young heart ceased to beat. I believe that God meant to teach all of us an important lesson, through the rapidity with which He called His faithful servant home. God used Father Martin as His instrument to impress the following lesson indelibly upon our minds: None of us who are here this morning know in which split second God will call us, just as He called Father Martin. I only hope and pray that we are as well prepared as Father Martin was, when God asks us to 'give an accounting of our stewardship.'

"Let me say in closing that Father Martin has not left us in spirit. We still possess his good example to emulate. We can also rest assured that Father Martin will always be at the throne of God, beseeching Him to shower His blessings upon those of us who loved Father Martin, and who were loved by him, in this life. We can repeat in all confidence the words which Saint Paul repeated in his First Epistle to the Corinthians: 'Death is swallowed up in victory!' "

November 14, 1950

I watched Abbot Cecil slowly and sedately leave the pulpit. He continued to rub his eyes with his handkerchief, as he had done throughout the sermon. When he had spoken of Karl as his son, he had seemed so emotionally distraught that it appeared he would not be able to continue. At the cemetery, he kept up the pretence. As he stood over the coffin in his mitre, rubbing eyes which were now red and swollen from the pressure he had applied, his black cope flowed bat-like in the breeze. *"Anima ejus et animae omnium fidelium defunctorum, per misericordiam Dei requiescant in pace,"* he prayed.

I kept repeating the same prayer. The only difference was that I meant it.

November 14, 1950

Although I thought that I was going to get some reading done tonight, no sooner had I sat down and opened a book than I was interrupted by a telephone call from Sister Margaret Mary. I suspect that I am going to have trouble with her. She asked me to come over to her office in the administration building, and when I told her that I was busy and would prefer to see her tomorrow morning, she said that an emergency had arisen and that she had to see me at once. When I got there, I found out that the emergency was a figment of her imagination.

She was waiting for me at the door of her office, and she was going to kiss my hand, just as she had done the first time we met. This time I managed to shove my hands into my pockets. She smiled when I did that and said: "You should permit me to greet you properly, Father. After all, it's been so long since I've seen you that we're almost strangers. Please sit down."

I did sit down, but I wasted no time in asking: "Sister, what *is* the emergency?"

"There are a number of problems," Sister Margaret Mary replied, suddenly becoming very serious. "You missed your classes last Thursday morning. When there is a funeral—as I understand there was on Thursday—or some other reason why you cannot meet with your classes, you should always let us know."

"I have already caught up with my lectures," I said. "I let the students know, and I didn't think that a substitute was necessary."

"Father, it is up to us to decide what is necessary at Holy Spirit College," Sister Margaret Mary informed me sharply.

"I'll remember that in the future, Sister."

"There is something else, Father. Where are your lesson plans?"

"I had no idea that college professors were supposed to provide lesson plans," I said. "I thought that was something the nitwits forced elementary and high school teachers to do. Frankly, I consider it rather degrading. If a person is incapable of taking care of his own lesson plans, I don't think he should be graduated from a college or hired by a school to teach. Once he has been hired, I think he should be permitted to do the job as he feels it should be done. This matter involves academic freedom."

"I'm not interested in your philosophy of education," Sister Margaret Mary snapped. "We require lesson plans here, and we expect you to provide them."

"That's something else that I'll remember, Sister."

"There is still another matter, Father. Sister Prudentia has been disturbed by complaints from some of our young nuns. Several of them do not like your lectures. They claim you accused the Church of practicing the principle of expediency rather than that of morality; thus causing society to suffer. I told Sister Prudentia you never could have said that. The Sisters obviously misunderstood you."

"The Sisters understood me. It's what I said."

Sister Margaret Mary grew red in the face. "You couldn't have said that, Father!"

"I said it, and it's true. I can't understand why the truth upsets people so much. The Church has made mistakes, and I think we should admit it. If we refuse to recognize our mistakes, we cannot correct them. It is the refusal to admit and correct our errors—not the disclosure of those errors—which causes grave harm to the Church."

The expression on Sister Margaret Mary's face seemed to alternate between anger and shame. She squirmed about in her chair for a while, and then she said: "I'm sorry, Father. You know that I'm sorry, don't you?"

"Sorry about what?"

"I was crabby with you."

"That's all right."

Suddenly she started to cry. "You're so good to me, Father," she sobbed. "Why are you so good to me?"

I didn't know what to say to her, so I didn't answer. She continued to cry, and as she did so, she looked at me very strangely. I could not help but notice how she was methodically rubbing her thighs together underneath her habit. Intermittently, she would stop and press her feet hard on the floor, and then her body would quiver all over.

Finally, she said: "I acted before like I didn't know you at all, but I do know you. I want you to understand that. Sister Prudentia doesn't know you, but I do. Do you believe that I know you?"

Once again, I wasn't quite sure what to say. "I'm glad that you understand the situation better now," I told her.

Then, before she could say anything else, I hurried out of her office.

December 15, 1950

I do not know if the academic world is this way everywhere, but the intrigue which goes on here at Holy Spirit College would make Machiavelli blush. The worst feature of all this is that the students suffer both academically and morally. Even the freshmen, who were admitted only a few months ago, are already masters of deceit and duplicity. I think it is very sad to find a situation of this nature in a Catholic institution, and I keep praying that something will happen to change it.

The root of the problem can be traced to the sentimental and sometimes unhealthy relationships which develop between students and the nuns who operate the college. Most students confide in at least one nun, who serves as a protectress. They know that if they complain about a lay faculty member or even a priest to their protectress, she will take action against that faculty member, even to the point of having him fired.

When a girl suspects that she is going to get a low grade, for example, she'll run to Sister and cleverly denounce the faculty member for something which has nothing to do with the grade. She'll even lie to her protectress that she's not the least bit concerned about her grade. She might say that the faculty member is not a good teacher—as though she would know!—or she might tell her protectress that the faculty member has said something against the Church; or in an extreme case, she might even accuse him of having tried to molest her sexually.

If formal charges are brought against a faculty member by the administration, the faculty member is never given the name of the student or students who lodged the complaint. He is told that it would be unethical for the administration to divulge such information. It is not considered unethical, however, to confront a faculty member with a charge and then not permit him to even so much as know who his accuser is. More often than not, the charges are vague and contradictory. A member of our English department will have to leave the faculty in January, because he was denounced by students on two charges: not presenting enough factual material during his lectures; presenting too much factual material during those same lectures.

When it comes to causing trouble for other faculty members, Father Sheehy is so much like the nuns that the only thing missing is the veil. He gossips with the students incessantly, and he is always inviting them to our office for tea and coffee. I was at Holy Spirit less than a week when the students tried to get me involved in the same sort of malicious nonsense. They began to complain both about nuns and about the lay faculty. I would have none of it. I told them that I'd be willing to discuss academic or spiritual matters with them at any time, but if they had anything at all to say about another faculty member, they should tell it directly to that person. Too few of my colleagues realize that if a student talks to them about somebody else, their turn is coming up next.

A great deal of the trouble is caused by departmental chairmen. At Holy Spirit College, departmental chairmen are

March 30, 1951

rotated every three years. This system was started by the administration in order to get rid of Sister Patricia Louise, a chairman in the English department. Since Sister Patricia Louise—a very wise, just, and highly competent nun—had seniority, the only way to remove her as chairman was to introduce the system of rotation.

If it were not for the harm that is being done, it would be funny to watch this system operate. The departmental chairmen become kings or queens for three years. While they were just ordinary faculty members before their elevation, they suddenly become omniscient and infallible in all things. They tell other faculty members what and how to teach, and they are constantly conniving with the students. At the end of three years, the old chairman miraculously loses all omniscience and infallibility, and the new chairman just as miraculously assumes all the attributes of God.

Frankly, I think it is impossible for an honest person to win in a system like this. Sister Prudentia and others resent the fact that I try to keep up a proper relationship with students and other faculty members. She has been telling my students that I am a very selfish man, who does not give freely of his time. In other words, I refuse to engage in gossip. A young nun, who interrupted my lecture yesterday, informed me publicly of Sister Prudentia's verdict regarding my selfishness. I didn't even bother to defend myself. In a situation of this kind, people usually believe what they want to believe.

Each night before retiring, I head for the chapel and ask the Good Lord to help me. Trying to be a good teacher is hard enough; but to survive the network of spies and other fiends in this place requires the special protection of Almighty God.

March 30, 1951

Today my students asked even more questions than usual. I still have the feeling that they are asking these questions because they were told to do so. I have an idea that someone in the administration hopes to use my answers against me. The questions are seldom relevant, and that fact alone makes me suspicious. I invariably answer them, though. I think it would be dishonest to do otherwise.

A student asked me whether the Church has been a leader in the fight for social justice. When I said no, she disagreed with me, citing *Rerum Novarum* and *Quadragesimo Anno*. I pointed out that those encyclicals not only came too late, but are ambiguous. I said that many authorities interpret them as favoring the rich over the poor. I added that when they are considered in their entirety, that would be my own interpretation. I admitted that a few statements in both encyclicals could be taken out of context to give the opposite impression, but I emphasized that they do not represent the main thesis of the encyclicals.

Next, someone asked me about the Church's leadership in education. I pointed out that over ninety-five percent of the people were illiterate during the Middle Ages, and yet the Church did nothing to remedy the situation. True, the Church did conduct schools, but they were for the privileged few. One of the students mentioned modern times, and I said that illiteracy is most common today in those places where the Church still retains much of her former influence and power. I quoted from the *Syllabus of Errors,* in which Pope Pius IX denounced the idea that the children of all classes should be educated. I added that in those places where others have won the right to educate the masses, the Church has followed her traditional policy of expediency by setting up her own system of schools. I said that the Church has not done this because she is interested in educating the masses, but because she fears that she will lose the masses if they are educated by those outside the Church.

Soon I was being asked about the Church and the position of women in society. I pointed out that almost all the Fathers of the Church had denounced women as tools of the Devil. I mentioned that wife-beating had been legal during the Middle Ages. I added that in those places where the Church still has considerable power, the position of women is usually as degraded as it was throughout the Middle Ages. I said that the fight for the rights of women has generally been led by those outside the Church.

Then someone brought up the question of the Church and slavery. I pointed out that the Church had once approved of slavery. I stated that Saint Augustine, for example, had given his approval, as had Saint Ambrose and Saint John Chrysostom. I informed the students that during the Middle Ages, popes, bishops, and monasteries owned many slaves. I added that for all practical purposes, the medieval system of serfdom itself was a form of slavery. I said that when the emancipation of serfs did occur in some places, the bishops and monasteries were the last to let their serfs go.

I imagine that there will be repercussions from what I said today, but I am not going to distort the truth for anyone. The Church has done a great deal for civilization, and I am proud to be identified with that part of her history. As for the other part, I am ashamed. Denying the truth is not going to mitigate the shame; nor in the long run, is it going to advance the cause of the Church in today's society. If we deny the truth, people will call us imbeciles and liars. I think we have been called those names often enough in the past.

April 5, 1951

Sister Margaret Mary asked to see me this morning, and sure enough, she brought up what I had told my class about *Rerum Novarum* and *Quadragesimo Anno*.

"Father, you are talking nonsense," she said. "In our own college, we teach that the workingman should be paid a just wage, and that's exactly what Pope Leo XIII and Pope Pius XI said should be done."

"But what is a just wage, Sister?" I asked her. "A just wage may mean a fairly good salary in a country where there is already a large measure of social justice, but in other places, it means only a few cents per day."

"I'm talking about our own country," she said.

"All right, let's consider our own country," I suggested. "In fact, let's have a look at this very college. It pays its lay faculty as little as it can get away with. It has convinced most faculty members—falsely, I might add—that it cannot afford to pay higher salaries, and that they are performing a Christian service by teaching here. There are some lay faculty mambers who get much higher salaries than others, simply because they refuse to be deceived and work for less. Then there are our janitors. They are paid twelve dollars each week. Would you say that the college pays a just wage?"

Sister Margaret Mary got angry. "Our janitors are alcoholics," she argued, "and they can't get a job anywhere else. If we gave them more money, they'd spend it on drink."

"The college is taking advantage of them," I countered. "No wonder they drink! If I were paid twelve dollars a week for working eight or ten hours a day, I'd drink, too. They are entitled to as much money as ony other man gets for doing a like amount of work."

"For being here such a short time, you seem to know all the dirt," Sister Margaret Mary snapped. "What we do here at Holy Spirit College is no concern of yours. You are one of our employees, too, Father— in case you have forgotten."

"I also happen to be a priest," I said, "and the welfare of *all* people is my concern."

"I heard that you even praised the French Revolution," Sister Margaret Mary complained.

"It had some good points," I said.

"The people who took part in the French Revolution were nothing but uncouth, murderous trash!" Sister Margaret Mary declared angrily.

"A revolution is always distinguished by impoliteness, Sister," I told her. "I have an idea that's because the ruling classes never bother to teach the people genteel manners."

Sister Margaret Mary sprang to her feet. "I'm just wasting my time talking to you," she snapped. "I think you need a psychiatrist."

I had to smile. "Sister, does everyone who disagrees with you need a psychiatrist?" I asked.

She stalked out of the office without answering me.

April 6, 1951

Late last night I received a telephone call from Sister Margaret Mary. She wanted me to come over to her office, but this time I refused, even though she kept insisting that a very serious emergency had come up. I told her that I would see her this morning, and that's what I did. Something tells me, though, that after our meeting today, my days at Holy Spirit College are numbered.

When I entered her office, Sister Margaret Mary was friendly enough. She offered me a seat and then asked: "Why wouldn't you see me last night?"

"It was late, and I had just taken a shower," I replied.

"And you were all bare," she drawled childishly.

"I was wearing pajamas and a robe," I said.

"You're still mad at me because of yesterday. I can tell. I'm sorry that I was crabby."

"It's all right."

"You're being good to me again, Father. Why are you so good to me?"

"I try to be good to everyone."

"But you are especially good to me! Sometimes I get so mad at you, though, that I could hit you with something. I think you say things just to get me upset so that you don't have to be serious with me. You don't like to be serious with me, do you?"

"I believe what I told you."

"I can never get you to change your mind, can I? You have such a strong will. In fact, you're strong all over, aren't you?"

When I did not answer her, she said: "You worry me, Father. You think too much about politics and social conditions. You know as well as I do that those things aren't important. Only God is important and how close we are to Him. I think you're too concerned about material things. You aren't detached like Saint John of the Cross, Saint Teresa of Avila, and the other great saints were. Sometimes I think it's pride that's holding you back. Instead of detaching yourself from the world, you want to solve all of its problems. You know that's impossible, Father."

"I'm not at all sure that Saint John of the Cross and Saint Teresa of Avila were so humble," I told her. "It seems to me that they made rules for everybody else, but they didn't follow those rules themselves. The writings of Saint Teresa clearly show that she was very much against any sort of freedom for her nuns. She said that if these nuns insisted on freedom, they were to be imprisoned, flogged, and fed bread and water. Saint Teresa herself, on the other hand, traveled all over the place, conversed with all kinds of people, and did exactly as she wanted."

"But saints are different," Sister Margaret Mary argued. "They do what God tells them to do."

"Maybe," I smiled.

"As proof of God's favor, some of the mystics even possessed the very wounds of Christ in their hands and feet," Sister Margaret Mary emphasized.

"Similar conditions have been produced under hypnosis," I said. "It's interesting that each stigmatic has the wounds where he or she *thinks* that Christ had them. One has them in the hands, for example, while another has them in the wrists."

Sister Margaret Mary shook her head sadly. "You're not happy, Father."

"I think I'm reasonably happy," I disagreed.

"But you're not happy like I am. I'm happy because I have something you don't have. You don't believe me when I say that I'm happy, do you?"

"Only you can say whether you are happy or not, Sister. Happiness means different things to different people."

"When I say that I'm happy, Father, I mean that I'm *really* happy."

"I suppose that's what most people mean when they say they're happy."

"But you're not happy like the saints were, Father."

"Some of the saints had such bad stomachs from shattered nerves that they vomited every day of their lives," I commented. "Some of them suffered from such terrible states of anxiety and melancholia that they never got a good night's sleep."

"Now you're doing what you always do," Sister Margaret Mary complained. "Why can't you forget about facts and logic? Why can't you just love?"

"I don't see where love and logic are incompatible," I said.

"Well then why can't we love one another, and through one

another, love God more?" she asked. "Many of the saints did that: such as Saint Clare and Saint Francis, Saint Catherine and Don Marabotto, Saint Jeanne de Chantal and Saint Francis de Sales. I think that God sent you here so that we could help one another to love. When Saint Teresa of Avila and Saint John of the Cross talked about the things of God, their bodies were so overpowered by love that they rose from the floor and touched the ceiling. Wouldn't it be something if that happened to us?"

"It certainly would be," I smiled.

"Now you're teasing me again," Sister Margaret Mary chided in her childish fashion. "Why do you like to tease me?"

I didn't reply. I noticed that she was methodically rubbing her thighs together and that her body was quivering.

"God sent you to me," she sighed, "and I'll love you even if you hurt me. I want you to be my spiritual director."

"I can't do that, Sister."

"I want you to hear my confession, Father."

"I can't hear your confession here," I told her. "It's against the laws of the Church."

She got up from her chair and knelt down at my feet. "Please, Father," she begged.

"I don't have my stole with me," I protested.

She embraced my legs. "Please, Father!" she pleaded. "Please, Father!"

I tried to get away from her, but she kept clinging to my legs. Finally, she started to stand up, but as she did so, she continued to grasp my body, touching each part of it.

I finally managed to push her away and to keep her at arms' length. "This is no good, Sister," I told her.

"But we love each other, Father."

"It could never work," I said.

She put her hands to her face and began to cry. Then, without another word, she left the office.

May 24, 1951

What I have been expecting for quite a while is definitely about to happen. I am going to be fired again. I was sitting in my office today when I noticed an envelope on my desk. I opened it and found a formal letter from Sister Prudentia, requesting my presence in her office at ten o'clock tomorrow.

"An important letter?" Father Sheehy asked from the desk next to mine.

"I think so," I replied. "Sister Prudentia wants to see me in the morning."

"I'll go with you," Father Sheehy said. "She wants to see me, too."

I smiled. "I'll have company then."

"I don't think that it will be a very pleasant meeting," Father Sheehy predicted. "I have reason to believe that Sister Prudentia is going to dismiss you from the college faculty."

"I'm not surprised."

A look of bewilderment flashed across Father Sheehy's face. "You don't seem very disturbed about it," he commented.

"I have been expecting it. I'm just surprised that it didn't come sooner."

"I've heard rumors that you will be assigned to Sacred Heart Church."

"That's my home parish."

"I happen to know that Bishop Connolly is not sending you there to please you, Father. He often sends Monsignor O'Shea his problems for straightening out. Monsignor O'Shea has been very successful at that sort of thing."

"Do you think I need straightening out, Father?" I asked.

"Yes, I do," Father Sheehy declared as though he had firm convictions on the matter. "Your behavior here at Holy Spirit College has been completely irresponsible, Father. I dislike saying this to a fellow priest, but you are considered something of a heretic."

I smiled. "What is the proper punishment for a heretic these days?" I asked. "Are you going to use the rack, the wheel, or the stake?"

"This is no joking matter," Father Sheehy stressed.

"I have never found the Inquisition very funny myself," I remarked.

May 25, 1951

When Father Sheehy and I arrived at Sister Prudentia's office this morning, Sister Prudentia and Sister Margaret Mary were already seated behind Sister Prudentia's long desk. Sister Prudentia offered Father Sheehy a chair to her right, and then she told me to take a seat in front of the desk. This seating arrangement itself made me feel as though I were on trial, with my three judges facing me from the opposite side of the desk.

Sister Prudentia spoke as snobbishly as ever. "You no doubt know why you are here, Father Faber," she said. "It is my duty—and a most unpleasant duty!—to inform you that your services are no longer required at Holy Spirit College. I have already informed your bishop of that fact. I have invited Father Sheehy to be here this morning because he is our chaplain, and Sister Margaret Mary, because she is head of your department. Do you have any objection to their presence?"

"No, Sister, I don't," I replied.

"What I have to tell you, Father, is not very pleasant, but we must proceed. From almost the moment you arrived at Holy Spirit College, you have caused dissension and discord. Father Sheehy felt compelled to inform me on numerous occasions that you were disturbing the minds of our students. As a specialist in theology, he considers many of your views heretical. He—"

"I really don't think all of this is necessary, Sister," Father Sheehy interrupted her. "I'm sure that Father Faber is familiar with my views."

"Not so fast, Father Sheehy," I spoke up. "I have no idea what my heretical opinions are. I would like you to list them for me."

"I can't pinpoint any specific heresy," Father Sheehy hedged. "It's just your whole attitude."

"Since when is an attitude heretical?" I asked him. "The truth is that I have never made one heretical statement in any of my lectures, and you know it."

"You are a fellow priest," Father Sheehy said, "and I don't want to be uncharitable."

"No, you just want to have a fellow priest condemned on

trumped-up charges!" I told him. "You don't know the meaning of the word *charity.*"

Sister Prudentia came to Father Sheehy's rescue by changing the subject. "The real reason for your dismissal, Father Faber, is that you are a poor teacher," she said. "Isn't that so, Sister Margaret Mary?"

"We have had many complaints," Sister Margaret Mary replied.

"Who complained?" I asked. Then I added: "I know you won't tell me. That would be *unethical,* wouldn't it?"

"It certainly would be," Sister Prudentia said. "We have an obligation to protect the confidences of our students."

"But apparently you are under no obligation to protect the human rights of a faculty member who has been slandered," I countered.

"I am going to have Sister Margaret Mary answer you," Sister Prudentia commented. "It is she who has the Ph.D. in history, and I am sure that she can tell you exactly where you went wrong."

"I have often discussed these matters with Father Faber," Sister Margaret Mary said, "and I do not think that any purpose will be served by going into them again."

I looked directly at Sister Margaret Mary. "Why don't you tell them where I went wrong, Sister?" I urged. "Tell them the *real* reason you don't want me in the department."

Sister Margaret Mary paled and averted her eyes. "I have nothing else to say," she stated.

From the expression on his face, I detected that Father Sheehy knew more about Sister Margaret Mary and the history department than I thought he did. "I think this matter should be dropped," he emphasized. "I'm sure that Father Faber realizes why he is being dismissed."

"I know the reasons," I said, "but they are not the reasons you have been giving me. Almost every responsible person in this entire college considers me a damn good teacher; and all of you know it. Let's have the real reasons."

Sister Prudentia grew red in the face. "I'll not listen to such

May 25, 1951

profanity!" she exclaimed. "Father, you should be ashamed of yourself."

"My God!" I sighed.

Sister Prudentia shook her head sadly. "I am afraid that we expected too much of you, Father," she said. "Our students come from the better families. Your background is quite different, and we should have realized that you would be unable to understand them. I suggest that you amend your ways, Father. I have the feeling that you are on your way to hell."

I got up from the chair. "If there are people like you three in heaven," I commented, "I'm sure that I'd be more comfortable in hell. But I have an idea that's not the case."

Although I could have said much more—especially in regard to Sister Margaret Mary—I left the office without doing so. I knew that nothing I might have said would have reversed the dismissal; and I saw no point in causing trouble for other people.

In a sense, I feel relieved. I never liked the idea of teaching, and I especially don't like snobs. I'll be happy to get out of Holy Spirit College and back into parochial work. These jobs with snob-appeal are not for me. I'll be glad to be working with some ordinary parishioners again.

PART EIGHT

June 7, 1951

The rumors which Father Sheehy had heard turned out to be correct. Today I received a letter from the chancellor, announcing that I am being appointed an assistant to Monsignor O'Shea at Sacred Heart Church. The appointment is to become effective on June 15.

I stopped by Sacred Heart this evening to see Monsignor O'Shea, who was friendlier than I had expected. He has not changed much since I attended Sacred Heart School as a boy. His huge stomach protrudes more, but his bearing is as arrogant as ever, and his voice just as gruff.

"You are young and inclined to be impetuous, Father," he said. "Bishop Connolly knows that you are inexperienced, and that is why he did not wish to penalize you for your mistakes." Monsignor smiled. "His Excellency has been sending me his problems of late. Father Calvin arrived a few months ago. Perhaps you know him."

When I told Monsignor that I had heard of Father Calvin but had never met him, he said: "When he was your age, he showed great promise. But then he made a retreat under some fanatical Jesuit from Canada—a rigorist—and nobody has been able to put up with him since. He's almost forty, and by that time, a man should have carved out his niche in the priesthood. Let Father Calvin's mistakes be a lesson to you. He is an example of what happens when priests think they know more than their bishops and pastors. Pride is at the root of it all."

"I have always heard that Father Calvin is a very humble man," I remarked.

It was evident that Monsignor did not appreciate my comment. "You heard wrong," he snapped. "He sometimes gives that impression, but that's because of his heretical ideas. He doesn't drink or smoke, and his shoes have holes in them because he usually walks instead of driving his car. But in the long run, I suppose it's just as well that he doesn't drive very much. He's so concerned about practicing poverty that his car is a pile of junk.

Some of his ideas on how to serve God are weird, to say the least. He kneels in church half the night praying."

"I fail to see the heresy, Monsignor," I said.

"Perhaps 'heresy' is too strong a word," Monsignor admitted. "It would probably be more correct to say that his ideas border on heresy. He doesn't think that we should count money and make public what the parishioners contribute. Somewhere or other, he got the crazy idea that a priest should not be a businessman. I don't know how he thinks a parish is supposed to function. He has another screwy idea that has been causing me a lot of trouble with our more patriotic parishioners. He doesn't think that Christians should fight in wars, and he has been advising young people to become conscientious objectors. His thinking is so simplistic that I suspect he's a mental case."

"He sounds like a very interesting person," I said.

Monsignor looked disappointed. "If I were you, Father, I wouldn't take up with him," he warned. "If you want a friend, get to know our other curate, Father Walsh. He's a priestly priest—a man worth emulating. By the time he reaches Father Calvin's age, he will be a monsignor. Some day—God willing!—he might even be a bishop. I'm sure you've heard of Father Walsh."

"I've read some of his articles in *The Catholic*," I said. "Hasn't he recently been made editor?"

"Just a few weeks ago," Monsignor beamed proudly. "I recommended it. Father Walsh is a very talented young man. I told him you were coming to Sacred Heart, and he promised to look after you."

When I did not comment, Monsignor changed the subject and offered me a drink.

June 15, 1951

This morning I met Father Walsh. He is a tall, thin, intense-looking man, with straight black hair and rimless spectacles. His voice is rather high-pitched, and there is something about the way he talks that reminds me of Sister Prudentia, the president of Holy Spirit College.

"Don't let Monsignor rattle you, Father," he told me. "He's

really a good Joe, and he'll give you every break he can. Just do your work. Whatever you do, don't disagree with him. He doesn't like that. He had a dreadful argument with Father Calvin this morning. But then Father Calvin is always causing trouble. He's such an oddball. He considers himself too good to have a cigarette or drink with his colleagues."

"I haven't met Father Calvin yet," I said. "Where is he now?"

"He's out visiting the hospital. He goes there every day. He could save time by taking his car, but he prefers to walk. Detachment from the luxuries of the world, you know. He is a disgrace to the priesthood, Father. His shoes have holes in them from walking so much. People have commented about it, but he doesn't bother to buy new ones."

"Yes, I know all that," I said. "Monsignor told me about it."

"I don't think you will see him at all today, Father. He's supposed to give the invocation at a banquet tonight, so he won't be here for supper. He will be instructing converts after that. Then he'll kneel in church half the night praying, as he always does."

"That's quite a schedule," I remarked.

"He's kept busy," Father Walsh admitted grudgingly, "but he doesn't do anything really important. He takes care of instructions, sick calls, confessions, census taking, and other routine matters. Monsignor doesn't trust him with important affairs. He usually assigns them to me. I had charge of the entire May Crowning last month. The theme was Mary in heaven, and the children of the parish portrayed the saints and angels. I had to see to it that appropriate costumes were provided for them. Then the altar boys got jealous because they thought the angels and saints were going to steal the show, so I had to place a quick order for some frilly surplices. The white, green, and red cassocks, *plus* the surplices, seemed to satisfy them. It was a lot of work, but worth it. Monsignor loved it."

"It must have been quite an affair."

"It was wonderful, Father. I love working with young people. Father Calvin gives our young people odd ideas, and then I have to spend my time straightening them out. I want to warn you about that, Father. Monsignor has placed me in charge of our young people, and if they have any problems, I am to take care of them. I hope I will have no trouble from you in that regard."

"I'll try to stay out of trouble, Father."

"Just so we understand each other from the beginning, Father."

Father Walsh looked at his wristwatch. "I still have a few minutes," he said. "I have an appointment with the doctor today."

"Have you been ill, Father?"

"I think I might have caught something. A few days ago, I was on a plane, and a Negro was sitting directly behind me. He was coughing. When I finally got to the airport, I bought a bottle of Listerine and used the whole thing gargling. But I don't think it helped. I've already had x-rays taken, and the doctor is going to give me a stomach examination this afternoon. You don't think he will stick his finger up my rectum, do you?"

"I have no idea what the doctor will do, Father."

"I heard that sometimes they do that. I hope he doesn't do it to me. I'd simply die! But I don't think he will, do you?"

"I hope not, Father."

"I don't think he will," Father Walsh repeated, apparently trying to reassure himself.

For a few moments, he seemed lost in thought, and then he said: "Do you know something, Father? I think you would look nice in a suit made by my tailor. You probably don't have much variety in your wardrobe."

"I don't need a suit," I told him.

"Don't worry about the cost!" he exclaimed. "People will be good to you if you are good to them. My car is a gift from a man in the parish. So far, I've been able to own a new one each year since I left the seminary. After all, we are professional people, Father, and we have to keep up. If we don't get a new car every year, we're not doing that. It's the same with clothing. Several very prominent women arrange to have suits and topcoats made for me. I'll tell you what I'm going to do for you, Father. Just yesterday a woman called my tailor and ordered another new suit for me. You can go to the tailor this time in my place. I don't think the woman would care. She doesn't even have to know about it."

"I really don't need a new suit, Father."

Father Walsh seemed very disappointed in me. He looked at his wristwatch again and said: "I have to run, Father. The doctor's appointment, you know. We'll talk again. All right? Think over what I said about the suit. It's yours if you want it."

Although I didn't tell him so, there was nothing to think over. I don't want the suit. When I read Father Walsh's articles in *The Catholic*, I always considered them superficial; and now I hold the same opinion of the man himself. I hope I'm not making a rash judgment, but I'm pretty sure that I'm not. Frankly, I don't think he has any idea what religion is all about. A new car every year! My God!

June 16, 1951

Something happened while I was hearing confessions this afternoon, which shows the harm that can be done by people who do not know how to instruct children properly. On the other hand, the incident presented me with an opportunity to help a child, and it is these opportunities which make all of the sacrifices involved in being a priest worthwhile.

A little girl was my last penitent of the afternoon. She confessed in a singsong voice, and I could tell that going to confession was still new to her. She confessed that she had missed her morning and evening prayers, that she had been disobedient to her parents, that she had gotten angry, and then she stopped without adding the customary ending to her confession. After waiting a few moments, I asked: "Are you finished?"

The little girl began to cry. "No, Father," she sobbed.

"Don't cry," I said gently. "You just take your time. If you can't think right away, I'll wait."

She continued to cry. "I touched myself," she sobbed, "and I'm going to hell."

"I'm sure you're not going to hell," I said.

"Sister said I would," the little girl cried. "Sister said the Devil would come and take me away and throw me in the fire."

"Now I'm sure that won't happen," I tried to assure her.

She kept crying, and everything I said was to no avail. Finally, I left my part of the confessional and opened the door which led to the penitent's section of the box. The little girl was still kneeling before the screen sobbing. I reached down and picked her up in my arms. I carried her through the church, into the vestibule. I sat down on the long bench in the vestibule, and placed her on my knee. I took out a handkerchief and wiped her eyes. "There," I said. "Everything's all right now."

But the little girl continued to cry. "I'm going to hell, and the Devil will get me with the pitchfork," she kept repeating.

"That just isn't true," I said. "You didn't do anything wrong, and you're not going to hell."

"Sister said so," the little girl sobbed.

"Now look," I said. "I'm a priest. Isn't that right?"

The little girl nodded her head.

"Priests are smarter than Sisters, aren't they?"

The little girl nodded again.

"Well then you should believe me when I tell you that you did nothing wrong. Isn't that right?"

"Yes, Father," she said, trying to stifle her sobs and catch her breath.

I wiped the little girl's face with my handkerchief again. "You will never go to hell," I said. "God loves you very much, and you will never go to hell. I want you to remember that. Always remember that the new priest told you that. Will you always remember?"

"Yes, Father," the little girl promised.

"Did you come to church all by yourself?" I asked.

"Yes, Father," she replied.

"Well you better go now. Your mother will be waiting for you."

I opened the big outer door of the church for her, and she tried to smile at me. "God bless you, honey," I called after her.

June 18, 1951

Although I had already spoken briefly with Father Calvin a number of times, this morning was the first time that we had an opportunity to talk at any length. I liked him when I first met him, and after our conversation today, I like him even more. He is a tall, handsome man, with a ready smile. The firm contour of his face shows that he is a man of prayer. In some ways, he reminds me of Monsignor Grosclaude.

"The Monday morning woes of an assistant!" he smiled when I entered the office this morning.

"How big is the weekly collection here?" I asked.

"Between three and four thousand dollars," he replied, "and it's mostly in pennies, nickels, dimes, and quarters. But we have to make sure that we record what everyone gives—even the children."

"I've heard that you're not very happy about the procedure," I said.

"How can I be?" he asked. "I believe there is more important work for a priest to do than count money. Priests neglect hungry, needy, and suffering souls all around them in order to devote most of their time to the dollar. And why? Like Monsignor, they want to be considered wise businessmen, join the right clubs, and mix with the other Babbitts of the city. Can you imagine Jesus being interested in such things?"

"You make us priests sound like materialists," I commented.

"That's exactly what most of us are."

"You just don't like to take care of the envelopes on Monday mornings," I smiled. "When Father Walsh finishes saying Mass, there will be three of us, and we'll be done in no time. You'll feel better then."

Father Calvin smiled back at me and said: "There will still be two of us, Father. Father Walsh never handles envelopes. In fact, you will discover that he doesn't do much of anything around here. Editing *The Catholic* takes up only a small part of his time, but Monsignor rarely asks him to do much else. I usually have to tabulate the collection alone, and because of all my other duties, I am seldom able to finish before Wednesday. Your predecessor, Father Boyle, helped occasionally. But he had a talent for raising money by putting on plays and operettas, and that's what Monsignor had him doing most of the time. I don't know what kind of talent you have, Father. Maybe you won't be helping very long either."

"I think you will discover that I'm not very talented," I smiled. "I understand that Father Walsh does a lot of work with the young people."

"He takes them swimming and to concerts, but he doesn't instruct them in religion," Father Calvin commented. "He forms sentimental attachments with the boys, bolsters his ego by exacting absolute obedience from them, and in general, indoctrinates them in everything that religion should not be."

"A great many priests do that," I remarked.

"Yet superiors rarely curtail the activities of priests like Father Walsh," Father Calvin observed. "Instead, they attempt to thwart the work of priests who desire to conform their lives to the gospel; who preach against worldliness and advise Christians to seek the kingdom of God. These priests are accused of wreaking havoc in the Church, and they are expected to keep silent about everything—from priests and sometimes even bishops who support mistresses on a lavish scale to those who live in dissipated luxury. Mentioning such matters is supposed to cause scandal. I think the scandal exists in doing these things rather than in discussing them."

"They say that you are something of a heretic," I smiled.

"They never come right out and make the charge," Father Calvin pointed out, "but they keep hinting at that possibility. Theologians have even done so in *The Ecclesiastical Review,* but they have never permitted me to answer my critics. They keep returning my letters and articles."

"I think they're afraid of you," I commented.

"That may well be," Father Calvin said, "but they're not being intellectually honest and fair. Tell me, Father, do you think that I am a heretic when I teach that the spiritual condition of Christians should be judged by their unworldliness of outlook, their deliberate simplicity of life in imitation of Jesus, their spirit of poverty and detachment, their spirit of mortification, their love of prayer, their readiness to serve their neighbor—especially the poor? Am I a heretic when I teach that it is wrong to plunder and slaughter one's brothers—including one's brothers in Christ—in meaningless and senseless wars? Am I a heretic when I condemn nationalism, which under the guise of patriotism, induces Christians to hate people who live in other countries?"

"I see no heresy in what you say," I answered, "but it does remind me very much of what a priest by the name of Arnold of Brescia said in the twelfth century. In the end, he was excommunicated by the Church and executed as a heretic."

"But there is one big difference," Father Calvin emphasized. "Despite my teachings—even my criticism of the clergy—I have never attacked the principle of authority, nor the right of superiors to command."

"In that, you remind me of Monsignor Grosclaude, my seminary rector and mentor," I told him.

"I consider Monsignor Grosclaude a kindred spirit," Father Calvin said. "But what do you believe, Father? Do you believe that Jesus was unafraid to condemn the rich and powerful? Do you believe that He was unafraid to denounce in vitriolic language the very leaders of the people? Do you believe that His love and goodness were chiefly for the poor and simple? Do you believe that He preached hatred of the world and riches, the danger of natural motives, and complete single-mindedness in the pursuit of goodness?"

"I do not know how anyone who has read the New Testament could believe anything else," I said.

"Exactly!" Father Calvin smiled. "You are an honest man, Father Faber."

June 27, 1951

There was a discussion at dinner this evening which seems to indicate that Monsignor O'Shea and Father Walsh are going to be on one side of most arguments, while Father Calvin and I are going to be on the other. It all began with an announcement by Father Walsh.

"I just wrote a special column for *The Catholic*," he said, "which deals with progress in the spiritual life."

"Oh did you now, Father?" Monsignor O'Shea asked benevolently. "I'll be looking forward to reading it."

"I wrote that a person can judge how well he is progressing in the spiritual life by the number of mortal sins he avoids," Father Walsh said. "I explained that a person is leading a saintly life when he not only avoids mortal sins and venial sins, but even faults and imperfections. I pointed out that the person who is really aiming for the heights of sanctity will even be careful about telling white lies. I showed that if a white lie is necessary, a person can avoid sin by devising a mental reservation or a circumlocution of some sort."

"It sounds like a fine article," Monsignor commented. "Why don't you ask Father Calvin and Father Faber for their opinion?"

"I'm always open to criticism," Father Walsh said with a show of magnanimity. "What do you think of it?"

"I don't see how anyone can begin to grow in the spiritual life by merely trying to avoid mortal or even venial sin," Father Calvin stated. "I believe that you have to start by eliminating worldly attachments, so that you can center all of your affection on God. Concentrating primarily on avoiding sin creates a mechanical Christianity, which when carefully analyzed, proves to be materialistic rather than spiritual."

"You have warped ideas on the spiritual life, Father Calvin," Monsignor observed sarcastically. "Because of your warped ideas, you are unable to perceive the soundness of what Father Walsh wrote."

"I think that Father Calvin is right," I said. "Avoiding white lies by using mental reservations or circumlocutions certainly does not help a person to grow spiritually. This is the very sort of external religion—of following the letter of the law rather than the spirit—which Christ condemned in the Pharisees."

"What you are saying is completely irrelevant, Father," Monsignor proclaimed dogmatically.

"I think it is quite relevant, Monsignor," I disagreed. "It shows that there is much more to religion than carrying out the perfunctory laws and forms which Father Walsh indicates are the essence of religion."

"You have a right to your opinion," Monsignor stated impatiently, "but you are wrong. I don't agree with you."

I knew that Father Calvin and I were right, but I decided to say no more. Father Walsh had an embarrassed look on his face. Besides, I thought it best to avoid Monsignor's ire by disagreeing with him further.

July 2, 1951

When we were tabulating the parish collection today, Father Calvin and I got to talking about the poor who live beyond the northern border of our parish. More than seventy percent of the people who live in that area are Negroes; and their plight is a sorry one, indeed. Not only are the houses infested with roaches and rats, but disease is rampant, and people are hungry much of the time.

We both knew that Monsignor would be against any plan to help, and Father Calvin felt that we would be unable to do anything really effective without his cooperation. It was then that I told him what I had been able to accomplish when I was an assistant at Saint Anne's. I explained how the parishioners themselves had taken charge of the program, and how they had opened their own homes to the poor and provided meals for shut-ins. Father Calvin thought that my plan was ingenious.

There was a hitch, though. Our parishioners did not live in the area where we wanted to help. I asked Father Calvin if he knew parishioners who would be willing to donate their time, money, or both. He said that he did. I then suggested that we rent a large building, where we would provide sleeping quarters for the homeless, a cafeteria for the hungry, and medical and legal aid for the indigent.

Father Calvin said that he knew a young Negro minister by the name of Reverend Haden, who would make a perfect director for the place. We decided that if we could persuade him to take charge, we would ask our parishioners to contribute their time and money directly to his efforts. He would organize and manage everything, while Father Calvin and I would merely serve as temporary advisers.

There was to be one stipulation, though. Everyone would be welcome regardless of religious beliefs or lack of them. There was to be no proselytizing of any kind; and none of the nonsense where an individual had to attend church services and pray before being permitted to eat.

"What will we call the place?" Father Calvin asked.

"How about Hospitality House?" I suggested.

Father Calvin liked the name.

September 20, 1951

Hospitality House will open its doors next week. We purchased the old Y.M.C.A. at the bargain price of a little over one hundred thousand dollars. People are really generous when they know that they are contributing to a good cause; and Father Calvin is an expert at convincing them. Maybe it's the holes in his shoes!

Five physicians and three lawyers have agreed to donate their time, two pharmacies in the area have promised to contribute free medical supplies, and there is going to be a nursery, which will provide care for the children of mothers who have to work. Father Calvin has even persuaded a number of stores to contribute food. Besides all that, we have been able to provide Reverend Haden with close to one hundred thousand dollars from the donations we have received. Part of that money will have to be used for further renovations to the building, but I still think we're off to a very good start.

It is something of a miracle that Father Calvin and I have been able to do most of this work on the one day off we get each week. We were laughing about it today. We feel like two secret agents. So far, neither Monsignor nor Father Walsh has discovered what we have been up to. It's surprising that somebody in the parish hasn't informed them yet; but maybe that's because we tell our helpers to always telephone Reverend Haden rather than the rectory. Anyway, God has been very good to us.

September 29, 1951

I suppose it had to happen eventually. Monsignor found out about Hospitality House. He didn't get his information from the parishioners, but through the newspapers. Hospitality House had its formal opening yesterday, and although Father Calvin and I were unable to attend because of our duties here, our names got into the papers.

October 1, 1951

Monsignor is furious. He said it was bad enough that we had opened the place, but he claimed we had committed a sin of sacrilege by placing a Protestant minister in charge. Moreover, the fact that we had purchased the old Y.M.C.A. building appalled him. He maintained that it had been used for heathen rites, and by purchasing it, we were propagating a false religion.

I kept telling him that Hospitality House was nonsectarian, but I'm afraid that just made him angrier. No explanation satisfied him. He continued to rant and rave that we had violated canon law and would ultimately be excommunicated from the Church.

He calmed down somewhat when Father Walsh assured him that Bishop Connolly would close the place immediately. But then Father Calvin pointed out that the bishop has no jurisdiction over Hospitality House, since it is controlled by a board of laymen, most of whom are Protestants. Now Monsignor's fury knew no bounds. When he could think of no other way to vent his anger, he rushed off to telephone the bishop.

Whatever Monsignor told the bishop must have been very effective. Within an hour after he had telephoned, both Father Calvin and I received calls from Father Malloy, the bishop's secretary. Father Malloy said that the bishop wants to see us early Monday morning.

October 1, 1951

Although Bishop Connolly shook my hand once or twice when I was in the seminary, and again when I was ordained to the priesthood, I met him formally for the first time today. Father Calvin, on the other hand, has known him for a long time. I rather like the man. He isn't corpulent—as are so many bishops—but ascetic in appearance. He is very animated in his movements and appears to be quite intelligent. It is obvious that he thinks much more than he speaks. He also seems to have a sense of humor. Throughout our conversation with him, he showed Father Calvin and me every consideration.

He made it clear, though, that he did not want anything like Hospitality House to happen again. "It is a commendable project," he told us, "but you are going to have every pastor in the diocese on my neck; and I can't have that. I want you to promise me that in the future you will undertake nothing like this without the authorization of Monsignor O'Shea."

We promised.

"Even though I don't agree with everything Monsignor O'Shea had to say on the subject," the bishop said, "I think he is quite right in being disturbed that you handed this project over to Reverend Haden. Since Catholics contributed most of the money, this should have been kept within the Church. Why did you handle it the way you did?"

"For two reasons," Father Calvin spoke up. "Reverend Haden understands the people of the area better than anyone I know; and we wanted to make certain that the project could continue after Monsignor O'Shea found out about it."

Bishop Connolly restrained a smile. "It was mostly the latter, though, wasn't it?"

We admitted that it was.

"Whose idea was it?" the bishop asked.

"I'll have to assume the responsibility," Father Calvin replied. "I have been in the priesthood much longer than Father Faber."

Bishop Connolly looked at me. "But it was really your idea, wasn't it, Father Faber?" he inquired. "You did something very similar when you were an assistant at Saint Anne's."

I glanced at Father Calvin. "I suppose you might call it a joint venture," I said, "although I did suggest the particular pattern we finally followed."

"Sometimes I think you are too clever for your own good, Father Faber," Bishop Connolly remarked. "Most people would say your schemes are crazy. The only trouble is they always work. No more scheming, Father!"

"All right, Bishop," I promised.

"And you, Father Calvin!" the bishop admonished. "I understand that because *The Ecclesiastical Review* will not publish your replies to your critics, your parents have set up a printing press in the basement of their home and have been circulating your letters and articles privately."

"That is true," Father Calvin admitted. "I don't think it is fair for theologians to insinuate that I am a heretic, and then not permit me to reply."

January 3, 1952

"I'm not the editor of *The Ecclesiastical Review*," the bishop said, "so I can't help what they do. But I am responsible for what you do, and I have been told that you are violating Canon 1385, 1, 2, by distributing these articles and letters without prior ecclesiastical permission. I realize that so far they have been sent only to other priests, but I must insist that you write to all of the priests who have received them, informing these priests that they are to return this material to you or dispose of it."

"Very well, Bishop," Father Calvin agreed, "but I am sure you are aware that my chief critics serve on the theological faculty of the Catholic University of America. I want you to know that I am willing to debate this matter with their entire theological faculty at any time and at any place."

"And you would win," the bishop said, "but I'm afraid that's not the point."

"If that's not the point, then I suppose that I'll just have to remain an obedient *heretic*," Father Calvin commented wryly.

This time the bishop managed a smile. "Poor Monsignor O'Shea," he lamented. "To be stuck with *both* of you! One would be enough. But please, Father Faber, don't suggest to Father Calvin that the two of you march around Sacred Heart Rectory with torches—as *you* marched around Juvenile Home—threatening to burn it down. I don't think Monsignor O'Shea could survive it."

When Father Calvin and I left the bishop's office, I had the feeling that Bishop Connolly's sympathies were with us. It was just a feeling, though. I can't be sure.

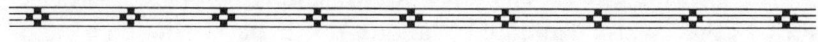

January 3, 1952

From all reports, Hospitality House is still doing very well. Father Calvin and I have not visited there since our discussion with the bishop, but we occasionally hear from Reverend Haden and others connected with the center. Monsignor now sees to it that Father Calvin and I are so busy that we would not have time to start a similar project—even if we had permission. We have to work on our day off, just to keep up. Father Walsh does practically nothing; nor does Monsignor. Father Calvin and I do all of the routine—and sometimes monotonous—work. But I don't mind. I still find the work preferable to teaching. Sometimes I can see that I'm actually helping people, and that is reward enough for me.

When things get too bad, I pray to Jesus in the Blessed Sacrament, and He puts me on my feet again. Father Calvin does the same thing. In fact, I often wonder if he gets any sleep at all. He sometimes spends the entire night praying before the Blessed Sacrament. I've already found him there at four or five o'clock in the morning, when I've made a visit to the church after returning from a sick call. He is certainly a man of prayer. Although I am younger than he is, I lack his stamina. I rarely get more than five or six hours of sleep at night, but I need at least four to keep functioning effectively. Father Calvin is lucky. I wish that I had his endurance.

May 5, 1952

It is always very difficult to discuss anything with Monsignor. If you do not agree with everything he has to say, you can't win. He becomes angry if you disagree with him, but he becomes angrier still if you refuse to comment on a controversial topic. I do think that I went too far today—perhaps I was even uncharitable—but I spoke the truth. This time, Monsignor's reaction was one of hurt. It just as easily could have been one of rage. I learned long ago that when you are dealing with Monsignor, you can always expect a reaction if you oppose him; but you can never be sure what form that reaction will take.

As always, the discussion started simply enough. "Isn't it sad," Father Walsh lamented, "about the little Catholic girl and that Jewish couple?"

"It is a tragedy," Monsignor remarked as he shook his head sadly. "I hope the Good Lord will enlighten the judges, so that they will give the dear little girl back to her mother. We should all pray for that decision."

"I am inclined to think the little girl is much better off where she is," I said. "She was adopted by the Jewish couple three years ago, right after she was born. Now her mother decides—or most likely, some unthinking priest decided for her—that the child should be brought up in a Catholic orphanage. The Jewish couple have even offered to rear the child as a Catholic, if only they can keep her. In so far as justice is concerned, everything is in their favor."

Monsignor O'Shea looked cunningly in the direction of Father Calvin. "And tell me now, Father Calvin, what do you think?" he asked. "Do you think that the little girl should be raised as a Catholic or as a Jew?"

"According to canon law," Father Calvin replied, "the child should be brought up as a Catholic. If the Jewish foster parents agree to that, I think it is in the child's best interests to remain with them."

"At least you take canon law into consideration," Monsignor commented sarcastically, "but I cannot say the same for Father Faber."

"I mentioned that they had offered to rear the child as a Catholic," I said. "I think that is taking canon law into consideration."

"But you did not emphasize the point, as Father Calvin did," Monsignor maintained. "Even so, you are both wrong in believing that the child, under *any* circumstances, should be brought up by Jews. The interests of the child will be protected best by the good nuns in a Catholic orphanage. The Jews should never have her!"

"I believe that you are too racially prejudiced, Monsignor, to see where justice really does lie in this case," I told him.

"At least I know how to address people who are my *superiors*," he retorted. "You haven't learned that yet."

Then, without another word, he stalked out of the room.

June 11, 1952

Every so often I have a really bizarre day here at Sacred Heart. Today was one of those days. A sailor, who is home on leave, was sent to the rectory by his mother, in the hope that one of the priests could reconcile him to the Church. He has not been attending Mass, and the problem seems to be that he is a very active homosexual. His mother knows about his homosexuality, and she apparently believes that religion can rid him of this condition.

As I was sitting in the office with him, trying to pinpoint his problem, he suddenly said to me: "I'm in love with you." I did my best to maintain my composure, but before I knew it, he was actually making physical advances. He is only about nineteen years old, and I didn't want to hit him, so I kept circling the desk, with him in pursuit. Fortunately, Father Calvin came into the office to pick up some papers, and that gave me an opportunity to extricate myself from the situation. I introduced the sailor to Father Calvin, and then told Father Calvin that he was just leaving. I offered to accompany him to the door.

When we reached the door, I had no idea what to say, so I told the sailor to attend my Mass tomorrow morning. I said that when he saw me in my vestments, he would think of me in an entirely different way. I had my doubts, though, since I was wearing my cassock when the foolishness began. He looked rather disappointed and commented that he would not have the time. It's just as well. I don't want him chasing me around the altar.

This is the first time I have had such an experience at Sacred Heart. There have been several women, but I find it easier to cope with them. I usually pretend that I do not understand what they have in mind, and so far, they have not tried too hard to enlighten me. Physicians have told me they have the same problem, so I guess it is one of the hazards involved in dealing with people on a very personal level. I always pray for such people. That's about all I can do.

June 27, 1952

I have seldom seen Monsignor O'Shea angrier than he was today. But this time he was angry at Father Phillips, an assistant chancellor of the diocese, rather than at any of us. A very prominent lawyer of the parish is scheduled to be married tomorrow, and since the marriage is to be a mixed marriage, forms had to be filled out and sent to the chancery. Because Monsignor considers the bridegroom so important, he handled the case personally.

This morning, however, a letter arrived in the mail from Father Phillips, along with the forms Monsignor had submitted. Father Phillips told Monsignor that the marriage could not proceed until new forms were on file at the chancery. He said that the parish stamp had not gone the entire way through the papers which Monsignor had sent him, and that made them invalid. Monsignor telephoned Father Phillips and offered to bring him new forms on Monday. Meanwhile, he requested permission to go ahead with the wedding tomorrow, as scheduled. Father Phillips refused, and Monsignor went into a rage.

After pacing the floor and damning Father Phillips for almost an hour, Monsignor finally made a special trip to the chancery and delivered the new forms personally. Then he immediately went to see the bishop, to protest his treatment at the hands of Father Phillips. I hope that Monsignor's action does some good. Most priests are treated with anything but kindness at the chancery; and when they dare to treat Monsignor the way they did today, one can easily imagine how they treat the ordinary curate.

I had a problem with Father Phillips myself a few weeks ago. I was certain that a particular marriage case would go through, so I put a specific date for the wedding on the forms. Father Phillips actually called me in and screamed at me. "What nerve, Father!" he yelled. "You have absolutely no respect for us. If you ever show such arrogance again, I shall inform the bishop."

I'm afraid that many lawyers are still pretty much like those Jesus criticized in the Bible—even though they happen to be canon lawyers, as is Father Phillips. They are all wrapped up in the letter of the law rather than the spirit.

February 10, 1953

This evening a woman came to me for advice. She has been married for nine years to a man she despises. From what she tells me, the marriage has been a nightmare. Her husband is apparently a sadist, who in addition to running around with other women, brutally beats her and their four children. On one occasion, he broke her jaw. On another, he brought a girl friend home to stay with him for several weeks; all the while forcing his wife to wait on both of them. When she complained, he locked her in a room for two days, refusing her food and water. Three times during their marriage, she contracted a venereal disease from him.

I carefully explained the laws of the Church to the woman, and I suggested a separation. Then she told me that she had an opportunity to marry someone else—a friend of her brother. When I raised an eyebrow, she quickly explained: "It's not what you think, Father. We have never even been alone together. He is just a good man who wants to help me. He has never been married before, has a good job, and would be a wonderful father to the children. If I don't take this opportunity to marry him, how am I going to support the children? I have very little education, and my husband is such a bum that once we're separated, I can expect nothing from him. He'll probably escape to another state—or even out of the country—just so he won't have to pay me anything."

"Is the man you're thinking of marrying a Catholic?" I asked her.

"Yes he is, Father."

"How would he feel about marrying you outside the Church?"

"It would bother him very much, Father, but he told me that he loves me enough to do it. He says that we could always get married in church if something happened to my husband."

"How do you feel about it?"

"I know that I would be living in sin," the woman replied dejectedly, "and it would worry me every day of my life. But what can I do?"

I looked into the woman's eyes, and I saw that she had suffered very much. "That is the official teaching of the Church," I told her, "but not everyone agrees with it. In the Gospel of Saint Matthew, Jesus says that 'whoever puts away his wife, *except for immorality*, and marries another, commits adultery.' The Church interprets this passage as meaning that if your spouse commits immorality, you have the right to a separation. In the past, however, certain local synods of the Catholic Church, on the basis of this text, have admitted adultery as a cause for divorce and remarriage. Schismatic Oriental churches have done the same, as have Protestant churches. Moreover, the Old Testament of the

Bible permits divorce. So you see, the whole thing is not so absolute as you might have thought."

"You do approve of divorce then, Father?" the woman asked hopefully.

"That's not what I'm saying," I told her. "What I am saying is that this is an exceptional case, and you must follow your own conscience. I do believe, though, that if you divorced and remarried, God might take a different view of the situation than would be taken by certain other people. God, after all, knows what is in your heart; and He is the ultimate judge.... I don't know whether I have helped you or not."

"You have, Father, and I can't tell you how grateful I am."

"Just try to work out a happy life for yourself and everybody else involved in your decision. That will be gratitude enough. May God bless you!"

August 18, 1953

When the newspaper arrived today, Monsignor O'Shea, Father Walsh, and I got into an argument over the name for a new bridge that the city is going to build. As Father Walsh scanned the newspaper, he remarked that because of Catholic protests, the bridge might not be named the Whitman Bridge after all. City Council was studying the possibility of naming it the Kilmer Bridge instead.

"I am glad they are using common sense," Monsignor said. "I protested to the mayor myself about the name they intended to give the bridge. Joyce Kilmer was not only a good Catholic, but he was a great patriot who lost his life in war. If he had written only *Trees*, that one poem would have made him America's greatest poet. Why shouldn't the bridge be named after him?"

"I can think of some very good reasons," I spoke up. "Every authority on poetry agrees that Walt Whitman was an infinitely better poet than Joyce Kilmer. A man does not become a great poet simply because he happens to be a patriot who died in war."

"That is beside the point," Father Walsh commented. "We all know that Whitman's writings are filthy and immoral; and that's all we need to know."

"Have you ever read *Leaves of Grass?*" I asked him.

"I wouldn't have such a filthy book in my possession," he replied, "and being a *censor librorum* for this diocese, I see many books."

"There is nothing filthy about *Leaves of Grass*," I maintained. Then I asked: "Do you keep a copy of the Bible in your possession, Father?"

Monsignor O'Shea's face grew red. "There is good reason for what's in the Bible," he stated in a shaky voice. "The authors of Sacred Scripture were just being realistic. But there is no excuse for Whitman. He was a grossly immoral man—even a pervert."

"The evidence for any such assumption is far from conclusive," I protested. "But even if it were so, that would not detract from his stature as a poet."

"He should have been taken out and shot before he had a chance to write all that filth," Monsignor snarled.

Even coming from someone like Monsignor, that statement stunned me. I decided that it was useless to say anything else.

January 4, 1954

There was quite a bit of excitement at the rectory this afternoon. It all started when a man appeared at the door and asked to see a priest. Mrs. Guzowsky, our housekeeper, escorted him into the office and rang for me.

I noticed when I entered the room that the man was quite agitated. At first, I thought he had been drinking. But when I could detect no intoxicant on his breath, I tried to get him to calm down and have a seat. He finally sat down, but he continued to talk very rapidly.

"I'm going crazy, Father," he said in an excited voice. "I want to rape every woman I see on the street. My wife and kids sit home while I go out with other women."

"Why have you been going with other women?" I asked him.

"That's how I know something's wrong with me, Father. My wife doesn't satisfy me."

January 4, 1954

"Why doesn't she satisfy you?"

"I like to beat naked women with wet towels."

"Where do you find women who will let you do that?"

"They are prostitutes, Father. I pay them extra for it."

"Does your wife know about this?"

"No, Father."

"Have you ever thought of seeing a doctor about your problem?"

"I know there's something wrong with me, but I don't know who to see."

"You need a psychiatrist to help you," I said. "I'll write down the name, address, and telephone number of a very good one."

"I can't afford to pay much money."

"That's all right. I'll talk to the doctor, and he won't charge you any more than you can afford."

The man got up to leave, and that's when the real surprise came. As he neared the door of the office, he suddenly whipped out a knife. Before I could get it away from him, he had slashed his wrists.

I called to the housekeeper to get some towels, and when she brought them, I told her to call the police and summon an ambulance. The man was bleeding profusely, and I did my best to control it. But once I had applied the towels to his wrists, he got away from me and ran out the front door of the rectory. Even though he was losing blood, he could really run. I know, because I ran after him. He had gone four blocks before I finally caught him.

Not only was it extremely cold outside, but neither of us had a coat. I tried to get the man inside a nearby store. That's when he fainted. I asked the proprietor of the store to call for the police and an ambulance again. While I waited, I kept trying to stop the bleeding; but I didn't have much luck.

When the police arrived, they took over. They strapped the man to a stretcher, placed him in the ambulance, and headed for the psychiatric hospital.

Poor guy! I've been praying for him. I just hope that he recovers from his wounds, and that they can do something about his mental condition. I intend to visit him at the hospital tomorrow. I'm also looking into what I can do for his wife and children.

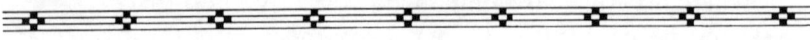

September 1, 1955

Monsignor O'Shea, Father Calvin, and I were sitting in the parlor this evening when Father Walsh hurried into the room, carrying a newspaper with him. "I have a copy of *The Catholic* here with me, Monsignor," he said, "and there is something in it which may be of interest to you. The paper won't be out officially for two more days, but the advantage of being the editor is that I am able to get a copy before anyone else does." Father Walsh smiled as he quickly unfolded the newspaper. "Your picture is on the front page, Monsignor."

"Oh is it now?" Monsignor responded benevolently.

"It tells all about the pope making you a prothonotary apostolic," Father Walsh related. "Just listen to these headlines: POPE ELEVATES MONSIGNOR PATRICK K. O'SHEA TO PROTHONOTARY APOSTOLIC. WITH THE EXCEPTION OF THE BISHOPS, MONSIGNOR O'SHEA WILL OUTRANK ALL THE CLERGY OF THE DIOCESE."

"It is really nothing," Monsignor said in a voice filled with emotion. "I am surprised they even put it in the paper."

"As soon as I heard about it," Father Walsh said, "I wrote the articles myself."

"It was very thoughtful of you, Father," Monsignor commented, now fairly beaming.

"Let me read you a paragraph or two from one of the articles," Father Walsh offered. " 'His Holiness, Our Holy Father the Pope, has bestowed on the Right Reverend Monsignor Patrick K. O'Shea, vicar-general of our diocese, the singular honor of prothonotary apostolic. Monsignor O'Shea's prelatial garb will now include violet-colored hose, cassock with fastened train, a violet silk belt with double pendant on the left side, a mantelletta over a rochet, a black biretta with a red tuft, red buttons and trimming on the cassock, and the same colored trimming on the mantelletta. Monsignor O'Shea will have the privilege of offering Solemn Pontifical Mass. While pontificating, Monsignor will be permitted to wear a pectoral cross with a red silk cord. He may also wear a mitre of plain silk or gold cloth. He may wear gloves and a ring set with a precious stone.' The article also mentions the schools at which you studied, Monsignor, and the high positions you have held in the diocese and community."

"It is a fine article," Monsignor commented, his voice still choked with emotion.

"After you are invested with the robes of your office, *The Catholic* is going to run a three-quarter-page picture of you in your new prelatial garb."

"I really don't deserve it, Father, but it is very thoughtful of you to see to all of this," Monsignor said.

"Have you made any plans for the investiture yet, Monsignor?" Father Walsh asked.

"It will be at eleven o'clock on the last Sunday of this month," Monsignor replied. "His Excellency, Bishop William J. Connolly, will invest me—of course. The two auxiliary bishops will also be present. I expect about sixty monsignori and over one hundred priests to attend. The chancellor, Monsignor Hogan, will read the apostolic brief. Following the investiture, I shall offer my First Solemn Pontifical Mass, with Bishop Connolly presiding at the throne. There are still a million and one details to be worked out. Incidentally, Father Walsh, I would like you to serve as deacon at the Pontifical Mass."

"It will be the greatest honor I have ever experienced, Monsignor," Father Walsh gushed. "Thank you very much for being kind enough to think of me."

"You are very welcome, Father," Monsignor smiled.

Although Father Calvin and I offered our congratulations, I knew exactly what Father Calvin was thinking. Monsignor was bad enough before. I hate to think what he is going to be like when he is parading around in a mitre, pectoral cross, ring, and all the rest.

Father Walsh lent me his copy of *The Catholic*, and I copied his description of Monsignor's new outfit from that. It is so complicated that I never would have remembered the details. I pity the poor seamstress who is going to have to put it all together.

December 18, 1955

Today a middle-aged man sought my advice. He looked very sad and troubled, and he finally got around to telling me about his real problem—homosexuality. He told me that he began the practice when he was about six years old. He said that he had been forced to perform the act by some older boys in his neighborhood. After the initial occurrence, they beat him severely if he refused them. This went on throughout his early years, and by the time he reached adolescence, he enjoyed such acts and was quite willing to engage in them. Consequently, he went on accommodating the boys during his high school years.

I asked him if he ever dated girls, and his reply was negative. It was also negative when I asked him whether he was attracted to women sexually. He told me that he had undergone psychiatric treatment for a long period of time, but the psychiatrist had finally given up on him. He added that he had tried going to Mass and Communion every day—as a priest had suggested—but that did not solve the problem either. He said that he still went to Mass each day, but he could no longer stay pure long enough to go to Communion.

He told me that he has been living with another man—a man somewhat younger—for about three years now. He was quite appalled when I asked him whether he was inclined to engage in such acts with children. He assured me that he had no such inclination. He added that if he were even so much as tempted in that direction, he would commit suicide. I believe him.

Finally, I told him: "Since you are apparently not harming anyone else, and since this is something over which you don't have much control, I can't see where you are committing any sin. I think you should try to get rid of your guilt and operate on the assumption that your acts are in no way sinful. I do not think that you should even mention this matter in confession, and I see no reason why you should not go to daily Communion. We are both aware of the Church's official position on this matter. But

April 26, 1956

throughout the New Testament, under particular circumstances, Christ made exceptions to certain laws. I think the circumstances in your case warrant an exception."

When I finished, the man had tears in his eyes. He told me that he had felt guilty and inferior throughout his life, and no other priest had ever spoken to him the way I did.

I went on to tell him that I considered him an excellent Christian, and I added that because of his suffering and his special sensitivity, he was quite capable of becoming a saint. I pointed out that all of us have at least one cross to bear in this life, and I told him that by imploring God's help in prayer, I was certain he would be able to bear the one society had imposed upon him.

I pray to God that I was of some help to him. If anyone ever deserved a little peace of mind, he does.

April 26, 1956

While Father Calvin and I instruct most converts, every so often someone with wealth or social position comes along, and Monsignor makes it a point to instruct such individuals himself. Monsignor instructs these people in his luxurious study. The drab, general office and two small alcoves are used for instructing those whom Monsignor does not consider especially important.

Tonight, Monsignor was busy instructing a Dr. Harris. After Dr. Harris had gone, I noticed that Monsignor seemed none too happy. Finally, he said to me: "Dr. Harris is engaged to Kathleen Daley. Attorney J. P. Daley is her father—and I might add—one of our best contributors. Dr. Harris is a non-Catholic, and I promised J.P. that I would bring him into the Church. But he is stubborn, and I haven't had much luck with him. Now I don't know what to do. If I follow custom, I have to marry them in the office where most of the mixed marriages are performed. But J.P. wants a big wedding for his daughter. I could make an exception and perform the marriage in my study. But since I already told J.P. that I thought I could convert Dr. Harris, I don't know what he'll think."

"You have quite a problem there, Monsignor," I commented,

trying my best through tone and facial expression to match the seriousness with which Monsignor viewed the predicament.

"I was thinking that maybe you could talk to him, Father. I've tried everything else. He's a proud man—too proud I fear to recognize the error of his ways and enter the true Church. He's arrogant, Father—extremely arrogant. I never should have taken him into my private study for instruction. That's where I think I made my mistake. If you are too informal with the laity, they become bold, Father. Bold, I tell you!" Monsignor paused here for emphasis before continuing. "I told Dr. Harris that you are a former college professor, and I think that impressed him. He said that he is willing to talk to you. I suggested that he stop by again tomorrow night. You know how it is, Father. We have to do the best we can for J.P."

"I am supposed to lead the rosary for Mrs. Hagerty tomorrow night," I said. "Her funeral is the day after tomorrow."

"Mrs. Hagerty isn't important now, Father—God rest her soul. It's the living we must think about. A member of her family can lead the rosary. I need you here." There was a note of desperation in Monsignor's voice. "This is our last chance, Father. I had Father Walsh speak to him last week, and do you know what he had the nerve to tell Father Walsh? He said that Father Walsh didn't know a thing about religion, and he doubted that he knew much of anything else either. Imagine him telling Father Walsh that—Father Walsh, a *censor librorum* for this diocese!"

"Poor Father Walsh," I commented.

"There's more, Father!" At this point, Monsignor's face grew livid. "He had the colossal nerve to tell me that I don't know any more than Father Walsh. Imagine him talking to me like that—me, the vicar-general of this diocese and next to the bishops themselves! I wouldn't put up with it, Father, if it weren't for my friend Daley. I would throw him right out into the street—doctor or no doctor."

"I don't know what I can do if he won't listen, Monsignor."

"Oh, he'll listen all right," Monsignor declared ruefully. "That's what's so exasperating about it all. He says that his mind is open, Father, but it's closed. I would have converted him long ago if he really had an open mind. I told him that, Father, and do you know what he told me? He said that if I had an open mind, he would have converted me long ago. Imagine that, Father! He would have converted me!"

I had to restrain a smile at the retort of the doctor. He sounded like anything but a dull fellow. I decided to have a talk with him. "I'll ask my friend, Father McHugh, to lead the rosary for Mrs. Hagerty," I told Monsignor, "and I'll do what I can for Dr. Harris."

Monsignor was very pleased.

April 27, 1956

Dr. Harris is a tall, dark, thin man. He arrived punctually at eight o'clock, just as Monsignor said he would. When we first began to talk, I detected that he considered his own profession vastly superior to that of a clergyman. He based much of his hostility to Catholicism in particular, and religion in general, on Christianity's historical opposition to science. He mentioned the Church's persecution of Bruno, Galileo, Bacon, and Vesalius.

I pointed out that churchmen originally opposed science because they believed that religion was under attack—an assumption which was often enough true. I also emphasized that the Church had changed its attitude in such matters.

This did not satisfy Dr. Harris. "I do not want to go back to the way medicine was practiced during the Middle Ages," he said. "In order to get rid of the imaginary devils which were thought to cause illnesses, patients were persuaded to consume feces, urine, body lice, the blood of rats, and pieces of paper with prayers written on them."

"I probably know more about the history of the Middle Ages than you do, Dr. Harris," I remarked.

"But you don't know anything about science," Dr. Harris countered. "You clergymen accept with relish the products of the very science you so often condemn; but you have not kept pace with the changing philosophies which the discoveries of science demand. You are savages riding in automobiles."

"Maybe I know a little bit about the history of science, too,"

I smiled. "I know, for example, that modern medical science is far from perfect—even though most doctors no longer believe that devils cause disease. In 1860, a famous physician by the name of Oliver Wendell Holmes said that except for a few good drugs—which, by the way, people other than physicians discovered—the whole of *materia medica* should be sunk to the bottom of the sea. He said that such a course of action would be all to the good for mankind, but much to the detriment of the fish."

"That was a long time ago," Dr. Harris commented.

"And the Middle Ages occurred hundreds of years before that," I reminded him. "Granted, there have been some improvements in medical science since the time of Holmes, but his statement still bears much validity today. A few months ago, a woman of this parish died after suffering for a year from aplastic anemia. Do you know how she contracted the disease? She had an ordinary cold, and some stupid doctor gave her an injection of chloramphenicol. You know as well as I do, Doctor, that similar and even worse incidents occur daily in the practice of modern medicine. If the woman had lived during the Middle Ages and been given a slug of urine for her cold, she most likely would have survived. It was modern medical science that killed her."

"You aren't being fair," Dr. Harris contended. "You aren't giving us credit for the really spectacular successes we achieve."

"I must admit that I'm not overawed by medical 'successes,' " I said. "Clergymen are officiating at funerals all the time. When one considers that almost ninety percent of your patients would get better whether they saw a doctor or not, and that you really help only a very small percentage of the other ten percent, your 'successes' are not all that spectacular."

I noticed that Dr. Harris was beginning to shift from an offensive to a defensive position. "Scientists are human," he stated rather lamely, "and they naturally make mistakes. But unlike the clergy, they don't go around persecuting people who disagree with them."

"Oh but they do!" I emphasized. "Physicians themselves opposed the most important advances of modern medicine. They persecuted men like Semmelweis, Pasteur, and Lister. The very same thing is going on in medicine right now. Unfortunately, human nature is such that professional people—like most other people—aren't especially anxious to embrace the truth."

"Although I cannot deny what you say," Dr. Harris conceded reluctantly, "that does not excuse your Church for opposing such obviously proper procedures as birth control, sterilization of the mentally defective, and therapeutic abortion."

"The Catholic Church's attitude is not so illogical—or uncivilized—as might appear at first glance," I pointed out, "provided that one accepts the point of view that God is still alive in the world, and that Divine Providence does intervene in the affairs of men. There is much wisdom in Catholicism, and I might add that the Church has had more experience in dealing with men than modern science has had."

"I still think the Church is being cruel and barbaric when it prevents people from receiving the best that modern medicine has to offer," Dr. Harris maintained.

"It all depends on whether or not what you have to offer really is *best*," I countered. "When it comes to birth control, sterilization, and abortion, the Church disagrees with you. . . . But tell me, Doctor, isn't it cruel and barbaric for the medical profession to hinder people—especially the poor—from receiving the *best* medical care? Because of greed, your profession has deliberately refused to train an adequate supply of physicians to take care of the population. Moreover, every day it permits people to die simply because they cannot afford to pay the fees you doctors demand for saving their lives. When it comes to science, it seems to me that you guys understand the science of the dollar better than you understand anything else."

"It's not fair to indict all physicians this way," Dr. Harris protested.

"I'm sure it isn't," I agreed, "and it's not fair to indict all clergymen the way you do either. We have as much education as you have, and yet we work for room and board, plus a few hundred dollars per year. Why do you think we do it? I do it because I can help people who cannot be helped in any other way."

"I think we're starting to get away from the topic of science," Dr. Harris pointed out.

"All right, let's return to it for a moment," I said. "If any age was ever the age of science, the twentieth century is; yet I doubt that there has ever been another century in which mankind has been forced to endure so much cruelty and barbarism. There have been constant wars over the material goods which science has helped produce, and in these wars, the most horrible weapons in history have been used—weapons which might conceivably destroy all life on earth; weapons developed by the very science you extol. While some segments of the world have benefited from modern technology—or so it seems, during this brief moment in history—the larger portion of the world has been the victim of these very benefits and suffers to a greater degree than ever before."

"I am beginning to think that you do know something about science," Dr. Harris smiled.

"I haven't even touched on the matter of technology destroying the balance of nature and progressively poisoning the entire earth," I smiled back at him. "The problem is that scientists have not assumed a humane responsibility for their discoveries and creations. They have too often moved ahead recklessly, without due regard for the effect their limited, immediate knowledge would have on the earth and its creatures. . . . So you see, Doctor, not only do savages wearing Roman collars ride in automobiles, but I suspect that there are other savages who ride with microscopes or volumes of statistics on the seat beside them; and perhaps even one or two with a stethoscope."

Dr. Harris smiled again. "I never meant to imply that *everyone* who wears a Roman collar is a savage," he said. "I have met a number of highly civilized clergymen. I think you might be one of them."

"But you do not want to become a Catholic."

"How can I? I don't believe in your religion."

"Do you believe in God?" I asked.

"No, I don't," Dr. Harris replied.

"So here we are," I smiled sadly.

"When are you going to try to convert me?" Dr. Harris asked.

August 11, 1956

"When are you going to tell me that I am proud, vain, and stupid? That was the pronouncement of your colleagues."

"No wonder you have a chip on your shoulder," I said. "I'm sorry about my colleagues. I guess I can't always help what they do any more than you can help what yours do. But I am not going to attempt to convert you. I just wanted to know what you believe. I could present arguments which would attempt to refute what you believe, but from talking to you, I do not think that you would accept them."

Dr. Harris looked puzzled and said nothing for a time. "Can't you advise me, Father?" he finally asked.

"I can if you want me to."

"Please do, Father."

"I can only advise you to love," I said. "Genuine love is such a rarity that it is sometimes worth the sacrifices necessary to bring it into reality. If you love Kathleen Daley enough, perhaps that love will enable you to share her faith. Scientific and philosophic truths are very important, but there is another kind of truth which is perhaps even more important; and that is the truth which pours forth from the human heart."

"You are an unusual man, Father," Dr. Harris told me. "Whatever my decision is, I want you to know that you did make a convert tonight."

And I believe I did. I have the feeling that Dr. Harris will become a Catholic. Before he left, there was something in his eyes which told me that. Monsignor Grosclaude once remarked that I could convert almost anybody to anything. This is quite unintentional on my part, but if true, it is a terrible responsibility. I often pray that when I do influence somebody, it is for his or her own good. As I knelt before the Blessed Sacrament tonight, that was once again my prayer.

August 11, 1956

It looks as though I'm in the doghouse again. When I finished saying Mass this morning, I found Monsignor waiting in the sacristy for me. "Why did you return the two-hundred-dollar check Attorney Daley sent to you?" he asked. "He called me last night and told me about it. You were very impolite, you know. A priest should have more polished manners."

"I did not do what I did either for money or for Attorney Daley," I said.

"But you did bring Dr. Harris into the Church," Monsignor countered, "and Attorney Daley only wanted to show you how happy he is. Refusing his gift set a dangerous precedent. He might get the idea that we are not in need of money here, or he might come to feel that it is improper to give gifts for the type of service you rendered. That is why I accepted the check he sent me and wrote him a note of gratitude. I think you could do that much, Father. You could send him a note and explain that you did not accept the money because you thought he might have need of it himself."

"I can't do that, Monsignor," I said. "I intended to do him no favor by instructing Dr. Harris, and I am not grateful for any money he sends me. In fact, I consider it something of an insult."

"An insult!" Monsignor grumbled.

"Yes, an insult, Monsignor," I declared. "It is as though things of the spirit can be obtained the same way he acquires everything else—with money."

"There is something else, Father," Monsignor said. "You did very good work in Dr. Harris's case, but then you turned right around and ruined everything in Mr. Wilson's case. He told me you embarrassed him by asking questions he couldn't answer. I might never be able to get him on his feet again."

"I think it is better for most people when he is off his feet," I remarked.

"Mr. Wilson is a very important man," Monsignor emphasized, "and we'll be fortunate if he joins the Church and becomes a member of this parish. But what do you do? You treat him as though he were some nobody. His friend happens to be Mr. Gallagher, the mortician, who is also upset about this matter. As you know, Father, Mr. Gallagher is one of our best contributors and a very influential man in the community."

"I don't care what Mr. Gallagher and Mr. Wilson are in the community, or how much money they have," I said. "I'm concerned with what they have spiritually, and from what I have seen, they don't have very much. I think they will require many more jolts—much more severe than the ones I tried to give them—before they even begin to learn the most elementary lesson of Christianity; namely, what constitutes a truly human being."

"Do you realize, Father, that the best members of this parish are moving away because of the Negro menace?" Monsignor asked angrily. "Do you realize that they are selling their beautiful homes to Negroes and that this will soon be a slum area? I have appealed to the city to stop these Negroes from moving in, but so far nothing has been done. Do you realize that Attorney Daley, Mr. Gallagher, and Mr. Wilson promised to help me prevent this black plague? Do you realize, Father, that our collection goes down every Sunday, and that soon we may be in desperate need of money? And yet you—you, Father, a simple curate—have the nerve to insult our best contributors. I won't stand for it, Father; I won't stand for it. Mark my words well! I won't stand for it!"

"Aside from the spiritual aspect of preaching the gospel to every creature—as Christ commanded us to do," I said, "it would be eminently realistic and practical to welcome the Negro. They are here to stay, and if we don't start to do something about winning them to the Catholic Church and to our parish, we'll soon be preaching to ourselves in an empty church."

"It is bad enough that they are in the neighborhood," Monsignor retorted angrily, "but they are not getting into this church while I am pastor here. If I have to preach before empty pews, I'll preach before empty pews. They'll never get in! Not as long as I'm pastor of Sacred Heart."

"I think you are being very unreasonable, Monsignor," I commented.

"Unreasonable! Unreasonable!" Monsignor complained indignantly. "I'll show you how *unreasonable* I am. Since we have not been taking in the money we should each Sunday, I have to find some other way of getting the money we need. Our diocesan assessment falls due in November. Therefore, Father Faber, I expect you to use your great reasoning ability and take charge of the carnival we are going to have in the last week of October. The spring carnival was not enough. We need a fall one, too. And if we need a winter one, we'll have a winter one! I hope you understand me. This should bring you down to earth and keep you from your dreaming for a while."

Although I could have brained him for his prejudice and stupidity, I made no reply.

November 4, 1956
Although I was heartbroken, I was not surprised when I heard today that Russian troops and tanks had made an end to Hungary's brief breath of freedom. I feel that the problem is not one of Communism, but of Russia—a larger and stronger nation—insisting that it continue to control a particular part of the world. It seems almost axiomatic that more powerful nations will always react in this manner.

For all of their criticism of Russian intervention, France, England, and the United States behave in similar fashion when what they have determined to be their spheres of influence are threatened. This situation is so sad and disappointing for those who still hope that people everywhere can live in freedom and peace. Naturally, national greed is at the root of it all; and like a cancer, it spreads to consume the vitals of all nations—eventually destroying even the predators themselves.

My prayers are with Cardinal Mindszenty, who has had to take refuge in the United States Embassy. Most of his years as a bishop have been spent in one kind of prison or another. First, he was imprisoned by Nazism, then by Communism; and I rather feel that if there had been any other kind of "ism" about, he would have been imprisoned by that also. In any system of government, the "crimes" of the Mindszentys are always the same. They demand freedom for themselves, for their people, and for their Church. May God be with him in this tragic hour!

March 2, 1957
There are times when it is especially difficult to be a priest; and for me, one of those times is when I hear confessions. On the one

March 2, 1957

hand, hearing confessions is a great joy, because I am able to help so many people. On the other, it is often a very lonely and agonizing experience, because I have to make so many weighty decisions which involve other people's lives. Today the experience was particularly agonizing.

A woman confessed that she had practiced birth control for the past month, and she was so distraught over the matter that she told me she had considered suicide. It took me quite a while to get her calmed down enough to ask some questions.

"Does your husband insist that you practice birth control?" I finally asked.

"No, Father," the woman replied, "but he does insist on having marital relations. I fought him off for a while, but then he began to stay out all night with other women. He told me what he was doing, and said he would continue to do it until I gave in. What could I do?"

"Is your husband a Catholic?"

"Yes, Father."

"How does he feel about practicing birth control?"

"It doesn't seem to bother him, Father. He always tells me that priests don't understand such things."

"How many children do you have?"

"Seven, Father. And I just can't have any more right now. My husband doesn't make enough money. I haven't been very well either."

"How long have you been married?"

"Eleven years."

"I think that seven children in eleven years are enough. Have you tried the rhythm method of birth control? It is permissible in your case."

"I tried it before, Father, and it didn't work. My doctor tried to help, but he finally decided that the rhythm method just won't work for me."

"All right," I said. "Now listen closely to what I am going to tell you."

"Yes, Father."

"I am convinced that in your particular case, there is absolutely no sin involved in practicing birth control; no matter what method you use. You can go right on doing as you have been doing during the past month. There is no sin."

At first, the woman was incredulous. "No sin at all, Father?" she asked.

"No sin at all," I assured her. "Do not even confess this matter when you come to confession in the future. Just forget all about it."

I talked with the woman some more, and before she left the confessional, she was quite happy.

But I cannot say the same for myself. I know that most priests would say I committed a sin by telling her what I did. Nevertheless, I keep trying to think of alternatives, and I can come up with none. I still feel that I have God on my side in this matter. But am I right? It is this unanswered—and perhaps unanswerable—question which continues to haunt me.

March 3, 1957

Even as I prayed before the Blessed Sacrament tonight, I still had the teachings of the Church in regard to sexual sin very much on my mind. From the theological standpoint, I do not see how the propriety of the laws can even be so much as questioned. They go back to the Old Testament itself, and were reaffirmed by Christ in the New. Indeed, some such laws are apparently necessary for the very development of civilization. If one were to deny their propriety and remain logical, he would have to conclude that Judaism and Christianity had been fraudulent religions—both in their God and in their teachings—from their inception until the present day.

Sections of the moral theology textbook, which I memorized in the seminary, keep coming back to me: *"Pollutio in se seu directe voluntaria est peccatum grave.... Sodomia est peccatum gravissimum, gravius fornicatione et simplici pollutione, tum qui est maxime contra naturam...."* Yes, but there must be exceptions. It is wrong to kill, but one has the right to kill in self-defense. It is wrong to steal, but one has the right—even the duty—to steal for himself and his family when faced with the alternative of starvation. So why should there not be exceptions to the laws which govern man's sexual activities?

I believe that the Church should very carefully delineate a number of exceptions to its laws involving divorce, masturbation, homosexuality, contraception, and abortion. Logic itself, not to mention the compassion shown by Christ during His life here on earth, makes it quite clear that such exceptions are in order. If the Church does not make these exceptions—exceptions which should still include personal unselfishness and humane altruism on the part of Christians—then I believe that demands are going to be made, even from within the Church, for the abolishment of the laws themselves. The basis for such demands will involve self-gratification, pride, the desire for power, greed, and a disrespect for all that is spiritual and sacred in human life. Once that movement takes hold, I fear for the future of the Church, for the dignity and welfare of man, and for Western Civilization itself.

July 2, 1958

Mrs. Guzowsky, our housekeeper, asked me today if I could find her a new job. Due to the illness of her mother, the salary she gets here is no longer sufficient to take care of medical and other expenses. Since both women are widows and there are no close relatives, she told me that she did not know what was going to happen to them if she did not find some way of making more money soon.

At first, I suggested that she talk to Monsignor. She said that she had already done that, and after a sound tongue-lashing, he had refused to give her one penny more. I knew that there was no sense in talking to Monsignor personally. If he said no, it was no. He never changed his mind.

I promised Mrs. Guzowsky that I would do what I could.

July 8, 1958

Success! I found Mrs. Guzowsky a job as hostess at a restaurant. Considering the work she has been doing here, the job will be quite easy. All she has to do is seat people, and see to it that they are waited on properly. Not only is the salary nearly twice the amount Monsignor has been paying her, but she will be able to spend more time at home with her sick mother.

Mr. Simon, the owner of the restaurant, is a friend of mine. I met him when his son was in the hospital. I try to talk to all of the children a little bit when I visit the hospitals, and I happened to be talking to Mr. Simon's son when Mr. Simon came into the room. We hit it off right away.

Mrs. Guzowsky was so happy that she cried when I told her. She is such a good cook that I really hate to see her go. But the new job will be much better for her, and that's what counts.

July 16, 1958

During the seven years I have been at Sacred Heart, there has always been quite a bit of bickering at dinner. But tonight there was a hassle that I'll remember for a long time to come. Everything started out normally enough. If there was one thing Monsignor demanded, it was that all of us be on time for the evening meal. I entered the dining room a few minutes before six. Father Calvin then arrived, and he was followed by Father Walsh, who took his place just before the big clock on the mantel began to strike the hour. As soon as the clock had begun to strike, Monsignor walked to the head of the table and said grace.

When we had seated ourselves, no one said a word. Monsignor had chosen to focus his eyes on his plate, and it was evident that he was in an ugly mood. We all knew from past experience that it was unwise to initiate a conversation at such times. He sat there rigidly for a few minutes, almost as though he were in a catatonic stupor. Then all of a sudden he began to beat the bell on the table with his fist.

The new housekeeper came running from the kitchen. "Yes, Monsignor?" she inquired nervously.

"I've told you a thousand times that I want you to serve my coffee before dinner," Monsignor shouted, banging his fist down on the table as though he were trying to represent the thousand times. "How often do I have to tell you?"

"I'm sorry, Monsignor," she apologized.

"Well don't stand there like an idiot!" Monsignor bellowed. "Get me my coffee!"

The housekeeper rushed into the kitchen and returned with the coffeepot. She stood next to Monsignor, the pot of coffee shaking in her hand.

"Well pour it!" Monsignor commanded. "Pour it! That's why I sent for you."

The woman tried to pour the coffee, but her hands continued to shake.

"You dumb-ox!" Monsignor shouted. "You're pouring the coffee all over the table."

The housekeeper was almost in tears. "I'm sorry, Monsignor," she said.

"I'm sorry, Monsignor, I'm sorry, Monsignor," he mocked. "A lot of good it does to be sorry! Get a cloth and wipe this mess up instantly."

The woman got a cloth and began to wipe Monsignor's cup and saucer, and then the tablecloth. Monsignor eyed her coldly. As she returned to the kitchen, he shouted after her: "Dumb-ox! Dumb-ox! Dumb-ox! If that ever happens again, I'll fire you. I'll fire you! I'll fire you! I'll fire you!"

Monsignor now stared at me. I felt his eyes on me, but I did not look up.

"This is all your fault, Father," he grumbled.

I realized that the remark was directed at me, but I still did not look up.

"Don't pretend you can't hear me!" Monsignor shouted. "I'm talking to you, Father Faber. At least be courteous enough to look at me when I talk to you."

My eyes met those of Monsignor.

"It was you who were responsible for letting those Jews at that restaurant take Mrs. Guzowsky away from us," he lectured angrily. "Now don't try to deny it! I happen to know for certain that you recommended her. You have no right to recommend anyone. Do you hear me, Father? No one! I am still the pastor of this parish."

"Mrs. Guzowsky needs the money the restaurant is paying

her, Monsignor," I stated calmly. "She has a sick mother to provide for, and she was not being paid enough for her work here."

"Not being paid enough!" Monsignor exclaimed indignantly. "I was paying that hunky every cent she was worth. Not being paid enough, indeed! The economy of this entire country is being wrecked by scrubwomen and millworkers who demand exorbitant wages for the menial work they do. They want more than bank presidents receive, and when they don't get it, they strike. The government shouldn't allow it. Those people should be jailed!"

"Mrs. Guzowsky is getting almost twice as much at the restaurant," I said, "and she doesn't have to work nearly so hard."

"I'll have the place boycotted!" Monsignor shouted. "I'll call the mayor and have the place boycotted! Then those Jews won't be able to pay that kind of money."

I made no reply. Instead, I looked down at my plate and began to eat again.

When Monsignor was in his present mood, even Father Walsh did not consider himself entirely safe from his ire, and he now attempted to divert Monsignor's attention to more pleasant matters. "The next issue of *The Catholic*," he said, "is going to contain a feature story on the Holy Father's elevation of Attorney Daley and Mr. Gallagher to knighthood."

"I'm glad to hear that," Monsignor responded, apparently somewhat mollified by Father Walsh's news. "They are fine men. I suggested their names to Bishop Connolly myself."

"In the following issue, we are going to do a feature on one of our new judges, Judge John McDonough, who was born in Ireland," Father Walsh announced.

This time Monsignor managed a smile. "*The Catholic* is a fine newspaper," he commented. "You are to be congratulated, Father Walsh."

Father Calvin had been wise enough to remain silent throughout the meal, but for some reason, I just couldn't keep quiet. Apparently I was still angry over what Monsignor had said about Mrs. Guzowsky, and over the manner in which he was treating the new housekeeper.

Anyway, I said: "I don't think that such propaganda should

July 16, 1958

appear in a Catholic newspaper. I am sick and tired of picking up *The Catholic* and seeing pictures of nuns being handed footballs by well-known football players, priests saying Mass and being served by baseball players, and afterwards being told in an article that the priests themselves were once either baseball stars, football stars, or state boxing champions. Such things have nothing to do with real religion. In fact, some of those activities, because of the greed and cruelty involved, are in opposition to genuine spirituality and the teachings of Christ. The fact that a judge was born in Ireland is irrelevant and not news. Such petty chauvinism has no place in a Catholic newspaper."

"I was born in Ireland," Monsignor proclaimed angrily, "and every really important Church figure in this country is of Irish descent. Irrelevant! Irrelevant, indeed!"

"Only the narrow-minded and prejudiced find it relevant," I said.

Monsignor O'Shea jumped to his feet and threw down his napkin. "The bishop will hear of this," he declared. "You have no respect for authority, Father Faber, and I no longer want you as my assistant. Even if *I* have to leave Sacred Heart, I won't remain under the same roof with you. I intend to tell the bishop that!"

I could see that even having said this was not enough for Monsignor. He was quite obviously searching for some more dramatic way to vent his rage.

Finally, he began to shout: "Dammit! Dammit! Dammit! You stupid ass, you! You won't get away with it! You won't get away with it!" Then suddenly he picked up the end of the tablecloth and gave it a violent pull, throwing food and dishes to the floor with a terrible crash.

The terrified housekeeper came running from the kitchen. "What happened?" she sobbed. "What happened?"

Monsignor darted from the room, and Father Walsh raced after him. "Be careful, Monsignor!" he called. "Your heart, Monsignor! Your heart! Be careful, Monsignor!"

Father Calvin and I brushed off some of the food and splinters of china which had spewed onto our cassocks. Then we got down on the floor and helped the distraught housekeeper pick up the food and broken pieces of glass.

PART NINE

July 17, 1958

When Monsignor O'Shea telephones the bishop, he gets prompt action. Monsignor Hogan, the chancellor, called this morning to inform me that I am being relieved of my duties at Sacred Heart. He ordered me to remain in residence here until I hear from the chancery. Just as when I was relieved of my duties at Saint Anne's and Juvenile Home after my first year in the priesthood, I'll be permitted to say Mass, but I'll not be allowed to do anything else. Once again, Monsignor Hogan expressed the hope that this respite from duties would enable me to ask God's guidance in prayer.

July 28, 1958

Monsignor O'Shea is finally speaking to me again, and I'm glad of that. I'm afraid that sometimes I think too abstractly, and what I present for the sake of argument or as a general principle is taken personally by people. It is true that I was angry at Monsignor, but I did not intend to hurt him; and I think that's what I did.

Although I am supposedly being punished and should be suffering, I'm really enjoying myself for a change. I've been doing a lot of reading, and since I've been overworked for a long time now, I'm getting what I feel is a much deserved rest. I am also able to devote more time to prayer, and I needed that, too. Prayer seems to clarify everything for me. Although I don't mean to be presumptuous, it seems that when I talk to God about my problems, I usually come away feeling that I really haven't done anything too seriously wrong. I have lacked prudence at times, but I think that even prudence can be carried too far.

The bishop probably sees things quite differently. Soon I'll know exactly how he feels. Father Malloy, the bishop's secretary, called this afternoon and said that the bishop wants to see me on Thursday morning. My suspension hasn't lasted very long, so I don't think he wants to see me about a new assignment. I suspect that he's really going to lower the boom this time.

July 30, 1958

I'm still somewhat staggered by the events of the day. Instead of criticizing me for my difficulties with Monsignor O'Shea, Bishop Connolly was all smiles. "I have decided to appoint you my secretary, Father," he told me. Although I could have fainted on the spot, I managed to keep my composure.

The bishop, noticing my bewilderment, said: "Monsignor Grosclaude and I were talking a few days ago, and your name came up. As you probably know, Monsignor Grosclaude thinks very highly of you. He keeps telling me that there is no better priest in the diocese. Since I don't think there is a better priest anywhere than Monsignor Grosclaude, I always take what he has to tell me very seriously. In short, I have decided to keep an eye on you myself for a while. My present secretary, Father Malloy, has been bored with the position for a long time now, so I am appointing him pastor of Holy Name Cathedral."

"Although I appreciate your kindness in appointing me," I responded, "I think I should tell you, Bishop, that I am probably going to be bored by the position, too. Besides, I have no idea what a bishop's secretary is supposed to do."

"I'm not being kind," Bishop Connolly stated. "I'm taking the word of Monsignor Grosclaude, who happens to know you much better than I do. Monsignor Grosclaude is an unusually perceptive individual, and he happens to think that you would make an excellent secretary."

"But I've had no experience," I protested.

"Your appointment does not become effective until August 16," the bishop informed me. "By that time, Father Malloy will have taught you everything you need to know."

I tried again. "I really didn't like teaching," I pointed out, "and I have an idea that I'm going to dislike sitting behind a desk all the time even more. I like to work among the people, Bishop."

Bishop Connolly smiled. "You'll see plenty of people here," he remarked, "perhaps many more than you'll want to see."

"But I like to work among ordinary people."

"We have many ordinary people right here in the chancery," the bishop smiled. "I'm one of them."

August 11, 1958

"I didn't mean—"

"I know exactly what you mean," the bishop said. "You like to minister to souls directly."

"That's true, Bishop. I like to hear confessions, visit the sick, help people in trouble—"

"I'll talk to Father Malloy," the bishop stated. "I'm sure that he'll permit you to help out with some of the work at the cathedral, if you wish."

"I would like that."

"There's something else to remember, Father. You'll be helping more people than you realize by working right here in the chancery. It's true that there will be a lot of paper work, but try to think of those papers as souls. Sometimes you can do much more for people by conscientiously handling their papers than by actually speaking to them."

"Whatever you wish, Bishop."

"Although I have heard considerable criticism of you," the bishop noted, "you are an obedient priest. If a priest is obedient, we can overlook many less important things. I would like to think that you will be happy in your work. If you're not, try to remember that all of the Church's work is necessary. Remember also that it is done for the love of God. Sometimes even bishops would like to be doing other things. But all of us have to do what God wants us to do."

He was right, and I knew it.

August 11, 1958

Many people have called to congratulate me on my new appointment. Apparently they consider the post quite important. Most of my classmates called, and the ones who knew about my suspension seem to be in a state of shock. Father Bill Fagan said that I am the only person he knows who can get ahead by displeasing important people. He then went on to make his usual acid comments. He said that if I can only displease Bishop Connolly enough in my new post, the pope is sure to make me a bishop. Then if, as bishop, I can displease the pope enough, they are sure to make me the first American pope.

Father Jim McHugh said he's now certain I am destined to become a bishop. He was quite serious. I suggested that he take a good look at me. I asked him if he could really envision me as a bishop. He admitted he couldn't envision it, but said that didn't matter, since he was unable to envision me as a bishop's secretary either. I told him that while Church officials make mistakes, they haven't lost their minds yet.

Poor Monsignor O'Shea looks as though he's seen a ghost. He still doesn't know what to make of the appointment. He told me to my face that the only assistant at Sacred Heart qualified for such a post is Father Walsh. I disagreed with him. I said that the only one qualified is Father Calvin. When I said that, he just gaped.

I was a little surprised to receive a call from Father Linehan of Saint Anne's. He was very effusive in congratulating me and in his praise for my work. I almost had to laugh when he said that he always knew I'd go places. I had a notion to ask him if he still thought I might be a Communist, but I restrained myself.

August 27, 1958

Being the bishop's secretary isn't as boring as I thought it was going to be. In fact, I'm usually much too busy to be bored. In addition to doing a great deal of paper work for the bishop, I have to arrange for all of his appointments and the functions at which he is going to be present. At times, he asks me to see people in his place. Although such meetings usually involve routine diocesan business, some of them are interesting enough.

I'm not in the chancery quite as much as I thought I was going to be. Today, for example, I accompanied the bishop to Saint Jude's Church, where he administered the sacrament of confirmation. Before we left, Monsignor Hayes, the pastor, offered the bishop three hundred dollars as a gift from the parish. The bishop refused the money, but suggested that it be offered to me, his secretary. I also declined the money.

On the way back to the chancery, Bishop Connolly asked why I had refused the money. He pointed out that I am terribly underpaid for all the work I do, and he said that Father Malloy had always been happy to accept the money. I told him that if I had accepted the gift, I would have felt as though I were being given money for spiritual services rendered. I added that I did not think that was proper. The bishop reflected for a while, and then he said: "I had never thought of it that way before, Father. You're right—of course. If I refuse and you refuse, then there will be no payment. That is what we are going to do from now on."

October 29, 1958

Many people have told me that they are disappointed in the election of Angelo Roncalli as Pope John XXIII. Even Bishop Connolly keeps lamenting that the new pope is almost eighty. I do not share their pessimism. Because Pope John has had an opportunity to acquire some degree of wisdom, I see his age as an asset rather than a liability.

Indeed, if people lived for at least two hundred years, I think we could make a real start at solving the problems which beset mankind. The way it is now, most men die at the very time they are beginning to grow in wisdom. On the other hand, the young, as they grow in experience, have a penchant for making all of the same mistakes their elders have already made. It is unfortunate, I think, that we do not have a greater respect for age. Through neglect, we turn old people into senile zombies at the very time we should be benefiting from what they have learned.

Apparently the election of Pope John came about by means of compromise. It is being said that when the cardinals could not agree on a younger man, they chose him, since they do not expect him to live very long. He would have been my choice regardless of age. He has had a varied and brilliant career. Moreover, he comes from a peasant family, which means he has spent some time close to the soil. I think this highly artificial age of ours needs leaders with a little earthy wisdom. His reign may be short, but that does not necessarily mean that it will be lacking in achievements.

The reign of Pope John's predecessor, Pope Pius XII, was one of the longest reigns in the history of the Church; yet I have never been impressed by his accomplishments. There are those who maintain that he spent much of his time trying to make certain that he would be canonized following his death. He did let it be known that he had experienced visions. He also arranged for his personal physician, who claimed to have knowledge about such matters, to embalm him in such a way that his body would never rot. The physician was something of a fraud, however, and the mummification turned out to be a colossal failure. The poor pope went stinking to his grave.

Still, from the historical standpoint, it is too early to assess Pius XII's life. As for the rest, it is really not for us to judge. He is now in the hands of God.

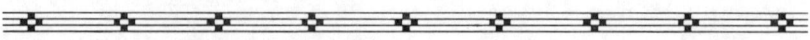

August 6, 1959

This morning I received a rather unusual call. A woman telephoned the chancery and requested that the bishop come to visit her. Her voice was barely audible, and when I asked her to speak a little louder, she said that she was ill and could not. She told me that it was because of her illness that she wanted to see the bishop. I took her name and address, pointed out that it would be impossible for the bishop to visit her, and said that I would see her this afternoon.

The woman's name is Rita Marie Bern. Before going to her place, I stopped at a florist and purchased a dozen yellow roses. From talking to her on the phone, I decided that she probably needed something to cheer her up.

Rita Marie lives on the fourth floor of a rather dilapidated apartment building. When I knocked at her door, I heard someone whisper: "Who is it?"

"It's Father Faber, Bishop Connolly's secretary," I replied.

I had to wait for almost fifteen minutes before the door opened very slowly and Rita Marie Bern appeared. For a while, I thought that I was seeing an apparition. Rita Marie dresses something like a nun. She wears a long, flowing, black choir robe, as well as a bandage around her throat, which resembles a wimple. Her eyebrows are dark, her eyes unusually large, and her nose long and well-shaped. Her long, black hair hangs loosely over her shoulders. She is very slender, and although her face is pale, she wears no make-up. Above all, she looks young and saintly. She is only of medium height, but her slenderness and the long, flowing choir robe make her seem tall and stately.

Rita Marie's room was simply furnished. There was a bed, a table and chairs, one easy chair, a refrigerator, a dresser, a shrine of the Virgin, and a crucifix on the wall. She surprised me by noticing that I was aware of the room. "They call me Lady Poverty," she smiled.

Before I sat down in the easy chair which Rita Marie offered me, I presented her with the flowers. As though not quite sure about them, she pointed to the roses and then to herself. "For me?" she whispered. When I nodded affirmatively, she beamed. As she walked toward the cupboard for a vase, I noticed that she had a bad limp. She placed the flowers in the vase and set it before the Virgin. "They are for Our Lady," she smiled.

"But I bought them for you," I said.

"Everything I own is Our Lady's."

"How long have you been sick?"

"I have had osteomyelitis since I was ten years old," she replied. "As you can see from the way I walk, the disease becomes progressively worse."

"Isn't there anything they can do?"

"Nothing!" Rita Marie smiled.

"What about your throat?"

"I have to keep it covered because it is draining. The doctors removed some tumors. God gave me the bone disease, but I asked Him for this."

"Why did you do that?"

Rita Marie beamed. "I did it for a priest I know," she answered. "He had incurable cancer. I asked God to give his cancer to me, because I could bear it better. God heard my prayers."

"Is the priest well now?"

"Certainly, Father," she smiled. "People often come to me for help—even priests and seminarians. I have been helping people ever since I became a Catholic."

"How long have you been a Catholic?"

"Nine years this month, Father. I was baptized when I was eighteen."

"What religion did you belong to previously?"

"I am Jewish."

"Your name doesn't sound Jewish."

"Our name was Bernstein. After my father died, my brother had it changed to Bern. He thought the new name would help him to get ahead. Before I was baptized, my first name was Rebecca. I always hated that name and was glad to change it to Rita Marie."

"How did your family feel when you became a Catholic?"

"They disowned me, Father. My brother and mother went to the rabbi, and he told them to throw me out of the house if I refused to return to the Jewish religion. I refused, and I'm glad I did. All my brother thinks about is a beautiful home and a new car every year. My mother used to be different, but now she's just like he is. They live only for the world. I couldn't live the way they do. If I had to live with them and didn't have this light which God has given me, I would have to kill myself. If I didn't believe there was something better to come, I would have done that long ago."

"Haven't you found that most Catholics are also very worldly?" I asked.

"Now you sound like my mother," Rita Marie smiled. "Some of her friends told her that if I had studied the Jewish religion as thoroughly as I had studied Catholicism, I could have become a fanatical Jew just as easily as a fanatical Catholic."

"Maybe they have a point," I said.

"I do what *God* tells me to do," Rita Marie emphasized. "He tells me to go out and nurse the poor and elderly at the County Home, and even though I can barely walk, I do it. He tells me to talk to the people who telephone me at all hours of the night with their problems, and I do it, even though I have to whisper. I want to leave part of myself to the world, and I can't do that by collecting money. I can do it only by helping others, as God directs me."

"I'm sure that God loves you very much," I commented. "But are you certain that there is no way in which you and your family can become reconciled? As you said yourself, your disease is becoming progressively worse. One of these days you are going to need a great deal of care."

"By giving up my Catholic faith, I could have all the care in the world," Rita Marie whispered. "My mother despises Christians. You should hear some of the stories she tells about the way Christians persecuted and tortured Jews."

"I can understand your mother's point of view," I said. "Her stories are probably quite true. I was once a history professor, and I'm very familiar with the way Christians treated Jews."

"You read too much, Father," Rita Marie commented rather sarcastically. "I don't have your learning. I have only the light which God has given me. I am like Saint Therese, the Little Flower of Jesus. She said that learned books gave her a headache and dried up her heart. Many priests—some of them with doctorates—come to me because I know secrets which have not been revealed to them. They call me the powerhouse. They say that they must come to me before they can perform their good works, since I bring down the necessary graces from heaven by my prayers and sacrifices."

For the moment, I could think of nothing else to say. It was obvious that I was not going to be able to reconcile Rita Marie Bern and her family. She would not attempt to understand them, and from what she had said, they were unwilling to understand her. I glanced at my watch and told her that I had to leave. I said that I would be back to visit her soon again.

Rita Marie looked at me and smiled as though to say she had not yet dismissed me. Then she hobbled over to the cupboard and got out a small purse. She flung the purse into my lap. "Open it, Father," she whispered.

The purse was empty.

"That's all I have in the world," she said. "There is nothing in the refrigerator. I'm ashamed I can't offer you anything. I don't eat solid foods, but there isn't even any juice left. I need new bandages, too."

"Does the St. Vincent de Paul Society give you any help?"

"They pay my rent, and I can't ask them to do any more. I don't want to go to the County Home. I could never live there.

This room isn't much, but it's the closest place I've had to home since I entered the Church. There's no place like home, Father."

"Have you tried to get help from the state?" I asked. "They do quite a bit to help the handicapped. They even pay for school. If you want me to, I'll see what can be done."

"If you can't help me yourself, don't tell me what to do," Rita Marie Bern snapped in her whispery voice, her face growing even paler in anger than it already was. "First you want me to go back to my family, and then you want me to get help from the state. I have been through all of those things—and more. You just don't want to help, and you are trying to push the burden onto somebody else."

I took out my checkbook and began to write. "I'm sorry you feel that way about it," I said. "I'll personally do all I can." I placed the check in the small purse and gave it to her.

Tears came to Rita Marie's eyes when she opened the purse and looked at the check. "The milk is spilt now," she whispered. "The milk is spilt!"

"Nothing is spilt," I tried to assure her.

Rita Marie smiled through the tears which were streaming down her face. "I couldn't accept it now," she whispered.

"I want you to," I said.

"You won't tell anyone else about this, will you?" she pleaded. "Some people would never understand. I am a symbol to them. That's why I can't ask them for money, and they would never understand if they knew I asked someone else."

"You don't have to worry," I said.

"Thank you, Father," Rita Marie sighed gratefully.

"If you need me for anything, just call."

"I'll pray for you, Father," she whispered.

October 25, 1960

I heard on the late news tonight that Martin Luther King has been jailed in Atlanta for leading sit-ins in an attempt to desegregate lunch counters. He is one man for whom I have only the deepest

February 9, 1962

admiration. It is hard to believe that someone can be jailed in America, simply because he adheres to the principle that a black man and a white man are sufficiently equal to sit side by side in a bus or restaurant.

The fact that Martin Luther King is a clergyman somewhat redeems us other clergymen—though not nearly enough. I hold the white clergy primarily responsible for the unhappy plight of the Negro in America. The clergy never should have permitted slavery to take root here in the first place. They should have condemned it as a heinous crime against humanity. Moreover, they should have declared it mortally sinful in the sight of God, and they should have refused membership in their churches to anyone who practiced or condoned it.

Certainly after the Civil War, the clergy should have taken the lead in educating the Negro and in integrating him into white society. They did not do any of these things, and they are very much to blame, consequently, for the problems all of us face today.

February 9, 1962

President Kennedy's announcement that he is giving more military assistance to South Vietnam makes me uneasy. I hope that he is not going to repeat the blunders made by Presidents Truman and Eisenhower—blunders which I feel are at least partially due to not knowing enough about history.

If we were wise, I believe that we would still try to win the friendship of Ho Chi Minh, the leader of North Vietnam. He would also be leader of the South, if the majority of people in the South were given a choice in the matter. The United States helped subvert the free elections for which the Geneva Accords of 1954 provided. This was done because President Eisenhower realized that Ho Chi Minh would have won in both the North and South if really free elections had been held.

Ho Chi Minh, after all, is revered as the George Washington of Vietnam. He freed his country from French colonialism. But instead of befriending him and the majority, the United States has been supporting a small segment of Vietnamese, most of whom are traitors who fought on the side of the French against their own people. All of this is ironic when one considers the fact that during the Second World War, Ho Chi Minh was an ally of the United States against the Japanese. After the war was over, he pleaded with President Truman to persuade the French not to reoccupy his country. Not only did his pleas go unheeded, but the United States helped the French by providing them with weapons and planes. Indeed, the United States even came close to providing troops.

The official excuse for all this has been that Ho Chi Minh is a Communist. Even if Communism were the major issue, it would still be immoral for the United States to attempt to force people to accept a government other than the one they want. The overwhelming majority of people in both North and South Vietnam want Ho Chi Minh, and they should have him, no matter what Americans think. After all, it is their country; not ours.

But Communism is not the real issue. How could it be? The United States has not intervened in Europe to prevent several countries there from being forced to accept Russian Communism, even though the majority of people in those countries oppose that form of government. Why should it then intervene in Vietnam? The answer lies quite apart from Communism. The United States wants to maintain a position of power in the area of Vietnam, and it wants to contain China.

Unfortunately, our national leaders fail to understand that they could best achieve these very objectives by supporting the cause of Ho Chi Minh. Nationalism is much more important than Communism in Ho Chi Minh's hierarchy of values. Like some other leaders of our time, he has been forced to embrace Communism as the only means available to him for freeing his country from colonialism and improving the living conditions of his people. It is significant that he quoted verbatim from the Declaration of Independence in his own declaration of 1945. It is equally significant that Mao Tse-tung has expressed his admiration for Washington, Jefferson, and Lincoln. It is with our present-day leadership that these men are disenchanted, and they are disenchanted because they believe that our leaders have betrayed the ideals of our founding fathers.

If only the patriots of other nations had been able to turn to the United States for help in their battle against colonialism and poverty—to the United States which was itself born in a revolution against colonialism—conditions in the world might be much happier for all of us. But not only has the United States steadfastly refused to help these patriots, it has actively helped their oppressors. Thus, they have had to turn to Communist nations for help, and in supplying this help, the Communist nations have naturally achieved varying degrees of power over them. I believe that the near-sighted approach of our national leaders—despite all their eloquent preachments against Communism—has done more than Russia itself to extend the domains of Communism.

July 23, 1962

Mr. Lawrence, our diocesan attorney, sought my advice this afternoon. His conscience was bothering him because of a decision he had made a month or so ago. The decision involves a priest by the name of Father Servaux. Father Servaux heads the Fathers of the Aquinas Institute, a community of priests who do educational and social work in the diocese.

At a party held one night at the Institute, Father Servaux is alleged to have made homosexual advances to one of the guests. The guest, who happens to be a good friend of Mr. Lawrence, got in touch with him. When Mr. Lawrence confronted Father Servaux with the accusation, Father Servaux said that he was unable to recall what had happened that night, since he was drunk. Mr. Lawrence then got together with other members of the Institute, and it was decided that if Father Servaux promised not to drink in the future—which he did—the matter would be dropped.

Now Mr. Lawrence did not know whether he had done the right thing or not, and he was thinking of informing the bishop. I told him that since he had already given his word to drop the matter, he had no choice but to follow that course of action. My advice seemed to satisfy him. Indeed, he appeared relieved. I am sure that he did not really want to bring the matter to the bishop's attention.

If the bishop had been informed about the incident, I know that he would have been heartsick. Bishop Connolly himself persuaded the Fathers to work in the diocese, and in a sense, they have been a pet project of his. Of late, though, he seems to be increasingly disappointed in them. They have turned out to be a group of snobs. They do not want to take people into their community unless they are Anglo-Saxon or French. When Bishop Connolly recommended a Slovak, they did not dare to offend the bishop by not accepting him. They made his life so miserable, however, that he left the community within two weeks.

Father Servaux himself comes from an ordinary enough family—his father is a coal miner—but he pretends that his background is one of money and social position. Before joining the Institute, he was a professor at a prestigious Catholic university. Even though he was older than most candidates for the priesthood, Bishop Connolly was so impressed with his credentials that he considered it a privilege to ordain him.

I visited the Institute only once, in the company of Bishop Connolly, and that was enough for me. For an entire hour before dinner, they served cocktails in the parlor. Fixtures were then lit in the dining room by a butler, and after an elegant meal, coffee was served in one of the exquisite drawing rooms. I kept asking myself how such worldly people could teach students anything about God and religion—indeed, how they could teach anyone anything at all!

In the event that Bishop Connolly ever found out about Father Servaux, I don't know what he would do. I do know that during the period I have been with him, he has never consented to see a priest involved in homosexuality. I have to see all of them, and that is never a pleasant task. A few months ago, a Franciscan friar, who freely admitted that he was a homosexual, tried to convince me that once the Church permitted priests to marry, homosexuality among priests would also be allowed.

June 22, 1963

Bishop Connolly has assigned me the responsibility of getting any priest or religious accused of homosexuality out of the diocese within twenty-four hours. While this procedure keeps most of the accused out of the hands of the law and avoids scandal for the Church, I do not approve of it. First of all, I do not think it is in the best interests of the accused, especially if he is not guilty. Secondly, Bishop Connolly recommends these men to bishops in distant dioceses, without telling those bishops what has transpired. Thus, he passes on his problems. This is very unfair to the other bishops, particularly in cases where children have been molested.

I have tried to talk over these problems with Bishop Connolly, but the homosexuality of priests and nuns is one matter that he adamantly refuses to discuss.

November 12, 1962

The reports which Bishop Connolly has been sending me from the Second Vatican Council sound very promising. I know that he was thinking of taking me with him, but apparently he decided that he needs me here in his absence. Monsignor Hogan, the chancellor, accompanied him, and I think it's time that Monsignor Hogan got away for a while. He has been working very hard, and the work he does is always so tedious.

Even before the Council, Pope John had already shown what an old man can do. Now I don't think that anyone has any doubts. The entire world loves him, chiefly because of his refreshing simplicity. He is a pope without pomp, and I think people have been sick of pomp for a long time now—especially in its churchmen. Pope John's heart is with the common man, and that's where every pope's heart should be. He is the most Christlike pope we have had in a long while.

June 22, 1963

I am still very sad about the death of Pope John. It is too bad that he did not live long enough to see the Second Vatican Council to its conclusion. I do believe that Pope Paul VI is going to prove himself an able successor. Bishop Connolly agrees with me. In fact, he thinks that Pope Paul is going to be even more popular than Pope John.

Although Bishop Connolly could very well be right, I wouldn't go as far as he does. Pope Paul has some enormously big shoes to fill. He strikes me as a good man and a humble man, but apparently he is not as gregarious as Pope John was. He seems to be more retiring and introverted. After Pope John, I am afraid that such a quality is not going to be an asset.

Moreover, I think there are recent developments in the Church which are going to cause him a great deal of trouble. I am already praying for him. I think he is going to need all of the support we can give him.

August 2, 1963

I had hoped to be able to attend the civil rights rally in Washington, D.C., on August 28, but Bishop Connolly turned thumbs down on the idea. It isn't that he is against civil rights. He just feels that a priest should not become involved in such partisan causes. He said that since most American Catholics are white, he could see no good reason for possibly offending the majority in order to please a very small minority. He went on to say that he did not think such rallies and marches accomplish much of anything anyway.

Naturally, I disagree with him, and I told him so. I stressed that the Church has the obligation to defend the human rights of all people, especially of minorities. I pointed out that at one period in history, Christians themselves were an infinitesimal minority. I said that the gospels clearly show that Christ expects us to spend most of our time on the poor and downtrodden, rather than on those who are quite capable of protecting themselves.

Bishop Connolly used the out that I have heard so many times from Church officials. He stated that while he approved of what I said in principle, he was against the methods being used. He said that laws were being broken, and he made it clear that he could

August 2, 1963

not countenance that. I asked him what methods he would advocate, and he suggested educating both whites and blacks to see things in truly Christian perspective. I pointed out that it was too late for that. I said that Negroes were unwilling to wait another hundred years, and I emphasized that I didn't blame them.

What never ceases to amaze me is that Bishop Connolly usually listens to my opinions and seems to respect them. He doesn't take suggestions from very many people. He was going to forbid all priests and religious to take part in the civil rights rally, but I talked him out of it. I told him that such an action could only do harm to the Church. I pointed out that it would not only turn priests and religious against their bishop, but it would turn the Negroes of our own diocese against him. He finally saw the wisdom in this.

I know that Father Calvin will be attending the rally. Since I talked Bishop Connolly into making him pastor of Saint Martin de Porres Church, he seems to be much more satisfied with his work in the priesthood. Saint Martin de Porres has the largest congregation of black Catholics in the diocese, and it is located in the ghetto, where Father Calvin feels the real action is right now.

I still wish that I could be marching with him, but in some ways, I feel that I am actually accomplishing more right where I am. If I were not Bishop Connolly's secretary, other priests and religious of the diocese would not be attending the rally. Moreover, Father Calvin, who is becoming increasingly important in the civil rights movement, would not be at Saint Martin de Porres Church.

Then, too, I often see my life as awaiting the right opportunity. When I get to feeling that I am not being socially active enough—as I often do these days—I try to meditate on the hidden life of Christ. According to a contemporary Biblical scholar, Christ spent thirty-five years in seclusion and preparation. The active part of His life lasted only a little more than two years. I think His example should tell all of us something about the real meaning of social involvement.

December 5, 1963

While I have been in favor of most decisions made by the Second Vatican Council, I am disappointed in the latest one, which concerns the Sacred Liturgy. I do not think it is a good idea to replace Latin with the vernacular in Catholic services. I know that Bishop Connolly feels exactly as I do about this matter, but other voices at the Council have obviously prevailed.

Latin has served as a symbol of the Church's unity and universality, and while the symbol does not constitute the reality, sometimes the reality itself withers without the symbol. Until now, a Catholic could attend Mass almost anywhere in the world, and feel perfectly at home in church. Without Latin, I do not see how this sense of belonging—this sense of universal oneness—is going to survive.

I think the abandonment of Latin is going to open up a Pandora's box of uncertainty, doubt, and confusion among the faithful. In the end, I believe it is going to weaken their faith in the Church itself. I have an idea that during the Protestant Reformation, when Catholics were persecuted in many parts of Christendom, the average Catholic probably died much more willingly for his Latin liturgy than for the pope.

To date, the church attendance record of Catholics in the United States has been vastly superior to that of Protestants. It remains to be seen whether that attendance will increase or decrease, once the language of the Mass is changed from Latin to the vernacular—the traditional liturgical language of Protestantism.

July 28, 1965

As President Johnson continues to increase the number of American troops in Vietnam, I grow more and more concerned. I feel that this involvement is immoral, and I believe that each succeeding day goes to prove that this is so. We are turning a guerrilla war, in which people fought with primitive weapons, into a war where poor, simple peasants suffer under the most sophisticated military technology the world has ever known. The students are right in protesting our participation in this war. While so many others are accepting the lies of the politicians, they are aware of the truth.

I have heard more talk recently that the American government was primarily responsible for the overthrow and murder of President Diem. Apparently Diem discovered that the Americans wanted to use him and other South Vietnamese politicians as instruments for exterminating other Asians. It is said that he balked at this and began secret negotiations with the North Vietnamese on his own. When the Americans found out, they decided that he was no longer behaving as a puppet should, and consequently had to be eliminated.

Shortly after the assassination of President Kennedy, members of Diem's family stated that since Kennedy himself had been involved in the murder of President Diem and his brother, he had gotten exactly what he deserved when Lee Harvey Oswald shot him. It is sad that the Diem family felt compelled to make such an accusation. There is so much that I admired about President Kennedy. Indeed, the entire world should be grateful for the wisdom he exercised in handling the Cuban missile crisis. Unfortunately for the world, he failed in regard to Vietnam.

September 5, 1965

I was saddened to learn of Dr. Albert Schweitzer's death. In losing him, mankind has lost a portion of its conscience. While he was sometimes criticized for not being entirely modern in his practice of medicine, I think that was one of the good things about him. He was able to meet people of a different race on their own terms, and serve them in a way they understood. His work takes on an added dimension in light of the troubled racial relations of our times. Too often a fellow human being is considered inferior, merely because he looks and lives differently than we do.

That is another of the tragedies about Vietnam. Our soldiers—indeed, our people!—often have little, if any, compunction in regard to killing Vietnamese. They look down on these people because their physical appearance and manner of living are different from our own. Moreover, most Vietnamese are poor in material goods; and in so far as the average American is concerned, that automatically brands them as being inferior. In reality, the culture of these people is often much more advanced than our own, for the very reason that material goods are not that important to them—just as they were not important to Jesus of Nazareth. People of real culture and nobility of soul are never impressed by material things; while barbarians invariably are.

Dr. Schweitzer was a builder. He revered life; and at the very time that so many others were destroying it, he was working quietly—ever so quietly!—to save it. During the many years he spent in Africa, he probably saved thousands of lives; both in the spiritual and physical sense. Yet, there is a certain irony in this. In just one day in Vietnam, more lives are being destroyed than Dr. Schweitzer was able to save during an entire lifetime of devoted and tireless labor.

November 28, 1966

The bishops of the United States have now decided that American Catholics will no longer have to abstain from meat on Fridays, except on the Fridays of Lent. Bishop Connolly voted against this proposal, and I think he was right in doing so. The decision can only further weaken the Catholic Church in America.

Much like Latin in the liturgy, abstaining from meat on Fridays has had a very important symbolic value for Catholics. For some—as unfortunate as that may have been—it was the very essence of their religion. As long as anyone can remember, Catholics have bravely withstood the ridicule of their Protestant friends and abstained on Fridays; all the while proudly proclaiming their unswerving loyalty to the Church.

Indeed, it was a mortal sin to eat meat on Fridays. The average Catholic, unsophisticated in theology, is naturally asking why this is no longer so. Then another question occurs to him. If it is no longer a mortal sin to eat meat on Fridays, then what about other actions that the Church defines as mortally sinful? Why can't rules in regard to these actions be abrogated just as easily?

It is especially unfortunate that the rules regarding Latin in the Mass and abstaining from meat on Fridays had to change when so many other turbulent transformations are taking place in society. These rules served as an anchor. They gave the average Catholic a feeling of stability, of security, of identifying with the changeless—indeed, of identifying with God Himself.

April 11, 1967

A man by the name of James Hannegan, who was recently expelled from the diocesan seminary, has been trying to see the bishop for more than two weeks now. Bishop Connolly steadfastly refuses to see him, so I asked the bishop if it would be all right if I saw him. The bishop gave his consent, and when Hannegan called again this morning, I set up an appointment for one o'clock this afternoon.

Hannegan was twenty minutes late for his appointment, so I had ample time to go through his dossier again. He had studied at Saint Mary's Seminary for eleven years. Although his grades were somewhat below average, he was considered a leader at the seminary. The past two years had been spent in constant conflict with those in authority.

According to the dossier, he was expelled for organizing a secret Mass at midnight in the seminary gymnasium. Two recent graduates of the seminary, wearing overalls, had concelebrated the Mass. Commercial bread rolls and wine had been used in the ceremony, prescribed rubrics had not been observed, and a jazz combo had provided music. During the consecration, Hannegan himself, wearing a red leotard, had done a dance in honor of the Holy Spirit. Moreover, he had been accused of rifling student files and bugging faculty meetings. He had denied the charges, but when other students, who were being falsely accused, put pressure on him, he confessed.

When Hannegan finally arrived, I didn't find him an especially likable person. I rose to greet him, but before I could offer him a seat, he had already sat down and was busily engaged in lighting a cigarette. He is a tall man, with rather handsome features, but much too heavy. I would guess that he weighs about two hundred and fifty pounds. The dance in the leotard must have been quite a sensation.

"It's about time that someone here finally condescended to see me," he stated rather belligerently.

"I condescend rather easily," I smiled. "What's the problem?"

"I think that should be perfectly obvious," he snapped. "I want to be reinstated in the seminary."

"The bishop will not permit it," I said. "In arranging for that bizarre Mass, you did something which only the pope could have allowed you to do. Even the National Conference of Catholic Bishops could not have authorized it."

"We had the concurrence of the Holy Spirit in what we did," Hannegan maintained.

"With connections like that, you don't need the bishop to get you reinstated," I smiled.

Hannegan completely ignored my remark. "I'm not a slave to any human power or hierarchy," he insisted. "If I were, I couldn't love freely. Love is something that cannot be demanded. It must be given. You and the bishop are living in the Dark Ages, Father. In the modern world, obedience in itself has no intrinsic value."

"Although I can think of certain instances where obedience does have value in itself," I said, "you are partly right. However, obedience has very positive value in so far as public order is concerned. Anyone can claim inspiration of the Holy Spirit and use that as a ruse for his actions. The result would be anarchy and the disappearance of individual freedom. Someone or some group, for example, might declare inspiration to the effect that you and I should be imprisoned or even murdered. Law—not anarchy—brings personal freedom."

"Love is what we need, Father; not law. You lack the spirit of the modern Church. You seem unaware of the great changes which have taken place."

"Yes, you can now join the Y.M.C.A.," I remarked in mock seriousness.

"I think the changes are more profound than that."

"I hope so," I smiled. "But I think we have to be on guard

April 11, 1967

against a tendency to destroy the past—the past which made us what we now are. The pope said that we must seek what is best rather than what is new, and I believe there is much wisdom in that. I think it precludes—among other things—dancing in a leotard before the altar."

"I'm not interested in what the pope said," Hannegan snapped. "I'm interested in what the Second Vatican Council had to say."

"You should read the decrees of the Second Vatican Council carefully," I told him. "Too many people comment on those decrees without reading them, or they read them haphazardly and imagine they see there what they would like to see. A careful study of the documents will indicate, I believe, that no really fundamental changes have been advocated."

"Then fundamental changes are needed," Hannegan maintained. "Nothing is being done to meet the needs of people in the Church today. We should reinterpret our faith so that it becomes relevant and authentic—especially to young people. Yet, when seminarians attend a Mass that will meet their needs, one of them is expelled; while the priests who officiated at the Mass are suspended. It is the Dark Ages all over again."

"I think that words like *need, relevant,* and *authentic* require analysis," I said. "You seem to be saying that if beliefs and customs which meet your needs do not exist, such beliefs and customs should be manufactured *ex nihilo*—even if they have no basis in truth. I believe that the terminology you use represents a state of mind which is too personal and self-seeking."

"I'm not the one who is selfish!" Hannegan protested.

"I think you are," I insisted. "By sublimating our own needs to those of others, we often discover that we were wrong in what we thought we needed. By sacrificing our own wants, we often learn that we are acting with relevance and authenticity for the very first time in our lives. On the other hand, when our supposed needs destroy—as they so frequently do today—we are usually astounded to discover that we really have no suitable substitute for what has been taken away."

"What you are really saying is that you are against freedom."

"Just the opposite!" I maintained. "Being too personal in expressing one's imagined needs can easily lead to a breakdown in order. You, for example, want to dance in a red leotard during the consecration of the Mass. Tomorrow, one of your friends might want to have sexual intercourse during the consecration. The result is one of two things: anarchy, which entails the loss of individual freedom; or a dictatorship imposed to rectify the situation, which also means a loss of freedom. But if I had to make a choice, I would choose dictatorship rather than anarchy; for even in dictatorship, I see more possibilities for individual freedom than in a system of complete savagery where people do whatever they want to do whenever they want to do it—all at the expense of somebody else."

"I think you misunderstand what I am proposing," Hannegan said. "Everything must be governed by the situation. Whatever is most loving in the situation is the right and good thing to do."

"But who makes the decision about the most loving thing to do in a situation?" I asked. "A computer?"

"In time, probably yes," he replied. "Experiments are now under way."

"Oh my God!" I exclaimed. "And you see no problems?"

"Why should I? By telling a person the most loving thing to do in a particular situation, the computer would enable him to choose for himself. Somebody else, under the guise of law, wouldn't be telling him what to do."

"But who is going to program the computer?" I asked. "As soon as any system at all is established, it is impossible to get away from that problem. Even if the system happens to be a relative one—such as you are suggesting—everything must be relative to other things. Consequently, *someone* will decide. The only question is who. Frankly, I think there is much more freedom under a system of formal law, if it is subject to change, and if it makes exceptions according to the situation."

"I don't think you understand what I am proposing, Father. Will you permit me to give an example?"

"Certainly."

"My example is from pioneer times. In one situation, a

woman and her four children, along with a large company of other people, are trying to escape pursuing Indians. One of the children is an infant who cries continuously. The mother is unable to stop the crying, and as a result, the entire group is captured and killed. In a similar situation, another woman, seeing that her crying baby is endangering the lives of everyone, kills the infant with her own hands. As a result, the entire group escapes. Which woman made the right decision, Father?"

"Which one do you think made the proper decision?"

"The second one, of course. A person who practices love has to act boldly and courageously. It is better that one person should die rather than many. Only a loving purpose, however, would ever justify such an act. A loving purpose can justify anything."

"I see many fallacies in your reasoning," I said, "but I'll point out only one or two. In the first place, how could the second group know for certain that the crying of the child would betray them? Perhaps all of them could have survived. But the biggest flaw is this: Why was it necessary to kill the baby in order to keep it quiet? Don't you think a gag might have been used? True, the baby might have strangled, but not necessarily so. Perhaps the gag could have been removed every so often. Or why was the baby not rendered unconscious by a blow to the head? True, this would have been risky, but the child might have had some chance. All I can say is: Lord deliver me from your method of showing love! . . . Or should I say Joseph Fletcher's method? That's where you got your example."

James Hannegan suddenly looked impressed. "I'm surprised that you've read Fletcher," he commented.

"Believe it or not, some of us older folks learned to read," I smiled.

"What I am really trying to say is that Jesus used love in making His decisions; not the petty legalisms in vogue during His time. When they were going to stone the woman taken in adultery—which happened to be the law—He asked the person who was without sin to cast the first stone."

"Jesus made exceptions and took exception to certain laws," I granted, "but He never said that law should not exist. Do you remember what He finally said to the woman?"

"Go and sin no more."

"Exactly! . . . There is something to be said for the ethical system which Fletcher outlines, but even Fletcher himself is incapable of applying it properly; as the examples given in his book show. The system can only be applied successfully by someone like Jesus."

"That's a big order!" Hannegan exclaimed.

"Yes, but very necessary," I said. "A period of purgation, of real suffering, of detachment from one's own pride and one's own will, of unconcern with the standards and judgment of the world—a dark night of the soul, if you will—are essential before such a system can be used justly and with love. That is why Jesus went to the desert. Without purgation, without suffering, without a quiet, contemplative spirit, the answers come much too easily, and they are usually the wrong answers. I believe that human life and human personality are too sacred to be dabbled in by people who lack the qualifications I have just mentioned. That is why the traditional concept of law—with all of its innumerable faults—is best in most instances."

"But you do believe, Father, that love is the answer?" It seemed that James Hannegan was speaking to me for the first time without rancour.

"Unselfish love, yes! If I didn't believe that, I wouldn't be sitting here."

"Do you think you could use that love to convince the bishop that he should reinstate me in the seminary?"

I smiled. "I'm afraid not," I said. "The bishop has already made up his mind. But I do think you might persuade another bishop to accept you, especially in a diocese where there is a great need for priests."

Hannegan suddenly turned belligerent again. "You mean out in the sticks, don't you?" he snapped. "I'm not going to go begging."

"That's up to you," I said. "You have been telling me how free you are. The choice is yours."

"I'm afraid the only remedy is to go to the newspapers,"

Hannegan threatened. "Many influential Catholics are concerned about paternalism, the lack of freedom, and poor student-faculty relations in the diocesan seminary."

"If you do that, Mr. Hannegan, we'll have to reveal everything we know about you. Moreover, I suspect that some of your actions would be regarded as criminal by the community. If you cause trouble for us, we'll bring charges against you and quite possibly have you arrested."

James Hannegan shook his head in wonder. "You are a bastard!" he exclaimed.

"And you are no gentleman," I smiled.

Hannegan laughed. "I'm sorry that I didn't meet you years ago," he said. "Do you mind if I come to see you occasionally?"

"Anytime that I can help," I offered. "But I don't want to sound too paternal."

"Meeting you was quite an experience," Hannegan said in farewell, all the while shaking my hand as though he were running for political office.

September 1, 1967

If only the pope would declare the war in Vietnam immoral and forbid Catholics to take part in it! Indeed, if even the American bishops took that stand, I think the war could be brought to an end. Instead, Cardinal Spellman calls the war Christ's War. Only God knows how a man of the cloth can make such a blasphemous statement.

Millions of innocent Vietnamese men, women, and children are being killed, horribly maimed, tortured, and made homeless, while their country is being turned into a wasteland. And for what? In the South, where the greater proportion of bombs are being dropped, most people would be unable to define either Communism or capitalism. All they want is to be let alone.

President Johnson, in defending the war, made the statement that the Vietnamese want what we have. A little thought would make it clear who wants what the other has. We now have almost five-hundred-thousand troops in Vietnam, while I have yet to see one Vietnamese soldier in America. The irony is that the Vietnamese are so poor and technologically unsophisticated that it would be utterly impossible for them to come here; nor would they want to do so. Yet, the mutilating and killing goes on, and our political leaders continue to lie about the war's causes and what is really happening in Vietnam.

I asked Bishop Connolly to forbid the Catholics of our diocese to take part in the war, but he refused. For the first time, he was actually appalled at one of my suggestions. It seems that all I can do now is pray.

May 23, 1968

This afternoon, Bishop Connolly invited me into his office and offered me a cigar. I knew from past experience that when he did that, he was disturbed about something. It wasn't long before he told me what the trouble was. Several of our priests had been arrested for staging a rally against the draft and burning draft cards. These were the same priests who had been involved in other protests against the war in Vietnam, and they also had been leaders of civil rights demonstrations. One of them was my friend, Father Calvin.

"What am I going to do about these priests?" Bishop Connolly asked in exasperation. "I am tempted to suspend them. They are disgracing the Church."

"I can only tell you what I would do," I said.

"That's what I'm asking you," the bishop commented, somewhat annoyed at my hedging.

"As their bishop, I would give them whatever comfort I could," I told him. "I would visit each of them in jail, and I would hire the best lawyers in the diocese for them."

Bishop Connolly, who did not seem the least bit surprised at my suggestion, said: "People are saying they are Communists, Father."

"That's a lot of hogwash," I emphasized. "We both know they're not Communists, and so do the people who make those crazy accusations."

May 23, 1968

"Many influential priests are making them."
"Like Monsignor O'Shea?"
"Yes," the bishop replied.
"Well you know what I think about that."
"Then why do these priests do such mad things?" he asked. "It seems that the entire priesthood is losing its mind."
"Maybe it's only beginning to gain its conscience," I said. "I'm not so sure that I'd go about it exactly as they are, but—"

The bishop cut me off: "No, Father! You would do something much more diabolical!"

We both laughed, and then I said: "It is our own leaders who are responsible for the spread of Communism, albeit unwittingly. Because they fail to see what is really going on in the world, they end up backing the wrong side in almost every important social issue. They use the taxpayers' money to keep in power the corrupt military regimes of Asia and Latin America, while those regimes, in turn, use their guns to suppress the just aspirations of a poor, suffering population."

"But why do the people of these countries always seem to lean toward Communism?" the bishop asked.

"They have no place else to go," I replied. "Not only do the capitalists reject them, but they supply the very weapons which enslave and kill them. As long as we have leaders who do not understand these things, the Communists do not have to worry about hiring agents; they already have them."

"You seem to have very definite views on the subject," Bishop Connolly remarked.

"You know I do, Bishop, and that's why you asked my opinion," I smiled. "I can assure you that the priests who have been arrested are doing more to *counteract* Communism than our leaders in government."

"But should priests break the law?" Bishop Connolly asked.

"Christ obeyed the law whenever He could," I said, "yet there were times when He had to protest against straining out the gnat but swallowing the camel."

"What you say is true," Bishop Connolly granted, "but shouldn't we start with the individual? Isn't that the root of the problem? And isn't that the real concern of the priesthood—the spiritual?"

"It is the most important part of the problem," I replied, "but the environment in which an individual has to live is very important, too. I think the Church needs a variety of workers. We need great spiritual guides, who will work to transform the minds and hearts of men; we need great humanitarians like Mother Teresa of India, who believes that we should love and care for the poor on a person-to-person basis; and we need men like Father Camillo Torres, who when there was no other way to help the hungry and oppressed, put aside his cassock, took up the gun of a guerrilla, and gave his life fighting for the poor he loved."

Although I could see that Bishop Connolly was moved, he said: "There must be *other* ways, Father. We have to use the democratic process. The way should be productive, but lawful and nonviolent."

"I share your sentiments, Bishop," I told him, "but sometimes there is no other way. I'm sure that all the men like Father Torres wish that there were. But in trying to free the oppressed, one is always going to provoke the wrath and opposition of the oppressors. This was true of Moses, David, Daniel, and the apostles. It was true of Christ; and He said it would be true of His followers."

Bishop Connolly sat thinking for a few moments, and then he said: "I don't believe that I should visit the jail. It would give the impression I am taking sides, and as a bishop, I don't feel I should do that. But I want you to go and report back to me."

"I'll be glad to do that, Bishop."

"When you see Father Calvin, you can tell him that the diocese is going to provide one hundred thousand dollars for his work among the poor. He needs a dispensary, recreation center, and so many other things. Tell him that I hope this grant from the diocese will help him get started."

"I'll do that," I said. "Although his methods may not always seem orthodox, I happen to know that he is a builder; not a destroyer."

"And what about you, Father?"

"I hope that I am the same."

"You would like to be in jail with the others, wouldn't you?"

"I'd try to avoid that part of it," I said.

"But if you weren't my secretary, you would be doing the work they're doing, wouldn't you?"

"I suppose I would," I admitted. "But long ago, I decided to serve where God wants me."

Bishop Connolly smiled. "I think God has done all of us a very *big* favor by wanting you to serve here," he commented.

There was just a tinge of sarcasm in his voice.

August 4, 1968

Bishop Connolly spoke in the cathedral this morning on the latest papal encyclical, *Humanae Vitae*. Because he upheld Pope Paul's position, a number of people attending the Mass tried to shout him down. Then, many people in the congregation stalked out. Those who remained applauded the bishop. Although the bishop was heartened somewhat by his supporters, he was crestfallen and bewildered by this unprecedented event. Indeed, he was physically sickened; so much so that he has been unable to eat today.

I must say that I have nothing but contempt for those who so rudely attacked the bishop. We are witnessing a strange and disquieting phenomenon these days. While more and more people are preaching freedom of conscience and expression for themselves, some of them are the very first to want to deny the same privilege to others. They expect everyone to listen respectfully to what they have to say, but when somebody else tries to have his say, they attempt to silence him.

There are many people, naturally, who disagree with the pope's position on contraception and abortion; but that is no reason for refusing to hear and consider it. Common courtesy would require that much. Then, too, one would expect all Catholics to be eager to hear what Christ's vicar on earth and the successors of the apostles have to say about such important issues.

While I myself have had difficulties in applying the papal teachings on contraception in certain situations, I can certainly understand the pope's reasoning. From a theological standpoint, it is quite sound. It has been the Church's position since its inception two thousand years ago. I am not so sure that the present age has such superior wisdom that these teachings can simply be abrogated. Even though they are not a matter of dogma, they bear such weighty authority that if they were denied now, one could quite logically ask why any teachings of the Church should be accepted; indeed, why the Church itself should continue to exist. I still wish that the Church would permit exceptions to some of its laws regarding sexual morality, but I see the laws themselves as necessary and worthwhile.

True, many scientists keep warning the world that if population is not kept under control by means of contraception and abortion, starvation for all of us is right around the corner. On the other hand, I have recently read a book by a world-renowned Oxford economist, which points out that if the world's land and resources were used properly, forty-seven billion people could be fed at the highest standard of living which currently exists in the United States.

The predictors of doom emphasize the hunger that already exists in the world; the deteriorating environment; the possible spread of world-wide pestilence due to modern methods of transportation; and the possibility that tensions caused by overcrowding will lead to biological and thermonuclear warfare. The trouble is that all of these real and potential disasters have been created by the scientists themselves; and one wonders if the problem can be solved by having scientists give us more of the specious reasoning which has already brought us to the very brink of annihilation.

For years, scientists have been ridiculing the Catholic Church, declaring that it is intellectually backward, reactionary, anti-life, and anti-man. Today, any really honest person has to consider the possibility that science and not the Church deserves those appellations. Naturally, the Church was wrong in opposing particular scientific theories which were quite correct; but perhaps the Church was prophetic in opposing the direction in which those theories were to eventually lead man.

All of the great religions have always had a healthy respect for nature; indeed, they have their very roots in nature. Monks and

Hindu holy men—so often pilloried by the scientists for their superstition—have not brought about the ecological imbalance in nature. They have not gobbled up our resources, and poisoned our air, water, and food. This has been done by our "brilliant," "progressive," "all-knowing" scientists themselves.

For two thousand years, the Church has served as a major influence—indeed, quite possibly the most important influence—in shaping and preserving Western civilization. The scientists, on the other hand, have been in control for a comparatively brief period of time; and already mankind faces annihilation. With this in mind, I believe that *Humanae Vitae* takes on an added perspective.

Perhaps once again, it is the Church, speaking through the pope, which is really pro-life and pro-man. Indeed, a cardinal principle of the universe is that nature—the most sensitive and perceptive of mothers—works instinctively to preserve herself. Perhaps, in the end, a mankind threatened with extinction by ecological imbalance and thermonuclear weapons, will be preserved only through numbers. Perhaps the increase in the populations of the world is nature's way of enabling a portion of mankind—sufficient for maintaining the species *Homo sapiens*—to survive a thermonuclear or ecological disaster. Perhaps the pope himself, in speaking out against contraception and abortion, is serving as nature's agent in this regard.

What I really fear in the world today is not the influence of the pope, but the brutality, greed, craze for power, and megalomania of the scientists. They are much more dangerous to freedom of thought and action than the Inquisition ever was. Indeed, the inquisitors presupposed freedom of thought and action. They believed that a man had a soul which could either be saved or damned by what he thought, said, and did. Contemporary science, on the other hand, is increasingly prone to view man as a soulless creature—an automaton—to be controlled by drugs, psychiatrists, mechanical devices, and granting or withholding financial appropriations from government. The pope has reason to be concerned that scientists, acting in behalf of governments, may soon be deciding such matters as which people are to be allowed to have children, and which babies and old people are to be killed.

In the days before the fall of the Roman Empire, the government sought to control its citizens by offering them bread, entertainment, and sexual license. Today, people are being offered the same things, with the same purpose in mind; but the offer is being made in the name of that prestigious secular god—science. It is much easier to control beasts than it is men, and already men are being debased to a degree that places them on an even lower level than the animals.

I was shocked to learn that many psychiatrists and psychologists not only have their patients sit in the nude during therapy sessions, but some of them—again under the guise of science—engage in sexual relations with them. Books are being written by psychologists which advise parents, in the interests of good mental hygiene, to provide sexual stimulation for their babies and young children.

The purveyors of such madness not only debase people by taking away their dignity as human beings, their sensitivity, their freedom—their very souls—but they make huge sums of money in the process. Like the pornographers who push their wares in the name of mental health, or the drug companies which promote universal contraception, they have a financial interest in what they are advocating. Meanwhile, mental illness continues to increase, as does violent crime and general savagery of every description. The social scientists—quite conveniently for themselves—fail to see the connection; but it is plain enough for any intelligent child to perceive.

Even Catholic social scientists have accused the pope of not taking into consideration the insights of modern psychology when he wrote *Humanae Vitae*. They, along with many theologians, have relegated the idea of sin to the fossil heap. More and more, they accept the simplistic notion of modern psychology and sociology that if something is done by enough people, or if it seems practical or advantageous for the moment, it is right.

If an individual, on the other hand, does something which is deemed improper by his brainwatchers or the government, he is said to be ill and in need of treatment. I think I would prefer the innermost recesses of Dante's hell in preference to some of the forms such "treatment"—a euphemism for brainwashing—takes. But there is still no talk of sin. Robots cannot sin in a sexual sense, or in any other way.

As I see it, that is the crucial point of *Humanae Vitae*. The pope is asking man to safeguard his right to be responsible for what he does or does not do. He is asking him to preserve his spiritual being; his very soul. I thank God for the courage displayed by the pope in giving us this unpopular document. It is much needed.

August 10, 1968

Poor Bishop Connolly! I really feel sorry for him. He is an excellent administrator, but he is living in an age which he finds incomprehensible. The doctor has been warning him about his high blood pressure, which I am sure would become normal if only he could solve the many problems that now beset the diocese.

This evening, more than a thousand people marched on the bishop's residence. From my suite on the top floor, I could hear them chanting their slogans when they were still blocks away. I went downstairs and tried to prepare the bishop as best I could for what was coming.

The crowd was made up mostly of Polish and Italian Americans. They were upset because Father Calvin has been leading open housing demonstrations in their neighborhoods. They carried two coffins. There was an inscription on one which read: FATHER CALVIN REST IN HELL. The other declared: GOD IS WHITE.

I told the bishop that I thought he should receive a delegation of no more than three members from the group. Since we already knew what the marchers wanted, I suggested that he be sympathetic but noncommittal, telling the representatives that the matter would be studied. The bishop, who seemed almost paralyzed with fear, decided that I was right.

I advised the bishop to remain inside while I went out to face the marchers, and once again, he agreed. After some more shouting and chanting, plus the singing of the national anthem, I finally got the bishop's message across. Three leaders of the march accompanied me inside the residence, and as they did so, a loud cheer went up.

The bishop, who had seemed so fearful only minutes before, surprised me by greeting the leaders of the march with great poise and dignity. He politely listened to their grievances, and the request that Father Calvin be transferred from his parish in the ghetto to a place where he would no longer be able to organize demonstrations. The delegation appeared satisfied with the bishop's expression of sympathy for their problems, and the promise that the matter would be carefully studied.

After the representatives had gone and the crowd had dispersed, Bishop Connolly seemed to be on the verge of collapse once again. "A younger man should have this post," he said. "I am going to submit my resignation to the pope."

"I don't think he would accept it," I told him. "No one could do a better job than you are doing. Both the Church and the diocese need you."

The bishop seemed to perk up somewhat at my compliment— a compliment which came from the heart. Although Bishop Connolly and I do not agree on every issue, I have grown to love the man. He is so very good and kind. He never gets enough sleep, simply because he is always trying to make his diocese a better place for everyone. Moreover, he does all this amid scant thanks and much criticism.

Bishop Connolly offered me a cigar and took one himself. "I can understand Father Calvin's concern for open housing," he said, "but the people who were here tonight have a legitimate complaint. They are poor people, and they have worked hard for their homes. Most of them will never be able to afford another one. Consider what happened to the Homewood section, Father, when blacks came in and whites started to move out. The homes there are now in shambles; and it's not safe for anyone to walk the streets—black or white. When a black family could not afford to buy a house, they pooled their funds with other black families. Now there are four or five families, with as many as thirty or forty people, living in a house that was meant for a family of five or six."

August 12, 1968

"I know," I told him.

"Besides that, all the people who were here tonight are Catholics, and they represent about thirty thousand other Catholics. Father Calvin's parish of Saint Martin de Porres has no more than five hundred members. Are we going to place the welfare of five hundred Catholics before that of thirty thousand?"

"I'm sure that Father Calvin is interested in all blacks—Catholic and non-Catholic," I pointed out. "Moreover, I think he is concerned about principles; not numbers. But I do think that whites, in this instance, are justified in their concern. The problem is not that the people moving into the area would be black, but that they would be culturally deprived. I'm sure that the more refined blacks would not want these people in their own areas, just as whites would not want other whites who had been similarly deprived. I think that you should talk to Father Calvin and try to arrange some sort of compromise. Perhaps the Poles and Italians could be persuaded to accept those black families which promise to live in separate homes, and whose moral standards are high."

"Will you talk to him as my representative, Father?" Bishop Connolly asked.

"Certainly," I said.

"I am indebted to you, Father, for all that you have done in this matter."

"You owe me nothing," I told him.

August 12, 1968

When I met with Father Calvin today, he was quite incensed. He felt that the bishop was making use of me to get him to do something he did not want to do. It took me a while to convince him otherwise. I'm sure now that Father Calvin has no idea how the bishop's mind works. I had to explain that the bishop wanted me to handle the matter for the very reason that he did not understand priests like Father Calvin, and did not want to be unfair.

Father Calvin was still angry and belligerent after the explanation. "What makes you think that *you* understand?" he asked. "I don't see how anybody who sits behind a desk all day can understand the sufferings of these people."

"You wouldn't have said that when we worked together at Sacred Heart," I told him.

"You were a lot different then," he grumbled.

"Was I?" I asked.

"All right, I'm sorry, Pete," he apologized. "I just happen to resent the fact that the bishop is concerned chiefly about the whites, merely because they contribute the most money to the Church."

"I think you're missing the point," I said. "You know as well as I do that the whites we are dealing with are not going to sit idly by and watch this happen. If the blacks move in under present circumstances, they are going to be bombed, burned out, and quite possibly shot."

"Those are risks we are prepared to take," Father Calvin declared. "I'll not call off the demonstrations."

"I don't want you to call them off if you can promise the bishop certain things," I said. "Remember, first of all, that we are dealing with poor whites; not wealthy ones. As regards economic status, they are not that far removed from the blacks you are trying to help. Can you promise the bishop that the area will not become another Homewood if open housing is put into effect? Can you promise that thirty or forty people will not be living in a house meant for one family? Can you promise that the neighborhood will be kept clean and tidy; that roaches, mice, and rats will be kept out? Can you promise that the area will not be turned into a shambles of broken windows and partially burned houses? Can you promise that the streets will be as safe to walk as they are today?"

"You know I can't do that, Pete."

"Well in God's name, man, why do you want to create another slum; another ghetto for both blacks and whites?" I asked. "What will that accomplish? The blacks will be no better off, and the whites will be worse off."

"What do *you* propose?"

"Why not compromise?" I asked. "Why not help both blacks and whites? Let's get together with black and white leaders to work out a plan whereby blacks of good moral character would be welcomed by their white neighbors."

"You mean blacks who have money, don't you?"

"No, I don't," I said. "I believe the neighborhood should be open to any black who will live decently and take care of his home properly. If he doesn't have the money, I think we should find ways to help him get it."

"I'm not convinced that's the right approach," Father Calvin stated. "These people have been discriminated against too long."

"I'm sure you know that I agree with you," I said. "But bringing blacks into a neighborhood where they are not welcome is not the best way either; nor is destroying the property of other poor people."

"All right," Father Calvin agreed reluctantly. "We'll try it your way for *now*. But it better work."

"I only ask that you try it," I said.

August 29, 1968

A compromise has finally been worked out between Father Calvin's blacks and the whites in adjacent areas. Only those blacks who are upright and highly responsible will be admitted to the white neighborhoods. On the other hand, Bishop Connolly has provided a fund from which poor blacks can borrow in order to purchase property in these neighborhoods. We also have set up a special committee of whites, which is to welcome the blacks, introduce them to other whites, and in every way possible, make them feel at home. The bishop has ordered that appropriate sermons be given in all Catholic churches located in the white neighborhoods. These sermons are to point out to the people that it is their Christian duty to welcome the blacks, and that if they do not do so, they are committing serious sin.

Father Calvin seems satisfied, although not exactly happy. He still has many serious misgivings. Frankly, I believe the plan is going to be successful. Even so, I have my fingers crossed.

The Diary of a Catholic Bishop

March 18, 1969

Father Kerwin, Catholic chaplain of the local VA hospital, had a long talk with Bishop Connolly today. After he left, the bishop called me into his office and told me about the terrible conditions which exist at the hospital. Bishop Connolly was appalled. He asked me to go right over to the hospital and look into the situation for him.

I found conditions to be exactly as Father Kerwin had described them to the bishop. The hospital is infested with rats, mice, and roaches. Those veterans who are paralyzed could quite easily be bitten by a rat and not know it. In order to prevent such occurrences, some of the veterans who are able to move around have been setting traps for the rodents.

Not only is the hospital dirty and the roofs leaky, but it is overcrowded and inadequately staffed. Patients who have damaged nervous systems are unable to do anything at all for themselves, and they often have to wait for hours before anyone gives them a drink of water. I saw a number of paralyzed veterans who were lying naked on their beds. They had been given baths, and after four hours, they were still waiting for someone to cover them up. I got so disgusted that I began making their beds and covering them myself. Finally, an aide came up and took over.

Most of the veterans are very bitter. A Vietnam veteran by the name of John Shipman told me: "I used to criticize the guys who went to Canada to avoid the draft, Father. I wouldn't do that now. I wish I had gone there myself. I used to love my country, but now I hate it. The more I think about it, the more I realize that all of the people I saw die in Vietnam died for nothing."

Dr. Altman, the administrator of the hospital, told me that he is unable to remedy the situation. He said that the government does not appropriate adequate funds for VA hospitals. He added that the local hospital is not an exception, but that VA hospitals are generally pretty bad throughout the country.

After visiting that place, I have decided that the more than fifty thousand American soldiers who have been killed in Vietnam are the lucky ones. I'm more concerned now about the three hundred thousand who have been wounded. Like most casualties

March 19, 1969

of this war, the boys at the hospital are simple souls. Almost all of them come from poorer families. The sons of government officials, and those born of wealthy families, are not being mangled in Vietnam.

The same holds true of South Vietnamese soldiers. The wealthy South Vietnamese—those who reap all of the benefits from their corrupt regime—keep their sons out of combat. Poor boys are forced to do the fighting. Thus, we have a situation wherein poor boys from America fight poor boys in Asia; and very few from either side would be able to properly define Communism or capitalism if their very lives depended on it.

March 19, 1969

Last night I was unable to sleep. I kept thinking about those unfortunate boys in the VA hospital. Then, about three o'clock in the morning, I had an idea. I don't know why it is, but my best ideas always seem to come during the night. I decided that a group of volunteers should be organized to help out at the hospital; and I thought I knew just the person to lead the group—Mrs. Russo. She was such a help in inaugurating and directing the project which cared for the needy when I was a curate at Saint Anne's. In fact, after nineteen years, she was still running that project as effectively as ever.

As soon as I saw the bishop this morning, I reported to him on my visit to the hospital. He said that he planned to telephone some senators and congressmen in regard to the situation. I told him about my talk with Dr. Altman, and pointed out that it most likely would be years—if then—before the bureaucracy acted to improve things. Finally, I gave him my idea about asking Mrs. Russo to organize a group of volunteers, who would help out each day at the hospital. He was all for it. In fact, he gave me the afternoon off to visit Mrs. Russo.

Mrs. Russo is a saint. She was so happy to see me again that she cried. She kept telling me how proud she was that I had become the bishop's secretary. "All of the people at Saint Anne's still think of you as their own son," she said. "When anything good happens to you, it happens to all of us."

She cried even more when I told her about conditions at the VA hospital; but this time the tears were not those of joy. "Don't worry, Father!" she repeated a number of times. "I'll take care of it!"

I ended up staying for a delicious supper of shrimp marinara and spaghetti. I talked some more about the VA hospital with Mrs. Russo, her husband, and their five children. I learned that the entire family had become involved in the project which helps the needy in Saint Anne's parish. By the time I left, I was convinced that Mrs. Russo and her family were quite capable of solving the problem at the VA hospital.

April 15, 1969

Mrs. Russo's group has been doing an excellent job at the VA hospital. There are now more than sixty volunteers working there. I asked Bishop Connolly if I could help out in my spare time, and although he granted permission, he was quite reluctant about it. He made it clear that he does not believe a priest should be doing such menial work. He said that he was granting my request only because he owed me something for getting the program started.

Frankly, I feel much more like a priest and a human being when I can actually touch the sick. So far, I have been able to spend two or three hours each day bathing patients, rubbing their backs, lifting them, emptying bedpans and urinals; and whenever it is requested, offering spiritual consolation as well. Maybe I should have been a doctor. So many people keep telling me that I have a healing touch. They say that patients seem to feel better just by having me around them. I don't know what it is. I do know that spiritual and physical consolation are more closely related than most people realize. Maybe all priests and ministers should study medicine.

I just wish that our political leaders would come to the hospital and see some of the boys there. If our president, senators, and congressmen spent a few days working in the VA hospitals, I think they would end the war in a hurry. The problem is that they never get close to the mangled flesh they have been so instrumental in creating. In fact, they seldom get close to the flesh at all.

November 28, 1969

Perhaps we should introduce a requirement that before anyone could serve as president, in the cabinet, or in Congress, he would first have to spend a few years working in our VA hospitals. I think that would work wonders in producing a more humane type of leader.

November 28, 1969

The more I hear about the massacre at Mylai, the more concerned I am about the future of our country. To think that American soldiers lined up unarmed old men, women, children—even babies —and wantonly murdered them! I'll never be able to forget the photographs: the old woman trying to protect her thirteen-year-old daughter from rape; the small boy attempting to shield his even smaller brother with his own body—and then all of them dead.

Some Americans are already justifying what happened on grounds that the soldiers were merely following orders. They completely ignore the fact that when the Nazis made exactly the same plea, we brought them to trial as war criminals. Others are saying that the soldiers acted as they did because a number of their comrades had recently been killed by stepping on land mines. Even if something could be said for this argument—and considering the enormity of what happened, I don't think it can—it avoids the much larger question. Why were the mines planted in the first place? To thwart an enemy, naturally, which had come thousands of miles to kill, maim, and burn.

Almost as terrifying as the massacre itself is the fact that once again we hear people—supposedly patriots—insinuating that those who tell the truth about such incidents are committing treason. The real treason is being committed by those who are responsible for such crimes, by those who conceal them, by those who defend them, and by those who don't want to talk about them. I pray to God that more people will wake up before it is too late.

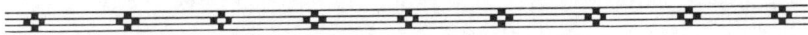

January 1, 1970

This morning I said Mass at Saint Paul's Church. Then I spent a few hours with the pastor, my old friend and mentor, Monsignor Grosclaude. I could think of no better way to begin the New Year. Although Monsignor Grosclaude must be close to seventy years old, he could easily pass for fifty. He seems to have the same vitality and magnetism he possessed when he was rector and spiritual director of the seminary. Saint Paul's itself is a testament to those qualities. When Monsignor Grosclaude became pastor twelve years ago, the parish was dying. Today it is one of the most thriving parishes in the diocese.

Even though Monsignor Grosclaude has had no official connection with the seminary since he became pastor of Saint Paul's, he has maintained a keen interest in what goes on there. He lamented the fact that there have been so many new rectors in recent years.

"It's not a good idea," he said. "A man needs time to learn the job. This business of changing the rector every year or two is not in the best interests of the students or the institution."

"I know," I commented, "but the bishop is rather desperate. There has been so much unrest among the students; and then, too, vocations have been declining at an incredible rate."

"Do you think that the appointment of Monsignor Wilt is going to make a difference?"

"I doubt it," I said. "Monsignor Wilt used to be too conservative, and now I think he's too liberal. I don't know if you've seen him lately, but his grey hair extends almost to his shoulders—what he has of it. He's completely bald in front. With his big belly, he looks like a sixty-year-old hip Santa Claus. If the seminarians appreciate humor, he's sure to be a smashing hit."

"I wouldn't worry about the hair," Monsignor Grosclaude smiled, "but what's beneath it. The bishop *had* to be desperate."

"Many people admire Monsignor Wilt as a progressive," I said. "He was responsible for a number of experiments at a liturgical conference I attended a few months ago. The most notable one was throwing paper plates from the balcony. The congregation then picked them up, tore them into pieces, and handed them to each other. This was called Communion."

January 1, 1970

"Good Lord!"

"I told them I thought it was a lot of nonsense, but since most of them considered it a truly transcendent religious experience, I was lucky to escape without being mobbed. If you disagree with these contemporary zealots, they really get mad. Their pettiness, arrogance, and conceit would make the original Pharisees blush. What worries me most is that they have no sense of humor."

"Have you heard about the Emergency Mass?" Monsignor Grosclaude asked.

"No. What's *that*?"

"It's the idea that if a priest is not present, anyone in the congregation can consecrate the bread and wine."

"Some of our colleagues are trying to put us out of business," I smiled.

"I've had priests tell me that unless all the people in the congregation love each other, the Eucharist is invalid. If that's the case, we're wasting our time anyway. I'm sure that no parish has that kind of harmony."

"It can all get pretty bizarre," I said. "Just a few days ago, Bishop Connolly was incensed to learn that three priests, attired in tuxedos and white gloves, had concelebrated a wedding Mass. Some priests insist on wearing dungarees or overalls when they say Mass. We even have one in the diocese who says Mass in a specially tailored cashmere coat."

"I'm very concerned about their disrespect for the Blessed Sacrament," Monsignor Grosclaude lamented. "This business of buying a loaf of ordinary bread, consecrating it, and then breaking off pieces which are handed to the congregation, is sacrilegious."

"They're like a bunch of kids playing house," I said.

"And what good does it do, son? People like Monsignor Wilt keep talking about making the Church relevant, especially to the young. But ever since all of these innovations began, the number of Catholics who attend religious services—especially young Catholics—has continued to decrease alarmingly."

"Small wonder!" I commented. "Our churches are no longer the quiet, reverent, prayerful places they once were, where an individual could really feel that he was communicating with God. Of late, when I've accompanied Bishop Connolly to the various churches for confirmation services, people have been so noisy that I've expected entrepreneurs selling hot dogs and popcorn to appear at any moment. It's all so very sad, especially since we could still be providing the peace, quiet, and privacy before God, which are so scarce in today's world. Before the changes, the priest conducted ceremonies, but the layman had to participate in them only to the extent he wished. His heart was always free to soar to God in the way that was best for him; whether that was through saying the rosary, reading his own favorite prayers, or personal meditation."

"The major problem, as I see it," Monsignor Grosclaude said, "is that the so-called revival which has been taking place in the Church is just the opposite of a spiritual revival. The changes have been chiefly external and superficial, while the individual soul has remained untouched. Indeed, Catholics are much more worldly than they were before. We don't see more prayer, humility, and mortification of the flesh; but we do see—especially among priests and nuns—an ever increasing secularism, self-righteousness, and appetite for material goods."

"You and Father Calvin have always been right about these things," I told him. "If people had listened to you years ago, the Church would be much better off today."

"Perhaps I get carried away, too, with my emphasis on spirituality," Monsignor Grosclaude smiled. Then he added: "But I fail to see religious progress when nuns shed their religious garb; when they dress in slacks and shorts; when they spend much of their time before the TV, all the while munching on pretzels, potato chips, and candy; when they smoke cigarettes, drink beer, and gulp whiskey; when they no longer pray, meditate, or sometimes even attend Mass. They keep talking about love, but I've been told that love doesn't include helping with the everyday chores. The housework and spiritual exercises are left for the nuns who don't love. Thank God there are still some of them left!"

"You forgot to mention the third way," I said.

Monsignor Grosclaude looked puzzled. "What way is that?" he asked.

"I thought you knew about it," I told him. "Some nuns and

priests have decided that they can remain in religion and still have a boyfriend or girl friend. Since they are neither married nor celibate, they call it the third way."

"Good Lord!" Monsignor Grosclaude exclaimed. "I hadn't heard about that."

"If you were working in the chancery, you would hear things like that every day," I said. "Not long ago, a Jesuit superior told Bishop Connolly that he was afraid all the Jesuits in his house might be arrested at any time, including himself. Some members of the group, who decided that cocktails were lower middle class, have replaced them with marijuana."

"Poor Bishop Connolly!"

"I know. . . . I'm concerned about his health."

"No wonder vocations are so scarce," Monsignor Grosclaude lamented. "At the very time young people are looking for an anchor, we've thrown out many of the really good things we've had to offer them. Have you read about the young people who have been forming religious communes, embracing the Ten Commandments, and rejecting the materialistic values of our society?"

"Yes, I have," I told him. "The really sad thing is that most priests and religious are opposed to the crazy changes which are being introduced into their lives. But they have no idea what to do about it. For one thing, the innovators are so much more vocal and aggressive than they. Then, too, most fear that there will be an even greater exodus from their ranks if they refuse to give the innovators everything they want."

"What interests me," Monsignor Grosclaude commented, "is that before the innovators took over, priests and nuns rarely left. Now many priests and religious are leaving for the very reason that they are dissatisfied with the changes which have been introduced. Some join stricter communities; but others return to the world, in the conviction that they can live a more spiritual life there than in a modern rectory, convent, or monastery."

"What do you see as our future, Monsignor?"

"Son, if I were to follow logic and human instinct, I'd say that the Church is dying. But then I recall the words of Jesus to his disciples: 'Behold, I am with you all days, even unto the consummation of the world.' If it were not for that promise, I wouldn't have much hope."

"Nor would I," I said.

May 30, 1970

There was quite a bit of excitement today. Father Malloy went away for the weekend, so I heard confessions for him at the cathedral this evening. About eight o'clock, a policeman opened the door to my part of the confessional and said: "Father, please come with me right away. A man has climbed onto the ledge of a hotel roof and is threatening to jump. He has been there for over an hour, and no one has been able to rescue him. A psychiatrist talked to him for a while, but it was no use. Somebody said the guy is a Catholic. We think maybe a priest can help."

Still wearing my cassock, I rushed outside with the policeman and jumped into the squad car. A policeman on motorcycle served as an escort, and with the siren blaring, we sped to the hotel. When we arrived, there was such a large crowd standing outside the building that several policemen had to clear a path for us.

As soon as we reached the hotel roof, a policeman handed me the bull horn he had been using and asked me to talk to the man on the ledge. I did, but the man refused to budge. Finally, over the protests of the police officers, I went out on the ledge myself.

Once I was on the ledge, I became aware that the crowd below was shouting insults at the man. They were actually trying to get him to jump. At first, I couldn't quite believe it. Then I began to feel a sudden revulsion for the human race. I wanted to shout back at them, but I immediately said a prayer, asking God to give me an unperturbed mind so that I could deal with the matter at hand.

When I got to within two feet of the man, I stopped. I did not want to startle him into jumping. The man was crying.

"They want me to jump, Father!" he kept repeating. "They want me to jump!"

"I know they do," I said, "but I don't. Neither does Our Lord. Give me your hand."

The man was about to take hold of my hand, but he hesitated, and then drew his hand back. "I have nothing to live for," he declared.

"You have God to live for," I told him. "He loves you so much that He has sent me out here to risk my own life in order to help you."

"They want me to jump, Father!" the man repeated again, as though he still found it difficult to comprehend that fact.

"Don't think about them," I said. "Just think about me. I'm here to help you."

The man finally took my hand, and I led him from the ledge onto the roof. Two policemen were going to handcuff him, but I stopped them. The man threw his arms around me and wept.

When I got him calmed down, I accompanied him and several of the policemen downstairs. I took him by the hand again as we made our way through the jeering crowd to the squad car. On the way to the hospital, he told me that his wife and two children had been killed when his home caught fire last week.

June 8, 1970

This afternoon, my old colleague, Sister Margaret Mary, and Father Neville, the current chaplain of Holy Spirit College, arrived at the chancery to keep an appointment with the bishop. I greeted them and ushered them into Bishop Connolly's office. Sister Margaret Mary seemed rather embarrassed to see me. I suppose she was thinking of our days together in the history department of Holy Spirit College. She no longer wears a religious habit or veil. Except for a small pin, she dresses as a laywoman. She is now known as Sister Marie Burke, having assumed the name she had before becoming a nun.

As soon as Father Neville and Sister Marie Burke had finished their business and left the chancery, Bishop Connolly asked to see me. He was furious. In all the years I've known him, he's never used such strong language. "Those damn fools want to be married," he said. "But that's not *all*. She intends to remain in the convent while they're living together as husband and wife, and he wants to continue as a priest in the diocese. Did you ever hear of anything so asinine?"

"The pope will never permit it," I remarked.

"Of course, he won't; and I told them so. But they want me to send their case to Rome, and I suppose I'll have to do it."

"It looks as though Sister Margaret Mary has finally gotten her man."

"What do you mean, Father?"

"Nothing important," I said. "I was just reminiscing."

"Holy Spirit College is much different from what it was when you were there," Bishop Connolly stated. "They're teaching heresy; and even the parents of students are complaining. They have a theology professor on the faculty who tells students that the Bible is mythology. I keep protesting to the administration, but they refuse to fire him."

"And they thought *I* was radical," I smiled.

"Father, right now I wish that I had a dozen priests like you there," the bishop said. "That trollop who was just here told me that she no longer believes in the institutional Church. She said that she is looking forward to the day when everyone attends Mass in private homes."

"If she doesn't believe in the institutional Church, why does she want to remain in the convent after she's married?" I asked.

"Ask her!" the bishop exclaimed. "You should know by now, Father, that these people have abandoned all logic. Madness reigns supreme!"

"What about Father Neville?"

"She did most of the talking for both of them. When I told her that I was certain the pope would refuse their request, she said: 'That's up to him! I can always get a job as a history professor, and Father Neville can teach theology at a secular university. We'll make a lot of money.'"

"So they'll make a lot of money," I commented. "It's amazing how she could have been a nun for so many years without learning the first thing about religion—even secular religion."

"It's pathetic," the bishop said.

"How times have changed!" I sighed.

And so they have—on the surface, at least. There is a woman in the English department of Holy Spirit College, a Mrs. Stone, who is really making a killing on the unrest which exists in the Church today. She has very conveniently become a convert to Catholicism—I suspect that economic motives influenced her from the beginning—and although she has no background in philosophy, theology, history, or even everyday religion, she is making a small fortune by attacking the institutional Church in articles and books.

Her pronouncements are absurd to anyone who is knowledgeable in religious matters; but that makes no difference to her followers, who are just as ignorant as she is. She frequently appears on TV, and it is always to propose some nonsensical scheme, which she tries to pass off as profound. Recently she suggested that the cathedral be turned into a recreation center. Bishop Connolly refers to her as "the crazy woman of Holy Spirit College." He has repeatedly asked the nuns to remove her from the faculty, but they grovel at her feet. Instead of firing her, they have recently named her a full professor, even though she has no doctorate—one of the requisites for such a promotion at the school.

But then, Sister Prudentia, the president of Holy Spirit College, has herself taken on a new dimension. Now known as Sister Rosemary Murphy, she no longer wears a veil or religious habit either. Also in keeping with the times, she has suddenly become interested in the poor. She is forever giving speeches on the subject. Indeed, one would think that the poor were her original discovery. She wanted to appropriate an entire building at Holy Spirit College as a center for rehabilitating drug addicts—another of her recent interests—but the bishop managed to thwart her plan. She promptly denounced him to the newspapers as being unchristian and unworthy of his office.

While I find any interest in the poor and suffering highly commendable, I have the feeling that the recent interest of people like Sister Rosemary Murphy is little more than a fad. It is fashionable to do these things at the moment, so they do them. I suspect that when such things are no longer fashionable, and no longer attract publicity, they'll be the first to return to the old ways. I believe that the former Sister Prudentia could despise the poor tomorrow, just as easily as she did yesterday. The problem is that I see no real commitment of heart in such people.

It is interesting, though, to observe how the ultraconservatives have become the ultraliberals. When anyone suggested to them several years ago what they themselves are advocating today, they were so outraged that they considered burning at the stake too good for that person. Extremes mark their lives. They are just as illogical in being liberals as they were in being conservatives. Although their views seem to have changed for the moment, these people remain as bigoted, narrow-minded, and unyielding as they ever were.

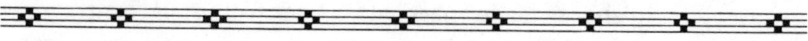

April 24, 1971

Today I said Mass at my alma mater, the diocesan seminary. I hadn't been back to Saint Mary's in years, but I kept hearing stories from priests who had. They told me that under the leadership of Monsignor Wilt, the place had become a complete madhouse. For one thing, they said that instead of cassocks, the priests and students now wore tight-fitting trousers and sweaters. Father Malloy was there on Holy Thursday and Good Friday, and he couldn't believe his eyes. He said that on Holy Thursday, as part of the religious services, a group of faculty and students did a dance in white leotards. On Good Friday, they did another dance, this time in black leotards. "My God, Father!" he told me. "I think they're all a bunch of fruits."

Several months ago, Father Huber, one of our diocesan priests working on his doctorate, took up residence at the seminary so that he would have peace and quiet to write his thesis. He stayed only a week. His room was located above the new barroom, and the racket not only prevented him from working, but it kept him awake. He said that every night there was a boisterous party going on until three or four in the morning.

My friend, Father Jim McHugh, had dinner at the seminary a few weeks ago. He told me that women were present at this dinner. Moreover, Monsignor Wilt had consumed so many martinis before the meal that he fell flat on his face when he got up to say grace. Since he was out cold, the vice-rector, who wasn't in very good shape himself, had to say the prayer. After the dinner was over, Father McHugh saw a number of seminarians take women to their rooms.

April 24, 1971

Apparently most—if not all—rules have now been abandoned at the seminary. The seminarians come and go pretty much as they please. Most of them have cars, and they even stay out at night if they wish. A number of them work all night. Attending religious services is optional. I understand that some of them never even attend Mass.

My own visit to the seminary this morning convinced me that everything I've heard is true. I was greeted at the door by a seminarian wearing a sweater and skintight trousers. He found Monsignor Wilt for me, who was attired exactly the same way. Poor Monsignor Wilt had bulges everywhere. He is too fat to dress like that. Then there was the long, grey hair that now hangs over his shoulders. The front part of his head is more bald than ever. I had a hard time keeping a straight face when I looked at him.

He was pleasant enough, though. He told me to pick out any chalice I wanted for saying Mass. Most of them were ceramic, but I managed to find a gold one. Then he asked me if I wanted to wear a robe. I thought he was offering to lend me a cassock, and I asked: "Do I need one?"

"Of course not, Father," he replied.

Then I found out that he thought I wanted to say Mass just wearing my suit. I told him that I preferred to wear the traditional vestments. I asked for an alb.

"We no longer use them, Father," he informed me. "We usually wear the Wittenberg robe."

Since he had no alb, I told him that I would wear the robe in its place; but I insisted on putting a stole and chasuble over it.

When I entered the chapel, I was astounded. There were several tables for saying Mass, but other than that, the place looked something like a setting for one of Eugene Ionesco's plays. All of the pews had been removed and replaced by stools. The stools faced a platform, from which sermons were given.

After I had said Mass, I mentioned to Monsignor Wilt that I hadn't seen many seminarians around. I asked him where they were.

"They're away for the weekend, Father," he replied nonchalantly.

I had a notion to ask him where they were and what they

were doing, but I knew he didn't know—or care. I did ask him where the Blessed Sacrament was kept, since it was obviously no longer kept in the chapel. He directed me to a repository down the hall.

When I got there, I tried to turn on a light, but the bulb was burned out. By leaving the door open, I could see that I was in a cubicle, barely big enough for two people to pray at a time. There was not even so much as a vigil light burning before the Blessed Sacrament. I knelt down and actually wept. "So this is where they have You, Dear Lord," I prayed.

I recalled my own days at Saint Mary's, when there were always a number of priests and seminarians kneeling before the Blessed Sacrament in the chapel. In fact, that was where many of us had gotten our daily strength. Without it, I don't think we could have persevered until ordination. I know I couldn't have.

Then I recalled something else. I was once talking to a Mohammedan who had recently visited Westminster Abbey in London. "What do you think of it?" I asked him.

"It's nothing," he replied. "It reminds me of a big mausoleum."

That's the way I feel about the new Saint Mary's Seminary.

May 2, 1971

Last night I was awakened by Mrs. Owens, our housekeeper, who told me that Bishop Connolly had been vomiting and was very ill. When I got to his quarters on the second floor, the bishop was experiencing difficulty in breathing, as well as excruciating pain in his chest. He also was suffering a great deal of pain in his left arm. I immediately telephoned Dr. Cappozzi, the bishop's personal physician, and told him that I thought the bishop had suffered a heart attack. Dr. Cappozzi said that he would be right over.

While I waited for the doctor, I did my best to comfort the bishop and to keep him calm. When Dr. Cappozzi finally arrived, he agreed that the bishop had probably suffered a heart attack. He gave him an injection of Demerol to relieve the pain. When the pain did not subside within an hour, he administered an injection of morphine sulfate. This second injection relieved most of the pain, and while the bishop was still awake, I anointed him. Then I recited some of his favorite prayers. Soon he was asleep.

"We are going to have to take him to the hospital," Dr. Cappozzi said. He telephoned Saint John's Hospital, requested an ambulance, and told them to prepare a place in the Coronary Care Unit for the bishop. He also telephoned Dr. Tracy, a cardiologist, and Dr. Morrison, a cardiovascular specialist, and asked them to come to the hospital.

I quickly got dressed before the ambulance came. Then both the doctor and I rode in back of the ambulance with the bishop. As we neared the hospital, the bishop woke up and began to insist that he was perfectly all right. When he asked to be taken back to his residence, Dr. Cappozzi finally told him that he had probably suffered a heart attack. The bishop then asked me to telephone Monsignor Grosclaude, and have him come to the hospital as soon as possible. I promised that I would.

When we reached the hospital, I was going to accompany the bishop into the Coronary Care Unit, but he requested again that I get in touch with Monsignor Grosclaude. I did as he wished, and Monsignor Grosclaude promised that he would try to be at the hospital within the hour.

By the time I entered the Coronary Care Unit, they were already attaching the bishop to the special monitoring devices. I heard the bishop ask: "What are my chances?"

One of the doctors replied: "At the moment, I think they are very good, Your Excellency. But you should try to rest now."

"After I have seen Monsignor Grosclaude," the bishop said.

The cardiologist and cardiovascular specialist had gone by the time Monsignor Grosclaude entered the Coronary Care Unit. He was pale and quite obviously worried. He shook hands with me, and then went over to the bed. "How are you, Bill?" he asked the bishop.

I was a little surprised at the informal way he addressed the bishop. I had never heard anybody call the bishop by his first name before.

"There's nothing wrong with me, Jerry," the bishop said. "Just a slight heart attack. I feel fine now. I should have stayed at home in my own bed."

"You are much better off here, Bill," Monsignor Grosclaude told him. "They have all of the equipment they need to help you."

Now the bishop said that he wanted to talk to Monsignor Grosclaude alone. He also requested stationery and a pen, stating that he wished to write some letters.

Dr. Cappozzi balked at this, but he could see that it was useless to argue. The doctor told one of the nurses to get the stationery and pen.

When Dr. Cappozzi and I got outside, the doctor said: "He needs rest. But what can I do? It is a very delicate matter to handle coronary patients. You have to be somewhat firm with them, but at the same time, you don't want to get them upset. That does more harm than good. Besides, how does one disagree with a bishop?"

"What are his chances, doctor?" I asked.

"It is too early to say," the doctor replied. "We should know better in about a week. So far, he's responding well. But in these cases, all of that expensive equipment in the Coronary Care Unit doesn't mean a whole lot. We doctors can't do very much either. It is in the hands of God."

When Monsignor Grosclaude came out of the Coronary Care Unit, Dr. Cappozzi went back inside. Monsignor Grosclaude had two letters with him. We sat down on a bench in the hall and talked for a while.

"They must be important letters," I remarked.

"They are, son," Monsignor Grosclaude said. "One is for the apostolic delegate. The other is addressed to the pope himself."

"It's strange that he didn't ask me to write them," I commented.

"He wanted to write them himself," Monsignor Grosclaude said. "I hope you don't mind that he had an old friend help him. There is so little I can do right now."

"Not at all," I told him. "Besides, you are doing a great deal for him in just being here. I'm sure that it makes him feel a whole lot better."

Monsignor Grosclaude and I discussed what to do next. Since all of the bishop's close relatives are dead, we arranged a schedule which would enable one of us to be near him at all times. Monsignor Grosclaude wanted to stay with me while I kept vigil throughout the night, but I persuaded him to go back to the rectory for some sleep. I said that I would remain during the night, and he could come back in the morning. Then I would get some sleep and return in the afternoon.

When Dr. Cappozzi came out of the Coronary Care Unit, he told us that the bishop was asleep. I then went outside with Monsignor Grosclaude, where I helped him flag a taxi. After he had gone, I went back inside the hospital.

Every hour or so, I looked in on the bishop, who continued to sleep. The rest of the time I spent in prayer.

May 5, 1971

This afternoon, shortly after I had relieved Monsignor Grosclaude, I was sitting in the corridor of the hospital, keeping my vigil, when I noticed several doctors rushing into the Coronary Care Unit. In a short while, Dr. Cappozzi came hurrying down the hall. "It's the bishop," he told me. "He has a pulmonary embolism."

"Can I see him?" I asked.

"You had better wait here for the time being," the doctor replied.

Within a few minutes, Dr. Cappozzi came out of the Coronary Care Unit. "The bishop wants to see you, Father," he said. "I don't think he's going to make it."

I was stunned. The bishop had been doing so well.

When I entered the Coronary Care Unit and approached the bishop's bed, I noticed that his face was ashen. He spoke quite clearly and coherently, though. I took his hand in both of mine. The doctors were working feverishly around him, and I asked if I was in their way. Before they could answer, the bishop said: "I don't care if you are in their way or not. I want you here. You can do me more good now than they can."

The bishop closed his eyes for a while, and I continued to hold his hand. When he opened them again, he looked at me and said: "I often wondered what my life would have been like if I had married. I never told you, but I have often told Monsignor Grosclaude that if I had married and had a son, I would have wanted him to be just like you—nothing different; nothing at all. When Jerry asked me to make you my secretary, he said that I would grow to love you; and he wasn't wrong. Jerry is sometimes wrong about worldly matters, but he is never wrong about anything which has to do with the human heart. I want you to know, Father, that you have been a good son to me. Even more important, despite your sporadic exuberance, you have been a good son to the Church."

"I have had three fathers during my lifetime," I told him. "My natural father, Monsignor Grosclaude, and you. I consider myself a very lucky man."

"Thank you," the bishop said.

Those were his last words. He closed his tear-filled eyes, and as I continued to hold his hand, he died.

I wept then, and I weep as I write this. Bishop Connolly really was a father to me. His heart gave out working for the Church he loved; and he worked for it at one of the most difficult times in its entire history—at a time when the Vandals were not only outside the gates, but inside the Church itself, striking at its very soul. For the most part, the world saw Bishop Connolly as a majestic figure, attired in a mitre and carrying a crozier. I also saw him as a majestic figure, but a figure without those trappings. I saw him as a kind and wise man who always did his best. May his good soul rest in peace! I am going to miss him.

PART TEN

May 28, 1971

Many people believe that Bishop O'Connor, one of our auxiliary bishops, will become the new bishop of the diocese. Most of that speculation is probably due to the fact that the pope named him apostolic administrator. Bishop O'Connor, on the other hand, has told me that he does not expect to receive the appointment. He feels that he lacks sufficient experience. Almost all of his work has been parochial in nature. Even as an auxiliary bishop, he mostly helped out with confirmations, and served as a stand-in when Bishop Connolly could not be present for some function which required a bishop. He still spends much of his time at Corpus Christi Church, where he has been pastor for over twenty years.

Since Bishop Connolly's death, I have gotten to know Bishop O'Connor rather well. He asked me to remain in the chancery as his secretary, and from what I have seen, he is being quite candid when he says that he knows almost nothing about administering a diocese. Although I consult him on all important matters, he always tells me: "Use your own judgment, Father. Do what Bishop Connolly would have done. You understand these things much better than I do."

When I asked Bishop O'Connor if he intends to move into the episcopal mansion, he told me that he was going to do absolutely nothing until the pope makes a decision. I suggested that I move out of the mansion, but he asked me to continue to live here and look after the place until a new bishop is appointed. So I've been keeping the housekeeper, Mrs. Owens, company. If I weren't here, she'd be all alone.

I suspect that Monsignor Hogan, the chancellor, will become our next bishop. He has had a great deal of experience in administration, and if a man from outside the diocese is not appointed, he could very well receive the post.

In any event, I have the feeling that my days as a bishop's secretary are coming to an end. The new bishop will probably choose another man; and that, of course, is his prerogative. As far as I'm concerned, it doesn't matter. I'm somewhat tired of the job, and I'll be glad to do something different for a change. I'll probably be appointed a pastor, and that's the kind of work I enjoy doing anyway. I hope that it will be a small parish, where I can really get to know the people and share their problems with them.

June 17, 1971

Today I chatted with Mrs. Stone, whom Bishop Connolly had always referred to as "the crazy woman of Holy Spirit College." She had been trying to see Bishop O'Connor for weeks, but he steadfastly refused to meet with her. She now belongs to the NAL, a very small but vocal group of Catholics who consider themselves reformers.

When Bishop O'Connor first mentioned Mrs. Stone and the NAL to me, I didn't know immediately which organization he meant. Instead of calling the organization by its correct name, the National Association of Laity, he dubbed it: "Nuts Are Loose." Although Bishop O'Connor made it clear that it was entirely up to me whether I met with Mrs. Stone or not, I thought that someone in the chancery should see her. Since no one else wanted to do it, I decided that it had to be me.

Mrs. Stone began by telling me that she and her group feel that the next bishop should not be appointed, but elected by the laity and priests of the diocese. I pointed out that while I personally believe that laity, clergy, and religious should be asked for their opinions, an election did not necessarily mean that the best person would be chosen. I tried to show her that the most popular person wasn't always the most qualified. Moreover, I said that collective prejudice was no better than individual prejudice. I emphasized that it was usually much worse, since there was often bigotry and complacency in numbers; as well as less opportunity to present grievances to a higher authority. I told her that Christ certainly wasn't chosen in an election; nor was Saint Peter.

Next we discussed the question of Catholic schools. Mrs. Stone is against any type of public support for these schools. Indeed, she thinks that they should be eliminated entirely. When I inquired into her reasons for this position, she said that private schools have no place in a democracy. I did my best to show her that private schools are one of the safeguards of democracy; that without a variety of opinions, real democracy ceases to exist. I pointed out that such diversity is especially essential today; at a time when national leaders are concealing the truth and manipulating public opinion to serve their own selfish interests.

From here, we went on to talk about the financial policies of the Catholic Church in America. She said that she and the NAL believe that finances should be controlled by the laity rather than by bishops. Once again, she mentioned elections, proposing that a national board be elected to supervise finances. When I asked her what purpose this would serve, she said the board would see to it that the Church did more to help the poor.

I tried to make her understand that just the opposite would occur. I pointed out that probably people who were monetary experts would be elected to the board. I added that they would most likely be very conservative and tight-fisted with Church funds; as is already the case with Protestant denominations which have such a system. Moreover, I told her that the system she proposed would take financial control away from the parishes and centralize it. Then if the entire Catholic Church in America centralized its resources, people would begin to fear her financial power. I stressed that this could only create additional enemies for the Church; while infinitely less would be done to help those in need.

Finally, we got to another matter very dear to Mrs. Stone's heart—abortions. She favors them and thinks the pope has no right to oppose them; at least without first inviting women to the Vatican in order to get their opinion. I tried to show her that a principle is involved here; and in so far as morality is concerned, it really does not matter what Mrs. Stone or any other woman happens to think. I told her that the Church has opposed abortions since its inception, two thousand years ago. I asked her if the pope has to consult all the thieves in the world before he can say that thievery is wrong; or all the murderers before he can declare that murder is wrong.

Mrs. Stone protested that this was something quite different. She said that a woman has a right to do what she wishes with her own body. I pointed out that certainly in the later stages of pregnancy, a body other than the woman's own—that of a child—is involved. I told her that when abortions were performed as late in pregnancy as they are now, it was undoubtedly a matter of murder. I emphasized that if these same babies had been born prematurely—and if they had been wanted by their parents—every effort would have been made to save their lives.

I mentioned the barbarity involved when aborted babies, still moving and trying to breathe, were packed in ice and sent to laboratories for experimentation and dissection. I also pointed out that cases have been reported where dissection was carried out while these babies were still alive. I cautioned her to consider what effect this callousness toward human life was going to have on society; especially on the young. I asked her what could be expected in the treatment of other people's children—particularly children in a place like Mylai—if Americans held the lives of their own children in such cheap regard. Then I quoted the words of Jesus: "Let the little children come to me, and do not hinder them, for of such is the kingdom of God."

Although I doubt that she understood what I was getting at, I tried to explain to Mrs. Stone that in one sense, women were no freer now that states permitted abortion than they had been when there were laws prohibiting it. After all, the state—not the woman—made the decision in both instances. I asked her if she had carefully weighed what this newest decision by the state might mean in the long run. I pointed out that vested interests were involved; that individual doctors were already making hundreds of thousands of dollars each year on abortions alone. I added that laws now being passed could very well be the hole in the dike. I asked her what guarantee we have that the state might not eventually permit the elimination of others deemed undesirable; such as the retarded, the mentally ill, the old, the handicapped—even war veterans.

Mrs. Stone appeared somewhat shaken by the time she left my office. Although I still think she has taken her particular position because it is a good way for her to make some money, I do believe that there are other Catholics who feel as she does and who are quite sincere. All I can do is pray for them and for the Church. Whether they realize it or not, in trying to "save" the Church, they are destroying it. They are much more dangerous to its survival than the old-time anti-Catholic bigots ever were.

July 1, 1971

What a shock! Official notification was received today that I am to become the new bishop of the diocese. At first, my reaction was one of sheer frustration and disappointment. I did not want to be bishop, and I could not understand how all of this had come about. I was tired of office work—especially so since Bishop Connolly's death—and I wanted to spend more time with the people.

I immediately went to see Monsignor Grosclaude at Saint Paul's Rectory. I told him that I was thinking of refusing the appointment.

"The one virtue you have always had as a priest," Monsignor Grosclaude said, "has been your obedience. Can you now refuse the express wish of the Holy Father, the Vicar of Christ?"

"But the people," I protested.

"Just think what you can do for the people *now*, son," Monsignor Grosclaude said. "Each bishop has his own style, and you will have yours. After all, you will be making the rules; and you will be free to see as many people as you want."

"Did the two letters Bishop Connolly wrote before his death have anything to do with this?" I asked.

"They could have had a great deal to do with it," Monsignor Grosclaude answered. "Bishop Connolly wanted you to succeed him. He had recommended you long before he had his heart attack. On the night of the attack, he insisted on reinforcing that recommendation by writing to the apostolic delegate and the pope. Although he tried to give the impression that he considered his illness insignificant, I don't think he ever expected to recover— even from the very beginning."

Monsignor Grosclaude and I continued to talk for hours, until I finally decided that he was right. Before leaving, I knelt down and asked him for his blessing, just as I had done many years ago, after finally deciding to become a priest. Following the blessing, I kissed his hand, exactly as I had done at that time. Once again, I felt very close to God and to the Church.

I am now convinced that I have an unusual opportunity to do great good for the people of the diocese and for the Church. I pray that God will give me the strength I need to serve Him and His people in this way. I want to be a good bishop—a bishop the people can love and approach with *all* their problems; both spiritual and material.

August 19, 1971

This has been quite a day. I am now a bishop, but I can honestly say that I don't remember ever having felt so tired before. I guess that I'll never learn to withstand pageantry, especially when I am the main attraction. It all began at nine o'clock this morning, and by the time I walked out of the cathedral, wearing a mitre and carrying a crozier, it was already past noon.

I have four newspapers here in front of me, which record the event in much detail. I'm not very happy about what they say. The articles are supposed to be about me, but I am unable to identify with them. They seem to be about somebody else.

All of the newspapers describe the procession which preceded the consecration. They speak of knights dressed in plumed hats "with capes over their shoulders and swords of silver at their side"; of two hundred policemen in their white gloves; of the governor, mayor, and senators; of monks in simple robes, with "white rochets, adorned with rich lace and red silk, reaching to the waist"; of monsignori who "approached in purple cassocks, over which they wore white rochets with lace and red cuffs, and black birettas highlighted by silken purple pompons"; of bishops, accompanied by their chaplains, who wore "purple cassocks, with purple birettas on their heads and crosses of gold on their breasts"; of legs "encased in white and gold buskins"; of Robert Cardinal McLaughlin, "a smile playing on his lips, dressed in the scarlet cappa magna, with long, flowing train—the train carried by a page."

Apparently the newspapers vied with each other to glamorize

both me and the event. A headline states: *CROZIER AND MITRE COME TO ONE-TIME ALTAR BOY*. Part of the article itself says: "A priest who knows Bishop Faber well has described him as a demon for work, a master of detail, a man with magnificent energy, a perfectionist. The priest says that he is generous to a fault, both with his time and money. According to the priest, he is broke. He gives everything away and doesn't have a nickel."

Another article in the same newspaper reads: "Bishop Peter Faber has ordered completion of his coat of arms. The coat of arms is used as a seal to authenticate episcopal acts. Every cardinal, archbishop, bishop, and abbot must have a coat designed. The symbolism for Bishop Faber's coat of arms centers about tongues of fire, and the bishop has chosen as his motto the words: *TO SERVE, NOT TO REIGN.*"

A reporter for one of the other newspapers wrote: "Bishop Peter Faber will wear two rings—one for ceremonial purposes and another for every day. The ceremonial ring—an oblong sapphire surrounded by a burst of tiny diamonds—is large enough to be worn over the prelatial gloves. The everyday ring—heavy in its massive gold setting—is identical but smaller. The rings were gifts of the new bishop's flock. Robert Cardinal McLaughlin, Bishop Faber's consecrator, presented him with two pectoral crosses. The everyday cross is studded with blue stones and diamonds. The ceremonial cross is more ornate."

One writer stated: "Robert Cardinal McLaughlin placed his hands on the head of the bishop-elect and said in a low voice: 'Receive the Holy Spirit.' In that moment, a metamorphosis of priest into bishop occurred." Another commented: "The scene of a mitred Bishop Faber, sitting on a throne, crozier held in a hand gloved in gold silk, seemed ages old; and the new bishop—had he not blinked his eyes—could have been not a living man, but a portrait from the Middle Ages."

Some of the photographs and their captions bother me even more than what the reporters wrote. Many of the captions are completely dishonest. I do not recall pausing for prayer before I entered the cathedral, yet a caption under my picture reads: *"A MOMENT OF PRAYER*—The Most Reverend Peter Faber meditates for a moment before entering the cathedral, where his solemn consecration as bishop took place."

At times, I was so confused by masters of ceremony and other people who were directing me that I didn't know what I was doing. Now I see the result. "Stand right there, Bishop Faber," a photographer had shouted. "And you, lady, kneel down and kiss his ring. That's it." The picture appears in a newspaper with the following caption: *"ACCEPTS HOMAGE—*A woman kneels to kiss the ring of the new bishop, who is holding the crozier, or shepherd's crook, that symbolizes the pastoral responsibilities of his new office."

So much of what happened today makes me feel like some kind of pompous fraud. Yet, if it is God's will for me, I have no right to complain. The tribulations of Job were infinitely worse.

I opened a drawer of my desk and took out the memento which Monsignor Grosclaude had given me to mark my ordination to the priesthood. The corpus of Jesus was still detached from the cross. For a moment, I held the corpus to the cross, but then I quickly separated them again. Then I kissed the corpus and the cross. "No, dear Jesus," I said. "I shall never put You back on the cross. At least *You* know that I did not want this. May Thy will be done!"

I put the corpus and cross back in the drawer. Then, although I had thought of keeping them, I flung all of the newspapers into the wastebasket.

August 20, 1971

I am not going to be able to write much today. Dr. Harris was here, and he wants me to get as much sleep as possible. Here I am a bishop, and the only thing different about me is that I have more stomach trouble. Although I have always had problems with my stomach, I have never bled before. Today was the first time for that, and Dr. Harris insists that I go into the hospital for some tests. I told him that it is probably nothing serious; only the excitement of yesterday. He remains unconvinced, though, so I promised him that I would enter Saint John's Hospital just as soon as I can attend to some of the more pressing diocesan affairs.

August 21, 1971

I retired very early last night, but when I couldn't sleep, I decided to begin taking care of some diocesan matters which I feel require immediate attention. For one thing, I telephoned Monsignor Grosclaude and asked him to come here to my residence at four o'clock today. I was a little late in keeping the appointment, however. I heard confessions this afternoon in the cathedral, and there were more penitents than I had anticipated. I apologized to Monsignor for my tardiness.

"Being late is one of the prerogatives of a bishop," Monsignor Grosclaude commented, a twinkle in his eyes. "A man in your position should never apologize. I thought I taught you better manners than that when you were in the seminary."

"The manners you taught me were flawless," I smiled, "and that is why I now have so few prerogatives and so many duties."

Monsignor Grosclaude laughed. "Is it really that bad, son?" he inquired. "Let me look at you. You do appear a bit weary. Sit down right here and tell me how you feel. What ever possessed you to hear confessions this afternoon after being ill last night? You should be resting. Does Dr. Harris know about this?"

"Maybe not about this," I smiled.

"Are you really any better?"

"I don't seem to be any worse.... What about your own health, Monsignor? How have you been?"

"I'm fine, son—fine for an old man, that is."

"You don't look like an old man," I told him. "Moreover, I happen to think that you are quite progressive in your views. That's why I want your advice."

"I'll help in any way I can."

"I've decided that something has to be done about Saint Mary's Seminary," I said. "More and more, I think that all of the troubles we have in the diocese begin and end there. If we can train good priests, then we can look forward to a healthy diocese. Otherwise, we'll have nothing but more disintegration."

"I quite agree with you, son."

"I have already decided that Monsignor Wilt has to go."

"Poor Monsignor Wilt!"

"I am going to ask him what other diocesan post he might want."

"Maybe he'll want to be head of the liturgical commission," Monsignor Grosclaude smiled.

"God forbid!" I sighed. "But seriously, Monsignor, how do you think we can improve things at the seminary?"

"After the office of bishop, I consider the position of rector to be the most important post in the diocese," Monsignor Grosclaude said. "Appointing a competent rector—someone the students could emulate—would be the first step. People seldom improve when they have no model other than themselves, and I'm afraid that's often the difficulty confronting young people today."

"There are those who feel that students should elect the rector," I commented.

"That's nonsense!" Monsignor Grosclaude exclaimed. "They'd end up electing somebody as immature as themselves—probably someone like Monsignor Wilt."

"I think you're right about that," I said. "There are still a number of priests at the seminary who know how to exercise good judgment, but naturally they're not the most popular. I understand that Monsignor Wilt recently asked the seminarians to write essays, evaluating their professors. Then he called in Father Mulhaney, who happens to be a fine man and an excellent professor, and told him that many of the students don't like him. 'We may not be able to renew your contract, Father,' Monsignor Wilt told him. 'You are like Jesus Christ. The students either love you or they despise you, and we just can't have that.' "

"Naturally!" Monsignor Grosclaude commented sardonically. "Monsignor Wilt wouldn't want to keep anyone too much like Jesus Christ around. Someone like that always makes idiots and fools uncomfortable."

"When the annual retreat was given at the seminary last March," I said, "the seminarians did not like what the retreat master was telling them, so they all walked out on him. That was the end of the retreat!"

"They never walked out on me," Monsignor Grosclaude smiled, "but they did manage to kick the kneelers and stamp their feet when I said something they didn't like. I'm sure you remember."

"I certainly do," I told him.

"In so far as people are concerned, nothing really changes very much—if at all," Monsignor Grosclaude said. "There are those today who think otherwise, however. They believe that every absurd scheme that comes along is pricelessly new. In truth, it is most often something quite old, tried many times before, and discarded because it did not work. It only seems new because people are ignorant of the past. Most of the change we think we see in life is due to truths being in and out of favor. Right now, I think we need some of the old truths back."

"So do I," I agreed. Then I asked: "What else can we do to improve the diocesan seminary, Monsignor, in addition to appointing a new rector?"

"I think it is time to stop trying novelty upon novelty," he replied. "That has done nothing but harm. I do believe, though, that individual thought and initiative should be encouraged. I wanted to do that when I was rector, but if you remember, I was thwarted at every turn."

"I remember well."

"I like the idea of seminars," Monsignor Grosclaude went on. "I also feel that the emphasis should be on individual, internal discipline; rather than on formal, external discipline. In one way or another, I would like to see all seminarians involved in actual pastoral practice. Perhaps some time should be spent in the community, helping with both secular and religious projects. Moreover, I do not think that honor students should have to attend formal classes if they can learn more through independent study. But most important of all, there must be an atmosphere of prayer, meditation, self-denial, and unworldliness. Without that, everything else will prove useless."

"Do you think that such a program will attract students?" I asked.

"I believe that young people are still idealistic, generous, and willing to sacrifice," Monsignor Grosclaude answered. "If we really give them that opportunity and throw out the nonsense, I have an idea that vocations will soar. Not only that, we'll be getting the best young people."

"Those are excellent suggestions, Monsignor. When do you want to start?"

"Start what, son?"

"I am asking you to return to Saint Mary's Seminary as rector."

Monsignor Grosclaude was stunned. "But I'm too old," he protested.

"I don't agree," I said. "Are you well enough to serve, and are you willing?"

"Yes, but—"

"Then I hereby appoint you."

Monsignor Grosclaude smiled. "Then so be it! It is God's will for me."

"With your approval, I am going to ask Father Calvin to assume the post of spiritual director at the seminary."

"Nothing could please me more," Monsignor Grosclaude said. "He is just the man I need to help me. He has a social conscience which will appeal to the young, and he has seen action in the field, which will be equally important to them. Moreover, he understands the necessity of genuine spirituality and discipline."

"I think we have a winning team."

"So do I," Monsignor Grosclaude smiled.

August 25, 1971

If only the days were longer! More and more, I find it impossible to get everything done which I plan to accomplish on a given day. I try to see everyone who wants to see me, and at the same time, I have to keep up with the many business matters which require my attention. If it were not for Monsignor O'Malley, my secretary, and for the chancellor and two auxiliary bishops, I would already be in the madhouse. I often feel guilty in having to ask them to work so hard, but I really have no choice. To further complicate the situation, I still have stomach trouble and occasional bleeding. Dr. Harris is furious because I keep refusing to go into the

August 25, 1971

hospital, but I don't think he realizes how important it is to take care of these diocesan matters first.

There are times when I really feel that I'm doing some good in my new job. Many young priests are now interested in helping the poor and oppressed, and I am doing everything possible to encourage them. I have already set aside over one million dollars of diocesan funds for that purpose. In addition, I have started an organization called Project Good Will. This organization will see to it that the diocese does not purchase anything from firms which practice racial, religious, social, or political discrimination. I have also been putting pressure on the board of realtors. I told the president this morning that if he does not present a reasonable plan for slum clearance by tomorrow, I am going to lead a march against the board myself.

Although it is no easy task, I am trying to satisfy—in what I hope is a constructive way—the demands of priests and religious who labor in the diocese. I am sure that all of them will be happy about many of my policies, while some of them will be disappointed in others. I have introduced a system of retirement benefits for the clergy; something which always should have existed. I'm sure that will make everybody happy. On the other hand, I have made a rule that all priests and nuns must wear religious garb in public, unless the nature of their work makes that impractical. Even though I am aware of the reasons some priests and nuns do not want to wear such clothing—the reasons sometimes being quite commendable—I believe that we are living in times when the garb itself is desirable as an authentic form of Christian witness. Yet, I am sure there will be opposition from a number of priests and religious.

I have also approved an association of priests for the diocese. I am aware, however, that some priests will want more power than the association provides for—especially in the placement of priests. I have decided to reserve to myself the right to make all appointments. On the other hand, I have formed a committee to advise me in this regard, and I have made it a rule that every priest must be consulted as to his wishes before any work is assigned to him.

Naturally there will be times when individual wishes will have to be sacrificed for the good of the Church. It is impossible to satisfy everyone, and at the same time to keep the Church functioning as it should.

Despite all the talk to the contrary, I remain unconvinced that a committee or an election always means freedom, democracy, love, and everything else that is noble, true, and good. Indeed, I have found through experience that just the opposite is often the case. Committees and elections can be extremely cold instruments, and they often ignore the rights of individuals. Moreover, priests on such committees are sometimes interested in promoting themselves and their friends rather than the individual who is up for their evaluation. Then there is always the matter of personal jealousy to consider. I still think that an honest bishop, who is not himself involved in the struggle for pastorates and other offices, is more likely to be impartial in his judgment.

Frankly, I doubt very much that a complete democratization of the Church would either strengthen it or stem the tide of defections by priests and religious. It is interesting, I think, that the defections only seem to increase as more committees are formed and more votes are cast. I still do not believe that priests and religious leave primarily because celibacy is required. Considering the fact that celibacy has traditionally been the rule, one must logically ask why so many more are leaving now than previously, while using that as their excuse. I believe that celibacy becomes an issue only as it relates to the increasing secularism among priests and religious. As their lives become more worldly and less God-centered, the blandishments of the flesh naturally become more desirable. If priests and religious really believe, if they are spiritually detached from worldliness and all that it implies, then celibacy becomes not a burden, but a badge of faith and commitment.

It is true that there have been and still are numerous abuses in the hierarchical system of the Church. There have been tyrants, and they still exist. But there has also been the right of appeal to higher authority—even, through one's conscience, to God Himself. I do not feel that replacing an individual tyrant with hundreds, thousands, or even millions of other tyrants, who act collectively, is going to solve anything. It can only make matters infinitely worse.

I do believe that the pope, bishops, priests, religious, and laity should labor together, in love, for the common good. I further believe that authority should mean only service, and I would like to see the day when common good and personal good become indistinguishable in the Church. I hope that I will be able to remain close to the priests, religious, and laity of the diocese; and that they will always consider themselves collaborators rather than subjects. I keep praying that God will give me the grace to achieve these ends.

August 27, 1971

This afternoon, I had an experience which has left me very sad. I had arranged for Monsignor O'Shea to come to my office at three o'clock. He arrived promptly enough, but I had not anticipated what occurred after that.

Monsignor O'Shea has a severe case of arthritis, and he supported himself with an old, gnarled cane. I rose to help him, but he shook his head negatively and remarked: "I can manage without your help, Bishop." I then offered him a chair, but he said: "You did not invite me here to be sociable, Bishop. Therefore, I prefer standing. Just apply the ax and permit me to depart."

"I am very sorry you feel that way, Monsignor," I told him. "You will always be welcome here. You have given much service to this diocese, and you have its gratitude."

"Your personal gratitude means nothing to me, Bishop. I would not lower myself to accept it. I want only the gratitude of God."

"I am sorry."

"Sorry that I want God's gratitude?"

"No, Monsignor O'Shea. Sorry that after all these years we cannot be friends. If you remember, you were the priest who baptized me. My parents often related how you, at that time, told them you would pray that I, too, one day would become a priest."

"I should have drowned you in the baptismal font—before it was too late! The best proof for the divinity of the Church is your presence in this office. If you do not destroy the Church, the entire world will have to finally accept the fact, once and for all, that its existence is safeguarded by the Holy Spirit. In the name of Saint Patrick and all the saints of heaven, how did they ever make you a bishop?"

"The very same question has occurred to me a number of times, Monsignor."

"Bishop Connolly was not the sort of man to want himself succeeded by someone like you. Bill Connolly was my kind of man. You must have voodooed him. Either that, or the poor man became deranged from senility or a stroke—God rest his soul!"

"Perhaps it is too bad that the clock cannot be turned back, Monsignor—too bad for both of us."

"I am not ashamed of my life, Bishop. I was never a cutthroat, devilish politician. The clock can stay where it is as far as I'm concerned. I suppose it is different for those who have a guilty conscience."

"From your attitude, I take it that you know why I sent for you, Monsignor."

"What sort of damn fool do you think I am? Of course I know why I am here. You are going to fire me. Why don't you do it and get it over with?"

"You are not making this very easy for me, Monsignor."

"And why should I make it easy for you? If you were the man your predecessor was, you would have told me already. He never beat around the bush—nor do I. But you are soft, and you always will be soft. That's what you really have against me. I'm as hard as this cane, and you're as soft as a jellyfish. That's the real reason you want to fire me—out of spite!"

"That isn't true, Monsignor. I am asking you to resign primarily because of your age. After all, you are eighty-nine."

"And what are the other reasons—the real reasons?"

"I have already given you the real reason, Monsignor—your age."

"It is spite! That's what it is."

September 1, 1971

I looked at the morose old man leaning on the cane, and I wanted to explain why spite was in no way involved. I wanted him to understand that curates and parishioners were insisting on his removal; that the parish was in serious financial trouble because of outmoded approaches; that there was some question as to whether Sacred Heart Church could even continue to exist, since the wealthy families had left the neighborhood, and Monsignor had done nothing to elicit the support of the poor. But after thinking about the matter for a few moments, I decided that it might be kinder to allow him to believe that personal spite was involved.

"I would like to name you pastor emeritus, Monsignor," I said. "In that way, you can continue to live at Sacred Heart."

"I am not going to have some fool appointed by you come in and tell me what to do, Bishop. No, thank you! I am leaving, and once I leave, they can bring me back to Sacred Heart in my coffin—not one second before."

"Perhaps you would prefer to live in the new diocesan home for retired priests."

"Where I live, Bishop Faber, is none of your business. I can tell you, though, that I intend to purchase a house and live alone. My only request is that you permit me to celebrate Mass there."

"That permission is granted. Can we help you financially?"

"I do not want your money, Bishop. And now, it is time to say good-bye."

Before I could stop him, he fell to his knees and kissed my episcopal ring.

"That wasn't necessary," I said as I tried to help him to his feet.

"I got down myself, and I shall get up myself," he proclaimed as he slowly and painfully raised himself to his feet. "And it *was* necessary, Bishop. I still love the Church—the Church as she always was, before fools like you began to tamper with her."

With that, he hobbled from the room.

September 1, 1971

The bleeding has been getting worse, and Dr. Harris convinced me that I should enter Saint John's Hospital tomorrow for some tests.

He suspects an ulcer, but he made it very clear that cancer is also a possibility. Probably a rest in the hospital will do me some good. I'm really not worried. I have noticed over the years that it is always God's plan which finally prevails. I'm in His hands and very much resigned to my fate.

September 4, 1971

Monsignor O'Malley, my secretary, brought my mail to the hospital today, and there was a letter for me from Maria Mannheim. Monsignor O'Malley generally opens all of my mail and sorts it, but because Maria's letter was marked personal, he had not opened it. It seems somewhat strange that after twenty-six years I still think of Maria as Maria Mannheim rather than as Mrs. James Carter. I wonder what Freud would have made of that?

No doubt Freud would have also had something to say about the fact that I am going to record this letter in my diary, but I have never been especially impressed with Freud's brand of psychological analysis. While he was right about some things, I think he was wrong about many others—particularly about those matters involving the human heart. Nevertheless, I continue to ask myself why I *really* want to incorporate Maria's letter into my diary. Some writers on the spiritual life would say that it is merely vanity on my part, but I am sure it is more than that.

I still remember my first day at the seminary and Monsignor Grosclaude's suggestion that I begin keeping a diary. He said that the diary would provide me with a record of my progress in the spiritual life. Indeed, he said that one day I might discover I had become a saint. While I know that I have not become a saint, I would like to think that my diary shows I have grown in love. In one way or another, I believe that everyone I have ever met has helped me to love better and to love more unselfishly. Perhaps Maria especially—or at least the memory of her—has helped me in this way. Just as Monsignor Grosclaude had predicted, my relationship with her did aid me in understanding other people. If it had not been for her, I would have failed many of the people I have been able to help.

Since there are no medical tests scheduled for today, I am

September 4, 1971

going to have ample time to write down Maria's words. Although I remember Maria in my prayers each day, I am happy to have this opportunity to spend more time reminiscing about her. I am recording her letter below.

Dear Peter,

You are often in my thoughts, and if I took pen in hand each time you come to mind, I would be writing daily. Unfortunately, I seem to have less time these days than ever for writing to dear friends, although I once thought there would be more time when the children were bigger. Even though Janet is married and Mark is away at school, my youngest son, Harry, and my three-year-old granddaughter, Denise—not to mention my husband—keep me fully occupied.

Harry will enter preparatory school next fall, but he will not follow in the footsteps of my father and husband. He will study music, and I think that decision would make my father very happy, because Harry is an outstanding musician. You probably remember what a stickler my father was for doing everything well, and he was particularly this way in respect to music, since he loved it so very much.

I suppose you wonder why I speak of my father in the past tense. You are probably unaware that he died three months ago. He was eighty-three, but he devoted himself to work until the end. He had just completed a massive new work in medieval history, and we placed a copy of the manuscript in the coffin with him.

My husband is carrying on my father's work. Several months ago, James was promoted to chairman of the history department at the university. He still spends much of his time in Washington. The highest officials of government continue to seek his advice.

Speaking of promotions, please accept my belated congratulations. My father would find it hard to believe that you have become a bishop. He always spoke of the fact that you had become a priest as some incredibly strange phenomenon, but your advancement to a bishopric would have really puzzled him. When his friends visited him, he often mentioned you as an example to illustrate a point. He always considered you his most interesting and—I might add—promising student.

I do not know if your new position makes you any happier, but if it does, then I am happy for you. You say so little in your own letters that it is difficult to know what you are thinking and whether you are satisfied or not. Your letters to me have been so much the same these many years that I could write them for you. You invariably inquire about my well-being, but you never say anything really concrete about yourself. Your weather report is always excellent, but I would so much rather hear about you. You did not even mention that you had become a bishop. I discovered that from reading the newspapers. Please remember I am your friend and would appreciate knowing more.

It seems that I always write to you at this time of year, near the beginning of fall. I do not like winter, but fall has always been my favorite time of year. It is a time when the turbulence of spring and the heat of summer have spent themselves, and a certain tranquility prevails. If you remember, it was in the summer we met. I often wonder what would have happened if it had been the fall. I think of you as one of those rare individuals who is able to understand and appreciate all the seasons of life, but for some reason, I see you happiest in the spring and summer.

Please, my dear bishop, find a few moments to tell me about yourself, for I shall no longer be satisfied with your weather reports. But even they are better than nothing.

Love,
Maria

September 6, 1971

Today I gave Dr. Harris permission to operate. The tests indicate that I have a stomach tumor. Although Dr. Harris hopes that it is not cancerous, nothing will be known for certain until the operation is completed.

Monsignor O'Malley was here today, and I did my best to give him the impression that the operation is going to be a minor one. There is no sense in worrying him about it.

Poor Monsignor O'Malley! Apparently Rita Marie Bern has been harassing him in an effort to get in touch with me. I asked him to visit her, explain that I have been ill, and try to help her with any problems she might have. I cautioned him to be kind.

I have also asked Monsignor O'Malley to look in on Helen Ryan, a little girl who has been suffering from leukemia. She is a member of Holy Name Cathedral, and for several months now, I have been taking Communion to her every week.

September 14, 1971

This evening I finally got to see Dr. Harris. He had been avoiding me ever since the operation. Two of his assistants came in each day, but I was unable to get any real information from them. They kept telling me to ask Dr. Harris. Dr. Harris, on the other hand, always managed not to appear. Today I insisted that he himself come to see me. But I already knew what was wrong, and why he had been avoiding me. I guess I really knew even before I entered the hospital.

I tried to put Dr. Harris at ease. Then I said: "It's cancer, isn't it?"

There were tears in Dr. Harris's eyes. "Carcinoma of the stomach," he replied. "Metastasis has occurred. I wanted you to get some rest before I told you."

"How long do I have, Bob?"

"Possibly a year," he answered. "It is rather difficult to say for certain. The gastroenterostomy should relieve some of your previous symptoms, and I think you will be fairly comfortable for a while."

I smiled at Dr. Harris. "Now it really wasn't that difficult to tell me, was it, Bob? . . . All it means is that I won't be a bishop very long, but then that's not important in terms of eternity. Forty-eight isn't such a bad age at which to begin preparing for death."

Dr. Harris looked away. "You'll never change," he said. "You're the same as you were that night I met you fifteen years ago. Nobody has a mind that works like yours. If I have ever met anyone with courage, you have it."

"Why should I be afraid to die?" I asked. "I have never feared life, and if anything is part of life, death certainly is."

"Among many other things, you are also a philosopher," Dr. Harris commented.

"Maybe," I smiled, "but I'm afraid it's all pretty homespun." Then thinking it was time to change the subject, I asked: "How are your wife and children?"

"Fine," Dr. Harris replied, "and I owe it all to you. Although I may have never told you so before, my marriage to Kathleen is the best thing that ever happened to me. The advice you gave me was the answer to everything."

"Thank you," I told him. "I like to look back and think that I have done some good."

"I just wish I could say that I've done half as much good as you have," Dr. Harris said. "I have saved men's lives, but you have saved their souls. I'm smart enough now to know which is more important. Did you know that my oldest son—your namesake, Peter—has just entered the seminary?"

"Saint Mary's?"

"Yes."

"He's very fortunate. Monsignor Grosclaude will look after him. He was my rector, you know."

"Yes, he told us that."

"I'll pray for your son."

"Do pray for all of us, Pete, but more than anything else, please pray for a miracle. We desperately need men like you—especially today."

"Don't worry," I smiled. "God has His own way of taking care of things."

October 4, 1971

When Monsignor Grosclaude came to visit me today, I told him that Dr. Harris had said I could go home in about two weeks. He was so happy with this news that I hesitated to tell him what I realized he had to know eventually. But after we had talked for quite a while, I finally told him. He was very shaken, but he tried—I'm sure for my sake—to remain calm.

"Does Monsignor O'Malley know?" he asked.

"No, Monsignor, he doesn't," I replied, "and I don't want him to. Besides the doctors, you are the only one who will know. I think it is best that way. The diocese will operate more smoothly."

"I think you're right, son."

"Dr. Harris seems to think that I have quite a bit of courage, Monsignor, but I'm not as convinced of that as he is. I'm all right now, but do you think that I'll have the spiritual strength to see this thing through to the end?"

"Yes, my son, you will have that strength and then some."

"Are you certain, Monsignor?"

"Have I ever told you an untruth?"

"No, my dear spiritual father, you never have."

I brushed the tears from my eyes, and noticed that Monsignor Grosclaude was doing likewise.

"We must be practical about this," I said. "These emotional outbursts don't help. I'm very sorry. With all of your good seminary training, I should have more control."

"I think you are being eminently practical about it, son," Monsignor Grosclaude told me, "and also quite courageous—if you will permit me to say so."

"I am appointing you executor of my estate, Monsignor. Burial is to be made in Resurrection Cemetery."

"Not in the cathedral crypt?" Monsignor Grosclaude asked.

"There is only one place left, and I want that reserved for the bishop who comes after me."

"I think Bishop Connolly intended that space for you, son."

"And I intend it for someone else."

"Very well."

"I have another request, Monsignor."

"Anything at all, son."

"I am going to stipulate in my will that you alone offer my funeral Mass. I want no knights in plumes and fancy uniforms—or anything else like that—if it reasonably can be avoided."

"I shall heed your request."

October 5, 1971

Today I wrote a long letter to the pope, telling him about my incurable illness, and asking that he appoint Monsignor Grosclaude to replace me at my death. I am recording here the last part of that letter: "There is one final favor that I would request of Your Holiness. I ask that Your Holiness give utmost consideration to naming Monsignor Jerome Grosclaude as my successor. He is staunchly loyal to the Church and to Your Holiness, and he possesses spirituality and wisdom of a kind that is essential if the Church is to survive the onslaughts of contemporary crises. I know that his age may be a problem, but men of even greater age, such as your illustrious predecessor, Pope John XXIII, have served the Church nobly. Indeed, if there were one gift I would leave to the Church I love so dearly, that gift would be Monsignor Grosclaude."

October 27, 1971

My chauffeur, Harold, picked me up at the hospital this afternoon and drove me home. On the way, we had one of our usual discussions. Harold has probably always considered himself something of a pundit, but now that the importance of the laity in the Church is being emphasized, there is no stopping him on ecclesiastical matters. He reads his daily newspaper carefully, and he always has advice—sometimes even directives—for me. Today Harold had qualms of conscience about my car.

"What's wrong with the car?" I asked.

"It's a Cadillac," he observed dourly.

"Yes, I've noticed that."

"I've heard that some of the bishops in Europe are going to get rid of their fancy cars," Harold noted rather pointedly.

"Oh I see," I smiled. "The reason I use this car is because my predecessor, Bishop Connolly, used it. In all the years that you drove for Bishop Connolly, did you ever have any trouble with it?"

"Well . . . no," Harold replied.

"I think that's very important," I said. "Then, too, the car is too old for a good trade. Keeping it is cheaper than buying another make."

"But do you think it's right for a bishop to be riding around like this?" Harold asked.

"Maybe not," I answered, trying hard to become poker-faced. "I think I'll take driving lessons, and get myself a small car."

"You mean you'll drive for yourself?"

"That's what I have in mind."

"But what about me?"

"We'll just have to discharge you."

"But I need the job, Bishop. I have a family to support."

"Then we'll keep you, but that means the Cadillac has to stay."

"I suppose you're right," Harold admitted reluctantly and rather peevishly.

"Sometime you should take out your Bible and read Matthew 11, 18," I suggested.

"What does it say?"

"I think it goes something like this: 'For John came neither eating nor drinking, and they say, "He has a devil!" The Son of Man came eating and drinking, and they say, "Behold a glutton and a wine-drinker, a friend of publicans and sinners!" And wisdom is justified by her children.'"

"What does that mean, Bishop?"

"I think it means that it is impossible to satisfy people."

"I guess you're right." Harold was silent for a few minutes, as though engrossed in thought, and then he said: "I didn't know you couldn't drive, Bishop."

"It's true."

"Why didn't you ever learn?"

"As a young man, I believed that a priest should walk, unless he absolutely needed a car to perform his duties properly. I always managed to get along without one."

"That still doesn't explain why you can't drive. I thought all rich kids learned to drive."

"Maybe I wasn't a rich kid."

"I always thought you were."

"Well, I wasn't."

Harold really had to turn that one over in his mind.

November 2, 1971

This evening, I asked Harold to drive me to Saint Michael's Abbey, which is located a short distance from the city. As our car approached the abbey church, a bell in the tower, which has rung on schedule for over a century and a half, rang out the hour. The giant spire of the church is surmounted by an illuminated cross. The cross seems to hover as a protective sign, high above the monastery and the city; and the spire itself resembles a huge, tapering pointer, which reminds onlookers of the symbol of peace and hope toward which it stretches. Especially at night, as bright light emanates from hundreds of windows, the abbey seems so strong, so placid, so permanent. Everything seems to proclaim: *DEATH CANNOT ENTER HERE.*

But death has entered there, and that is the reason I have visited the abbey cemetery on All Souls' Day for more than twenty years. When we arrived at the cemetery, I asked Harold to wait in the car for me. As I walked alone through the graveyard, hundreds of flickering candles illuminated the tombstones. Relatives and friends of the deceased had lit candles inside lamps—the custom on All Souls' Day—and placed them on the graves. At the end of a row of graves, I picked up a lamp and carried it with me. I finally stopped at one of the graves and held the lamp close to a plain iron cross, which served as a marker. *FATHER MARTIN WRIGHT,* the iron cross read.

Karl Wright! How well I remembered him—the adventurous and mystical companion of my youth. I looked down at the earth which covered his grave. It was the same earth that covered all of the graves. The earth made no distinction between prelate and simple monk, between rich and poor. It covered all alike. The earth outlasted even the bronze vault and bronze coffin. The earth remained, and in time, it made all material things equal.

Father Martin's choice had been fraught with idealism, but like so many human choices—idealistic and otherwise—it had ultimately crumbled into dust. I asked myself what would have happened if Father Martin had chosen differently. Indeed, what if I myself had made another choice?

I could not speak for Father Martin. I could speak only for myself. I knew that even if I could have gone back and done things differently, I would not have wanted to do so. I have learned that the place where one serves is not really that important—whether it be in the bustling world or in the comparative solitude of a monastic cell. Although the distant place, with its untried blandishments, always appears more appealing to the untrained eye, I now know that goodness and evil exist not in any one place or the other, but in the hearts of men.

Place, time—even man himself—are impermanent. Only the earth remains forever. That is the tragedy of man, but also the source and proof of his towering endurance, nobility, and destiny. Of necessity, man dies—no matter how well he has built—and all of his handiwork is ultimately engulfed by the earth, from which it has sprung in the springtime of life. But I still believe that the moment of building—that spark of divine, godlike creation—is reward sufficient for the fleeting hours, days, months, and years.

As I stood before Father Martin's grave, I knew that I was standing there for the last time. I knelt down and kissed the iron cross. "No, I have not forgotten you, my dear friend," I said. "Soon we shall be together again."

November 27, 1971

Unfortunately, my health would not permit me to attend the meeting of the National Conference of Catholic Bishops. I doubt, though, that either my presence or vote would have done much good anyway. Several bishops were courageous enough to speak out on some of the real issues which confront the United States and the world, but their voices were muffled by the official documents which came to be promulgated.

In many ways, the National Conference was similar to the recent Synod of Bishops held in Rome. At that meeting, men like Archbishop Alberto of the Philippines emphasized many of the real issues, but compromise and an attempt to placate everybody —especially the world's leaders—prevailed. It was heartening to read that the Synod recognized the fact that the poor are being exploited and made to suffer by wealthy nations, as well as by wealthy individuals. But the platitudes never became specific; the nations and individuals involved were never named. Indeed, much of the phraseology is so general that it is subject to diametrically different interpretations.

The National Conference of Catholic Bishops likewise went out of its way to avoid offending the politicians, businessmen, and militarists, who are primarily responsible for wreaking havoc in the world. While my colleagues—after all these years!— finally got around to saying that the war in Vietnam is wrong and should be brought to a prompt end, they were very careful to couch their words in such a way that they did not tread on the toes of those in power. They spoke of the people "who have borne the heaviest burden of this war," but they identified them as being "the young men who chose conscientiously to serve in the Armed Forces, many of whom lost life or limb." Statements such as these made nonsense out of the really good things the bishops did say.

Since when have the military personnel of the United States done most of the suffering in Southeast Asia? Anyone with even a modicum of common sense knows that the airmen who drop the bombs, or the soldiers who shoot at anything that moves, are not doing the real suffering. The real sufferers are the victims of these and similar actions: the burned children, the debauched and disfigured women, the tortured old men, and the millions who have been uprooted from their homes.

My colleagues, the bishops, did not once denounce the perpetrators of all this suffering. They did not recall our Catholic chaplains from Southeast Asia, thereby removing religious sanction for what is happening there. They did not even urge the chaplains to inform our soldiers that because the war is intrinsically immoral, they are automatically committing the sin of murder, as well as other heinous sins, by serving in Vietnam.

My fellow bishops in no way condemned our president and other leaders for their sinful policy of Vietnamization. Although the current war in Southeast Asia has always been an American war by proxy, this policy is making it even more so. I pray that our people will not be deceived. I hope that even when Americans are no longer being killed in Southeast Asia, there will still be vast numbers of our citizens who will be noble and courageous enough to oppose the selfish and immoral militaristic policies of our government: policies that provide the weapons and monetary incentives which result in the maiming and killing of people in other lands.

There are still other matters on which my colleagues should

have spoken out. They should have condemned President Nixon's concept of a voluntary army. It is just another ruse to silence public opposition to the administration's war policies. Naturally, poor boys rather than the rich would join such an army, since only the poor would be in need of the financial inducements being offered.

Once such an army of mercenaries existed, it would be much more difficult for the moral segment of the American public to oppose wars like the one in Vietnam. Since even the sons of middle-income families would be able to escape military service, I am afraid that it would be only too easy for the majority of Americans to close their eyes to the moral issues involved in future American military exploits.

The wealthy, on the other hand, not only gain financially from such bloodshed, but they possess the political power to either create or end these wars. When there was no longer even a remote danger that their own sons might be drawn into the conflicts, and when no pressure at all was being brought to bear on them by a large and influential part of the population, many of them would probably do even more than they do now to encourage new military adventures.

Indeed, the American bishops should have condemned in general the exploitation of the poor and middle-income families of America by the rich. They should have condemned the fact that our government today is only too often aligned with the moneyed interests against the average citizen. They should have condemned as immoral a system in which the rich not only pay little or no taxes, but often receive subsidies from moneys which are collected as taxes from the ordinary citizen. They certainly should have condemned those officials of government who are deliberately lying to the public in order to protect and enhance their own positions; officials who have been putting horrendous pressures of every description on honest individuals in an attempt to prevent them from telling the truth.

I feel that my fellow bishops were much too bland in what they had to say. They lacked the courage of Old-Testament Biblical prophets, of John the Baptist, indeed of Christ Himself;

none of whom were afraid to condemn sin in high places. I am so disappointed in their dereliction of duty that I am going to issue a pastoral letter of my own. I am working very hard on the preparation of this document, and I am going to read it personally from the pulpit of the cathedral on New Year's Day. I have already arranged for newsmen to be present. The letter is going to be something of a spiritual bomb, and I have an idea that its explosion will be heard around the world.

December 22, 1971

As soon as I got out of the hospital, I once again began taking Communion to eight-year-old Helen Ryan. Early this morning, I received a call from Mrs. Ryan, who told me she thought Helen was dying. I said that I would be right over.

During the many months that I have been visiting the Ryans, I have come to admire their faith and courage. Even before Helen became ill with leukemia, Mrs. Ryan had experienced her share of troubles. She became a widow within a few months after her marriage, and because she had loved her husband so much, she refused to even consider the possibility of marrying again. From everything that she has told me, he was a fine man. He died of complications which followed an operation for appendicitis. Since that time, Mrs. Ryan has supported herself and Helen by working as a domestic.

It was still dark outside and snowing when Harold drove me to the Ryan home, which is located in one of the poorest sections of the city. Mrs. Ryan met me at the door with a lighted candle, and after I had removed my topcoat, led me into Helen's room. She had placed a small table beside Helen's bed, with articles on it which were used in anointing the sick. Two candles on the table, one on either side of a crucifix, cast flickering shadows over the emaciated form breathing heavily on the bed.

After I had placed the Blessed Sacrament on the table, Mrs. Ryan extinguished the candle she was carrying, and we both knelt down for a few moments of prayer. Then I took a bottle of holy water from the table and sprinkled it as I said the prescribed prayers, blessing the little girl, her mother, and the room itself.

"She seems to be asleep," I commented.

"She keeps slipping off to sleep and waking up again," Mrs. Ryan said. "She's been doing that all night."

"Do you think I should disturb her?"

"I want you to, Bishop, and so does Helen. She has been waiting for you."

Large sores covered the little girl's face and arms. Only her breathing told me that she was still alive. "Helen," I called softly as I took her by the hand. "Helen."

Helen stirred slightly and opened her eyes.

"It's Bishop Faber, Helen. I've come to give you Holy Communion."

"Bishop," the little girl sighed weakly.

"Do you know who this is, Helen?"

"You are the nice priest," Helen answered dreamily. "Mommy said you would come."

"How do you feel?"

"I hurt all over," Helen replied, slowly moving her dry, cracked lips.

I took a piece of cotton from the table, dipped it in a dish of water, and moistened her lips. "You are going to get well very soon now," I promised. "You won't hurt any more."

"I don't care about the hurt, Bishop. Jesus hurt when He was on the cross. I am going to heaven to be with Jesus."

"Do you want to go to heaven?"

"Yes, Bishop, but before I go to heaven, I want to see Santa Claus. Mommy said he was going to bring me a great big doll."

"I am sure that he will. You would like that, wouldn't you?"

"Yes, Bishop."

"I am going to give you Holy Communion now, Helen. When Jesus comes into your heart, ask Him to take all the hurt away. If you do that, He will, and you won't hurt any more."

"Yes, Bishop," the little girl tried to smile.

While Mrs. Ryan knelt beside the bed, I placed the Host on Helen's tongue. She was having difficulty in swallowing, so I took a teaspoon and a glass of water from the table. I fed her a little water, and she managed to swallow. Following Communion, I anointed her with holy oil. Then I read the apostolic blessing over her. Soon she was asleep again.

Mrs. Ryan and I quietly left the room and went into the parlor, where we talked for a short while. When we went back into Helen's room, she was dead.

Mrs. Ryan threw herself down at the side of the bed and embraced Helen's lifeless body. I walked to the doorway and stood there. I watched as the candles on either side of the crucifix cast shadows over the pathetic figure of Mrs. Ryan sobbing over her dead child. I stood there for a long time, and then I walked over to the bed again.

"Come, Mrs. Ryan," I said gently. "It's time to go into the other room now." I helped her into the parlor and got her to sit down on the sofa. "Can I get you anything?" I asked.

Mrs. Ryan shook her head and continued to cry.

I sat down on the sofa beside her. I think I said all of the things a priest usually says at such a time, but nothing seemed to help. Finally I said: "Perhaps today is the time to take stock of your blessings, Mrs. Ryan. You have really known what it is to love and to be loved. Many people pass through an entire lifetime without being so fortunate. It did not last as long as you wanted it to last, but it was there. Many people who have lived long lives with those whom they wanted to love, and by whom they wanted to be loved, would envy you."

I felt that my words were finally beginning to reach her, and I went on: "I know that you have suffered, and even though suffering is bitter, you should be glad that you have suffered. It is only through suffering that we learn so many things that we, as human beings, need to know. Through suffering we learn how to better understand the sufferings of our fellow human beings; we learn how to love better, and we love with a love that is more pure. There are so many people in the world who need love, Mrs. Ryan, and you will find, because of your own suffering, that one day you will be able to love those people better. I think that is God's plan for you: to keep on loving and to keep growing in love."

Mrs. Ryan continued to sob softly, but for one instant her

tear-filled eyes met mine, and I knew that I had spoken something at last which she understood.

December 24, 1971

The strangest thing happened to me tonight. I think I may have had a vision. I intended to concelebrate midnight Mass in the cathedral, but I finally asked Bishop O'Connor to take my place. After supper, the pain in my stomach and back became much worse, and I had to take some of the medicine which Dr. Harris prescribed for such occasions.

I spent most of the evening reading in my bedroom. Then I turned out the lights and went to the window. As I peered into the darkness, I remembered the days of my early childhood, when for the first time, my parents took me to see the crib in the parish church. While we knelt before the manger, my father and mother had explained the different statues to me: the Christ Child, Mary, Joseph, the Wise Men, the shepherds, the animals. I recalled gazing at the manger in childlike awe. There was something so reassuring; something so peaceful about the simplicity of the scene. Then I thought how wonderful it would be if one could spend his entire life kneeling before the manger and contemplating its serene mysteries. But that was for only once each year. The lives of men were not—and could not be—spent before the manger.

Suddenly, as I continued to stand there at the window, the manger I had visited as a child appeared before me. But this time, the manger was engulfed by fire, and the statue of the Christ Child had become alive and was moving about in the flames. Then the Christ Child smiled entreatingly through the flames and stretched out His hands toward me. I stretched out my own hands toward the Christ Child, but I could not reach Him. Then I saw the smile leave the face of the Christ Child, and He disintegrated into a mass of molten wax.

I was much saddened by what I had seen, and I was about to turn away from the window. Then, all of a sudden, the wax began to spontaneously reconstitute itself. After assuming a number of grotesque forms, the Christ Child gradually became whole once again. He was much larger, stronger, and more beautiful than He had ever been before. Once again He reached out to me, and this time, for only an instant, I was able to touch His hand. Then He disappeared.

When I finally turned away from the window and put on the lights again, I was filled with joy.

Tonight I can go to bed happy.